As I lay in bed I anxiously wondered, What had we done to cause all this nasty gossip about us?

Cary and I were twins, brother and sister, born minutes apart. He and I had been connected in our mother's womb, and birth was a great separation from each other as well as from her. . . .

As we grew older, Cary just naturally hovered about me, protected me. Being twins, it took only a glance or a touch for us to communicate a fear or a happy idea. Perhaps our friends resented this magical connection; perhaps they were jealous and that was why they wanted to hurt us. It was easy for them to turn Cary's devotion to me into something dirty.

And then a more fearful voice, tiny, hiding in the back of my mind, stepped up to say, "Maybe Cary was so angry because he realized some of what they said was true . . . he was too devoted to you. . . ."

Alone now, feeling anger and confusion, as well as shame, I thought of Cary above me, shut up in his attic workshop. It was very quiet, but I thought I could hear him crying. I listened hard, but it was silent again. The wind had died down, yet there was still enough of it to make the walls creak. Outside, the moon played peekaboo with the parting clouds. The surf rose and fell against the dark sand, resembling a giant wet hand stroking the earth. Night was our respite, the time to put aside the trials and torments of the day and then welcome sleep like a cherished friend.

I closed my eyes and prayed and waited for the surprise of morning. . . .

V.C. Andrews® Books

Published by POCKET BOOKS

For orders other than by individual consumers, Pocket Books grants a discount on the purchase of **10 or more** copies of single titles for special markets or premium use. For further details, please write to the Vice-President of Special Markets, Pocket Books, 1633 Broadway, New York, NY 10019-6785, 8th Floor.

For information on how individual consumers can place orders, please write to Mail Order Department, Simon & Schuster Inc., 200 Old Tappan Road, Old Tappan, NJ 07675.

V.C.ANDREWS®

Music in
the Night

POCKET **STAR** BOOKS
New York   London   Toronto   Sydney   Tokyo   Singapore

Following the death of Virginia Andrews, the Andrews family worked with a carefully selected writer to organize and complete Virginia Andrews' stories and to create additional novels, of which this is one, inspired by her storytelling genius.

This book is a work of fiction. Names, characters, places and incidents are products of the author's imagination or are used fictitiously. Any resemblance to actual events or locales or persons, living or dead, is entirely coincidental.

An *Original* Publication of POCKET BOOKS

 A Pocket Star Book published by
POCKET BOOKS, a division of Simon & Schuster Inc.
1230 Avenue of the Americas, New York, NY 10020

ISBN: 0-671-53474-2

First Pocket Books paperback printing March 1998

10 9 8 7 6 5 4 3 2 1

V.C. Andrews is a registered trademark of the Virginia C. Andrews Trust.

POCKET STAR BOOKS and colophon are registered trademarks of Simon & Schuster Inc.

Tip-in illustration by Lisa Falkenstern

Printed in the U.S.A.

Prologue
ಜ

A long time ago, I lived a fairy tale life. There was always magic around me: magic in the stars, magic in the ocean and magic in the sand. At night when we were only ten years old, Cary and I would lie back on our blankets on the deck of our daddy's lobster boat and gaze up at the heavens, pretending we were falling into outer space, flying past this planet and that, circling moons and reaching out to touch the stars. We permitted our minds to wander and imagine. We said anything we wanted to each other, never ashamed or too embarrassed to reveal our most secret thoughts, our dreams, our intimate questions.

We were twins, but Cary liked to call himself my older brother because, according to Papa, he was born two minutes and twenty-nine seconds before me. He behaved like an older brother from the moment he could crawl and protect me. He cried when I was unhappy and he laughed when he heard me laugh, even if he didn't know why I was laughing. When I asked him about that once, he said the sound of my laughter was music to him and it pleased him so much, he couldn't help but smile and then laugh, too. It was as if we were enchanted children who heard our own

1

songs, melodies that were sung to us by the sea we loved so much.

As far back as I can remember, there was always magic in the water. Cary could wade in and come walking out with the most spectacular seaweed, starfish, clamshells, seashells, and even things he claimed had washed across the ocean from other countries to us. When it came to the ocean, I believed anything he said. Sometimes I thought Cary must have been born with seawater in his veins. No one loved it as much, even when it was nasty and wild.

What discoveries Daddy let us keep, we kept in either Cary's room or mine. We decided everything had some sort of power to it, whether it was the power to grant us a wish or the power to make us healthier or happier just by touching it. We assigned an enchanted quality to each thing we found.

When I was twelve and I wore a necklace made from the tiny seashells we had found, my friends at school were amazed at the way I identified each and every shell, explaining how this one could drive away sadness or that one could make the dark clouds move on. They laughed and shook their heads and said Cary and I were simply foolish and even immature. It was time we grew up and put away childish ideas. There was no magic in these things for them.

But to me there was even magic in a grain of sand. Cary and I once sat beside each other and let the sand fall through our fingers, pretending each grain was a tiny world unto itself. Inside it lived people like us, too tiny to ever be seen, even with a strong microscope.

"Be careful where you step," we told our friends when they were with us on the beach. "You might crush a whole country."

They grimaced with confusion, shook their heads and walked on, leaving us behind, enveloped by our own imaginative pictures, pictures no one else wanted to share. We were inseparable for so long, I guess people thought we had been born attached. Some of my jealous girlfriends once made up a story about me, claiming I had a long scar down the side of my body from my underarm to my waist and Cary had the same scar on his body. It was where we supposedly had been connected at birth.

Sometimes, I thought, maybe it's true, that from the moment we entered this world, our separating had begun, a slow and painful process. It was a separation Cary fought much harder than I did as we grew older.

As a very young girl and even when I first entered my junior high school years, I was comfortable, happy and grateful for Cary's devotion to me. Other brothers and sisters I knew argued and occasionally insulted each other, often in public! Cary never said a really bad thing to me, and if he spoke to me in a manner that suggested he was impatient or annoyed with me, he immediately regretted it afterward.

I knew that other girls fixed their flirtatious gazes at Cary and competed with each other for his attention. It wasn't just a sister's prejudice for me to say Cary was handsome. From the first day he could cast a rope or carry a pail, he accompanied Daddy on the lobster boat and helped in the cranberry bog. He always had a dark tan that brought out the emeralds in his green eyes, and he loved to wear his rich dark hair long, the strands lying softly over the right side of his forehead, just above his eyebrow. It looked so much like silk, girls were jealous and all of them longed to run their fingers through it.

My brother carried himself firmly with the demeanor of a confident little man, even when he was just in grade school. Other boys used to make fun of the way he held up his head and shoulders, striding alongside me with his gaze firmly fixed on where we were headed, his lips tight. Soon, however, they started to envy him, and girls in our classes just naturally thought of him as older, more mature.

Frustrated by their failure to win his attention and interest, however, they eventually found comfort in making fun of us. By the time we were in high school, they were calling Cary "Grandpa." He didn't seem to care or even notice. I was sure it bothered me more than it bothered him, and it wasn't unless someone physically got into his face or insulted me in front of him that Cary reacted, almost always violently. It didn't matter if the other boy was bigger or even if there were more than one. Cary's temper was as quick and as devastating as a hurricane. His eyes became glassy and his lips were stretched so tightly they formed white spots in the corners. Anyone who challenged him directly knew they were in for a fight.

Of course, Cary would get into trouble, no matter how justified his reaction was. It was he who had lost his temper and usually he who dealt the most damage to his opponents. Almost every time he was suspended from school, Daddy gave him a beating and confined him to his room, but nothing Daddy could do and no punishment the school could impose would deter him if he believed my honor was somehow compromised.

With such a devoted and loyal protector watching over me, other boys kept their distance. It wasn't until I entered high school that I realized how untouchable I had become in their eyes. Many girls my age had crushes on boys or had boyfriends, but no boy dared pass me a note in class, and none joined me in the hallways to walk from one class to another, much less walk me home. I walked with some girlfriends or with Cary, and if I walked with girls, Cary usually followed behind us like my guard dog.

When I reached sophomore year, however, I, like most of my girlfriends, wanted a boy who showed serious interest in me. There was a boy named Stephen Daniels, who had lived in Provincetown only a year, who I thought was very handsome. I wanted him to talk to me, to walk with me, and even ask me to go on a date. I thought he wanted to because he was always looking at me, but he never did. All my girlfriends at the time told me he wanted to, but said he wouldn't because of my brother. Stephen was afraid of Cary.

I mentioned it to Cary and he said Stephen Daniels was stupid and would go out with any girl if that girl gave him what he wanted. He said he knew that from listening to him in the boys' locker room. Later, I found out Cary had actually walked up to him and put his face an inch from Stephen's, threatening to break his neck if he should so much as look twice at me. Naturally, I was disappointed, but I couldn't help wondering if Cary had been right.

In the evenings after we had done our homework and helped Mommy with May, our younger sister who had been born deaf and was attending a special school for the handicapped, Cary and I would talk about some of the other kids at school. No matter what girlfriend of mine I mentioned to him, he found fault with her. The only girl he didn't criticize was Theresa Patterson, Roy Patterson's oldest child. Theresa's father, Roy, worked with Daddy on the lobster boat. The Pattersons were Bravas, half African-American, half Portuguese. The other students looked down their noses at them, especially the ones who came from so-called blue-blooded families, families who were able to trace their lineage back to the Pilgrims, families like Grandma Olivia's, Daddy's mother, who ruled over us like a dowager queen.

Cary liked Theresa and enjoyed being friends with her because he liked the way she and her Brava friends defied the other students. When I asked him if he could ever think of Theresa as a girlfriend, he raised his eyebrows as if I had said the silliest thing and replied, "Don't be stupid, Laura. Theresa's like another sister to me."

I suppose she was, but as I grew older and felt Cary's shadow over my shoulder more and more, I began to wish he found some other girl to win his attention. I did my best to recommend this one or that, but nothing I said made him act any differently toward them. If anything, when I mentioned a possible girlfriend for him, that girl suddenly became ugly or stupid in his eyes. I realized it might be better if I just let nature take its course.

Only, nature didn't.

I used to think nature just missed Cary. She walked by one day while he was out on the lobster boat or something. Other boys his age were trying to get dates, hanging out in town, showing off to get a girl's attention, asking girls to do things with them; but Cary . . . Cary spent all his free time with me or his model boats upstairs in his attic workshop, a room just above mine.

Finally, one day at lunch I mentioned my growing concern to Theresa. She rolled her dark eyes and looked at me as if I had just been hatched.

"Don't you hear all the talk behind your back? All the whispering and gossip? There isn't a girl in this school who thinks Cary's normal, Laura; and most of the boys have their doubts about *you*. They don't talk to me about it, but I hear what they say."

"What do you mean? What sort of things are they saying about us?" I asked, trembling in anticipation.

"They're saying you and your brother are like boyfriend and girlfriend, Laura," she replied hesitantly.

My heart skipped a beat and I remember looking around the cafeteria that day and thinking everyone was looking at us, their eyes full of contempt. I shook my head, the deeper realizations taking shape like some dark, ugly beast who had crawled out of a nightmare into my daytime thoughts.

"Look at you," Theresa continued. "You're fifteen now and one of the prettiest girls in this school, but do you have a boyfriend? No. Anyone asking you to the school dances? No. If you go, you go with Cary."

"But—"

"There are no buts, Laura. It's because of Cary," she said. "Because of the way he dotes on you. I'm sorry," she added. "I really thought you knew and didn't care."

"What am I going to do?" I moaned.

She nudged me with her shoulder like she usually did when she was going to say something nasty about one of the other girls in school.

"Get him a girlfriend who'll stir up his hormones and you'll be fine," she said.

I remember she got up to join her Brava friends and I sat there, suddenly feeling very alone and unhappy. Cary came

6

walking into the cafeteria quickly, spotted me, and marched over.

"Sorry I'm late," he said. "Mr. Corkren kept me after class about my homework again. What's going on?" He looked closely at me when I didn't respond. "Did something happen?"

I just shook my head. I wondered how I could tell him and not hurt him.

I put it off and never really tried to make him understand until the year after, when Robert Royce and his family bought the old Sea Marina Hotel and Robert entered school.

For me and Robert, it was love at first sight and that brought with it a special kind of magic Cary couldn't share.

Somehow I had to make him understand and accept. I had to show him how to separate himself from me.

I only hoped it was possible.

1

Young Love

All day my heart had been beating faster than normal, thumping so hard I was sure Cary heard the echo in my chest. When I walked, it was as if my feet didn't touch the ground. I was floating along on a cloud of air, bouncing with a spring in my step. I was positive I had woken this morning with a smile on my face, and sure enough when I looked at myself in my vanity table mirror, I saw my cheeks were flushed with excitement, the excitement of wonderful dreams that continued into my waking moments, dreams that carried me on a magical carpet like some Arabian princess floating through volumes and volumes of enchantment.

Everything around me took on a new and different glow. Colors I had grown used to were brighter, richer, sharper. Every normal sound became part of a grand symphony, whether it was simply the creak in the stairs as I descended to help Mommy with breakfast, or the clink of dishes and pans, the splash of water running in the sink, the opening and closing of the refrigerator and stove, or the tap of Daddy's, May's, and Cary's footsteps in the hallway, and all

9

their voices. Their voices suddenly became a chorus behind the music.

"You look very nice today, dear," Mommy said at breakfast. Daddy glanced at me and nodded. I held my breath because I was wearing just a touch of lipstick, and Daddy hated makeup on a woman. He said it was the devil's touch and an honest woman never tried to fool a man by using paint on her face.

I had chosen my brightest blue dress with the white collar and I wore my gold charm bracelet, the one Mommy and Daddy had recently given me on my sixteenth birthday. They had given Cary an expensive pocket watch on a gold chain that played "Onward Christian Soldiers" when he flipped open its lid.

Cary looked up from his bowl of oatmeal.

"Aren't you afraid you'll swallow some of that lipstick?" he asked, sending a bolt of ominous lightning through my morning of warm sunshine.

I looked at Daddy, but he just snapped the newspaper and glanced at the headlines. Then I threw Cary my most angry look and he went back to his oatmeal.

When we stepped outside to start for school, I stopped in the doorway, felt the sunshine on my face, and closed my eyes. I embraced my books against my breasts, wishing that none of this was a dream.

"What are you doing?" Cary asked sharply. "You want May to be late for school?"

"I'm sorry," I said, skipping forward to join them. He held May's hand firmly in his own. My little sister, locked in her silence, gazed up at me with a twinkle in her eyes, as if she knew it all, as if she had poked her pretty little face into one of my dreams last night and saw my happiness. I took her other hand and we continued down the street. I felt like Alice in Wonderland.

"You're behaving just like all the other dumb girls in our school," Cary muttered, and threw me a look of reprimand. "Making a fool of yourself over some boy."

I only smiled back at him. Today, I thought, today, I am

surrounded by protective sylphs, tiny fairy-like creatures who would deflect any arrows of unhappiness away from me.

There were clouds in the sky, but to me it was all blue. Although it was early May, there was a chill in the air, the residue of yesterday's nor'easter. The whitecaps sprouted on the surface of the sea like water lilies, and even this far away from the shore, we could hear the surf roaring in. In the sunlight, the sand was the color of autumn gold. The terns looked like they were tiptoeing over uncovered treasure as they searched for their morning meal.

My hair was pinned back, but some loose strands whipped gently at my forehead and cheeks. May wore a light blue hairband that kept her hair neatly in place.

Cary couldn't care less how his hair looked when he entered school. He would just run his fingers through it and not even go into the boys room like all the other young men to brush and comb in front of mirrors. Instead, he would accompany me to my locker and wait until I had my books before going on to his own. He would stand there even when Robert Royce joined me, and he would glare unhappily, suspiciously, hardly talking, lingering alongside or just behind us like an angry storm cloud. It was the only thing that put darkness in my heart these days.

"Stop daydreaming and watch where you're walking," Cary ordered as a car sped past us.

The invasion of tourists had begun in small ways. The entire Cape was busier now on weekends, but traffic during the week was still at a lazy crawl down Commercial Street. Our route in the morning took us down side streets to May's school. At the gate we each kissed her and signed our good-byes, Cary putting on his best Daddy-like face to warn her to behave herself, as if she ever needed a warning. There was no one sweeter, no one more gentle and fragile and loving than our May. Although Doctor Nolan assured us her deafness had nothing to do with it, May's growth was impeded. She was bright and intelligent, always doing well in school, but she was so tiny for her age, her facial features as diminutive as a doll's, her hands so small they barely covered Cary's or my palms when we held them.

All of us protected and loved her dearly, but sometimes I would catch Daddy gazing at her, unaware that anyone was looking at him, and I would see the most terrible expression of sadness on his face, his eyes glazed with trapped tears, his lower lip trembling just enough to be noticed. Then he would become aware of what he was doing, and he would snap into a firm posture, wiping away any emotion from his face. I never saw Daddy really cry, and the only times I saw him with his head down was when he was praying or after a particularly hard day of fishing.

At her school, May turned back after she had started through the gate and smiled at me impishly as she signed: "Don't kiss Robert too much." She giggled and ran into the building with the other children. I glanced at Cary, but he pretended not to have seen her and started off, his steps so deliberate I thought he would leave footprints in the sidewalk.

It was Friday, and tonight was the school's spring dance. For the first time in my life, I would have a real date for a school party. Robert Royce had asked me. It was to be our first formal date. Up until now, we had just met in places by accident or after we had timidly suggested to each other we might be someplace at the given time.

Robert had enrolled in our school in late February. His parents had purchased the Sea Marina, a hotel with fifty rooms on the northwest end of town. As soon as spring came, they had begun the restoration of the old resort, repairing, painting, planting, and pruning the landscape. Robert was an only child, so there were no other children to help Charles and Jayne Royce. Robert explained that his family had put most of their money into the purchase of the property and had to do most of the work themselves. Because of that, he went home directly after school most days and was very busy on the weekends, especially now that the summer season was fast approaching.

I had hoped Cary would find Robert's devotion to his

family and their business admirable. He and Robert really had a lot in common, but from the moment Robert had the courage to step up to me in the hallway and begin a conversation right in front of Cary, Cary's eyes grew small and dark whenever Robert was around me.

Robert always tried to include him in conversation, but Cary's responses were short, sometimes not much more than a grunt or a shrug. I was afraid Robert would be either frightened away or bothered so much by Cary's behavior that he would stop speaking to me and walking with me, but instead he grew bolder and even took a break from working on the hotel and visited me at home one Saturday.

Cary had gone to the dock to work on the lobster boat engine with Daddy and Roy Patterson. I introduced Robert to Mommy and to May, and May fell in love with him faster than I had. Robert was good at picking up signing, too. Before he left that day, he had learned to say "hello," "good-bye," and "I'm very, very hungry."

Later, when Cary returned and Mommy told him and Daddy I had had company, Cary turned white and then bright red when he asked me why I hadn't brought him down to the dock.

"I didn't want to interrupt you," I explained. Actually, I was grateful for the privacy, for not having Cary hovering over us.

He looked hurt and then angry.

"Ashamed of what we do?" he asked.

"Of course not," I protested. "And besides, you've spoken to Robert. You know he's not like that. He doesn't come from a snobby family, Cary. If anyone's family is snobby, it's ours."

Cary grunted, reluctant to admit I was right.

"He probably knew I was down at the dock all day," he muttered.

"What? Why would that matter, Cary?"

"It matters," he said. "Believe me, all these guys take advantage, Laura. You're just too trusting. It's why I have to look out for you," he declared.

"No, you don't, not with Robert, and I am not too trusting, Cary Logan. You don't know everything there is to know about me, and you certainly know nothing about romance," I flared, and stomped up to my room, closing the door behind me.

After my heart stopped pounding and I grew calm, I lay back and thought about my wonderful afternoon with Robert, walking on the beach, holding his hand, just talking. We told each other about ourselves, our favorite foods and colors and books. He was surprised that we didn't have a television set, but he refused to criticize Daddy when he learned it was Daddy's decision.

"Your father's probably right," he said. "You do read more than anyone I know and you're a great student."

He smiled that sort of smile that embeds itself in your mind, prints itself on the surface of your memory, embossed behind your eyelids whenever you close them and think about him. He had azure-blue eyes that turned opaque whenever he spoke deeply or seriously to me, but when he smiled, his eyes brightened as if they had drawn sunshine into them. It was the sort of smile that warmed your heart, infectious, sweeping away any cobwebs of gloom.

Robert was about an inch taller than Cary and just as broad-shouldered. He had longer arms, but was not as muscular. He wore his light brown hair short and always neatly brushed at the sides with just a slight wave in front. Because he was a year older and a senior, we didn't have any classes together, but I knew he was a good student and his teachers liked him because he was polite and inquisitive.

Cary had never been a very good student. He wore school like a pair of pants two sizes too small, reluctant to get in, struggling to be comfortable, relieved when the end-of-the-day bell rang. He hated being shut up and regimented by the clock and the rules. He was truly a fish out of water.

Consequently, Robert Royce's success in school was another thing Cary resented. He hated whenever Robert and I got into discussions about history or a book we'd read

for class. To Cary, it was as if we had begun to speak in a
different language. On a few occasions, however, Robert did
try to talk about his family's problems with the hotel,
construction difficulties, the use of tools and paints, things
Cary understood and appreciated. Almost as reluctant as
someone sitting in a dentist's chair, Cary would settle into
conversation, offering his suggestions as dryly and as
quickly as he could.

Later, Cary would tell me Robert should stick to quizzes
in history and leave the real work to men more qualified.
That only brought a smile to my face and a look of
confusion to Cary's.

"What?" he demanded. "What is so funny now, Laura? I
swear, you walk around with a stupid grin on your face all
the time these days. You just don't know how silly you
look."

"You simply can't admit you like him, can you, Cary?" I
said, and he reddened.

"I don't," he insisted. "There's nothing to admit."

Despite this gloomy prognosis, I hoped and prayed Cary
would eventually become friends with Robert, especially
after he had asked me to the school dance. Mommy really
liked Robert, but Daddy hadn't met him yet and I knew he
wouldn't give me permission to go to the dance with him
until he had, so the Saturday after he had asked me, I
invited him to the house for lunch.

Robert charmed Mommy again by bringing her a box of
candy. Cary called it a bribe, but I patiently explained it was
only a polite gesture, something people invited to lunch or
dinner often do. As usual, he grunted and turned away
rather than admit I might be right.

At lunch, Robert sat beside me and across from Cary,
who kept his eyes down and refused to talk. We began our
meal as usual with a reading from the Bible. I had warned
Robert that was something Daddy always did. Daddy
paused when he opened the holy book and gazed at Robert.

"Perhaps our guest has a suggestion," he said. Cary
started to smile. It was Daddy's little test. He was always

lecturing us that young people were slipping into sin faster because they didn't know their Bible.

Robert thought a moment and said, "I like Matthew, Chapter Seven." Daddy raised his eyebrows. He glanced at Cary, who suddenly looked glum.

"You know that one, Cary?" Daddy asked.

Cary was silent and then Daddy handed Robert the Bible.

Robert opened it, smiled at me, and glanced at Cary before beginning in a soft, silky voice.

"'Judge not, that ye be not judged. For with what judgment ye judge, ye shall be judged . . .'"

He read on and then looked up. Daddy nodded.

"Good," he said. "Good words to remember."

"Yes sir, they are," Robert said, and Daddy and he began a conversation about the tourist business, the old Sea Marina and how Daddy remembered it. I was afraid Daddy would take off on his and Grandma Olivia's favorite pet peeve—how the tourists were ruining the Cape—but he was civil and said nothing critical.

Cary sulked with his back against the chair, only speaking when he wanted someone to pass him a dish.

Robert confessed that he knew little about the lobster fishing business, and even less about the sea and boats.

"We've been so busy fixing up the place, I haven't had much time for anything else," he explained.

"That's all right. Your parents need you first. Maybe after lunch, you can come down to the dock and see our rig," Daddy said and looked at Cary. But after lunch Cary claimed he had work to do on one of his models and had spent enough time on the boat that week anyway.

I took May's hand and Robert took her other hand the way Cary always did. The three of us followed Daddy down to the dock. I turned and looked back at the house and thought I saw Cary looking out of an upstairs window. For a moment I felt like bursting into tears, but Robert's smile drove that feeling away quickly and we continued on.

Most important, Daddy approved of Robert that day

and so tonight I would be attending the school dance with my very first boyfriend. The school was buzzing like a beehive all day long. Everyone was fidgety in their seat in class and the cafeteria sounded like a hundred more students had enrolled that morning. Only Cary moved like a somber mourner through the halls, his face gray, his eyes dark. He sat silently, eating mechanically in the cafeteria.

"Why don't you ask Millie Stargel to the dance tonight, Cary?" I suggested when Robert and I sat down with him. "I know no one has asked her yet."

Cary stopped chewing and looked at me with such pain in his eyes, I got a huge lump in my throat and couldn't swallow for a moment.

"Millie Stargel?" He laughed. It was a wild, loud, and frightening laugh. "Whose idea was that, *his?*" he said, nodding at Robert.

"No, I just thought—"

"She's a pretty girl," Robert said, "and I bet she'd love to go."

"So why don't you ask her?" Cary retorted.

Robert smiled softly and gazed at me.

"I've already got a date," he said.

"Then why are you looking at other girls?" Cary shot back at him.

"I'm not. I was only saying—"

"See, I warned you," Cary said to me and got up. "These dances are stupid anyway," he said. "Hanging out in the school gym is not my idea of fun. If I go on a date, I'm not going to bring her back to this place."

"Cary," I called as he started away. He just glared back and continued out of the cafeteria.

"He'll be all right," Robert said, and put his hand over mine. "One day he'll meet someone and his heart will pound just like mine did when I first looked at you."

I nodded.

But I didn't have as much confidence in something like that happening to Cary anytime soon.

Not for a moment. And I knew that until Cary was happy, I would have a very hard time being happy myself.

It seemed to me Cary deliberately walked a great deal slower than usual when we left school. He didn't have to be a genius to see how eager I was to get back to the house.

"May will be waiting for us," I complained. "I'm not waiting for you to catch up," I added.

"So go on by yourself," he said, and I hurried away.

May was actually just coming out of her school when I arrived. I signed for her to hurry and we started for home. Cary was so far behind, he was still out of sight of May's school. May asked where he was and I told her he was being a brat. She looked back, confused, but she didn't slow down. She knew why I was hurrying home and she was almost as excited as I was. When we got to our house she asked if she could help me get ready for the dance and I signed back that I would need all the help I could get. May laughed and signed that she thought I was already beautiful, so I wouldn't be needing much help at all.

Despite May's words of encouragement, I wanted to do something special with my hair. I had shown Mommy a picture of a girl in *Seventeen* and told her I wanted to style my hair that way. She said she would help. She was almost as good at it as a regular beautician. So after I showered and washed my hair, I sat at my vanity table and Mommy began to brush out my hair and trim it. May sat on the stool beside me and watched, her eyes full of excitement. She was full of questions.

Why, she wanted to know, did I have to change the way my hair looked?

"This is a special occasion," I told her. "I want to try to look as good as I can."

"Oh, you'll be beautiful, Laura," Mommy said. "You're the prettiest girl in the school."

"Oh Mommy."

"You are. Cary says so."

18

"He's . . . prejudiced," I said.

"I remember there was a girl named Elaine Whiting when I was in school. She was so pretty everyone thought she would become a movie star. All the boys tried so hard to be the first to ask her to the school dances. I never saw her without every hair being in place and there wasn't a boy whose head didn't spin when she walked by. I bet it's the same for you," Mommy said with a wonderfully happy smile on her face. She was looking at me in the mirror, but her eyes seemed to be focused on her own fantasy. I could tell that neither she nor Daddy had ever heard a nasty whisper about Cary and me. It would just break her heart if she knew what some of the students in the school thought. Ugly rumors could be like infectious diseases, corrupting, rotting, sickening even the most healthy of souls.

"Which boys did you go to dances with, Mommy?" I asked her.

"Oh, no one ever asked me. I was what you would call a wallflower," she said with a smile.

"I'm sure you weren't, Mommy."

"I was frightfully shy, especially around boys. I was glad when my father and Samuel planned my marriage to your father."

"What? Your marriage was arranged?"

"Well, I guess you could call it that, though it really wasn't as bad as it sounds. Our fathers discussed it and I guess Grandpa Samuel told your father and he decided I would do, and he began to take an interest in me.

She paused and laughed at a memory.

"What?"

"I was just remembering the first time your father spoke to me. I was coming home from work at Gray's Pharmacy and he slowed down in his truck and asked if I wanted a ride. I knew who he was. Everyone knew who the Logans were. Anyway, I didn't reply. I kept walking, afraid to even turn my head toward him. He drove ahead and then stopped and waited until I reached him and he leaned out

19

and asked me again. I shook my head without speaking and kept walking.''

"Then what happened?" I asked, breath bated.

"He drove off and I thought that was the end of it, but when I turned the corner and started down the street toward my home, there he was. He had parked his truck and was leaning against the door, waiting for me. I tell you I was terrified," she admitted and then glanced at May, who was tilting her head, wondering what Mommy was talking about for so long.

"I almost turned around and went the other way, but I kept walking, and when I reached him, he stood up and said, 'I'm glad you didn't accept my offer out of hand, Sara. Shows you're not a frivolous young lady. Your father and mine have been talking about how we would make a good couple. I'd like permission to come calling on you next Saturday, properly.'

"Well, that just took my breath away," she said. "You see, I had no idea of my father's plan up until then. I didn't even know he and Samuel Logan were friends. Well, once I recovered, your father asked, 'Do I have your permission?' and I nodded. 'Thank you,' he said and drove off, leaving me standing there with the most befuddled look on my face, I'm sure."

"Did he come calling the following Saturday?"

"He did and then we began to go out on dates. Our fathers had discussed our marriage, but Jacob didn't bring me to see Olivia for some time. She wasn't exactly demanding he bring me up to the house," she added.

"Why not?"

"I think Olivia Logan had someone else in mind for your father, someone more . . . wealthy, someone with a social position," she said. "But Grandpa Samuel had gone ahead and discussed it with my father and Jacob took a liking to me, so that was that. No matter," she said with a small wave of her hand. "That's all in the past now. Let's get back to your hair," she said excitedly.

"Did you have a nice wedding, Mommy?" I asked, not

ready to give up the first glimpse I'd gotten into my parents' early life together.

"It was a simple wedding at Olivia and Samuel's home. Judge Childs married us."

"I never heard you talk about your honeymoon, Mommy."

"That's because I didn't have one."

"You didn't?"

"Not really. Your father had to go back to work the next day. We told ourselves we would take a vacation soon, but we didn't. Life," she said with a sigh, "life just takes over. Before I knew it, I was pregnant with you and Cary. Don't look so sad, Laura," she said, gazing at me in the mirror. "I'm not an unhappy woman."

"I know you're not, Mommy, but I just wish you had a chance to travel, to have some fun, to leave Provincetown just once. No one in our family ever leaves here. . . . No one except Uncle Chester and Aunt Haille. Mommy, I never understood why Daddy stopped talking to Uncle Chester and why Uncle Chester and Aunt Haille left Provincetown," I said.

"You know your father doesn't want us talking about them, Laura."

"I know, but—"

"This is such a happy time. Please, dear," she begged. She closed her eyes and then opened them as she often did when she wanted to just forget or skip over something unpleasant. I didn't want to make her uncomfortable, but Uncle Chester and Aunt Haille remained the big mystery in our family, and I just naturally wondered what had complicated their love affair and marriage to make them outcasts in our family.

But Mommy was right: Tonight was not the time to press for answers.

"Okay, Mommy," I said. She looked grateful. I smiled and turned to May, who was signing and demanding to know what all the talk was about. I told her as much as I could. While I was signing, I heard the creak in the floorboards above and realized Cary was in his attic work-shop. I glanced up at the ceiling, thinking about him, thinking about how he would spend one of my most wonderful nights, alone and bitter.

Suddenly, I saw what looked like a pinhole of light in the ceiling. My breath caught and I brought my hand to my chest.

"What's wrong, dear?" Mommy asked.

"What? Nothing," I said. "That looks fine, Mommy. I better lay out my clothes now," I said quickly.

She stepped back and nodded. I glanced up at the ceiling again. The light was gone, as if someone had covered the hole. Why hadn't I ever noticed it before? I wondered. My fingers trembled as I sifted through my closet to find my most beautiful dress, the pink taffeta Mommy had made for me. It was the only formal dress I owned.

It was a good dancing dress, too. All week I had been practicing dancing with it on. May sat on the bed and watched and then, when she got up her nerve, joined and imitated me. We laughed and grew dizzy.

Now I thought about the hole in the ceiling and wondered if Cary had been watching us all that time. Did he feel so left out? Was that why he would do that? How long had the hole been there? The thought of Cary watching me muddled my brain for a moment, and I just stood there, holding the dress.

"Are you happy with the dress, Laura?" Mommy asked. "I know it's not as expensive as some of the dresses other girls will be wearing."

"What? Oh. Yes, Mommy. I just love this dress."

I took it out of the closet and lay it on the bed. Then I took out my shoes.

"Well," Mommy said, "I'd better get downstairs and work on dinner for your father, Cary, and May. Call me when you're all ready," she said. "I can't wait to see you. Oh, and I want you to wear my necklace tonight," she said.

I started to shake my head. Mommy's necklace was her only really expensive piece of jewelry. Even her wedding ring was not that expensive, because Daddy thought it was a waste of money to buy something elaborate when a mere silver band would serve the same purpose.

"I can't, Mommy."

"Sure you can, honey. When do I get a chance to wear it? I want you to wear it for me, okay?"

I nodded hesitantly.

"Come along, May," she signed, "and help me with dinner tonight. Laura has too much to do."

"Oh, I can help, Mommy."

"No you can't, honey. I told you, I never went to a school dance, but I wanted to very much. Tonight," she said with a deep sigh, "you're going for me, too."

"Oh Mommy, thank you," I said. She held out her arms and I hugged her back.

I felt tears prickling under my lids and quickly kissed her cheek and turned away to take a deep breath. After she and May had left, I sat at my vanity table and began to paint my fingernails. I started to daydream, imagining what it was going to be like to be dancing in Robert's arms, floating under the balloons and the lights, feeling him holding me close, occasionally brushing his lips over my hair.

A deep creak in the ceiling pulled me from my reverie and reminded me of the peephole in my ceiling. I gazed up at it and then I got up and went into the bathroom. I was angry, but then I began to feel sorry for Cary. I knew I was shutting him out of a part in my life, a part he could never enter again, yet he had to understand that I was growing up and the things that once amused me, amused us, were no longer enough. *He'll soon realize it,* I convinced myself. *He has to.* In the meantime, I didn't want to do anything else to break his heart.

My thoughts returned to the dance. I was so excited, I had to lie down and rest before I got dressed. I know I dozed for nearly an hour before my eyes snapped open and I sat up, frightened I had slept too long. I was only asleep for twenty minutes, but still I hurried to put on my dress. Then I put on a little more lipstick than ever before and perfected my hair before taking a deep breath and gazing at myself in the mirror.

Was I really pretty, as pretty as Mommy claimed? Robert thought I was and, of course, Cary did, too, but I never felt like the girl Mommy had described. I never thought all the boys were looking my way or that I had even turned a single head. I wasn't ugly, I decided, but I was no raving, movie-actress beauty. I had to keep my feet on the ground and not let my ego swell like so many other girls I knew at school.

Everyone was just finishing dinner when I went downstairs. Mommy slapped her hands together and cried out as soon as I entered the dining room. Daddy sat back, nodding, and May was smiling from ear to ear. Cary wore a strange, dark look.

"You're beautiful, honey. Just beautiful. Isn't she, Jacob?" Mommy said.

"Vanity is a sin, Sara. She looks fine, but there's no reason to blow her so full of steam she explodes," Daddy chastised. However, he wore a very proud expression as well.

"Now you just wait right there," Mommy said, and she hurried out of the dining room.

"How do I look, Cary?" I asked him. I couldn't stand the fact that he wouldn't look my way.

"Fine," he said quickly and dropped his gaze to his plate.

"I might have thought you'd be going to the dance, too," Daddy told him.

"It's stupid," Cary muttered.

"How's that?"

"I'm not interested in any old dance," he snapped. Daddy's eyebrows lifted.

"Well, it's a well-chaperoned affair, isn't it? Teachers are there, right?"

"What's that matter, Dad?" Cary said with a smirk. "Teachers are in school, too, but kids smoke in the bathrooms and do other things."

"What other things?"

"Other things," Cary said, realizing he was digging himself a hole he might not easily climb out of. He looked to me, but I said nothing. "Dumb things kids do."

"Laura's a good girl," Daddy said, looking at me. "She wouldn't do anything to embarrass this family."

Cary smirked and looked away.

"Of course I won't, Daddy," I said, my eyes fixed on Cary. Mommy returned, her necklace in hand.

"I wanted her to wear this tonight, Jacob," she said, looking to him for his approval. He nodded slightly and she put it on me, fastening it and then running her fingers over the garnets and sparkling diamond. "Doesn't it look nice on her?"

"Be careful with that," Daddy warned.

"I will. Thank you, Mommy."

We heard the doorbell.

"That'll be Robert," I said.

"Oh, she should have a shawl, don't you think, Jacob?"

"Sure. It's getting pretty nippy these nights," Daddy said.

Mommy went to the closet to get hers for me and I went to the door to let Robert in.

He looked terribly handsome in his jacket and tie. He was carrying a small box in his hands.

"It's a corsage," he declared.

"Oh, that's very thoughtful," Mommy said. Robert signed a hello to May, who beamed beside me. Then he opened the box and took out the corsage of red roses, my favorite. They matched the garnets perfectly.

"You'll have to pin it on," I told him. He looked at Mommy helplessly for a moment and then tried, but his fingers were clumsy with his nervousness.

"I'll do it," Mommy said, coming to our rescue. Robert smiled with relief and stepped back to watch her pin it on me.

"There, that's very pretty," Mommy said.

"Thank you, Mommy."

"We should get moving," Robert said. "Don't want to miss the opening dance."

"Have a wonderful time," Mommy said. Daddy came up behind her and looked at Robert.

"You look fine, boy," he said. "Now remember," he added with a scowl, "I want her home before midnight."

"Yes, sir," Robert said.

I looked for Cary, but he hadn't come out of the dining room.

"Good night, Cary," I called. There was no response. I flashed a weak smile at Mommy, who nodded, her face full of light, her eyes brighter than ever, and then Robert and I stepped out into the night.

He opened the car door for me and I got in. He hurried around and got behind the wheel.

"Well, I guess I have the prettiest date at the dance tonight," he said and turned to me. "Laura, you look more beautiful than I ever dreamed."

"Thank you, Robert. You're very handsome yourself."

"I guess we'll knock 'em dead then," he predicted and started the engine.

As we backed out, I looked toward the front door, half expecting to see Cary, but he wasn't anywhere to be seen.

2
ॐ

I Could Have Danced
All Night

"Oh, Robert," I said the moment we walked into the school gymnasium and saw how wonderfully the dance committee had decorated, "I wish Cary had come. He wouldn't be so down on the dance if he saw what they've done to this place. It looks like a real ballroom!"

"I don't think that's really what kept him from coming, Laura," Robert said softly. He smiled sympathetically, his eyes soft and gentle. I nodded, knowing he was right.

There was a makeshift stage directly in front of us for the four-piece band. They were already playing, and the floor was crowded with dancers. Above us, ribbons of crepe paper crisscrossed around mounds of multicolored balloons with long tails of tinsel. At the far right, there were long tables with red, green, and blue paper tablecloths set up for the food, and to the left and down the sides of the gymnasium, there were tables with the same color paper tablecloths and chairs. A large poster on the left wall read: WELCOME TO THE ANNUAL SPRING FESTIVAL.

Everyone was dressed up, some of the girls in dresses so formal and expensive-looking, I was sure Mommy would feel what she had made for me was inadequate, even though

I thought my dress was just perfect. However, I was happy now that I had agreed to wear Mommy's necklace. Many of the girls wore earrings, necklaces, bracelets, and rings on most of their fingers. It looked like a contest to see who could be the most overdressed.

"Well," Robert said after we put my shawl on a chair and set my purse aside, "why don't we join the fun?"

He led me onto the dance floor and we began dancing. As we moved across the crowded floor, I felt as if everyone's eyes were on us. When I let my gaze shift from Robert's, I saw some of the girls in my class gathered in a small pack, watching us with twisted smiles on their faces. I felt a tightness in my stomach.

The music was loud and fast. I hoped I didn't look foolish, but Robert seemed pleased. He was a very good dancer and I started to imitate some of his movements with my arms and hips. As long as I concentrated on him, fixed my eyes on his, I felt secure and comfortable. He had such an air of confidence about him. There was enough for me to share.

When there was a pause between songs, we stopped, embraced each other, and laughed. He turned me toward the punch bowl, waving to some of the boys he knew and they waved back, giving Robert the thumbs-up sign to indicate they approved.

"We're going to have fun tonight," he promised, his eyes full of excitement. "We're going to dance until our feet beg for mercy."

"Did I do all right out there?" I asked.

"Are you kidding? If they have a dance contest, we're entering," he said.

"Robert Royce, we are not." Just the thought of such a thing took my breath away.

We drank some punch and ate some chips with cheese dip. Marsha Winslow and the class president, Adam Jackson, joined us. Marsha was in charge of the party. She was a tall, attractive girl who spoke with a slightly nasal tone, as if she were looking down her nose at the rest of the world. She carried a clipboard.

"Excuse me," she said, "but we don't have any record of your paying for your tickets."

"What? Of course you do. I gave the money to Betty Hargate," Robert said.

"Betty has you down, but not Laura," she replied.

"That's ridiculous."

"Are you calling Marsha ridiculous?" Adam asked. "You know, she doesn't get paid for doing all this work that makes it possible for everyone else to enjoy themselves. She's just doing her job."

"I'm not calling her ridiculous. I'm just saying . . . where is Betty? There she is." Robert pointed. "Let's call her over," he suggested.

"Good idea," Adam said, and he waved at Betty, who was standing with Lorraine Rudolph. The two hurried over.

"What's up?" Betty demanded impatiently, her hand on her hip. It was as if she had been asked to wallow with the undesirables.

"Robert Royce claims," Marsha said, rolling her eyes, "that he paid for Laura, too, but that's not indicated on the sheet I have."

"I gave you the money in the cafeteria last Tuesday," Robert insisted. "Remember?"

"Whatever is written on the paper is what I received," Betty said in a singsong, smug voice. "I don't have to steal party ticket money."

"I didn't say you stole it," Robert cried, growing increasingly frustrated.

"I only have one ticket marked off after your name," Marsha repeated. "That means you paid for only one ticket."

"I can't believe this," Robert said.

"Are you sure you just didn't *think* you paid for Laura? Maybe you weren't sure she was going with you last Tuesday," Lorraine quipped, a tight smile on her lips. She shifted her eyes to Adam and back to Robert.

29

"Of course, I'm sure. I paid," Robert maintained.

"All the money checks out," Marsha said.

"That means we don't have more money than tickets issued," Adam added.

"I know what it means," Robert said.

"Do you have the tickets, Robert?" I whispered. He thought a moment and then nodded with a confident smile, pulling them out of the inside of his sports jacket.

"If I didn't pay for them, how did I get them?" he asked Marsha, thrusting the tickets in front of her face.

She gazed at the tickets and then looked at her clipboard again.

"I don't understand," she said.

"Maybe Betty gave him two tickets and he promised to give her the money for the second one later," Adam suggested.

"Yes," Betty said quickly. "That's it."

"No, it's not and you know it," Robert insisted.

"Betty's too responsible to give out tickets and not collect the money for them," I suggested calmly. Everyone paused and gazed at me a moment. "Someone just made a simple mistake."

"Well . . ." Marsha glanced at Adam.

"I don't think Robert would steal a dance ticket, do you?" I followed.

"I hope not," Betty blurted.

"We'll straighten it out later," Marsha said. "Right now, we're all wasting time when we should be having fun."

"Exactly," Adam said, taking her arm. "To the dance floor, Madam Chairman."

The others laughed and then left with them.

"That was a pretty stupid bit of meanness," Robert said, glaring after them.

"Maybe it was just an honest mistake, Robert."

He continued to glare in their direction, just daring one of them to look back at us.

"Somehow, I doubt it," he said. "Those kind don't make honest mistakes."

"Let's not let them ruin our night, Robert," I said, touching his hand. He relaxed, smiled at me, and nodded.

"Right. Shall we?" he asked, taking the punch glass from my hand and putting it on one of the tables.

We returned to the dance floor. It didn't take us long to get lost in the music and each other. We soon forgot about the ticket incident and danced until I declared my feet were really begging for mercy. Robert laughed and suggested it was time we had something to eat anyway.

"I guess we've worked up an appetite."

We got in line and filled our plates. Some of the girls in my English class complimented me on my dancing, and girls who had come together without dates gathered around Robert, commenting on his dancing ability too.

Theresa Patterson was there with some of her Brava friends. They kept to themselves, but Theresa gave me a bright, friendly smile when I waved.

As I looked over the endless plates of food I had to give the devils their due: Betty and Marsha had planned a wonderful party. There were steamed clams, of course, and all sorts of chicken dishes, including Southern fried, bowls of tricolor pasta, salads, plates of fruit, loaves of Portuguese bread, rolls, and a table of desserts that would surely be the first to be picked clean.

When we were satisfied we'd taken a bit of everything to sample, Robert and I sat with some of his friends and their dates. Everyone was so excited, they all talked at once. I really was having the time of my life, and when Robert leaned over to give me a small, quick kiss on the cheek, I blushed and told him how much fun I was having.

"I'm so glad," he said. "I was worried when Cary was so negative about the dance. I thought he might—"

"Might what?"

"Talk you out of coming," Robert confessed.

"He could never do that. We may be twins, but I still have a mind of my own, Robert."

"That's good," he said, smiling.

"You should know that by now, and if you don't, you will

31

soon," I promised. Even I was surprised at how seductively it came out. His eyes widened with his smile. I turned away quickly, afraid I would become so crimson, everyone at the table would notice.

After we ate, the music got slower and the lights grew dim. I liked this kind of dancing more because I could rest my head against Robert's shoulder and feel his arms around me. We swayed to the rhythm, neither of us wanting to spoil the moment by talking. Occasionally, I felt his lips on my forehead and hair. My heart pounded so hard, I was sure he could feel it against his chest.

"I'm so glad you came to the dance with me, Laura," he whispered.

"Me too," I said.

"Maybe . . . we can leave a little earlier and just take a ride along the shore. It's a beautiful night," he said.

"I'd like that, Robert."

We moved through the shadows and light. I was dazzled by the glow of the round lanterns, and for a while, it was as if Robert and I were the only ones at the dance. Everyone else just faded away.

That is until I heard Janet Parker's sharp, cold laugh right behind us and turned to see her standing with Adam Jackson, Marsha, Betty, and Lorraine. Brad Laughton and Grant Simpson had joined them as well. Why weren't they dancing? I wondered. Did they come here just to watch and make fun of others? They kept looking our way and laughing.

"What's with them now?" Robert muttered.

"I don't care," I said, but he couldn't stop gazing at them, his eyes filling more and more with fury.

"It's got something to do with us," he said sharply and stopped dancing.

"Robert, forget about them."

"I'd like to know what's so damn funny," he said, taking my hand and crossing the dance floor toward them. They parted, expecting we would walk in between them, but Robert paused.

"Why don't you let us in on your little joke," he said sharply.

"Excuse me?" Adam said with his self-satisfied smirk. "You want to hear a little joke?"

They all laughed.

"What is it with you people?" Robert pursued. I tried to tug his hand, but he was determined to have his say. "Are you trying to ruin our good time? I feel sorry for you if that's all you have to keep you occupied."

"Are you kidding me?" Adam said, surprised that anyone would dare question his actions.

"Well?"

"We just wondered why Laura's brother didn't come to the dance. Couldn't he afford a ticket?" Lorraine asked.

"Robert could have bought him one the same way he bought Laura's," Adam suggested.

"That's not funny," Robert said, stepping toward him. Adam took a step back and held up his hands.

"Hey, take it easy. You wanted to hear a little joke, didn't you?"

"That's not a joke. You're a joke," Robert shot back.

"Whoa, buddy," Brad said. Robert's glare put him back a step, too. They all looked so shallow and cowardly to me, despite their expensive clothing and jewels.

"Come on, Robert," I said. "Let's not waste any more of our time on them."

"The reason we were wondering about your brother," Janet said, "is Grant just came in from having a cigarette and said he saw him loitering in the parking lot."

"What?"

"That's right. He's out there in the cold, dreaming of being in here with his sister," Brad blurted.

Robert's arm shot out so quickly, I didn't realize he had moved until I saw his hand bounce off Brad's chest, sending him back so awkwardly he lost his balance and landed hard on the gym floor. Some of the kids around him started to laugh. He turned red, but after scurrying back to his feet, he kept his distance.

"That was very rude," Betty exclaimed. "Maybe where you come from that happens all the time, but we aren't allowed to do that at our parties." Her eyes widened and she groaned. "Oh no! Mr. Rosner's coming across the floor already. He'll make us cut the party short if there's any wild or stupid stuff and I worked hard to make this a success!" she cried, her mouth twisted and distorted.

"What's going on here?" Mr. Rosner demanded, his hands on his hips. He looked from Brad to Robert and then at the others.

"Just a silly joke, Mr. Rosner," Adam said, smoothly cutting in front of him. "It's nothing. We're all cool."

Mr. Rosner studied everyone and although he wasn't satisfied, nodded.

"I don't want to see any roughhousing," he warned.

"You won't," Adam said. "I guarantee it, sir. As class president, I'll take full responsibility."

"I'm sure you will, Mr. Jackson," Mr. Rosner said. When his eyes fixed on me, he calmed down. "You all look very nice," he said, "and up until now, this has been a very nice affair. I hope you'll continue to make us proud of you."

"Thank you, Mr. Rosner," Lorraine said sweetly. I saw the corner of his mouth twitch as he turned and started away.

"That was close," Adam said, glaring at Robert.

"It wasn't his fault," I said.

"No, that's for sure," Betty said. "Actually, we all feel sorry for him."

"What's that supposed to mean?" Robert demanded.

"Robert, come on," I pleaded, desperate to get Robert away before they could elaborate on their ugly rumors.

"No, what's it supposed to mean?" he pursued.

"Why don't you go out and ask her brother?" Janet quipped and they all started to smile.

"Shall we dance?" Adam asked Marsha, holding out his hand.

"Anything to get away from this incestuous atmosphere,"

she said and they all laughed as they broke up to go their separate ways and leave us standing alone.

"Spoiled, rich—"

"It's all right, Robert. Let's not pay attention to them."

He nodded and then looked at me.

"Do you think Grant was telling the truth? Do you think Cary's hanging around out there?"

"I hope not," I said. "I'm sure he made it up just to hurt us."

Robert forced a smile.

"If you want to go for that ride now," he said finally, "it's fine with me. The air is getting stale in here."

"Yes, I would," I answered him in what I hoped was a cheery tone of voice.

His mood softened.

"Great. I want to be sure to get you home before twelve," he said. "I wouldn't want your father mad at me."

"Most of the time, Daddy's growl is worse than his bite," I said.

"I'm not worried about being bitten; I'm worried about being forbidden," Robert said, slipping his hand into mine, "forbidden to see you."

Our eyes met and I felt a warm glow travel from my stomach to my heart. Was it possible to want to be with anyone more than I wanted to be with Robert? I didn't think so. Surely, this was what love was, and it had happened to me so soon after we had set our eyes on each other, it must be true love. Did that mean it was written in the stars like it had been for Romeo and Juliet? That was fine, as long as we didn't have the same destiny, I thought.

We started out of the gymnasium, gazing back only once to see Betty and Adam looking our way and laughing. It filled me with dread because it was as if they knew something I didn't.

There were some students huddled in the shadows and smoking outside, but I didn't see Cary anywhere. I released the breath I had held in my lungs and walked quickly across the front of the school toward the parking lot. We got into Robert's car and glanced at each other, both of us feeling nervous and excited. Robert took a deep breath and started the car. Then he turned to me.

"You all right with this?" he asked softly.

"Yes, Robert." I slid over to be closer to him and he smiled.

We drove out of the parking lot slowly. I looked back once and thought I saw a shadow scurrying away from a car. In a moment, the shadow disappeared in the darkness and was lost.

"You see something?"

"No," I said, shaking my head and turning back.

We drove quietly for a while, following the road out to the Point.

"I know the artist who lives down that road," I said, when we passed a beach road. "His name's Kenneth Childs. He's Judge Childs's son."

"I've heard of him," Robert said. "In fact, I think we have one of his paintings in the hotel. It was there when we bought the place."

"Most likely. He is one of our most famous artists. He's a nice man, but keeps to himself. Some people call him a hermit."

"I'd still like to meet him. I like his painting in the hotel," Robert said, putting his arm around my shoulders as he slowed the car.

"I took a few exploratory rides down this way recently," he said.

"Oh? And for what reason?" I teased.

"Just to see the countryside," he claimed with an impish little smile.

Moments later he turned down a narrow beach road and then switched off the headlights as he continued a few yards farther. Darkness closed in behind us and on both sides, but before us was the ocean, with the dazzling sea of stars above it and the moonwalk that went to the end of the world.

36

Many times before, Cary and I had sat in the darkness and looked up at the vastness of space with all the stars twinkling, but it never set my heart pounding as it did this night while I leaned against Robert's shoulder, feeling his breath on my hair and then on my forehead before his lips gently touched my ears, my cheeks, and my eyes. I turned to bring my lips to his and we shared a long, soft kiss.

"Laura," he said, stroking my hair. He put his cheek to mine and whispered in my ear. "When I first saw you in school, I felt as if your face was immediately printed in my mind. That first day, I looked for you everywhere, and if I changed classes and didn't see you, I was sick with disappointment."

"I noticed you, too, but I didn't think you were looking at me in a special way."

"That was because I was too shy to say anything. I thought you would take one good look at my face and know I had fallen head over heels. I was afraid you would laugh at me."

"I never would."

"I know that now," he said, putting the tips of his fingers on my lips. "But I didn't know it until I spoke to you and saw how wonderful you really were. I was walking around in a daydream, even at home. I remember I walked right into the kitchen door and bumped my forehead. My father thought I was taking drugs or something. Then my mother looked at me and said, 'He met a girl. I don't know anything else that would turn a boy his age into a clumsy, absent-minded oaf.'"

"She said that?"

"My mother has a great sense of humor," Robert said. "I can't wait for you to meet her."

"Does she meet all your girlfriends?" I asked. He smiled.

"I haven't had many girlfriends, and never one like you," he replied. "Before you, what I felt for other girls was a schoolboy's crush, but when I look at you, Laura, I know it's for real. I hope you feel the same way."

"I do, Robert," I said. "I really do," I added, and we

kissed again. This time he kept kissing me, moving his lips down to my neck. I closed my eyes and let my head rest against his shoulder. His hands moved along my ribs, over my dress, his fingers sliding over the material and then up to my breasts. At first, I instinctively brought my hands up to stop him, but the tingle was so pleasant and warmed me so wonderfully, I let him continue.

Robert sensed my hesitation and then my quick surrender. It made him kiss me faster, harder, longer, his lips rushing over mine before going to my neck, while his hands lifted my breasts, his thumbs riding over the crests of them, caressing my budding nipples.

A soft moan left my lips and I felt Robert gently push me down. He was over me, his fingers finding the zipper behind my dress and carefully moving it down my back. I lifted my arms and he helped me fold the top of my dress to my waist. My eyes were closed as his fingers continued to explore until they unfastened my bra. For a long, delicious moment, my heart pounding, I thought I might die from anticipation and then, when his lips came down upon me, I thought I'd die of pleasure.

The rush of excitement crashed against my better judgment. I knew I should tell him to slow down, but I felt like I was floating, gently undulating on a wave of passion, a wave that was carrying me out too far. "Wait," I heard myself say finally. "We're moving too quickly, Robert. I'm afraid."

He lifted himself from me and I saw him above me, his eyes closed. He took a deep breath and caught hold of the wild passion that was pulling him forward, too.

"You're right, Laura," he said. "I just couldn't stop myself."

"I know a lot of girls wouldn't stop you, Robert. I understand if you're angry with me."

"No," he said, smiling. "It's just the opposite. I want us to be something special, very special. I want us to move as quickly as we both want to move, and love as we both want to love. I want this to last, Laura. I really do love you."

I nodded.

"I love you, too, Robert." I reached up for him again, but he shook his head and pulled my bra down over my breasts.

"If we don't stop now, I won't be able to, Laura," he confessed. He leaned back against the car door and I sat up and fixed my clothes. He had to help me with my dress zipper.

Then we just sat there in each other's arms, listening to our hearts calm themselves, kissing gently every once in a while, and talking softly about the stars, our love, our dreams. Suddenly, Robert looked at his watch.

"Wow, I didn't realize how long we've been here. We had better get going or you'll be late for your curfew."

He started the engine and put the car into reverse. We heard the tires spin, but the car didn't move.

"What the . . ."

He gunned the engine and the tires squealed, kicking up more sand that slapped at the belly of the car, but still we didn't move. He put the car into drive and tried to move forward, then back, rocking the vehicle, but that didn't work either.

"Oh no," he moaned. He reached over to open the glove compartment to take out a flashlight. Then he got out and shined the light on the rear tires. "I dug a hole in the sand. I didn't realize it was so soft here!"

"Robert, what are we going to do?"

"I'll have to run back until I can find a house with lights on and make a call to a tow truck. I'm sorry. I've ruined everything. There's no way we can explain . . ."

Suddenly, a set of headlights brightened up the sky. Robert brought his hand to his forehead to shade his eyes.

"What the hell . . . Who?"

"Who is it, Robert?" I asked, terrified.

"I can't make him out yet, but . . . I think it's Cary!" he declared after another moment.

I turned to look. I would never mistake that silhouetted form. It was Cary walking along the beach road, his truck headlights on behind him.

"Cary!" I cried as soon as he drew close enough.

"Got yourself in a bit of trouble, I see," Cary said with his hands on his hips, gazing down at the wheels.

"Yes, I didn't realize—"

"That's because you aren't from around here," he said disdainfully. "You think these roads are like the old dirt back roads where you took your other girlfriends, huh?"

"No," Robert protested, but Cary just turned to me.

"This was stupid, Laura," he said to me. "I thought you knew better."

"What are you doing here, Cary? How did you find us?"

"I saw you leave the school dance and thought you were going home. When you kept going toward the Point . . . well, just lucky for you I decided to trail along for a while."

A while? I thought. We'd been here a long time. What was he doing all that time?

He turned to Robert. "I'll back my truck in. I've got a chain on it. We'll hook it to the axle and pull you out. Get in and put the car in neutral," he ordered. Robert got back into the car quickly. "And make sure you don't have any brakes on," Cary warned before returning to his truck.

"I can't believe . . . your brother," Robert mumbled. We turned and watched Cary turn the truck around and then back it up toward us. He approached with the chain and crawled under Robert's car. "Why would he follow us like this?" Robert whispered.

"Lucky for us he did," I replied, choosing not to even think about his question at the moment.

"It's all set," Cary called. "Get ready."

He returned to the truck and slowly drove forward. We felt Robert's car jerk and then lift out of the holes he had dug with the tires. The car bounced along the beach road until we were on more solid ground. Cary stopped and returned to detach his chain.

Robert stepped out.

"Thanks a lot," he said sheepishly.

"I didn't do it for you. I did it for Laura," Cary replied. He stepped over to my side of the car. "You better come home with me, Laura," he said.

"I'll take her home," Robert said.

"It looks like it's safer if she drives with me," Cary said, and even in the darkness, I could see Robert turn bright red.

"If I don't come home with Robert, Daddy will wonder why, Cary."

"So?"

"You're not going to tell him about this," I pleaded.

"No, of course not," he said quickly. "Okay, but it's getting late," he warned. He looked at Robert. "And I'm not going to hang around here to bail you out again."

He strutted back to his truck and then drove away. Robert got back into the car and pulled out, driving slowly.

"Why did he follow us, Laura?"

"He was bored, I suppose," I said. It was weak, but it was all I could think to say.

"Was he there all the time, sitting in his truck right behind us? Watching us? Spying on us?"

I started to speak, but just shook my head instead.

"Those idiots back at the dance were right, you know. He was in the parking lot. You've got to help him, Laura. You've got to help him realize you can't be his little sister forever," Robert said.

"I know, Robert. Let's not talk about it right now, please," I begged. Just thinking about Cary's weird obsession with Robert and me brought tears to my eyes and put a lump in my throat.

"Okay," he said, and we were both uncomfortably silent until my house came into view.

"I'm sorry for what happened," Robert said after he parked in our driveway. "Cary was right to bawl me out for it. I just hope it didn't ruin your night."

"No, it didn't. I had a wonderful time, Robert. Really, I did."

"Me too," he said. "I'll call you tomorrow, okay?"

"Let me call you. It'll be easier that way," I said.

"Okay. If that's what you want." He looked worried.

"I'll call. I promise," I said. He smiled and we kissed

quickly before I hopped out of his car. "Thanks for a wonderful evening, Robert."

"Good night, Laura."

I closed the door and looked over at Cary's truck. He was already in the house. When I entered, I found Daddy had waited up for me and was sitting in the living room reading. He looked up from his book. I held my breath, wondering whether Cary had decided to say something after all.

"Have a good time?" Daddy asked.

"Yes, Daddy. It was very nice."

"Everybody behaved themselves?"

"Yes, Daddy."

He nodded and then lowered his voice.

"Your brother didn't come home much earlier than you. I think he's got a secret girlfriend. Am I right?" he asked quickly, unable to keep the hope from his voice.

I felt the blood drain from my face as I shook my head. I hated lying to Daddy.

"I don't know, Daddy. He's never mentioned any girl to me," I said.

Daddy stared at me a moment and then shrugged.

"Oh well," he said, "he'll tell us when he wants to. I just hope it's not someone he thinks we'd be ashamed of." Daddy continued to gaze at me with questioning eyes.

I pressed my teeth on my lower lip and shook my head.

"I don't know, Daddy." How I wished it were true that Cary had found a girlfriend, I thought sadly.

"Well," Daddy said, looking at the clock on the mantel, "young Mr. Royce brought you home on time. That's good." He sighed deeply and stretched out his arms. "It is late though, so I guess I'll go to sleep, too," he added and yawned. "Don't forget we're all going to Grandma Olivia and Grandpa Samuel's tomorrow for brunch."

"Okay. Good night, Daddy," I said, happy to get away from his questioning eyes.

I hurried up the stairs. Pausing on the landing, I saw the door to Cary's room was closed and quickly went into my own room, closing the door behind me. I leaned against it and caught my breath. It was only then that I finally felt myself relax with relief.

Unwilling to take off my party dress just yet, I went to my bed and sat there for a while, thinking about the magical night Robert and I had shared. What an evening, I thought, and then my memories of Robert's kisses, Robert's embrace and touch returned, washing over me in a warm reverie. I lay back with a sigh and closed my eyes, thinking about his hands on my breasts, his lips making me tingle. As I thought about him, I moved my hands to where his had been. I started to undress. In moments, I was naked, standing in front of my mirror, gazing dreamily at myself, imagining Robert beside me. Finally, my fatigue hit me and I went to the bathroom to rinse off my makeup. It felt good to crawl under my blanket and snuggle up.

Despite it all, I thought, it was a wonderful night. It really was. I reached over and turned off the small lamp beside my bed and dropped my head to the pillow. The sound of the floor above creaking popped my eyes open and drove away my sweet thoughts. I held my breath and listened. It was Cary, for I heard him open the attic room door, drop the ladder, and descend as quietly as he could.

He had been up there the whole time, maybe peeping through that hole at me, I thought. I felt my body grow hot with embarrassment as my blood rushed toward the surface of my skin. How much had he seen? We had stopped bathing and sharing the bathroom when we were seven or eight, and I began to demand my privacy even more when I began to develop breasts. Cary's curious eyes had made me feel self-conscious. It wasn't long afterward that I stopped walking around in front of him in my underwear. Even then, the way he looked at me and my changing body made me uncomfortable.

I got up and went to my door, opening it slightly to peer out as he returned the ladder. I started to open the door wider and then hesitated. If I confronted him, I'd only bring more embarrassment to myself, I thought. It was late, I told myself; it wasn't the time for this.

I closed the door ever so softly and waited until I heard him go into his room. Then I went back to bed and lay there with my eyes open, trying desperately to drive the troubled thoughts from my mind so I could think only of Robert and our wonderful night together.

But when I turned on my side and closed my eyes, I saw only Cary's angry face after he had emerged from the darkness behind us, his truck headlights casting him in an eerie silhouette. I finally drifted to sleep, only to find that Cary was in my nightmares, along with the distorted faces of my classmates, whispering, leering, laughing, chasing me toward the roaring sea. Everything was so vivid. I woke in a sweat after the first wave washed over me in my dream. My heart was pounding. I sat up quickly and had to hold my hand over my heart and take deep breaths. Finally, I got up and went to the bathroom to splash my face with cold water.

Whenever Cary and I had a nightmare, we would share it the next morning. It was a way we both had to drive the demons out of our hearts, to comfort each other. For the first time, I couldn't tell him about my dream. This time, I had to find a way to drive the demons out myself.

3
&

Trouble's Brewing

Cary sat sullenly at the breakfast table the next morning. We exchanged few words, but most of the time when he looked at me, I thought I could see the accusations in his eyes. I didn't believe he had any right to make me feel guilty and I refused to act ashamed. If anyone should be ashamed, he should, I thought, following me around at night, peeping through holes in the ceiling.

Mommy was eager to hear about the dance, and I was thankful that at least she could share my happiness. As I spoke, I signed to May, describing the decorations, the food, the music. Of course, I left out the unpleasantness over the ticket and mentioned nothing about Cary pulling Robert's car out of the sand.

"I thought you went to the dance, too, Cary," Daddy said when there was a pause.

"Hardly," Cary said disdainfully.

"Then where were you, boy? It was pretty late when I heard you come in and hurry up those stairs."

"I just met some friends at the Bean Bag," he said quickly.

"How can you hang around a custard stand all night?" Daddy continued.

Cary shot a glance at me to see if I would say anything, and I looked down at my plate.

"We were just hanging out," Cary said. "I didn't realize how late it got."

Daddy shook his head.

"I don't know what you all have to talk about so much that you lose track of time."

"You can pass a lot of time jawin', Jacob," Mommy said, "like when you get together with Pat O'Reilly."

"That's different. We talk about business," Daddy retorted, reddening at the criticism. It was enough to end the topic, for which both Cary and I were grateful.

While we waited to go to brunch at Grandma Olivia's, I took May out to the beach and made some drawings while she sat beside me, asking me questions about my date and about Robert. Drawing was something I did to help relax, just like needlework. I drew pictures of all of us, some from memory, some from things I saw at the moment. Everyone who saw my drawings thought they were very good. I once showed them to Kenneth Childs, who said I might consider taking art classes and developing my talent. I never thought I was good enough to do that, and wasting time trying to be someone I couldn't be was something Daddy convinced me was sinful.

"God grants us enough time to do something worthy with ourselves. Procrastination, chasing foolish dreams, that's what the devil would like us to do," he had said.

I wasn't fixed on anything yet, but I had been thinking lately that I might become a teacher, maybe even a teacher in a school for the handicapped. It made me feel special and filled me with so much pleasure when I was able to teach May something and see her eyes brighten with understanding. I felt as though I had broken through a thick wall, no matter how small the achievement, and I thought I could do this successfully with other handicapped children.

While we were sitting on the beach, drawing and talking, Daddy and Cary went by on their way to the dock.

"We're just going to check on the lobster traps," Daddy explained. Cary stood by, silent, still somewhat sullen. "We

46

won't be long, Laura. You should get yourself and May ready soon."

We always dressed up for brunch at Grandma Olivia's. In fact, we never went there without treating the visit as if it were a special occasion. This was easy for Grandma Olivia, since she was always formally dressed. Even when she was working in her garden, she had her hair pinned properly and wore outfits that most would save for trips into town or visits with company. Grandpa Samuel usually wore a sports jacket and slacks, along with a cravat or a tie. Their home was kept immaculate, everything in its proper place. As children, we were forbidden to wander in the rooms and were terrified of touching anything.

"Okay, Daddy," I said and folded my drawing pad. I signed to May and she folded hers as well. As we headed for the house, I thought this would be the best and maybe only time I would get to call Robert. I was sure he was on pins and needles, worrying about what might have happened after I entered the house last night.

Robert's mother answered.

"Oh hello," she said with enthusiasm, after I had introduced myself. "From the way Robert's been acting this morning, I'd say you and he had a wonderful time last night. I have to say everything to him twice," she added with a little laugh. I heard Robert complaining in the background. "I'd better give him the phone before he throws a fit."

"Hi," he said. "My mother's in one of her hilarious moods today."

"I can't wait to meet her," I said.

"I'll introduce you . . . *as long as you know she'll say anything,*" he added in a voice meant for her ears. He paused and then in a lower voice, asked how things were.

"Everything's fine," I said. "My father was waiting up and I could tell he was relieved that I made it home before curfew. And Cary didn't say anything," I added, knowing he was waiting to hear about that most of all.

"Your father was waiting up? I guess it would have been disastrous if Cary hadn't come to the rescue, but I still can't get over his following us, Laura. Have you talked to him about it?"

"Not yet, Robert. I'm waiting for the right time."

"Don't put it off, Laura," he warned.

"I won't," I said in a little voice. It wasn't something I looked forward to doing.

"I can't wait to see you again," he added in a softer tone.

"Me neither. I'm going to my grandmother's for brunch in a little while. I've got to get ready and then help May get dressed."

"Okay. Thanks for the call," he said in a voice that sent shivers all the way to my toes.

"I couldn't wait," I confessed shyly.

"I'm glad," he said and we both hung up. I hurried upstairs to dress and help May pick out something that wouldn't make Grandma Olivia shake her head disapprovingly.

Grandma Olivia was always uncomfortable around May. We all knew that the signing unnerved her: She said all those hands bending and turning through the air, fingers jabbing, made her stomach jump. She resisted learning any of it and consequently spoke to her youngest grandchild only through an interpreter, usually me or Cary.

Although Mommy seemed to look forward to Grandma Olivia's brunches and dinners, she was always nervous the day of the visit. Mommy reminded me of someone who was preparing for an audition. Pains were taken over how all of us dressed, how well our hair was brushed, our shoes shined, and we were always, even now, reminded about the rules of behavior when at Grandma Olivia's home, including what not to say and what to say. If one of us didn't pass Grandma Olivia's inspection, Daddy usually blamed Mommy, so we did our best to live up to expectations.

We all ended up looking like different people when we were all dressed up, especially May and I, since Grandma Olivia didn't like women to wear their hair loose and down. She said that it made them look like witches, so I had to use bobby pins and combs to wrap my hair neatly, and even May wore a little French twist. Although the old-fashioned hairdos added years to our age, we didn't look overly grown-up, since makeup was strictly forbidden, even for Mommy. She didn't even wear lipstick.

Despite all this, I did look forward to going. Grandma Olivia usually had wonderful things to eat. I especially loved the tiny cakes with frosting and jelly in the center, and even now, even though we were really grown-up, Grandpa Samuel always gave me and Cary, along with May, crisp five-dollar bills when we left.

I had one particular dress that always seemed the most acceptable to Grandma Olivia. It was a navy blue dress with a white collar that buttoned at the base of my throat. Although I had other, equally dowdy dresses, for some reason this one always brought a smile to Grandma Olivia's grim face.

When I stood before the mirror, I reminded myself to keep my shoulders back and my head up, as if I were balancing a book on top. One of Grandma Olivia's pet peeves was the way young people slouched. She claimed posture showed character and embellished good health.

I never told anyone except Cary, but I actually felt sorry for Grandma Olivia. Sure, she had a big, beautiful house filled with extravagant furniture, paintings, and decorations. Her dinners were elaborate and served on expensive china with fine crystal glasses and real silverware.

Yet for all her extravagance, her important acquaintances, and her gala affairs, Grandma Olivia never looked happy to me. If anything, I thought she was trapped by her wealth and position. How sad it must be, I concluded, to go through your life never letting your hair down, never walking barefoot on the beach, never just being lazy or having a potluck dinner; in short, never doing anything spontaneously, but always first having to go through the proper arrangements, as if your whole life had to be lived according to Emily Post.

I knew very little about my grandmother's past. She never volunteered any information and rarely, if ever, told any stories, unless of course, they were to illustrate and support some rule of behavior. Whenever I asked Mommy questions about Grandma Olivia, Mommy would shake her head and say, "Your grandmother had a difficult childhood because of the problems caused by her sister Belinda." What those problems were and how they had made Grandma Olivia's life difficult was left a mystery. Belinda had problems with alcohol when she was younger and eventually ended up in a rest home nearby. Whenever I visited with her, she told me stories and made references to her and Grandma Olivia's youth, but her stories were almost impossible to understand because Aunt Belinda confused the past and the present, mixing up people and places. Sometimes when she saw me, she called me Sara, thinking I was my mother, and once, recently, she called me Haille.

I know Grandma Olivia did not approve of my visiting Aunt Belinda. She treated her sister as if she were poisonous and could infect one of us with her outlandish stories and statements. I rarely brought up her name in front of Grandma Olivia because I knew what sort of reaction I would receive.

With all these no-no's and strict rules to follow, Cary, May, and I practically tiptoed around the big house and grounds, keeping our voices low and keeping ourselves as much out of sight and out of mind as possible.

After we were all dressed, Daddy looked us over as if we were lining up for parade inspection. He straightened Cary's tie and brushed down May's skirt after he spotted a tiny crease.

"I can have her take it off and iron it, Jacob," Mommy offered.

"It's all right," he said. "We'll be late. Let's get started."

The three of us got into the backseat, Cary sitting on one end and me on the other with May between us. He gazed out the window and didn't look at me once during the ride over to Grandma Olivia and Grandpa Samuel's.

"What a pretty spring day," Mommy said as we headed down Route 6. Grandma Olivia's house was midway between Provincetown and North Truro. From the outside, my grandparents' house looked far from cold and impersonal. It was a large two-story, clapboard covered home with a wide-planked whitewashed front door. Over the door was a fan-shaped window of colored glass and, though I'm sure it was meant to be decorative, Cary and I always joked about it looking like a big gloomy frown warning visitors to stay away.

Grandma Olivia was very proud of her home, claiming it was prestigious because of its historic past.

"The original portion of this house was built around 1780," she declared to every new visitor. She usually added, "That was when the prosperous families began to build some of the more fashionable buildings in colonial America. Today," she would continue in that sharp, critical tone of voice of hers, "wealthy people sacrifice classic fashion for ostentation."

The grounds around the house were also beautiful and well taken care of. The carpet-like green lawn was always immaculate, and the flower garden was dazzling with its hydrangeas, pansies, roses, and geraniums. There was even a small duck pond with a dozen or so ducks in it. In front of the house were two large, blooming red maple trees. Between them on the far right was a bench swing with a canopy over it, although I don't think anyone but Cary, May, or I ever used it.

We saw Judge Childs's car parked in the circular driveway when we pulled in. Judge Childs was a frequent guest, especially for Sunday brunch. He was my grandparents' closest old friend. The judge was retired, but Grandma Olivia always stressed the fact that he still had friends in high places and was very influential.

After we got out of the car, Mommy gave us another once-over, straightening May's clothes and again trying to brush out any creases.

Daddy rang the doorbell, and Grandma Olivia's house-keeper, Loretta, answered the door. For as long as I could remember, Loretta had worked for Grandma Olivia and Grandpa Samuel, but she never looked terribly happy about it.

"Everyone is in the sitting room," she declared without much emotion and stepped back to allow us in.

We entered like one of the duck families in the pond, Daddy first, Mommy right behind him, and then the three of us trailing in single file.

There was a short, marble-floored entryway with paintings on both sides, seascapes of the Cape and boats and portraits of sailors. The house was always full of the perfumed aroma of flowers, even in the wintertime.

The sitting room was the first room on the right. It had the look of a showcase in a furniture store window. The oak wood floor was kept so polished, Cary and I used to pretend that we could go ice skating over it. There was a large rug between the pair of beige sofas and under the large dark maple coffee table. Beside both settees were matching maple end tables. On every table, on every shelf, there were expensive-looking crystal pieces, vases and, occasionally, pictures in silver and gold frames of Grandpa Samuel and Grandma Olivia when they were younger, and some pictures of Daddy, Mommy, as well as one group picture of me, Cary, and May taken four years ago. There were no pictures of the ostracized Uncle Chester and Aunt Haille. Bringing up their names in this house was the same as uttering a profanity.

Everything always looked brand new to me. Every piece of metal glittered, as did every piece of glass. The windows were so clean, you couldn't tell if they were open or closed unless you walked right up to them.

Grandma Olivia was in her high-back chair looking like a queen granting an audience when we entered the sitting room. She wore an elegant rose silk dress with a large cameo above her left breast, a piece we knew was an heirloom, handed down from her grandmother on her father's side. Her hair was pulled back in a severe bun with a pearl comb decorated with small diamonds.

Grandpa Samuel sat rather casually compared to Grandma Olivia. He had his legs crossed, a tall glass of whiskey and soda in his hand. He wore a light brown suit and looked his usual dapper self. His face broke into a wide, warm smile as soon as we entered the room.

"Here they are," he declared, "and a pretty handsome and beautiful group of grandchildren, too, hey Nelson?"

Judge Childs nodded. He sat across from Grandpa Samuel on Grandma Olivia's right side. The Judge was a distinguished-looking, elderly man with gray hair shot through with some of his original light brown color. It was neatly trimmed and parted on the right side. He wore a dark blue suit and a bow tie. Despite his age, I thought he was still a rather handsome man. His face was full and his complexion robust, with wrinkles only across his forehead. He had light brown eyes that dazzled with a glow more characteristic of a man half his age.

"Absolutely, Samuel. You and Olivia are very lucky people. Hello, Jacob, Sara," the Judge said.

Mommy nodded and smiled.

"We've got Bloody Marys, if you like," Grandpa said.

"No thank you," Daddy said quickly.

"I know you like Blood Marys, Sara," Grandpa followed, with a twinkle in his eyes. Mommy glanced quickly at Daddy, who was as close to a scowl as could be.

"Oh, I don't think so, just yet, Pa," she replied.

"When are you going to loosen up that collar you have around your wife's neck, Jacob?" Grandpa said, and the Judge smiled.

"That's an inappropriate remark," Grandma Olivia declared. "Especially in front of the children," she added firmly. "Loretta," she snapped, "please take the children into the kitchen and give them some lemonade while we wait for brunch to be served."

"Yes, ma'am," Loretta said.

Grandma Olivia thought it was inappropriate for young people to sit and listen to the older people converse. While we were standing in the doorway beside and behind Mommy and Daddy, she had been looking us over. She nodded at Daddy.

"The children look very nice," she offered Mommy, who beamed immediately. "Now don't go wandering outside and getting messed up," she called after us. "We'll call you to the dining room in a little while. Sit down, Jacob. You're making me nervous standing there like that. Sara."

They moved quickly and Loretta led us away. She gave us the lemonade and then, as we had done many times before, we went out back to the gazebo. Cary stood staring out toward the ocean while I entertained May. Finally, he turned to me, his eyes narrowed as if he were in pain.

"You go down a dirt road like that your first date with a guy. It doesn't look nice. It makes you look like . . . look like . . . an easy target," he said. "I just knew he was going to do that; I just knew it," he claimed and turned back toward the sea.

"First, I'm not an easy target, Cary Logan. I don't do what I don't want to do and we didn't do anything wrong, for your information. Robert is a complete gentleman."

"Ha," he said.

"You don't know him, Cary."

"You'll see," Cary predicted. "Tomorrow they'll be chattering about you in the locker room and Royce will be bragging about how easy you were."

"He will not! And it's dreadful of you to say that he would. You're just . . . just jealous," I accused. His shoulders stiffened and he turned, his face turning pink.

"What's that supposed to mean?"

"You don't have a girlfriend and you don't go out on dates, so—"

"So *what?*"

"So, you're jealous that I do."

"Dates," he said, curling up the right corner of his mouth. "Some dates."

I realized that May had been reading my lips and watching my face. She looked very confused. I tried smiling at her, but she turned and looked at Cary, her eyebrows raising as she gazed at me again. She didn't see us argue often.

"We'll talk about it later," I said.

"There's nothing to talk about," Cary retorted.

"Why did you follow us?"

"Why?" He shook his head. "I went to the dance to see what it was like and then, when I saw you two leave early, I just knew I had better keep my eye on you. Lucky for you, I did. I can't believe you have the nerve to question me. If it weren't for me, you wouldn't have made it home in time for curfew."

"You've got to let me—"

"Let you *what*, Laura? Go on. What?"

"Grow up," I said.

He stared, blinking rapidly, and then turned to the ocean again.

"I appreciate your concern, but I need my space, too, Cary."

"Fine," he said through gritted teeth.

He spun around and glared at the house, his anger spilling over like water boiling out of a pot. "I don't know why we have to wait around for them to stop gossiping. I'm hungry. We hardly had anything for breakfast this morning."

"So, go tell Grandma," I challenged.

He pounded up the steps to the door, nearly ripping it off the hinges when he pulled it open. May tugged on my hand and started to sign her questions.

"Cary's hungry," I explained. "He wants to see how much longer before we eat."

She stared after him and then glanced at me, her suspicious eyes small and troubled. I lowered my shoulders in defeat. Why did my most wonderful, new relationship have to bring such sadness? Why couldn't Cary be happy for me? I was near tears and had to turn away from May before she saw my sadness.

Whatever Cary did inside sped things along, because a few moments later, Loretta appeared to say it was time we came in to eat.

It was as wonderful a brunch as ever, with chunks of lobster in Alfredo sauce, shrimp cocktail, delicious home fries, salads filled with almost every vegetable imaginable, and as usual, great desserts, including my favorite, the multilayered, multicolored petit fours.

Afterward, the men went for their walk along the beach, Judge Childs and Grandpa lighting up their cigars. They took Cary along with Daddy, and Mommy, May, and I were left behind with Grandma Olivia.

Mommy started to tell Grandma about my date and how pretty I looked, when Grandma suddenly rose from her chair.

"I'd like to speak with Laura," she said, interrupting Mommy in midsentence, "if you don't mind, Sara."

"What? Oh. No. Why should I mind?" Mommy stuttered and gazed about the big room helplessly. Grandma Olivia was already to the door of the sitting room.

"Come along, Laura," she commanded. I looked at Mommy, who only shook her head, her eyes wide with surprise. I caught up with Grandma in the hallway, heading toward the back door.

"Why can't Mommy hear what we say, Grandma?" I asked nervously.

"We'll go out to the gazebo," she replied, ignoring my question. "I need some air and a little walk after that meal anyway," she said.

"It was a terrific brunch, Grandma."

"The coleslaw was rather bitter this time," she complained. We left the house, walked down the pathway to the gazebo, and sat on the bench.

"Mommy and May should come out, too," I said. "It's so beautiful, hardly a cloud in the sky."

I gazed down the beach and saw the four men walking, little puffs of smoke from Grandpa's and Judge Childs's mouths caught and dissipated in the breeze. Cary was a few steps behind the adults, his head down.

"We'll send for them in a moment," Grandma Olivia said. "Now that you are obviously becoming a young woman with a woman's . . . interests, I thought it was time we had a little talk, Laura. I don't mean to interfere, but I don't think your mother is prepared for this sort of discussion," she added.

"What kind of a discussion is that, Grandma?"

"A woman-to-woman discussion," she replied, "where one woman has vast experience and wisdom to give to another, younger woman. Although she would have the same good intentions, your mother doesn't have my background, my breeding. She's not as aware of the dangers."

"Dangers?"

I stopped smiling and sat back. I suddenly felt as if my wonderful brunch had all tightened into a small, hard ball at the base of my stomach.

"I don't understand, Grandma. What dangers?"

"You're interested in someone, I understand, and you've actually gone out on a formal date with this person?" she began, her eyes small, but fixed on me with that same intensity that stopped laughter and wiped smiles off faces.

"Oh," I said with some relief. "Yes. He's a very nice young man. His name's—"

"I know his name," she said quickly. "I know of his family and what they do. I know he's been to your home for lunch and you went to the school dance with him last night."

My eyes widened with surprise. I smiled at Grandma Olivia's interest in my social life. She had never asked any questions about it before or cared whether I had gone to a school dance or not. I always thought that sort of thing wasn't significant enough to matter to her.

"I'm sorry I haven't had a chance to tell you about him, Grandma," I told her. Finally, she and I would have a nice grandmother-granddaughter talk, I thought, and imagined she wanted to tell me about her own childhood romances.

"There isn't much that goes on in this town that I don't know and there is nothing that involves my family and the family name that I won't eventually find out about," she declared. "I may not discuss it with you, but I know how well you're doing in school and how much your teachers like you. I know how you are a great help to your mother, and how you've been a respectful, obedient daughter. That's why I think it's so important we have this conversation," she continued.

I widened my smile and nodded.

"You're much too young to get deeply involved with any one young man, especially one who comes from a family of some questionable character."

"What?" The little bubble of delight that had started to fill within me suddenly popped.

"Don't interrupt, Laura. Just listen and learn. The Logans, and my family, the Gordons, go back to the Pilgrims, as you know. We have a strong, highly respected lineage. We are looked up to in this community; we are people of worth, status, and that brings with it more responsibility. We have been and remain models of proper behavior, models of respectability. My father taught me years and years ago that the first and most important and valuable thing you own is your reputation.

"You and Cary have been born with a gift. That gift is your family name. You've inherited literally hundreds of years of highly valued reputation. It will open doors for you, gain you respect, and place you high on the ladder of status, but you have a big responsibility, Laura, and that responsibility is to uphold the respectability, the value of our family name.

"Because of that," she continued, "there is a magnifying glass over you and your actions." She flashed a cold smile. "Up until now, you have done nothing even to slightly tarnish our family name, and I'd like to keep it that way. I want you to immediately end this acquaintance. These people are not up to your standard," she concluded. "I intend to discuss it with your father before the day is over as well," she said. She sat back, obviously waiting for my reaction.

For a moment I thought the words would get caught in my throat and my voice wouldn't work. Despite the silvery, soft breeze blowing in from the ocean, I felt as though I had fallen into a furnace. My face was flushed, my heart, although pounding, seemed to have sunken in my chest, the *thump, thump, thump* barely felt through my body. I shook my head.

"I don't know what you've been told, Grandma, but it's

all a mistake. Robert Royce is a very, very nice young man, Grandma. He—"

"He comes from a family of innkeepers," she said, practically spitting out the words, as if they were bitter in her mouth. "Do you know what an innkeeper is, Laura? How they started to be? These are people who had nothing, no family name, no reputation. Practically destitute, they open their own homes to strangers, clean up after them, wash their toilets and sinks, serve them food, cater to the wishes of complete and utter strangers, and worst of all, they contribute, are responsible for the pollution and destruction of the Cape.

"Fine homes, beautiful landscapes are all being marred by these . . . these motel and hotel chains. Anyone who can afford the price of a cheap bed can come here and enjoy what we, who built this, who founded it, created and made elegant. You have no business consorting with someone of that ilk, Laura. I absolutely forbid you to continue seeing this . . . this person. He will only bring you down."

"Please, Grandma," I said, choking back my tears, "don't talk like that."

She tightened her lips.

"You must get a hold of yourself, Laura. You must become mature, strong, beat down any foolish little lusts and remember who you are.

"Unfortunately," she said with a deep sigh, "we've already had a terrible time maintaining our family honor because of my sister and your Uncle Chester, but that has been remedied. We don't need something else to disgrace us and weaken our family's reputation."

"Remedied? Your son has left the family. We're not permitted to mention his name in your presence. I don't understand all of it, Grandma. You never talk about him, but don't you ever miss him?"

"He made a choice and one that is unfortunately best for everyone," she said sternly. "I'm not here to discuss the dead. I'm here to discuss you, the living."

"The dead?"

"Laura," she said firmly, "do you understand what I've been trying to tell you?"

"No, Grandma, I don't. I just met Robert. I like him. He's been very nice to me and we had a wonderful time at the school dance. I didn't agree to marry him . . . yet," I said, and her eyebrows rose so fast and so high, I thought they might leave her face.

"You would never marry such a person," she stated, her fear and anxiety deepening the lines in her face.

"I don't judge people by their bank accounts, Grandma," I said. I meant it as a matter of fact, but she pulled her head back as if I had reached across the gazebo and slapped her.

"I don't either, Laura. That's the point I'm trying to make and the point you're missing. Many of these so-called nouveaux riches are resort businesspeople. They have money, but they don't have class or reputation. They never will, no matter how fat their bank accounts become."

"But . . . didn't you ever like anyone who wasn't from an old and respectable family, Grandma? Not even when you were growing up?"

"Of course not," she said. "I wouldn't permit myself to like someone like that."

"That's not something you can permit yourself to do and not to do, Grandma," I said, smiling. "It's something magical. Surely, when you were my age—"

"I was never a foolish young woman, Laura, never like any of these empty-headed girls nowadays. My father wouldn't have tolerated it anyway, especially with my sister being such a disgrace. It would have destroyed him if both his daughters . . ." She paused to pull herself up tight again. "This is all beside the point. We're not here to discuss my past; we're here to discuss your future and the future of the family's reputation," she insisted.

"Can't you remember what it was like to be my age? You couldn't have worried about all this back then."

"Of course I worried about all this." She shook her head. "I knew I should have taken more of a role in your upbringing. Sara . . . Sara is just not equipped and she has too much to do with your crippled sister."

"May is not crippled, Grandma. She has a handicap, but it hasn't stopped her from being a good student and doing most of the things other young girls her age can do. She's very helpful around the house, does her chores, looks after her own things. She's far from a burden to Mommy, Grandma. If you would just let me teach you some sign language, you could talk with her directly and see for yourself how bright and wonderful she is."

"Ridiculous. I have no time for that sort of thing. Besides, you all shield her too much because of this . . . this imperfection. She should be made to expect no favors and she certainly shouldn't be babied. Only then will she have the strength to stand up to her deformity."

"It's not a deformity," I insisted. "And May is smart and strong enough to live a good life with her handicap."

"I didn't bring you out here to waste time on this topic, Laura. I brought you out here to give you the benefit of my years of wisdom and my sense of family responsibility. Unfortunately, I am the one who has to have all the strength in this family. Your grandfather is becoming more and more forgetful. I'm afraid he's falling into his dotage and will end up in a rest home sooner rather than later."

"Grandpa? He looks wonderful."

"You don't live with him," she replied dryly. "Anyway, I hope you have heard some of what I have said and will behave properly, doing the right thing."

"I like Robert Royce, Grandma. I'm not going to hurt him by telling him he's not good enough for the Logans," I said softly, but firmly.

She stared at me a moment and then slowly shook her head.

"I expected more from you, Laura. You leave me no choice but to speak to your father about this."

I felt the tears come to my eyes.

"Daddy likes Robert, too," I said, but I knew how strong my grandmother's influence was on my father. Usually, her words were like Gospel. "Please don't say anything bad about him."

"If I have your word that you will not do anything hasty or foolish with this person," she said. "Too many young people today think nothing of embarrassing their families."

"Of course, I won't."

"Very well. We'll see how things progress. Someday, you will be grateful for what I've said to you today, Laura. You'll look back and laugh at yourself for being so foolish."

She looked confident of that, but inside, I thought, *No, Grandma, I'll never be grateful for your telling me that magic between people is merely empty-headed foolishness. I'll never be grateful for your telling me that people have to be judged by their family lineage instead of the content of their character, that status is more important than anything, even honest feelings. No, Grandma, I won't be grateful; I'll always be full of pity, and not for myself, but for you.*

I said none of this, of course. Instead, I sat silently watching her look toward the beach where the men were making their way back to the house.

"It looks like the great minds have settled the problems of the world and are returning," she said dryly. "Why don't you ask your mother and sister to come out now."

I rose quickly.

"When I was your age, I always thanked my elders for taking the effort and time to talk to me and share with me their wisdom, Laura," she said as I started away. I paused and turned back slowly.

"I know you want only happiness for me, Grandma. I thank you for that," I said.

It didn't please her enough. She gave me the most chilling and piercing look I could remember, a look that sent me hurrying into the house to get Mommy.

4
🕮

A Sign from Above

*D*uring the days that followed, an uneasy truce developed between Cary and myself. He continually tried to maintain an air of anger and disapproval, once again trying to prove that he knew more than I did about dating. He would talk to me through May, signing and delivering his lectures aloud, even though we both knew she could hear nothing. He claimed May needed to learn what to do and what *not* to do on dates, since I had obviously never been taught the rules. He sounded like Daddy, complaining about young people being too forward, too advanced for their age. At times, when he put on Daddy's face and took on Daddy's voice, I was afraid I would laugh, so I had to turn away to hide my smile. Cary didn't have to imitate Daddy's temper. He had one of his own that was bad enough.

"Now that you're getting older, May," he lectured, shifting his eyes to me, "you have to be careful you don't waste your time on foolish boys or boys who think of girls as trophies and not as people."

"She doesn't have any idea what you're talking about, Cary," I said.

"That's more reason to talk to her now, before it's too

late. You're a big influence on her," he growled. "A negative one," he added.

"What's that supposed to mean, Cary?"

"Just what it means. What she sees you do, she'll think is the best thing to do, the right thing to do."

"I haven't done anything in front of her that I shouldn't," I protested.

"Maybe not yet," he muttered.

He was infuriating, but it was better for me to bite my lip and swallow back my words. He simply continued to make his speeches, talking about boys as if they were poisonous. Poor little May was smart enough and sensitive enough to know she shouldn't contradict him, but she looked to me continually to see if I would reinforce or challenge anything Cary said. I said nothing and looked away. Later, when we were alone, she asked me why Cary was so mad at the boys in school. I told her he was just trying to protect her; he was worried about her. She fixed her large hazel eyes on me and waited for me to say more, but I couldn't.

Sadness was like a spider weaving a web around us. Cary's face of gloom cast long shadows in our house. Whenever he entered a room May and I were in, her eyes swung from me to him and back to me in anticipation of some nasty wave that might drown us all in a sea of depression. Cary spent more and more of his time alone, up in his attic workshop. At school, he stayed to himself, even in the cafeteria. Sometimes, he sat with some of the boys from other fishermen families, but his eyes were always on Robert and me, making me feel self-conscious, making me feel guilty for every laugh, every smile, and especially, every touch.

Robert tried to be friendly toward Cary, tried to have conversations with him, but Cary would only respond in monosyllabic grunts, usually hurrying off or simply ignoring him. I told Robert it would just take time. I told him to be patient, that once Cary saw how nice Robert was, he would stop being so protective and concerned.

"I suppose if I had a sister who looked like you, I'd be walking around with a shotgun over my shoulder, too," he told me. It brought a smile to my face and laughter to my lips. Robert had a way of parting the clouds and bringing the sunshine into every desolate moment. I had never known anyone as hopeful or as cheerful. After I met his parents, I decided it was because of them, because they appeared to be so happy and in love themselves.

"A flower blooms best in a happy pot," Aunt Belinda once told me when I visited her at the home. I thought she was referring to Grandma Olivia not being a flower that showed much bloom. I thought she was complaining about her own family life, but I couldn't get her to explain any of the things she said. Most of the time, she would just follow something with a laugh and the words would float from us and dissipate like smoke.

I met Robert's parents one afternoon when school was ended early because of a teachers' conference. I asked Cary if he wanted to come along to see how Robert's parents were fixing up the Sea Marina.

"Why would I want to waste time looking at a run-down tourist hovel?" Cary snapped in response. "And why would you?"

"It's not run-down anymore, Cary, and it's certainly not a hovel."

"Who's picking up May?" he countered.

"I will, if you want," I said.

"If I want? You used to care about your little sister," he remarked coldly.

"You know I care about her, Cary. That's not fair. I said I would pick her up."

"Never mind. You'll probably forget; you'll probably be too distracted by loverboy, and she'll be standing there alone and afraid," he said.

"I'm never that distracted, Cary, but even if I were, May could come home herself easily."

"Sure, and not hear a car when she goes to cross the road."

"She knows how to cross a road."

"I don't think going to see some junk house for tourists is

more important than May's safety," he said. "I'll look after her."

He turned and marched off before I could respond and left me simmering, my hands pressed into tight fists at my sides, my stomach feeling as if it had been twisted and turned inside out. The way some of the other students were looking at me as they passed me in the hallway made me think I had ribbons of steam coming from my ears.

"Are you feeling all right?" Robert asked me when we left school that afternoon. "You haven't said a word."

"I'm fine," I said. "It's just . . . my brother gets me so angry sometimes, I feel like screaming."

"Maybe you should, Laura. Maybe it's time you let him know just how you really feel," Robert said.

"Maybe."

I looked at him, at his face full of concern, and I knew that he was right.

"I'd better wipe the frown out of my face before I meet your parents," I said, "or they'll think you've chosen a witch for a girlfriend."

He laughed and we got into his car and drove to the Sea Marina.

Although the building itself had been neglected, the property on which it lay was prime seaside real estate. Only the front of the hotel had any real lawn. The rear was sandy beach with a pathway that led to a small dock. At one time, the hotel had a sailboat, but it was long gone. All that was left were two rowboats, neither looking very seaworthy, both covered with mildew and both with small leaks. Robert's parents had been concentrating on the building itself, replacing broken shutters, worn, cracked, and broken porch floorboards, painting the walls, repairing the kitchen, putting down new flooring, and replacing the bedding, sitting room furniture, lamps, and electrical fixtures.

"My father's always been pretty handy," Robert told me as we drove up. His father was on a ladder, repairing a loose clapboard.

I knew that the Sea Marina had once been one of the most

interesting houses in the area. It had been built as a mansion for a Captain Bellwood, who had developed a successful whaling business when sperm oil was in great demand. As with many great houses, the family lost its fortune and eventually converted the home into a rooming house for tourists. A sign bearing the words THE SEA MARINA was slapped over the entry doors and a new history for the building began. It was never well kept and four or five years ago was finally shut down. Robert explained that the bank had foreclosed on the inn and Robert's parents were able to buy it cheaply enough to have money left over to restore it.

It was a three-story building with twenty-two rooms available for renting. Robert and his parents lived in the downstairs rear of the house. Above the roof was a large cupola with a round dormer. The house had been constructed with a great deal of decorative detail, cresting along the roof line, a widow's walk, paired windows above the front doors, bay windows on the lower floor, and a one-story porch with carved railings and posts. The entire outside of the building had to be stripped and sanded before it was repainted. The cement steps that had cracked and chipped were replaced, as were a half dozen cracked and broken windows. I had ridden my bike past the Sea Marina before and knew how run-down it was before Robert's parents began this prodigious remodeling. It was no wonder he was occupied and working so much of the time.

Mr. Royce saw us drive up and waved. Immediately I saw that Robert had inherited his smile from his father. When we drew closer and he came down the ladder, I also noticed that Robert shared his blue eyes as well. His father was an inch or so taller, with the same lean, muscular frame.

"What are you hooky players up to?" he asked.

"I told you school was out early today, Dad," Robert said. His father winked at me.

"Yeah, he told me, but can I believe him?"

"Yes you can, Mr. Royce," I said quickly and he laughed.

"I see you have a loyal partner there, Robert. You going to introduce us or just stand there looking foolish?"

"This is Laura Logan, Dad. Laura, my father, Bob Hope."

"Bob Hope? If I was that good a comedian, do you think I'd be out here sweating over clapboard? Hi, Laura. Well, what do you think so far?" he said, stepping back, his hands on his hips. We all looked up at the Sea Marina.

"It's looking very good, Mr. Royce. It's going to be beautiful."

"Thank you. Robert's had a hand in all this, but you should see what his mother's accomplished inside."

"Come on," Robert said.

"It's nice meeting you, Mr. Royce."

He smiled and gave Robert a look of approval that broadened his shoulders even more.

"Feel free to drop by anytime, Laura. We could always use another hand clutching a paint brush," he said.

"Dad!" Robert protested.

"I'd like to," I said. "It looks like fun."

"Fun? You call this fun?" he joked. "I like this girl, Robert."

"Bye, Dad," Robert said, rolling his eyes and seizing my hand. "Come on, let's meet my mother," he added in a deep, low voice, filling me with trepidation.

We went up the front stairs and inside. Unlike the outside, the inside of the inn looked like it needed weeks and weeks more of work. The floors were still bare, the walls in the sitting room had only been sanded down and prepped for paint, wires hung from ceilings waiting for their fixtures, and doors were still off their hinges, lying against the walls like impatient guests waiting to be checked in.

"Ma!" Robert called from the hallway. We heard what sounded like a collapsing tower of pots and pans and then a curse. "Uh-oh," Robert said. He widened his eyes and held on to my hand as we continued down the hallway toward what had to be the kitchen.

Robert's mother was sitting on the kitchen floor, her face buried in her hands. Pots and pans were scattered around her. She wore a pair of jeans and a flannel shirt knotted at the bottom, the sleeves rolled to her elbows. Her hair, Robert's color, was tied in a ponytail. When she lifted her face from her palms, I saw she had the same soft, perfect features as her son. Even though she was obviously upset at the moment, she had the complexion and youthful glint in her eyes that made her seem ten years younger.

When she focused on us, she smirked, and leaned back on her hands.

"Welcome to the Sea Marina," she said. "Dinner," she continued in a style imitating an English butler, "will be slightly delayed due to catastrophe."

"What happened?" Robert asked.

"Those shelves I put up decided I had put them in the wrong place and rebelled," she explained and pointed to where the brackets had come out of the wall.

"I told you I would do that today," Robert said.

"I didn't think it was going to be a big deal. Obviously, I underestimated the weight of my cookery." She gazed at me and then smiled. "Are you the new cook?"

"What?"

"Ma, you know who this is," Robert said impatiently.

"Oh? Oh," she added and jumped to her feet, brushing off her jeans. "The lobster girl."

"What?"

"Ma!"

"Hi, I'm Jayne Royce," she said, coming forward to shake my hand. "Robert has told me everything about you, so I don't have to ask you a single question."

"Ma."

"Ma, ma. He sounds like a confused sheep. It's ba, ba, Robert. Come on," she said, taking my hand, "let me show you my jewel."

I looked back helplessly as she pulled me along, back through the hallway and into the dining room, so far the only finished room I'd seen. It had a long, dark maple table with very comfortable-looking captain's chairs. There was a silver candelabra and very pretty placemats that looked hand-stitched. There were two teardrop chandeliers that sparkled like ice in the sun, and a large oil painting of a whaling vessel in pursuit was on the far wall. Hanging across the room was another oil painting that I recognized as one of Kenneth Childs's earlier works. It was a beach scene with terns just starting their turn toward the setting sun.

"Well?"

"It's beautiful, Mrs. Royce."

"Please call me Jayne. I call my mother-in-law Mrs. Royce."

I laughed as Robert came up beside us.

"You want to see the dock?" he asked.

"Why would she want to see the dock? It's uglier than a one-eyed bulldog in heat."

"Ma."

"Maybe we should help your mother with those shelves, Robert," I suggested.

"Now here is a girl I could grow to adopt. When you're ready to run away from home, this is the place," she said. "She's very pretty, Robert. You didn't exaggerate."

"Mmm—"

"Don't say it. Wait a minute, Robert," she said, pressing her forefinger into her cheek as she feigned deep thought. "I have it. Why don't you call me Mrs. Royce," she suggested and I laughed. "Come on," she said, taking my hand again, "we'll go back to the kitchen and you can tell me all about life on Cape Cod while I pick up my pots and pans."

I looked at Robert, who shrugged.

"I guess we'll help Mrs. Royce," he said and we all laughed.

It was a wonderful afternoon. I never thought I would enjoy working so much. They wanted me to stay for dinner, but I didn't think it would be right on such short notice. I explained how I usually helped my mother make dinner and should be getting home.

Despite all the restoration work ahead of them, the Royces were happy and confident. The atmosphere of camaraderie, the sense of partnership among them, made me envious.

Robert's parents seemed so much younger than mine and so much more relaxed. I felt their love for each other and how concerned they were for each other's happiness. *No wonder Robert has such a warm and hopeful personality,* I thought.

"Well," he said as we drove away, "I warned you my mother was a character."

"I love her, Robert. She's great."

"Yeah, I guess I'm lucky," he said. "And now," he added, looking at me, "I'm even luckier."

Because the school year was approaching its end, studying for exams and preparing our last projects was very important. Although Robert and I didn't share any classes, we thought it might be fun to study together. For that purpose, he came to my house the following Saturday. I had already told my mother and mentioned it to Daddy just before Robert was due to arrive. Daddy and May were playing a game of checkers in the living room at the time. He paused and turned to me.

"Seems you're becoming the talk of the town, you and your boyfriend, Laura," Daddy said.

"No we're not, Daddy." I started to laugh at the idea.

"Grandma Olivia thinks so," he added. "You know how all the news worms its way up to her."

"I know." I grimaced in expectation of what Grandma Olivia had told him.

"Maybe you're getting a little too serious too fast," Daddy suggested.

"I'm not, really, Daddy."

"Everyone's expecting you'll go off to college, Laura. Not many Logans have. Your mother tells me you've shown some interest in becoming a teacher."

"I *will* become a teacher, Daddy."

"Lots of girls make plans and then meet someone and lose their heads, Laura," he warned.

"I'm not lots of girls, Daddy. I'm me," I said.

He nodded, his eyes softening. Daddy never liked chastising me and on more than one occasion, Cary suffered because of that. Poor Cary was always blamed for things we did together, no matter how much I protested and defended him. Daddy believed because Cary was a boy, he should be more responsible.

Once, when we were only ten and we had gone down to the beach at night and gotten ourselves soaked, he took the strap to Cary. I shouted and cried outside the door to Cary's room. Afterward, I went in and put some soothing cream on his welts. He never cried nor complained and when I did, moaning that I should have gotten at least half of the beating, he looked at me and said, "What for, Laura? I can bear it for both of us. I'm happy to take your half."

Because Cary was always so devoted to me, it was hard seeing him upset and angry now. I felt like a rubber band being stretched from both sides, fearful I would soon snap. I wanted Cary to be happy, too; but I wasn't willing to make myself and Robert unhappy in the process. I was hoping Cary would accept Robert soon and we would all be happy together.

Daddy said no more about my relationship with Robert and he didn't oppose our studying together at the house. Cary didn't say anything nasty about Robert coming over, as I thought he might, so I asked him if he wanted to study with us.

"I'm not going to waste my time on that," he replied.

"It's not a waste of time, Cary. I know you're not doing well in some of your classes."

"What of it? I'm not going to college. You are. I'll be working with Dad in our business, where I belong," he snapped.

"You know you want to build boats, Cary. It would be good for you to go to college and take some courses in engineering and design."

"I don't need to sit in some stuffy college classroom full of snobby kids just to learn what I already know," he said.

He did know an awful lot about boats. He had never had

reading difficulties when it came to that, and there wasn't a boat, a design, or a concept of which he wasn't aware. Daddy was proud of the way Cary could hold his own in a discussion about our boat or about sailing whenever Daddy's friends were around. Some of them even took to asking Cary for advice.

"If you change your mind—"

"I won't," he declared. "I have things to do at the dock."

Robert had to work until after lunch, but around two-thirty, he drove up. I was waiting for him on the front stoop. Mommy and May had gone into town to do some shopping.

"Hi," he said, getting out quickly, his books and notebooks under his arm. We exchanged a quick kiss. "I hated leaving; there's still so much work to do, but my mother practically threw me out. So," he said, "where shall we go?"

"Up to my room," I said. I had been planning on studying there and had my own work set out. "We'll be less distracted. It's too beautiful today and if we stay out here, we won't get a thing done."

It was one of those warm days when the breeze seemed like lips gently brushing my cheeks and the clouds hung lazily under a turquoise sky. The sea conspired with the golden sand to tempt me into daydreams, beckoning with its soft spray and dazzling whitecaps.

"Good idea," he said, his eyes full of more love and devotion than an ocean could hold.

I had never had a boy in my room before. Just the idea of it put butterflies in my stomach. We paused when we entered the foyer.

"Your mother's not home?"

"She took May shopping. My father and Cary are down at the dock."

"Oh." He looked embarrassed, shy about being with me in my empty house.

I took his hand.

"Come on," I said. "We've got a lot to do."

I led him upstairs and into my room. I had made the

room spotless, polishing and cleaning all morning. Twice, Cary had looked in with a dark expression of disapproval on his face.

"This is a nice room," Robert said. He entered and looked at my posters of rock and movie stars. "Who gave you all these?" he asked, indicating the shelves crowded with stuffed animals and ceramic dolls. There was a collection of ceramic and pewter cats on one shelf as well.

"Daddy, Mommy, and Cary, for birthdays, special occasions," I replied. He smiled at the small table with a miniature tea set and a big doll in a chair.

"You don't still play with this, do you?" he teased.

"Sometimes. With May," I added.

He laughed and approached my canopy bed.

"Looks very comfortable."

"You can sit on it," I said and he did, bouncing and smiling.

The bedding, comforter, and pillows all matched the mauve shade of the canopy, and at the center of the two fluffy pillows was a large stuffed cat. He reached out to pet it.

"It looks so real, I had to be sure," he said.

I went to my desk, where I had an open notebook beside a pile of school textbooks.

"I've been going over my history notes."

He got up quickly and looked over my shoulder.

"I got an A in that class," he bragged, "but don't ask me anything now. It went in and then out again."

We both laughed.

"Nice view," he said, walking toward the open window beside my bed.

"We came up here to get away from all that," I reminded him gently.

"Right, right."

"You can have that chair," I said, pointing to the one beside the desk.

"Thank you, Miss Logan," he said with a short bow.

He sat and opened his math book.

"I hate these formulas," he muttered, but didn't lift his eyes from the page.

We both worked silently. Occasionally we would look up, our gazes would meet, and we would smile and look down again quickly.

"Would you like something cold to drink?" I offered, after finishing a section of notes.

"Sure."

"Cranberry juice okay?"

"Fine," he said.

"I'll be right back."

I hurried out and down the stairs, put ice cubes in the glasses, and brought them back up filled with our home-made cranberry juice. Robert was lying on my bed, his hands behind his head, gazing up at the canopy when I returned. I paused, smiling.

"Sorry," he said, sitting up guiltily. "It just looked so inviting."

"No, it's all right." I handed him his juice.

"It's good," he said.

I sat beside him and drank my own.

"Why do they make us take final exams just when it gets so beautiful outside? It's cruel," he said and I laughed.

"It's the end of the school year, Robert. What do you expect?"

"A little more consideration," he kidded.

We gazed at each other. I felt my heart begin to pound as he leaned closer and closer until our lips met.

"I've been wanting to do that for the last hour," he said.

"Me, too."

He took the glass from my hand and put it along with his own on the nightstand. Then he turned to me and we kissed again, this time embracing. I let myself fall back slowly, gently, and he lay down beside me, stroking my hair, kissing my cheeks.

"You're on my mind day and night," he said. "You're the first thing I think about when I wake up and the last before I close my eyes to sleep. On the days we don't see each other I hate the hours until we do."

He kissed me again, this time his hands moving over my shoulders. He brought his lips to my neck, and it was like electricity had exploded from inside my heart, speeding through every vein, to the tips of my toes and back up to my heart again. I took his head in my hands and kissed his hair while he moved his lips down, over my collarbone, unbuttoning the first and second buttons on my blouse, and then kissing the tops of my breasts, unbuttoning another button and another until he could peel away my blouse.

I let him unfasten my bra and lift it away so he could bring his lips to my tingling nipples. *I should stop him,* I thought, but I didn't. He moaned my name and his hands moved over my thighs and lifted my skirt so he could press his palms to my thighs. I put my own hands over them and held his there.

"Laura, Laura," he whispered, "I love you so much."

"I love you, too, Robert."

I let his hands go and they moved to my panties. My heart felt like a clenched fist, pounding at the inside of my chest as if it wanted to get out. When his hands moved over my hipbone and down, I uttered a small cry.

When I was younger and read novels in which girls were seduced or went too far, I swore I would never be like them, no matter how handsome the boy or how much I thought I loved him. How, I wondered, could your body make you do things you didn't want to do? How could any pleasure be so great that you would disregard all your warnings to yourself and surrender? Yet that was what was happening to me. I was moving faster and faster toward the point of no return, that moment when I would be like a swimmer who had gone out too far and was now at the mercy of the waves.

It was like one wave after another, one overwhelming, undulating sensation after another, sweeping me away from the shore of caution.

"Robert," I pleaded, "if we don't stop, we won't stop."

"I can't help wanting you, Laura."

"We're not ready yet, Robert. Let's be ready. Please," I

pleaded, knowing if he refused, if he kissed me one more time or touched me one more time, I would simply fall back and throw caution to the wind.

He held his breath and then pulled back. I lay there, breathless. Robert stepped off the bed and closed his pants. I hadn't even realized he had unzipped them.

Suddenly, I heard a deep, long creak in the ceiling and my heart stopped.

"Wait," I said, pulling him back under the canopy.

"What?" He studied my face. "Do you want me to—"

"No, no, just be quiet for a minute," I ordered.

"What?" He smiled with confusion. "Why?"

There was another creak and then another, then . . . footsteps.

"Cary's upstairs," I said in a low voice.

Robert's eyes widened.

"Huh? Why didn't you tell me?"

"I didn't know he was there."

"I never heard him come in and go upstairs, Laura. And your door's open. We would have seen him go by, wouldn't we? Or," he added with a dreadful pause, "he went by while we were . . . occupied."

"No, he must have been there the whole time, Robert. We would have heard him coming in and up the steps. Those steps creak so loud it sounds like Cary might step right through them sometimes."

Robert shook his head.

"I don't understand. I thought no one was home. You said—"

"I guess he came back when I was outside waiting for you."

"So?" Robert said, shrugging after another moment's thought. "He's been upstairs. What of it? No harm done. We'll just get back to the books." He smiled.

How could I explain? How could I tell him about the peephole in the ceiling, when I couldn't face Cary about it myself? Now I had to, I thought. More than ever, now I had to.

"But first," Robert said, "I'd better cool off." He went into the bathroom.

I rose and went to my doorway, listening. Cary was as silent as a ghost now.

"Okay," Robert said, emerging, "let's get back at it."

I looked once more at the attic doorway and then I returned to my desk.

We did study and talked and studied some more. We made plans for the summer months, and Robert talked about his college plans, his desire to become an architect. His drawings were all over the bulletin boards in the art classroom.

"Actually, you and Cary have a lot more in common than Cary wants to admit," I said. "I bet you could design a boat he would like."

"Maybe. I would for the fun of it, if I didn't think he would bite my head off," Robert said.

"He won't. He and I are going to have a real heart-to-heart talk," I promised.

The front door slammed and we heard Mommy and May talking in excited voices.

"It's getting late. I'd better get back. I'll just go down and say hello to your mother. Cary's still upstairs?" he asked.

"Yes," I said, gazing at the ceiling and the hole that, fortunately, Robert had not noticed.

We went downstairs and Robert talked to Mommy and signed to May for a while. He learned some new words with her and then I walked him out to his car.

"See you tomorrow," he said. "I'll get away in the afternoon for that walk on the beach."

"Okay."

He gave me a quick kiss and got into his car. I stood there and watched him disappear, until I heard the front door open and close behind me. Cary stood there, glaring at me. He started down the steps toward the beach and the dock.

"Just a minute, Cary," I said.

"What?"

"We have to talk," I said.

"I have nothing to say. I have to get to the boat."

"Well, I have something to say, Cary Logan, and you'd better stop and listen."

He paused and reluctantly turned toward me.

"Talk about what?"

"About the ceiling in my room," I said and walked toward him.

5

Maiden Voyage

Cary turned away and continued toward the dock, walking very slowly. I walked beside him without speaking for a while. It was hard to think of the right words with which to begin.

"You snuck up there, didn't you, Cary? You knew Robert was coming over so you snuck back into the house and up into your attic workshop to spy on us," I said as softly and as calmly as I could.

"You're crazy," he said. "I had something to finish and just went up there. It's not my fault you didn't know I was up there. Anyway," he said, stopping and spinning around on me, "why are you so worried? You do something you're ashamed of?"

"Did I, Cary?"

He stared at me a moment, his eyes blazing.

"Well? Did I?"

"How would I know?" he said, marching over the sand faster now. I ran to catch up with him.

"How would you know? You would look through that peephole, Cary. That's how you would know."

"What?" He stopped again, his hands on his hips. "Peep-hole?"

"You know what I'm talking about, Cary Logan. If you want, we'll go right back to the house and to my room and I'll point it out to you."

He tried to stare me down again, but this time his eyes shifted guiltily away and his face turned a bright shade of pink.

"Oh," he said, nodding, "I know what you're talking about. There was a knothole in the wood that fell through a while ago."

"A knothole?"

"Yeah," he said. "I just noticed it myself the other day. You think I have nothing better to do than go up there and peep down at you and your boyfriend?"

"I hope you have better things to do," I said, "and if you tell me you didn't do it and you don't do it, I'll believe you," I said.

"I just forgot to fix it, that's all," he said. "I was going to plug it up with some wood glue the other day," he added, looking grateful for being allowed to come up with an explanation. "I just got too involved in what I was doing and forgot."

"Okay," I said.

"I can't believe you would accuse me of such a thing," he continued, now on the offensive.

"Why shouldn't I think it, Cary? You treat me as if I'm some sort of fallen woman now, just because I'm seeing Robert, who, I might add, you have no good reason not to like. He's done nothing to you."

"He and his family are part of the resort business, bringing those tourists up here," Cary said bitterly.

"You know we need the tourists, and that's not you talking anyway. It's Grandma Olivia. Who would buy Daddy's lobsters if there were no tourists, and who would buy our cranberries if people didn't want the products from the Cape? Why do they buy them? It's because we're a famous resort region in America, and it's time everyone accepted that. The only people who don't are those who've inherited so much money, they don't care about anyone else."

"You ought to go work for the chamber of commerce or the tourist bureau," he quipped.

"Maybe I will."

"You would not." He thought a moment. "Would you?"

"I don't intend to, but I wouldn't turn it down out of hand," I said. "It's all beside the point, Cary. You have to judge people for who they are and not for what their parents do or what their grandparents did. Don't be such a Codsnob," I warned.

He couldn't help but smile because that was a term he and I had invented when we were much younger. He looked away.

"I just don't want anyone taking advantage of you, Laura. You're very trusting and innocent."

"Oh, and you're a man of the world, Cary Logan? Since when?"

"I know what boys are looking for these days," he said sharply.

"Robert's not like that."

"How do you know?"

"I think I would know better than you would, Cary, unless you were eavesdropping on every one of our conversations and spying on every one of our dates," I said. "Are you?"

"No," he said.

"So? Then tell me why you won't at least give Robert a chance. You'll be surprised at how much you two have in common, Cary. You both work for your parents. You may not respect what his parents do as much as you respect what Daddy does, but Robert is devoted to his father's business, just as you're devoted to Daddy's. Nothing's been handed to him on a silver platter, just as nothing's been handed to you. You both work hard for everything you have. You're both stronger and better people than the other boys in our school," I said.

I saw from the twinkle in his eyes that he liked that very much.

"Robert wants to be an architect someday. He's very interested in the work you do with boats, too. Few of your other so-called friends even care. None of them ever come to see your workshop."

"I don't ask them to," he said.

"But why don't you? Because you don't think they're sincere in their interest, that's why. Well, Robert is," I said.

He smirked.

"You've bought this guy, hook, line, and sinker, it seems."

"Cary, can't you have enough faith in me to trust my judgment this one time? You used to respect the things I said and believed," I wailed.

Tears flooded my eyes. When he looked at my face his face softened.

"I'm not saying I don't believe in you, Laura."

He looked at the ocean pensively and then turned back to me.

"Okay, I'll give him a chance," he said. "If that's what you want."

"I do."

"Fine. Now I've got to get down to the dock. I promised I'd help Dad," he said.

"You've got to start studying for exams, Cary," I called as he started away.

He just waved back at me without turning and continued to walk past the pink wild beach grass, strands of his hair lifting in the wind. I stood there watching him for a few moments and then made my way back to the house, feeling I had won some sort of victory, but not sure what it was.

However, the following Monday at school, things were different. Cary was friendly to Robert, so friendly, in fact, that even I was taken by surprise.

"Laura tells me about all the work you and your folks are

doing on the Sea Marina. I'd like to check it out one of these days," Cary offered, glancing at me quickly after he had said it.

"Great," Robert said. "I could sure use some advice about the dock. It has to be reinforced, only I'm not sure how to go about it."

"Maybe Wednesday," Cary said, "after school." He turned to me. "We'll pick up May and take her along."

"She'd love that," I said, bursting with so much happiness, I thought I might explode.

"We'll have to tell Ma," Cary said. "Let's not mention it to Dad," he added in a lower voice. I nodded.

Despite my father's need to have a market for his lobsters and his cranberries, he parroted Grandma Olivia's complaints about the tourist industry and the damage it had done and would continue to do to the Cape. I was grateful Cary hadn't brought it up in front of Robert, but I was always on pins and needles when talk turned to tourists and the effects they had on our town. It was a subject Cary and Robert would have to agree not to agree about.

That afternoon, Cary joined Robert and me in the cafeteria for lunch. Robert asked him some questions about boats and Cary talked right through the warning bell. Every once in a while, Robert glanced at me, his eyes wide with surprise. I simply sat there, holding my breath, afraid that if I uttered a word or moved a muscle, I might break the magic spell.

But it didn't break. On the way home from school that day, Cary offered that he might have been wrong about Robert.

"Maybe it's because he's not from around here," he said. "At least he doesn't follow Adam Jackson and that crowd. He asked me to give him some sailing lessons. Maybe this coming weekend," he thought aloud.

I bit down on my lip and nodded. I felt like someone tiptoeing over a floor of fragile glass, afraid that if I stepped down a little too hard, it would all crack, shatter and break around me.

"You can come along, too, if you want," he said.

"That sounds like fun, Cary."

"We'll wait and see how the weather is. As for it being fun, that will depend on how good a student he is."

"Robert said he definitely could get away from his work at the hotel?" I asked.

"Well, I promised I'd help him stain the inn's back deck on Thursday. I've got some time," Cary said.

"You would?" I couldn't believe what I was hearing. "I mean, you do? I mean—"

"It's no big deal, Laura. If he holds his own, we'll finish in an hour," Cary said, with more than a hint of challenge in his voice.

On Wednesday, as Cary had promised, we picked up May and went to the Sea Marina. I introduced May to Robert's mother and taught her some sign language to use while Cary and Robert went out back with Robert's father to look at the dock. Whatever Cary recommended pleased and impressed Robert's father, who had only high praise for Cary afterward. We all enjoyed some cold lemonade on the front porch, while Cary and Robert's father continued their talk about the building repairs.

May loved Robert's mother, who gave her an inexpensive watch, still in working order, she had found in a dresser drawer in one of the rooms when they had first taken over the property. It had Roman numerals and a pearl-like casing with a thin, leather strap. May was so excited about it, she walked all the way home with her wrist raised so she could admire it better.

"Daddy's going to ask her about that," Cary warned. "We can't tell May to lie."

To both of us, May was so precious and special, the very thought of having her do something even slightly sinful was upsetting. No one was purer in spirit.

"Let her tell the truth, Cary. We haven't done anything wrong. It's just being a good Christian to help other people. If Daddy says anything, we'll remind him of 1 Corinthians 13, 'And though I bestow all my goods to feed the poor, and though I give my body to be burned, and have not charity, it profiteth me nothing.' "

Cary laughed.

"Serves him right for having us read the Bible every night before dinner," he said.

Daddy did ask about the watch, but he didn't understand May's answer and asked me. I told him the truth. He was quiet for a moment.

"I don't like her taking things from strangers, Laura," he said.

"Mrs. Royce isn't a stranger anymore, Daddy, at least to me," I added. He didn't look happy, but he let it go and May kept the watch.

On Thursday, Cary went home with Robert and helped him stain the rear deck. I didn't go along, but I was so nervous about the two of them together without me around that I couldn't do anything but stare out the window and wait for Cary to come home. True to his word, he wasn't gone much more than an hour. I hurried downstairs to greet him at the door.

"You finished it already?" I asked as he stepped up to our porch.

"What's the big deal?" he said with a shrug. "Painting a hull, now that's a big deal."

"Did Robert think it was as easy as you did?" I asked. I was really asking if they had gotten along.

"He held his own," Cary replied. "I guess I'll spend a few hours teaching him something about sailing on Saturday," he added. "If you want to come along—"

"Oh, Cary," I cried and embraced him. "Thank you." I gave him a quick kiss on the cheek.

He stood there, frozen for a moment. It was almost as if my kiss had burned him. We hadn't kissed each other for some time, both of us self-conscious about it. But I was like springwater gushing. I couldn't help it.

"It's no big deal," Cary said almost angrily. "I'd do it for anyone," he said. "I have to wash up."

He hurried past me and up the stairs.

I knew I should be happy; I should feel very good about it all, but there was a cold chill in the air. It was as if Cary had left his shadow behind and that shadow lingered over me, blocking out the sun.

The next day at school, Robert announced that his parents insisted he take off all of Saturday.

"They said I haven't had a whole day off since we all arrived, and since we're ahead of schedule . . ."

"That's wonderful. Why don't we have a picnic on the beach, Cary?" I suggested.

"All right. Here's the plan. We'll do the sailing lessons late in the morning and then stop to picnic on the beach around Logan's Cove."

"Logan's Cove? Where's that?" Robert asked. Cary and I exchanged smiles.

"It's our secret place," I said. "Cary and I named it Logan's Cove because practically no one else goes there."

"It's about a half mile north of the bog," Cary said. "We don't have to worry about tourists bothering us."

"Oh," Robert said with a twinkle in his eye. "Sounds secluded. I can't wait."

After our Bible reading at dinner that night, Daddy paused before cutting the bread and glanced at me.

"I hear you hope to make your landlubber seaworthy," he said. I looked at Cary for a hint as to what Daddy was really thinking, but Cary's face was a closed book, unreadable.

"We're going to give him a lesson with the *Sunfish*," I said.

"We?" Cary asked with a smile.

"I'm a good sailor, too, Cary Logan. You've said that yourself."

"Yeah, I have, but you don't do it enough to be a good teacher," he explained. Daddy liked that and laughed. Then he grew serious.

"If you take May along, I don't want her in the *Sunfish* while you're teaching him, Cary."

"Of course not, Dad," Cary said.

Even though the *Sunfish* was only big enough to seat two,
May was so small, we usually took her with us when Cary
and I went sailing. I had already promised her she would be
part of our picnic.

"May and I will sit on shore and watch them, Daddy.
Don't worry."

He grunted, which was as close to an approval as we
would get.

"The weather looks promising," Cary said. Daddy agreed
and that was all that was said about it. I was too excited to
keep it all bottled up. May sat in my room as I planned the
picnic. My hands moved with my thoughts as I paraded
back and forth, listing the things we would bring and the
food I needed to prepare.

"Maybe I should make shrimp salad. Cary loves my
shrimp salad. We could barbecue though, couldn't we?
Should we do hamburgers or grill some lobster? We'll need
salads and oh, I should make my lemon cake, don't you
think? Robert is going to be so surprised when he learns
what a good cook I am. What?" I asked May when she
started to sign. "Oh, games. Yes, we'll bring something for
you and I to do while they're out in the *Sunfish*. No, I'd be
too embarrassed to let him see my drawings, May. We'll
bring Chinese checkers, okay? And Cary's Frisbee. I'm
worried about what I should make. I'll talk to Mommy
about it tomorrow. No, let's go talk to her now," I said and
reached down for May's little hand. She flew up to her feet
and followed behind me as I went downstairs to talk with
Mommy.

On Saturday morning as Mommy and I packed the picnic
basket, Cary grumbled at us from the breakfast table.

"I don't know why we're not just having sandwiches and
cranberry juice like we usually do," he said. "This isn't
exactly the Blessing of the Fleet," he added with a laugh. He
was referring to an annual event on the Cape when boats
were decorated with pennants and priests lead a procession
from the church. Everyone dressed up and there was very
elaborate food and drink.

"Just like a man," Mommy said, "complaining and mocking until he sinks his teeth in and then he quiets down like a church mouse at sermon."

I laughed and Cary turned crimson.

A little over an hour later, Robert arrived. He was dressed in a pair of new sneakers, khaki pants, and a crisp white shirt. His preppy sailor outfit was topped off by a jaunty sailor cap. Cary, who wore a pair of torn shorts, and was barefoot and shirtless, laughed.

"What do you think we're sailing, a yacht?" he joked.

"No, but I thought I'd get into the swing of things," Robert replied, undaunted by Cary's ridicule.

"And you look very nice, Robert," I said. I was wearing a pink sundress over my bathing suit and thought that Robert and I looked like the perfect couple.

"Sailing's work," Cary followed sternly. "You're going to mess up that pretty-boy outfit."

"That's all right," Robert said. "It's not like I have many chances to wear these clothes. Hey, what's all that?" he asked, nodding at the big picnic basket.

"She made a feast," Cary said.

"Gee, Laura, you didn't have to go all out like that . . . but thanks!" Robert said.

"Let's get started. We're missing some good wind," Cary said gruffly, obviously eager to change the subject. May carried our towels and Robert offered to carry the blanket.

The weather was with us: A gentle breeze barely nudged the foamy white clouds along the azure sky. South of us, the sea was already peppered with sailboats.

"Looks like a perfect day for sailing," Robert commented as we trekked over the sand toward our dock.

"Oh, and you know what a perfect day for sailing is?" Cary shot back over his shoulder.

"Me? I know as much about sailing as I do about . . . nuclear physics," Robert replied. "I don't even understand how you get the boat to move."

"The wind gets the boat to move," Cary said. I could tell his mood was already softening and I smiled to myself. Cary was in his glory, talking about the things he loved the most: sailing and boats. "You set the sail at a ninety-degree angle to the longitudinal axis of the boat, keeping the power of the wind on the sail's back surface. That's called running before the wind. In sailing off the wind, the sails are set at a forty-five-degree angle from the axis of the craft. This way, the wind exerts a pulling rather than pushing action, understand?"

"I will when I see it, I guess," Robert said, smiling at me. Cary glanced back.

"This won't work if you don't pay attention and concentrate," he said stiffly.

"I will," Robert promised. "Sorry."

"The wind flows at a great rate of speed along the forward surface of the sail, creating an area of lower pressure ahead of the sail. Understand?"

"Yes. I mean, aye, aye."

Cary shook his head.

"I must be crazy."

"He's paying attention, Cary," I insisted.

"We'll see."

"I just don't understand why the wind doesn't turn the boat over if the sail is at a forty-five-degree angle," Robert said. Cary stopped walking and turned.

"It would if the hull were perfectly flat. Every sailboat has a fixed keel that acts as a flat longitudinal plane to prevent the boat from moving sideways," Cary explained, illustrating with his hands.

"Oh. But if we're moving with a forty-five-degree angle, how do you get the boat to go in the direction you want it to go?" Robert asked. Cary's eyes filled with that glint of pleasure he always had when talking boats. I was glad Robert was asking questions.

"By sailing on the wind, a sailboat makes a course about forty-five degrees away from the wind direction. First you go to the left and then you go to the right, zigzagging. It's called tacking. You should know the terms so you'll know what I mean when I show you and tell you to do something. Coming about means shifting from one tack to the other. We'll do it with the rudder, pointing the bow up into the wind and then away from the wind on the opposite tack, or steering away from the direction of the wind until the sails fill from the other side."

Robert nodded, but I could see he wasn't clear on what Cary was explaining.

"In fore-and-aft rigged vessels—"

"Fore-and-aft?"

"You don't even know what that means?"

"I think I do. Is fore the front?"

"Great."

Robert smiled.

"In fore-and-aft rigged vessels, this maneuver is called jibing, and in square-rigged it's called wearing. If we start to lose control, I'll say we're broaching, understand?"

"Lose control?"

"It can happen," Cary said dryly.

"What happens?"

"We turn over and you fall into the sea and mess up your fancy outfit," Cary said, turned, and walked on. Robert looked at me.

"Don't worry, he won't let our boat turn over," I said. "He hasn't ever."

"That's reassuring," Robert remarked and we followed with May at our side.

May and I set the blanket out on a nice flat spot in Logan's Cove while Robert and Cary launched the *Sunfish*. I had brought along Daddy's binoculars so we could watch them from shore. I knew that once Cary had boarded our boat and set sail, he would be all business. He was really a very good instructor and expert at reading the wind.

They went back and forth, the *Sunfish* bouncing over the waves and looking as if it was running smoothly each time. When I gazed through the glasses, I saw Cary lecturing, pointing, and adjusting, directing Robert to make this turn and that, explaining as they went along. Even so, a few times, they did come close to capsizing when Robert was at the rudder and controlling the sail.

May and I played a few games of Chinese checkers, searched the beach for interesting seashells and waded out along the jetty of slippery rocks, searching for tiny crabs. The terns flew around us and followed us everywhere, especially when we returned to the blanket. They knew about picnics, anticipated crumbs, and eyed us cautiously.

Nearly two and a half hours later, Cary brought the *Sunfish* around and headed for Logan's Cove. They beached where we had set up our blanket. Robert's clothes were soaked, but he looked exhilarated.

"How did he do?" I asked as they made their way up to us.

"Fair to middling," Cary said without much enthusiasm.

"It takes lots of practice," I said. I looked closer at Robert's face. His cheeks and forehead were beginning to look sunburned, but the back of his neck was the reddest, deep crimson. "Oh, Robert, you should have worn some sunblock. You're going to be hurting tomorrow."

"Yeah, I'm going to regret not putting any on. I feel crisp as burnt toast," he said. He gazed at Cary. "How come you're not burnt?"

"I've been out there so long, my skin's used to the sun," he said. "Anyway, I'm starving. Let's eat," he added.

May and I took out the food and as we ate, Robert described his sailing lesson, revealing that Cary had been screaming, "You're broaching!" more than half the time. "I think I finally got the hang of it toward the end, huh, Cary?"

"You're getting there," Cary said. "Actually," he reluctantly offered, "for a landlubber, you didn't do too badly."

"Thanks," Robert said. He was practically beaming. "You're not so bad yourself for an old sea dog."

"Old sea dog, huh?"

"You *are* a bit bowlegged," Robert kidded. I laughed.

"I am not." Cary stood up. "Am I, Laura?"

"Only just a little, Cary," I said hesitantly.

"Is that so? Well, I've got perfect balance on or off land," Cary bragged.

Robert laughed.

"Want to find out, big shot?" Cary challenged. Robert glanced at me.

"Cary, no," I said.

"He's the one who claims to be perfect," Cary said.

"What's your challenge?" Robert asked.

"Ever hear of Indian wrestling?"

"Sure. I'm the Eastern United States champion," Robert bragged.

"Will you two stop? We still have dessert to eat. Sit, Cary," I ordered, pointing to his spot on the blanket.

"We have to earn it first," Cary taunted. "Champ?"

Cary took his stance, his hand out. The object was to pull the opponent so far off balance that he fell. I knew Cary was very good at it, probably from doing balancing acts on boats during heavy seas.

Robert jumped to his feet. May laughed and clapped her hands in anticipation.

"You're going to mess up that sailing costume even more," Cary warned.

"We'll see."

"Will you two stop?" I pleaded. My heart began to pound. Whenever egos came into question, especially masculine egos, there was always trouble.

Robert grabbed Cary's hand, took his stance, and the struggle began. Both were strong. Their forearms bulged and their shoulders strained. Robert surprised me with his balance and I could tell Cary was amazed as well. He had thought he would make short work of Robert. Both nearly toppled the other and then Robert faked a thrust forward and pulled Cary so hard, Cary lost his footing and fell face forward, unable to catch himself before he fell face first into the sand. When he pushed himself up, his cheeks were blistered with sand, as were his chest and legs.

"And still champion of the East Coast, Robert Royce," Robert cried, holding his hands high. May laughed. Cary's eyes met mine and I knew this was not going to end well.

"Let's have a rematch," he demanded.

"You'll have to speak to my manager," Robert said, nodding at me.

"Cary, please, stop. Let's have dessert."

"I don't need dessert. Come on. You were just lucky, Royce," Cary declared. He took his stance and held out his hand. Robert looked at me. I shook my head but he shrugged.

"I can't pass up a challenge," he said. "I have my fans to consider."

"Great." I slammed the basket cover down and sulked as they started their struggle.

It went as before, both nearly toppling the other. Cary was much more intense this time, his determination twisting his mouth and filling his eyes with fire. Once again, Robert made a good feint, only this time when he pulled back, Cary fell forward onto him and the two of them toppled to the sand.

"Tie," I cried, happy it was over, but they didn't let go of each other. The test of strength continued on the ground. Robert laughed and Cary tugged his arm, pushing him back to the sand. In response, Robert clutched Cary's ankle and pulled him to the sand. Then the two of them grappled, turning and twisting, one over the other.

"STOP IT!" I screamed. I stood up. May did, too. "If you two don't stop, I'm leaving."

They grunted, neither relinquishing his hold on the other. The struggle continued. I grabbed May's hand and she looked back over her shoulder as I pulled her away. I marched over the beach and back to our house, leaving the two muscle men grunting and groaning in the sand.

Thanks to their stupid male egos, what could have been a perfectly wonderful afternoon was ruined. Mommy and Daddy had gone to town, so I didn't have to answer any questions. Instead, I went upstairs to my room, May trailing along, wondering what had gone wrong.

"Boys!" I signed angrily. "They can be such idiots. They were getting along so well and now this. I'm tired of it. You're lucky. You still treat boys as if they had cooties."

"Not anymore, Laura. I like a boy in my class," she confessed.

"Don't tell him," I advised. I was feeling so bitter and angry. I seized my latest needlework and sat by the window jabbing the needle in and out of the cloth.

A short time later, I saw Robert and Cary. They weren't walking side by side until they reached the house. Then they stopped and spoke to each other quietly.

"Thanks for ruining the picnic," I hollered out the window. The two looked up.

"We were just fooling around, Laura," Cary claimed. "Why did you run off like that?"

"You weren't fooling around. You're both just two idiots," I declared. "I don't care if I do anything with either of you again."

"Laura," Robert pleaded. "It was just . . ."

I folded my arms and sat back so neither of them could see me. I didn't hear them come into the house and I didn't hear Robert drive off, but I held my curiosity on a tight leash and didn't look out the window. *They're planning something,* I thought, and suddenly heard the two of them singing beneath my window. To the tune of "My Darlin' Clementine," they sang, "We are sorry, we are sorry, we are sorry for what we did. We feel lost and gone forever, oh our darlin' Laura Logan." They repeated it until I stuck my head out and saw the two of them, now with their arms around each other's shoulders, gazing up at me.

I couldn't help but laugh.

"Are we forgiven?" Robert asked.

"You shouldn't be, but you are," I said with a smile.

"Then, can we have our dessert now?" Cary followed. "We worked up another appetite."

"Oh, now the feast makes sense, huh? Come on in," I said, delighted that they had come to a truce.

I signed to May, explaining what was happening now. She shook her head with confusion.

"Being grown-up is going to be harder than I thought," she replied and I laughed.

After dessert, Cary went back to the beach to dock the *Sunfish* and I walked Robert to his car to say good-bye.

"I had a great time. I'm really sorry about our ruining it for you, Laura."

"I'm just happy you and Cary are getting along, Robert. I just hope you two will stay that way."

"We will," he promised. "You're really a good cook," he said. "I enjoyed the picnic."

"Thank you."

He paused and I saw he was thinking of something that was taking a great deal of courage to say, so I helped.

"What is it, Robert?"

"I was just wondering. My parents are going to Boston next Saturday to buy some things for our place. I'm not going," he explained. "How would you like to come over to the hotel and maybe we could make dinner together? We could pretend we were the owners and we had a hotel full of guests and—"

"I don't know," I said, looking back at the house and wondering what I would say to Daddy. Robert looked very disappointed.

"Oh, well, it was just an idea," he said, opening the car door.

"I guess there's nothing wrong with my going to dinner at your house," I said. "I'll tell the truth: You invited me."

"That *is* the truth," he said, encouraged.

"It's not lying if I don't mention that your parents are away."

"No, it's not lying."

"I'll work it out," I promised.

"Great. What should I make?"

"I'll think about it and let you know during the week," I said.

"It'll be like we're married," he said and leaned out to kiss me. "I love you, Laura," he whispered.

"I love you, too," I said and he started the engine, backed out, waved, and drove away over a road dappled with sunlight and shadows.

Perhaps some day we would be married, I daydreamed, and then I thought about Grandma Olivia. She probably wouldn't attend the wedding. She might even excommunicate me from the family as she did her own son, Chester, but like Uncle Chester, that was a chance I was willing to take and a price I was willing to pay for the one I loved.

However, I had no idea just how powerful Grandma Olivia was and how much she could raise the costs.

6
∞

Hopelessly Devoted

Despite their wrestling match on the beach, Cary and Robert remained friends, and Cary even went over to the Sea Marina in the middle of the week and helped Robert and his father with some of the refurbishing of the dock. On Thursday, we had a bad storm. The rain fell so hard the drops were bouncing on the streets, pounding the windows and roofs, making the walls of our house beat like the outside of a drum. Daddy couldn't go out on his lobster boat, so he drove us to and from school just to have something to do. It was dark and dreary and unusually cold for this time of year. It didn't begin to clear up until late Friday afternoon.

"At least we know we did a good job on the dock," Robert told me in the cafeteria, "thanks to Cary. The storm didn't have any effect on it at all."

Cary blushed at the compliment. The three of us had been inseparable over the past week. I could see we were becoming the subject of idle chatter, some of the more jealous girls dipping into their dark wells of innuendo and nastiness to bring up new vicious rumors. Someone left a note stuck in the door of my hall locker. It read, *Does Grandpa sit and watch while you and Robert kiss?"*

I ripped it into a dozen pieces, afraid of what Cary would do if he saw it. He didn't mention anything, but I sensed that he was getting ugly notes as well. If anyone bothered Robert, he didn't tell me either. However, on Friday morning, just before lunch, Cary got into a fight with Peter Thomas in the boys' locker room. Whatever Peter said put Cary into a wild rage. He bloodied Peter's nose and gave him a welt on his forehead.

I asked Cary what had happened, but he wouldn't talk about it. He wouldn't say anything in the principal's office, and once again, he was suspended for fighting. The school called Mommy and Daddy, and when they came to pick us up, Mommy cried in front of Cary, which was punishment enough. During the drive home, he sat with his head lowered and listened while Daddy spoke softly, almost like a man pronouncing a death sentence on a convict.

"You're not a boy anymore, Cary. You do a man's work. You've been doing it for some time now. When you're a boy, your parents are judge and jury. They're your government, your court judges, and they pass sentence on your bad deeds. But now, you have to live with yourself and what you do. You have to be responsible for your actions and answer to a higher voice than mine. You hurt all of us and you have to live with that. If they decide to throw you out of school, that will be that."

"It wasn't my fault, Dad," Cary protested.

"Why wasn't it? You beat that boy good."

"He had it coming to him."

"Why?" Daddy pursued. Cary just shook his head.

"He had it coming to him."

"Well, when they make you judge and jury, you can decide that, but for now, you'll sit home instead of being in class where you need to be the most."

Daddy looked to me to see if I could add anything to clear up the mystery. I just shook my head.

"I'm tired," Daddy said as soon as we got home. "I'm going up to bed early tonight."

"I'll send up some supper for you, Jacob," Mommy called after him.

The air was so thick with gloom, I thought we'd have to slice our way through the sadness. May, locked up in her world of silence, nevertheless sensed the tension, and sat at Cary's feet, gazing up at him with big, sad eyes from time to time, which only made him feel more miserable. He skipped supper, too, and went up to his attic hideaway.

I heard him moving furniture and when I looked up at my ceiling, I saw he had put something over the hole. Then he was quiet.

I often went up to Cary's workshop to watch him work on his models. It was a small room because of the way the roof slanted, but he had a nice-sized table where he worked on his model ships. The ships he had completed were lined up on half a dozen shelves. He was most proud of his sailing ships, and they held center stage on each of the shelves.

When he'd been silent for over half an hour, I went up to see him. He sat with his back to me and continued to work.

"What's that?" I asked.

"A replica of the HMS *Victory,* the flagship of the British admiral Horatio Nelson," he said. "I feel like working on war ships these days."

"Cary, what happened between you and Peter? Please, tell me."

"What's the difference? It's over and done," he said.

"Is it over, Cary?"

He turned and I saw his eyes were bloodshot.

"It won't be over until we're both out of there, Laura," he fired back at me.

"Why?" I pursued. He returned to his model and worked.

"Cary, I want to know. Why won't it be over?"

"Because they won't stop," he mumbled. "They enjoy doing it too much."

"Doing what?"

"Belittling me, belittling you, saying disgusting things about us."

"What things?" I asked, anticipating the answer. Little

butterflies of panic fluttered in my stomach when he turned toward me again.

"Things like, 'Do you and Robert take turns? Do you pick a card to see who goes first? Or do you go at it all at once?' You happy now, now that you know?" He looked so strange, and I couldn't tell if it was rage or sadness shining brightly in his eyes.

"No," I said, "but you've got to ignore them, Cary. They're just spiteful and mean."

"I won't ignore them. I'll stuff their garbage words down their garbage mouths," he vowed.

"But you don't win in the end, Cary," I said softly. "You're the one suspended from school."

"It doesn't matter. I get some satisfaction and at least they know they'll have to pay and pay dearly for every remark," he said. Then he fixed his glare on me. "No one's said anything to you? Bothered you?" He got his answer with my silence. "You wouldn't tell me anyway," he said.

"No, because look at what happens," I said. "You want some supper? I'll bring something up."

"I'm not hungry."

I started down the ladder.

"Laura," he called.

"What?"

"Don't let anyone make fun of you when I'm not in school."

"They won't," I said. He went back to his model ship.

Robert called to find out what had happened and express his sympathy. I was afraid that if he knew the whole truth, he, too, would get into fights and then I would be responsible for the two of them doing badly in school.

"You're still coming over tomorrow night, aren't you, Laura?" Robert asked.

"Yes," I said, even though I knew I would regret leaving Cary locked up in his own dark, unhappy world.

"I'll be there by five, okay?"

"Okay."

That night I lay awake for the longest time with my eyes

wide open, thinking. What terrible things had we done to cause all the nasty gossip about us? We were twins, born minutes apart. We had been connected in our mother's womb and birth was a great separation from each other as well as from her. When we were younger, we did cling to each other more than most brothers and sisters, even those close in age. I couldn't recall a day or a night when we were apart. I was sure most of our friends believed that when one of them said something to one of us, the other would soon know it. They all sensed that there were no secrets I would keep from Cary or he from me. He just naturally hovered about me, protected me as we grew older. Being twins, it took only a glance or a look for us to communicate a fear or a happy idea.

Perhaps our friends resented this magical connection; perhaps they were jealous and that was why they wanted to hurt us. It was easy for them to turn Cary's devotion to me into something dirty and sick.

And then, a more fearful voice, tiny, hiding in the back of my mind, stepped up to say, "Maybe Cary was so angry because he realized some of what they said was true. . . . He was too devoted to you. Maybe he realized his own problem and maybe his violence was his way of trying to deny it."

I turned over in bed and buried my face in the pillow to shut off that tiny voice and the memories it evoked. Memories of strange looks, lingering touches, intimate words that were meant for lovers, not siblings. I was afraid for Cary, afraid that if I gave this tiny voice even an iota of credence, I would avoid Cary's eyes, find his touch burning, flee from being alone with him. The separation that had begun the day we were born would reach its final stage, and soon Cary, my poor beloved brother, would be alone.

I cried for him, feeling anger and confusion, as well as shame. He was still above me, shut up in his attic workshop. It was very quiet, but I thought I heard him crying. I listened hard, but it was silent again. The wind had died down, yet there was still enough of it to make the walls creak. Outside, the moon played peekaboo with the parting clouds. The surf rose and fell against the dark sand, resembling a giant wet hand reaching out of the ocean, crawling out onto the sand. Night was our respite, the time to put aside the trials and torments of the day, to rest our weary bones and stuff our troubled thoughts into dark corners and then welcome sleep like a long-cherished friend.

I closed my eyes and prayed and waited for the surprise of morning.

The next day, Daddy and Cary went to work right after breakfast and were gone almost all day. They were just coming home when Robert pulled in to pick me up for our date. Both Daddy and Cary knew I was going to Robert's for dinner, but not even Cary knew that Robert's parents had left for Boston and wouldn't be home until late the next day.

With all the trouble circling our lives recently, I was eager to leave our gloomy house. I felt guilty about not telling Daddy and Mommy that Robert's parents wouldn't be there, but I knew if I did, Daddy would scowl and say he didn't think it would be proper.

Instead I waved good-bye to the both of them and got into Robert's car.

"You all right?" he asked.

I forced a small smile, took a deep breath, and nodded.

"Yes, fine," I said.

Robert squeezed my hand gently and then backed out of the driveway. A moment later, we were headed toward the inn and our romantic evening. The Royces had done a lot of work since I'd visited last, and I could tell as we pulled into the driveway that their work was almost complete. Robert gave me the grand tour, taking me from the sitting room to the office and then showing me some of the guest suites. All of them were beautifully decorated, bright and airy, especially the rooms that looked out at the beach and ocean. With its new paint, flooring, wall covering, fixtures, and furniture, the Sea Marina now ranked up there with some of our finest inns.

"We're advertising in the big newspapers and magazines," Robert explained. "Mom and Dad are very hopeful."

"As they should be," I said. "You and your parents did a wonderful job, Robert."

"Thank you."

Being alone in the refurbished, sparkling new inn made us both somewhat nervous. Without realizing it, we were being formal and very polite. Robert opened doors for me and kept his hand on my back as we climbed the stairs. We avoided each other's eyes and talked only about the inn, the grounds, and the upcoming tourist season. It was almost as if we were strangers who had just met.

"I guess we should think about dinner. I bought everything you told me we'd need," he said, and we headed for the kitchen, where we both worked on the preparations. I had him peel potatoes and heat up pots of water for vegetables while I breaded and sautéed flounder fillets.

Robert had already set the dining room table. He had their finest china and silverware laid out, with linen napkins and crystal goblets beside them. There were tall, white candles in the two candelabra in the center of the table. Over the new sound system that had been piped into most rooms downstairs, he played soft romantic music.

"Do your parents know all about this, Robert?" I asked.

"Oh sure," he said. "Mom suggested I use our nicest stuff. Although, I didn't tell them about this," he added and produced a chilled bottle of Portuguese wine. "I thought it would be all right. This *is* a special occasion," he added.

I nodded and went back to our dinner preparations. When everything was ready, I told him to light the candles and sit at the table. I would bring in the meal.

"Let me help," he said, but I insisted and he went into the dining room.

I brought in the food and Robert poured glasses of wine. Shyly we made a toast to the Sea Marina.

"May she have a successful maiden voyage," Robert declared.

We began to eat. Robert raved about everything. We laughed, drank more wine, and pretended first we were the owners and then the guests.

"This is our honeymoon," he suggested. "Where are we from?"

"New York. No, the Midwest. That way we haven't seen the ocean," I followed.

"And now that we have, we're enchanted."

"We don't want to leave. Ever."

He changed his posture, trying to take on the demeanor of an older, stuffy businessman.

"I'm even thinking of looking for work here. Did I tell you, my dear?"

I imitated Grandma Olivia and looked down my nose at him.

"No, you didn't."

"I looked at a small beach house yesterday. Nothing elaborate, but it has a wonderful view. It would be a great place to raise children. They would have the world's biggest sandbox," he said.

"Sandbox? My children won't be permitted to dirty their little hands and feet in any old sandbox."

We laughed and drank more wine.

Suddenly, Robert reached across the table and put his hand over mine, fixing his warm eyes on me and giving me that wonderful winsome smile.

"Have I told you how happy I am, how utterly complete I feel whenever I'm with you, Laura? It's as if the world was created just for you and me. There's no one else and all the beauty is ours alone to behold."

Whether it was the wine or his words that brought an exciting, warm tingle to my stomach, I do not know. All I was certain of was that I felt like I was overflowing with love for Robert, and I never wanted to let go of his hand or this moment. He leaned over to kiss me, a short, soft kiss, so tender and gentle, it was more like the kiss in a dream.

"Laura," he said. "How lucky I am to have found you."

"Me, too," I said, barely above a whisper.

He held on to my hand and then slowly, ever so slowly, he stood up and pulled me with him. Again he kissed me. It was the sort of kiss that grew deeper with each moment, became more demanding and ended only because we were both out of breath. He brought his face to mine and let his lips glide over my cheek and to my ear where he nibbled gently and then whispered, "Shall we go to our room, darling?"

Our room! The thought of it was both thrilling and frightening at the same time. My heart began beating frantically as Robert led me from the dining room to the stairway and to a suite that looked over the beach and the sea.

Entering the room, we were both so nervous we couldn't speak. Standing in front of me, Robert unbuttoned his shirt and took it off, dropping it on the chair. My fingers, as if they had minds of their own, went to my blouse and, though trembling, undid each button. Slowly, I took off my blouse and let it drop beside Robert's shirt on the chair. He smiled and stepped forward to kiss me, his hands moving behind my back to undo my bra.

My heart pounded.

Robert undid his pants and sat on the bed to take off his shoes and socks. I watched him with eyes wide as he removed his pants and folded them over the back of the chair.

The wind made the curtains dance and the ocean outside roared against the beach, but all I really heard was the thumping of my own heart.

I unzipped my skirt, slipped it down my legs and placed it over Robert's pants. Then I took off my sandals and he rose to embrace me. We kissed again, and again it was a long, demanding kiss that took our breath away.

"Laura," he whispered.

I didn't look down, but I felt him move his hands to his waist. I kept my eyes closed as he stepped out of his briefs and then gently lowered my panties. I stepped out of them as if I were stepping gingerly into a warm bath.

For a long moment, we didn't touch, we didn't move. It was as if we had brought each other to the brink, to the cliff from which we could never turn back once we stepped forward.

"You're the most beautiful woman in the world, Laura. I love you so much, my heart aches."

Wave after wave of warnings drifted over me, but my body was tingling and the voices of restraint were dying under the rush of desire. I threw all caution aside and made the eventful step forward. Suddenly Robert's hands were on my hips and his lips were pressed to mine, our bodies touching. Everywhere. And yet, we still couldn't get enough of each other. Our legs had to rub against each other, our stomachs, chests. Our hands had to stroke all over until we were clinging to each other like two people holding on for dear life.

Before we knew it, we were in bed, our heads comfortably resting against the fluffy pillows, our bodies entwined under the cool sheets.

"Don't worry," Robert whispered. "I'm prepared."

I closed my eyes and drifted, my head spinning as I waited. Moments later, I felt his lips on my stomach. He worked his way up, between my breasts, over them and then to my mouth as he moved gracefully between my legs.

"Robert," I said weakly, almost too weakly for him to hear.

"This really is our honeymoon," he said before we joined.

I moaned, I cried, I grasped his hair so hard I was sure he was in pain, but he didn't resist or complain. I felt tears streaming down my cheeks and when he felt them, he kissed them away. When it was over, we lay there, still entwined, both of us breathing hard.

Then I gazed down and saw the blood on the bed sheet.

"Oh no, look," I said.

"Don't worry. I'll take care of that." He started to smile.

I pulled away from him, spinning around and pressing my face to the pillow.

"Laura," he said, pressing his palm to my back. "I love you, Laura."

I felt like I had fallen back to earth, like I had been traveling on a cloud, and suddenly, it turned gray and somber and began to rain down on the Sea Marina, releasing me along with the raindrops. My heart was still pounding, but my mind was clearing, the thoughts rushing in like water that had found an opening.

We had done it; I had gone too far; I had lost control. Or had I simply wanted it as much as Robert? Was it a sin to want it? Was all that Daddy taught and preached true, and would he take one look at me and read the sin in my eyes? Would it break his heart?

I thought about Cary, too: about his distrust of all the boys who looked at me or spoke to me. Nothing would convince him that this was good and pure and beautiful. He would say I had simply become someone's little trophy.

"Laura, what's wrong?" Robert asked softly.

"I don't know what came over me. Why . . . how . . ."

"Laura, we didn't do anything wrong. We love each other. Don't start feeling guilty."

"Why shouldn't I feel guilty, Robert?" I snapped and got up to gather my clothes. "This is exactly what everyone would have thought would happen if I came here and spent the evening with you alone. Every accusing eye and word, every sneer—"

"But we didn't do anything wrong. We love each other, want each other."

"I drank too much wine," I said, flailing about for an excuse.

"You don't mean that, Laura. You don't mean the only reason you made love to me like you did was because you got drunk." Robert lay there, looking at me with such pain in his eyes.

"I don't know what I mean," I wailed. "I just feel like we went too far, that we ruined something true and pure."

"That's foolish."

"It's not foolish to me, Robert!" I cried.

"Okay, okay," he said, holding up his hands. "I'm sorry. I didn't mean you were foolish, but you know in your heart, this was what you wanted, too."

"That's just it. Maybe I did, but maybe I was wrong to want it."

"You weren't wrong," he insisted.

"That's something boys usually say," I shot back.

"Not this boy. I say what's true and good for us. I don't

find myself in bed with every girl I meet and I don't fall in love with every girl I meet, but I fell in love with you."

I put on my sandals and looked at him.

"I'd better go home," I said.

"Laura—"

"Please, Robert. I just want to go home."

"You're punishing yourself unfairly," he said, rising. He started to dress.

"I'll go down and clean up while you dress," I said. "You better do something about the bed sheet, too."

"It's all right. I can do it later."

I left anyway and hurried down the stairs. I was already clearing the table when he caught up with me. He seized my wrist.

"I said I'd do that, Laura. Stop this. Stop punishing yourself."

I tried to swallow, but couldn't. I just stood there, nodding softly. He embraced me and held me, stroking my hair.

"Laura, Laura, Laura," he sang. "If I thought I made you unhappy . . ."

"I'm all right," I said, straightening. "Just take me home. I'll feel better after I get some sleep."

"That's right. Things always look better in the morning, don't they?"

"Not always," I said prophetically. I looked back at the dining room table. Our dinner had been so beautiful, so dream-like. Then why was I so confused, so twisted with mixed feelings?

All the way home, Robert cajoled, pleaded, begged me not to think poorly of him or myself. He repeated his love for me and swore he would go to the ends of the earth to follow me if he had to. He said he would rather walk on fire than hurt me in any way ever.

I tried to talk, but all my words got jumbled and stuck in my throat. All I did was look out the window at the dark ocean and the crashing waves. I didn't understand my own feelings. How could I explain them to him?

"Give me some time," I told him when we arrived at my house.

Sadly, he nodded.

"I was hoping this would be a special night . . ."

"It was," I said. I kissed him quickly on the cheek and ran to the front door. I didn't turn back to wave. I went inside and up to my room before anyone could see my face. Then I went to the bathroom and threw cold water on my cheeks.

"Laura? Is that you, honey?" I heard Mommy call from my doorway.

"Yes, Mommy."

"Everything all right?"

"Yes, Mommy. I just had to go to the bathroom," I said. "I'm fine."

"Okay. Would you like some hot chocolate?"

"No, Mommy. I ate and drank enough."

"Oh. Is Mrs. Royce a good cook?"

I swallowed and closed my eyes. Robert had told me she was a good cook.

"Yes, Mommy," I said. I felt like I had stuck pins in my own throat. No one believed in me more than Mommy and no one would refuse more to believe I had lied or been deceitful.

"That's nice, dear. You can tell me all about it tomorrow, if you want. Good night, Laura."

"Good night, Mommy."

I heard her go to her room. Then I took a deep breath and got ready for bed. I tossed and turned all night, seeing myself in a rowboat that was being flung from one wave to another, the sky black and full of cold rain. Out of the storm clouds Daddy's face appeared, raging. A long finger of accusation pointed at me from the heavens.

"You have sinned," he bellowed. It was a chant caught in the wind. "You have sinned."

I woke up in a cold sweat.

"I haven't sinned. I haven't. I love Robert and he loves me. That's not a sin. That's—"

I pressed my hand to my mouth, embarrassed to find

myself talking aloud. Slowly, I lowered my head to the pillow and stared into the darkness until my eyelids grew so heavy again, I couldn't keep them open.

Sunlight burst into my room like a bird crashing madly into the window. My eyes snapped open and I sat up quickly. I had perspired so much during the night, my nightgown was cold and wet. I pulled it off my body quickly and went in to take a warm shower, turning my face into the water and letting it pound on my closed eyes and cheeks.

No one but Cary seemed to notice how quiet I was at breakfast. Daddy was excited about a new location he had discovered for lobster fishing and talk of the day's work dominated the conversation. Every once in a while, Cary glanced at me and I could see from the way he studied me that he sensed something was wrong. Every time his questioning gaze met mine I glanced away quickly. I was eager for everyone to finish eating so I could escape to the kitchen to help Mommy clean up.

Cary poked his head through the kitchen doorway just as Mommy and I were finishing.

"I'm going over to the bog," he said, "if you and May want to come along."

"Go ahead, dear," Mommy said. "We're almost done."

"I—"

"I know it's not as exciting as it used to be," Cary snapped. "Forget it."

"No!" I cried. He looked back, surprised.

"I'd like to go, too. I'll get May."

We joined him outside and the three of us, just as we used to, walked over the beach to our cranberry bog. It was all in blossom and looked like a pale pink ocean.

"Daddy says it will be a fair crop this year, but no record breaker," Cary remarked. He leaned over and inspected some of the blossoms.

We didn't harvest until the fall and even with everyone helping it was still quite a process. It was Cary's job to run one of the harvesting machines. He had been doing it since he was ten.

"Looks healthy," he remarked. He gave May a blossom. Then he sat and put a twig in his mouth as he gazed out at the ocean. "So how was your dinner? Are you a member of their family yet?"

"No, Cary. And you don't have to be so sarcastic. We had a nice dinner," I added quickly.

"Um." He glanced at me. "Everything all right?"

"Yes," I said.

"You don't look all that happy this morning."

"I've been thinking about a lot of things," I said.

"Oh?"

"Things I have to work out for myself," I added. He grimaced.

"Used to be a time when you and I trusted each other with our problems, Laura."

"It's not that I don't trust you, Cary. Sometimes girls have to deal with girl issues, issues boys just won't be able to understand."

"Sure," he said, his mouth twisted with skepticism.

"I'm telling you the truth, Cary Logan. You don't have to sneer at everything I say."

"You mean you're not going to discuss this with your precious boyfriend?"

"Cary!"

"What?"

"Nothing," I said, shaking my head, my tears escaping from the corners of my eyes.

"What is it, Laura?" he asked with a face full of concern.

"Boys are just . . . boys!" I cried and got up. I tried running down the sandhill, but sand has a way of giving and I know I looked clumsy and foolish, nearly losing my balance as I hurried back to the house.

All that day I found myself bursting into tears for no apparent reason or warning. I tried to hide my face and spent most of my time alone in my room under the guise of studying for finals. The truth was my eyes just floated over the pages of my notes, my mind not grasping any of the lessons. Robert called, but I kept our conversation short and I heard the unhappiness in his voice when I ended the call.

I returned to my room and my mind once again returned to the night before.

Why? I demanded of my annoying conscience, why should I feel any guilt? I love Robert and I believe he loves me. What we did all people who are in love do.

But other people wait until the proper time, until they are blessed and until they swear their love and loyalty before God in a church, my conscience, in Daddy's voice, replied.

No. I shook my head. Love is what's holy, not words pronounced by a priest. Love, pure and simple.

Is it love? Can you be so sure, so positive? Will you be in love like this next year? Will Robert?

Yes, yes, yes, I shouted in my thoughts.

Suddenly there was a gentle knock on my door. I quickly wiped away my tears with the back of my hand.

"Who is it?"

Cary opened the door and leaned in.

"Laura, if I did anything or said anything to hurt your feelings today, I'm sorry," he said. "I just wanted you to know that before you went to sleep."

"You didn't," I said. "But thanks."

"Good. Night, Laura."

"Good night, Cary."

He closed the door and walked softly away.

During the following week, Robert would leave a letter in my locker at the end of every day. Each letter declared his love for me more than the letter he had previously written.

I want to apologize to you, Laura, but I tell myself what we did was not wrong and neither you nor I should feel guilty about it. I love you and only you and making love is only another way of saying it. There's no one to forgive, he added.

I tied his letters up and kept them hidden in my desk at home, reading and rereading them so much, I thought the words were starting to fade. I wanted to believe every word he wrote and everything he said to me. I wanted that more than anything and I fought hard to silence the voice of conscience that berated me and threatened me with the punishments of damnation.

Every night that week at dinner, Daddy seemed to pick the readings from the Bible as if he knew what was going on in my mind. One night Isaiah, Chapter 1: "Ah sinful nation, a people laden with iniquity, a seed of evildoers, children that are corrupters . . ."

I looked down at my lap and when I looked up, I felt the heat in my face and Cary's penetrating gaze, his face still full of questions and concern.

The next night it was my turn and Daddy asked me to read from Romans, 8. I began, but my voice cracked when I read, ". . . for to be carnally minded is death; but to be spiritually minded is life and peace . . ."

My throat closed and I had to stop, pretending to be choking on something I had nibbled before we sat at the table. I drank some water and Cary scooped up the Bible and completed the reading for me. Daddy looked at me with troubled eyes.

"Are you all right, Laura?" Mommy asked.

"Yes, Mommy."

"Maybe you're working too hard on your schoolwork," she said. "You should take a day off and maybe go sailing or enjoy the beach."

"I'll see, Mommy," I said. "I'll be fine."

Robert's letters kept coming, his pleading growing more frantic as I continued to remain aloof in school. He was absent on Thursday and, since Cary was already eating with friends, I sat with Theresa Patterson in the cafeteria.

"You look lost without Robert," she said. "Where is he?"

"He's . . . I don't know. I guess he wasn't feeling well this morning."

Theresa's dark eyes searched my face and then she moved a little closer.

"There are a lot of girls who are jealous of you, Laura. Most of them would steal him away if they could. Can they?" she asked with a small smile on her lips.

"I don't own him, Theresa. No one owns anybody else," I replied.

She shook her head.

"That's not the right answer, Laura. You should be a tiger when it comes to holding on to your man. See Maggie Williams there. She'd jump you and tear out your hair you so much as batted your eyelashes at Artrus. Everything all right with you and Robert?" she finally asked.

"Yes," I said.

"I know that boy dotes on you, Laura. That's why the other girls were making all that hissing about you and him and Cary. They're jealous. Good," she said. "I like to see them eat their hearts out," she added, glaring at the girls across the room, the ones who would never be seen sitting beside a Brava.

She turned back to me.

"You make that boy happy, Laura, he'll make you happy. Know what I mean?" she said, winking.

I shook my head.

"If you're a good lover, your lover is good to you," she said and laughed. "Never mind. I don't want to pry. But I warn you," she sang, "you turn your back on him once, and Robert Royce is going to be snatched away."

Was she right? I wondered. Was Robert losing patience with me? Would he turn away? And would I regret it, forever?

If only these answers were as easy as the answers that came to me on my final exams, I thought, life would be so simple.

7
℘

A Woman's Heart

Once, when I was much younger, I looked up and saw Mommy staring at me while we were both sitting on the porch and doing needlework.

"What's wrong, Mommy?" I asked because she had the strangest, soft smile on her face. She looked like a little girl, amazed at some wonder of nature.

"Oh, nothing, dear," she said. "I was just thinking how much you remind me of Belinda sometimes."

Then, as if she realized she had said something blasphemous, she bit down on her lower lip and shook her head vigorously.

"Don't ever tell anyone I said that, especially your Grandma Olivia, Laura. I shouldn't have said that. You don't really look like Belinda. Not at all," she emphasized and went back to her needlework.

Although I never mentioned it to anyone, not even Cary, I never forgot Mommy had said it, and whenever I had any opportunity to look at a picture of Aunt Belinda, I searched her face for similarities.

Then, one day, on a whim, I asked Cary to take me to the rest home. He refused at first. For us it was as off limits as a

116

local bar. It was pretty much understood that Aunt Belinda was an embarrassment to our family and she was so mentally confused, it would be a waste of time to speak to her. If I asked about her, Daddy would say, "It's not your affair. Forget about her." Nevertheless, probably because of the remark Mommy had let slip from her lips and the curiosity it had stirred in me, I wanted to meet Aunt Belinda.

Finally, Cary agreed to drive me there one day, but he refused to follow me inside.

"I'll wait out here for you," he said. "Don't be more than a half hour."

That was my first visit. It was our secret for a long time. He drove me there one other time, but that was months ago. Neither of us spoke much about Aunt Belinda. Cary didn't ask any questions about my visits. It was as if he thought it was so forbidden a subject, even to show curiosity was a sin. He would rather act as if it never happened.

Occasionally, because it had been done so many times before in conversation, he would make a remark like, "That's something only crazy Aunt Belinda would do or say." She was truly a skeleton dangling in our family closet.

The day of my conversation with Theresa in the cafeteria, I asked Cary to drive me to the rest home.

"What? Why? You haven't been there for months," he said.

"I know. I feel sorry for her, Cary, but I want to talk to her about other things."

"What other things?"

"Things," I said. "If you won't do it, I'll have to ask Robert," I said. That was enough to cause him to make a decision quickly.

"I'll do it, but I won't go in with you."

"I know. I'd rather that you didn't anyway," I said.

He looked at me with a face full of curiosity, but he just shook his head.

"You've been acting really strange these past few days,

Laura. Sometimes keeping a secret buried so long can make it fester like a sore," he warned.

"I'll be all right, Cary. Just do me this favor. Please."

It was almost impossible for Cary to refuse me anything if I asked him strongly enough.

"As soon as we get May home, we'll go up, but it can't be for long, Laura. You know we can't let Daddy know."

"I know. I think that's wrong. She's really a very lonely, sweet old lady and no threat to anyone," I said.

He didn't reply. We picked up May from school and walked home quickly. Then he and I got into the truck and drove to the rest home.

We rode for nearly a half hour before Cary turned up a side road heavy with pine, wild apple, and scrub oak. It seemed fitting that our aunt who was kept a secret and whose past was to be forgotten had been put in such an isolated place.

The rest home had a pretty setting. The ocean was directly behind it and the grounds in front of the building consisted of a long, rolling lawn with benches, a rock garden, and some fountains.

The Wedgwood-blue home was a three-story building with a front porch the width of the building. Behind the building there was an elaborate garden, more benches and fountains, and a gazebo twice the size of Grandma Olivia's. There were some full red maple trees, more scrub oak and pine, and the pathways were lined with trimmed bushes. I had spent my second visit with Aunt Belinda out among the gardens.

After he shut off the engine, Cary turned to me.

"Remember. Not more than thirty minutes," he ordered, tapping his watch. "We want to get back before Daddy gets home and starts asking questions."

"Okay, okay."

I got out and walked the flagstone walkway to the short row of steps. I glanced back at Cary, who stared at me with a face the picture of worry. He looked about as if he were afraid to be caught here, as if he were the driver for a gang of bank robbers.

I entered the building. The lobby had light blue curtains, a blonde oak slat wood floor with dark blue oval area rugs. There were large paintings of country scenes and ocean scenes, some with fishermen, some simply with sailboats. The cushioned chairs and settees were all done in a light blue floral pattern. There were small wooden tables, book and magazine racks, and several rocking chairs were lined up in front of the large, brick fireplace.

There were only a few residents seated, a pair of elderly gentlemen playing checkers, with the rest just reading or talking softly. I didn't see Aunt Belinda.

The receptionist turned from a nurse and hurried toward me.

"Yes?"

"I'd like to see my aunt, Belinda Gordon. I've been here before," I said. "My name's Laura Logan."

"Oh, yes." She turned to the nurse. "Do you know where Belinda Gordon is at the moment, Jenny?"

"She's in her room. I brought her there about ten minutes ago."

"Is she all right?" I asked quickly.

"She was tired. She spent almost the whole day outside," the nurse said. "Come on. I'll take you to see her," she offered with a smile.

I followed her down the corridor through another door to Aunt Belinda's room.

She was sitting in her chair, her eyes closed. The moment after we appeared in her doorway, her eyes snapped open and she blinked rapidly.

"There's someone here to see you, Belinda," the nurse said. I stepped into the room.

"Hello, Aunt Belinda. It's Laura. Jacob and Sara's daughter," I added when her face registered no recognition.

She smiled.

"Oh, yes. Laura."

I pulled the chair near the window closer to her and sat. "How are you feeling?"

Aunt Belinda was no taller than Grandma Olivia. If anything, she was an inch or so shorter. They both had small features, but I thought Aunt Belinda was prettier. She had sapphire-blue eyes, which even here were brighter, happier. Her smile was softer. There was a childlike innocence to her, despite the tales of promiscuity and the notoriety of her youth.

"I'm a little tired today. How is your family?" she asked.

"Everyone's fine, Aunt Belinda."

"You're Jacob's daughter?"

"Yes," I said, smiling. Just as before, she had trouble remembering the details.

"Jacob has how many children?"

"Three, Aunt Belinda. I have a twin brother, Cary, and a younger sister, May, remember? Don't you remember me coming to see you before?"

"Oh, yes," she said. She stared a moment and then leaned forward. "Have you seen Haille, then?" she asked in a whisper, her eyes on the doorway.

"No, Aunt Belinda. I have never met Haille."

"Oh. Well . . . isn't it a nice day?" she said, gazing out the window.

"I came to see you, Aunt Belinda, because last time you were telling me about the first time you fell in love, really in love. Remember?"

"Oh? Oh, yes," she said with a smile. "I remember." Her face grew darker. "It was a forbidden love, a love to be kept in the shadows, full of whispers and stolen kisses. When we saw each other in public, we couldn't show our feelings. Then I lost him," she added sadly. "I lost him forever and ever."

"But how did you know it was love, Aunt Belinda?"

"Oh, it was love all right. Why? Did Olivia say something again? She's always telling on me, running to Daddy and whining that Belinda did this and Belinda did that. Well, she's not so lily-pure."

She pouted.

"No, Grandma Olivia didn't say anything, Aunt Belinda. I just wanted to hear about love. Somehow, for some reason, I think you know more about it than anyone else in my family," I added, more to myself than to her, but she perked up.

"I do." She leaned forward and took my hand. "I've been in love many times."

"Many times? But I thought there was only one great love of your life. That's what you told me the last time," I said, not hiding my disappointment.

"There was, but I lost him and then forever after I was always looking for him," she explained.

"Always looking for him? I don't understand, Aunt Belinda. Where did you look?"

She laughed.

"Wouldn't you like to know?" Her eyes grew small, suspicious. "Did Olivia send you here to find out?"

"Oh no, Aunt Belinda. She has no idea I'm here."

She stared, skeptical, and then nodded softly.

"Every time I fall in love with someone, Olivia falls in love with him, too. She always says she was first, that he liked her first and I stole him away by being promiscuous. Well, no one likes her because she's a cold fish. She won't even hold hands in public! You can run back and tell her I said that, if you want."

"I won't tell her anything you say to me, Aunt Belinda," I assured her.

"If you love someone," she continued, "you're not afraid to touch him or have him touch you. Olivia says that's ridiculous. She says it's not necessary to touch all the time and she hates kissing. Oh, she'll deny that; she'll say she kisses in private, but she doesn't. I know. Young men have told me. She turns away all the time." She laughed and then leaned forward again. "You know what I heard Samuel told someone? He told them she won't make love with the lights on and never with the covers off. Like she has something someone is dying to see."

She paused and looked at me closely again.

"What did you say your name was, dear?"

"I'm Laura, Aunt Belinda. Sara and Jacob's daughter Laura. How can you be in love so many times, Aunt Belinda? Isn't love something special?"

"It always was, every time," she replied. She pulled in the corners of her mouth and nodded. "You just make sure they respect you and treat you like a lady. Don't let him know you love him right away. Let him twist and torment himself and then," she said with a wide smile, "when you finally say yes, he will think you have given him the world.

"I was in love once," she added wistfully. "A long time ago, a sweet boy, handsome. He thought the sun rose and set on my moods. 'When you're sad,' he said, 'you bring the rain clouds. But when you smile, the sun is bright and strong.'

"Wasn't that sweet? It's poetry. He wrote poetry. Olivia found the poems and tore them up. She said if I complained, she would show them to Daddy and he would see what I was up to.

"I wasn't up to anything. I just . . . wanted someone to love me and I wanted to love him."

She paused, took a deep breath, and then looked at me again.

"You remind me of someone," she said and blinked rapidly for a moment. Her expression changed. It was as if she had just set eyes on me. "Do you know my sister Olivia Logan? Her maiden name was Gordon, same as mine," she said with a light, thin laugh.

"I'm your niece, Aunt Belinda. I'm Jacob's daughter, Grandma Olivia's Jacob."

"Yes," she said. She smiled. "How pretty you are. Are you a schoolgirl?"

"Yes, I'm in high school."

"And you have a boyfriend, or do you have many boyfriends?"

"Just one," I said.

She looked out the window.

"I'm waiting for him. I sit here by the window every day and I wait. He promised he would return, you know. And he would bring me flowers and candy. They don't want me to have any candy," she whispered, gazing at the door. "But he hides it in the flowers."

She brought her hand to her mouth and giggled like a little girl.

Then, she suddenly started to hum.

"Aunt Belinda?"

She continued to hum and stare out the window.

"I'm going, Aunt Belinda," I said, rising. She paused and looked at me.

"You tell Olivia I'm not sorry. She's the one who should be sorry. If it weren't for her, he'd still be my boyfriend. We would be out there," she said, gazing at the garden, "walking hand in hand and he would be telling me sweet things."

She returned to her humming and staring.

I leaned over and kissed her on the cheek, but she didn't seem to feel it. I paused in the doorway and gazed back at her. She looked so small and alone, left only with her memories and haunted by her regrets and losses.

That would never be me, I pledged. No one will keep me from my love.

"Well?" Cary said after I got into the truck and we started away. "Did you get what you wanted from her?"

"Yes," I said.

"What was that?"

"An answer to a question."

"What question?" he asked, glancing at me. "Laura?"

"Something only a woman would understand," I said.

"Oh brother. That stuff again."

"Yes, Cary, that stuff again," I said and pressed my forehead against the window as we bounced over the road and onto the main highway. Cary accelerated, blowing air out of his tight lips and shaking his head.

"It's all because of him," he muttered.

"What?"

"Nothing," he growled and tightened his shoulders as he turned himself away and drove faster.

When we got home, I thanked him and hurried toward the house, Cary right behind me.

"Robert called," Mommy said as we entered. Cary looked at me and then ran up the stairs, pounding the steps so hard, the entire staircase shook.

"Thank you, Mommy. I'll be right in to help with dinner," I said and went to the phone.

"Where were you today?" I asked as soon as Robert said hello.

"I had such a headache this morning, Mom thought I was coming down with the flu or something. She said I had a little fever and gave me some aspirin and told me to take the day off. Normally, I'd have to be chained to the bed, but things haven't been too normal. Did you miss me?"

"Of course. I wouldn't have asked if I hadn't."

"How are you doing? You looked so distracted after school yesterday. I hardly had a chance to say a word and I don't think you heard anything I said anyway."

"It's all right, Robert. I've just had so much on my mind with finals and stuff."

"Stuff means me, right?"

"Yes."

"I still love you, Laura. You can refuse to answer my letters, grunt after everything I say in school, but I won't stop loving you."

"I know. I don't want you to," I said.

"Really?"

"Of course. How do you feel now?"

"I'm getting better fast," he said. "I'll be in school tomorrow. Laura, can't we see each other soon?"

"Yes."

"This weekend?" he asked hopefully.

"Yes, Robert. I would like that."

"Great," he said with relief. "I'll—we'll plan tomorrow, okay?"

"Okay, Robert. I've got to go help Mommy with dinner."

"I'll be at your locker tomorrow morning, probably before you," he said with a laugh. "I love you, Laura."

As soon as I cradled the receiver, Daddy entered. He took one look at me and then tilted his head with curiosity.

"What's going on, Laura?"

"Nothing, Daddy. I'm just going to help Mommy with dinner. Did you have a good day?"

"Fair to middling. Where's Cary?"

"Upstairs."

"In the attic again, I suppose. That boy should have been born a bat so he could live in a belfry," Daddy muttered and went to wash up for dinner.

After dinner Mommy insisted I go up and study and not waste time helping her with the cleanup.

"Besides," she said, signing to May, "May's big enough to help out by herself now."

Up in my room, I began to worry that I had lost my ability to concentrate and would do poorer than I expected on my finals. If I continued to do as well as I had, I would be my class's valedictorian next year. I knew how important that was to Mommy and especially to Grandma Olivia.

I hadn't been at my desk long before I heard the phone ring. I listened, wondering if Robert was calling again. No one called me to the phone, so I went back to my notes. Then I heard Daddy's heavy steps on the stairway. I looked up because I sensed he had stopped at my door. He knocked.

"Yes?"

He opened it and stood there, his hands on his hips.

Daddy always seemed to feel out of place in my room. My things were too dainty, too sparkling for him to touch. Even though he gave money to Mommy and approved of the gifts, the stuffed animals, the dolls, and ceramics, he looked uncomfortable around them. When I was just a little girl, not much older than May, Daddy rarely came into my room. He always said his good-night from the doorway. Once or twice he came to my bedside when I had a fever and when I had the measles.

125

"Laura, where did you go today?" he demanded.

"You mean after school?" I replied.

"You know what I mean, Laura," he said, his voice dripping with disappointment. I never lied to Daddy face-to-face and I wasn't about to now.

"I went to see Aunt Belinda," I admitted.

"Who took you there, Cary or Robert Royce?"

"Daddy—"

"Who took you there, Laura?"

"I took her," Cary confessed from his attic doorway.

Daddy spun around and glared up at him.

"You know I told you distinctly never to go there, Cary."

I never knew Daddy had strictly forbidden him. It made me feel worse for asking him to do it.

"He didn't go in, Daddy. I went in to see her myself. Cary waited in the truck and he didn't want to take me. I made him."

"You can't make a young man Cary's age do anything he doesn't want to do," Daddy said.

"She didn't make me," Cary said.

"You turn those truck keys over to me, Cary. I don't want you using it until I say again, hear?"

"Okay," Cary said. "Here." He tossed them down and Daddy caught them in his right hand, which only turned up the fury in his eyes another notch. Then he looked at me.

"I thought we were clear on this matter, Laura. I thought you understood I didn't want you going up there, that it disturbed your grandmother."

"But why, Daddy? I don't understand how it disturbs anyone for me to go see a lonely old lady."

"It's family business," he said.

"So? I'm part of the family. Why can't I visit her?"

"Belinda is the black sheep of the family. It's a matter of reputation, family honor," he said.

"Why is she the black sheep?"

"I don't have to go into details, Laura. She was not a good girl, a decent girl. She gave Grandma Olivia's father and mother a lot of grief and that behavior continued long after they were gone, only then it fell on Grandma Olivia's shoulders. She's done right by her and that's that. It's embarrassing to me to have to learn my children disobeyed me. It says in the Bible, honor thy father and thy mother, Laura. It's a sin not to. Remember that," he warned.

"But—"

"There are no buts. I absolutely forbid you to go up there again, understand? Do you?" Daddy demanded.

The tears that came to my eyes blurred my vision. Daddy looked out of focus, but his anger was so great, his face so red, I couldn't look away.

"Yes, Daddy."

"I hope this is the end of it and I never get another phone call from your grandmother about it. She's very upset."

I shook my head.

"It also says 'For if ye forgive men their trespasses, your heavenly Father will also forgive you . . .'"

"Don't quote Scripture to me, Laura. I know Scripture and I know you should obey your father," Daddy said, his face so crimson now I thought his blood pressure must be sky-high.

"Okay, Daddy."

"Let it be," he said.

I nodded and looked down. I heard Cary slam his attic door shut. It sounded like a gunshot in the house. Daddy turned and descended the stairs, each of his steps sounding like a judge's gavel, pronouncing harder and harder sentences on all of us.

It was difficult to get back to my studying. It took all the concentration I could muster, but I was finally able to run through a few chapters and go over some quizzes before I got too tired to focus any longer. After I crawled into bed and put out the lights, I heard Cary come down the ladder. I got up quickly and went to the doorway. He was just turning to go to his room.

"Cary . . ."

"What?" he snapped.

"I'm sorry about what happened with Daddy."

"I told you it would. I don't know why you had to go up there, why it was so important right now," he said. "Girl stuff," he added and started toward his room.

"Cary!" I called, but he continued walking away from me. He closed the door hard.

I never felt more like crawling under my blanket and disappearing.

I apologized again to Cary in the morning when we walked to school.

"Forget about it, Laura," he said. "You know Dad. He'll calm down and it will be all right again."

"I just don't understand it, Cary. If you met Aunt Belinda once, you would see what a sweet little old lady she is. She can't be a threat to anyone and I'm sure she doesn't even remember half the things she was accused of doing."

"It's not our business," Cary said.

"But why isn't it, Cary? We're members of this family. Why can't we ask questions and express our opinions, too? We're old enough now," I insisted.

"It's the way it is," he replied. Then he stopped walking and spun on me. "Somehow all this is because of you and Robert, isn't it? It has to do with your great love affair, right?"

I blushed before I could utter a reply.

"You don't have to answer. I know the answer," he said, walking ahead. We had just dropped off May when he quickened his steps and kept in front of me the rest of the way to school. As soon as Cary saw Robert waiting at my locker, he glared at me and then hurried away to join his own friends.

"Something wrong?" Robert asked immediately. He looked after Cary, who was plowing through other students, knocking shoulders, and clearing a path.

"I'll tell you about it later," I said and organized my books and notebooks for another day of school.

Cary remained distant, barely looking at me in classes or in the hallways. He sat with his friends in the cafeteria and I sat with Robert. It was then that I told him about Cary and me getting into trouble for visiting my forbidden aunt.

"How weird," Robert said. "No one will tell you exactly why she's off limits?"

"No one thinks we're old enough yet," I muttered.

"I've got relatives I haven't seen, but it's only because they're wrapped up in their own lives. My mother calls them the funeral family." He laughed at my look of puzzlement.

"Funeral family?"

"We see them only at the funerals of other family members. She says as far as she knows, these people have only black clothing."

He laughed and I smiled.

"That's better," he said. "That's more like my Laura. Do you want to go to the movies this weekend? I can splurge. My father paid me back wages. I can take you to dinner, too. I can even afford the Captain's Table!"

"I'll see," I said and then quickly added, "what my father says. I want to go."

"Good," Robert said, slipping his hand under the table to take hold of mine. He squeezed it gently. "Good."

I wanted to wait until a little more time passed before I asked Daddy's permission to go to dinner and a movie with Robert. Fortunately, over the next few days, Daddy's mood improved because he was enjoying a good lobster catch and there was talk that the prices for the cranberries would go up in time for our harvest this year. One night after dinner and after I helped Mommy clean up, I stopped in the living room and asked him if it would be all right for Robert to take me to a movie.

"And dinner first," I added.

"Dinner?" Daddy's eyebrows rose. "The tourist season hasn't even started yet really, and he's got money to waste?"

I smiled.

"He doesn't think it's a waste to take me to dinner, Daddy," I said.

Daddy shook his head.

"When I was your age, going to a restaurant was something I did only with my parents."

"It's different now, Daddy."

"Aye, that it is, and not all for the better."

"It's just a date, Daddy. I'm old enough to go on dates," I said softly, giving him my best smile.

"Ask your mother about it," he said finally. This was the same as him saying it was all right. Of course, I knew Mommy would approve.

I told Robert the next day at school, which made him very happy. We were both back to our old selves, holding hands, laughing, enjoying our time together. I felt a whole new energy, and I was eager now to face my exams and end the year on a high note.

When Cary, Robert, and I left the building at the end of the day, however, we were surprised to see Grandma Olivia's Rolls-Royce in front of the school and Raymond waiting beside it. He waved as soon as he spotted us.

"What's going on?" I wondered aloud.

"Your grandmother would like to see you, Miss Laura," Raymond said.

"See me?"

"She asked me to bring you up to the house right after school."

I looked at Cary, whose gaze dropped to his feet.

"I'll see about May," he said and started off.

"Something wrong?" Robert asked me.

"I don't know. I'll call you tonight," I promised and got into the luxurious automobile. I hadn't ridden in it all that much and never before alone. I felt self-conscious about driving off in a chauffeured Rolls with other students looking after me.

When we arrived, I went right inside and found Grandma Olivia alone in the living room, seated in her favorite chair, her thin-framed glasses on her pearl chain resting against her bosom. She had been reading the society pages in the Boston newspaper and set it aside.

"Hello, Grandma. You wanted to see me?"

"You can sit over there, Laura," she said, nodding at the sofa across from her. I sat and waited as she pulled her shoulders up.

"Is this about my visiting Aunt Belinda?" I asked quickly.

"No, not directly," she said, pursing her lips for a long moment. "You and I, you'll recall, had what I thought was a very important conversation. I was hoping you had listened to what I said and would behave accordingly. That you would be a source of family pride and accomplishment and continue to be a good daughter, a good granddaughter. But you have chosen, it seems, to fly in the face of all my words of wisdom and be defiant."

"It's about Robert," I said, nodding. "I told you, Grandma, that he is a very nice young man and I—"

"Nice young men don't invite impressionable young women to their homes when their parents are away and seduce them," she spat.

For a moment I could swear my heart actually stopped. I know I felt faint.

"What?"

"Don't deny it. I can see it's true in your face and denying it only makes it worse."

"Who—I don't understand." Did she have spies everywhere? Was every living soul in this town on her payroll?

"There's nothing to understand. What you've done and what you seem bent on continuing to do is disgraceful. I want it put to an end tonight. I will not say a word of this to your father and your mother if you obey, but if you don't—"

I shook my head and stood.

"Sit down, I'm not finished with this conversation, Laura."

"I won't listen. I don't want to hear another word, Grandma. You don't understand and you have no right to run my life like this."

"Of course I do," she replied, as if I had spoken the silliest words. "I'm responsible for the health and welfare of this family."

"Why?"

"Why?" She laughed. "Why? I'll tell you why," she said, fixing her eyes on me and narrowing them into slits, "because the men in it are not capable of it. They've never been capable of it, and the other women haven't the stamina or the backbone.

"Now, back to what I was saying. You are apparently seeing so much of this boy and being so openly intimate with him, you have people talking. Some of my closest friends have come to me and—"

"You have people spying on me, Grandma? Am I being followed?"

"Of course not, but they have eyes. They have ears and they know how important the family reputation is to me," she said.

"They're just gossips who have nothing else to do with their lives," I cried. "I'm no princess, Grandma, and you're not a queen. We're not royalty because we can trace our family lineage back to the first settlers here. We're just like everyone else. We put our shoes on one at a time," I said, the tears streaming so freely down my cheeks, they dripped off my chin.

"Have you no self-respect?" she hissed. "Don't you care at all about what you do to my family name?"

"Your family name?"

"Our family name. I explained how important that is, how reputation—"

I straightened my shoulders to match hers.

"I'm not doing anything I'm ashamed of, Grandma Olivia. I have a personal life and I'm old enough to make my own decisions about it."

"That's idiotic talk. Age has nothing to do with it. There are people twice your age who are twice as foolish and some of them are in this family," she said.

"How do you know you're always right about everything, Grandma?"

"It's my unfortunate destiny to be right about everything," she said calmly, resting her hands on the arms of the chair, "because with that comes the awesome responsibility of looking after the family."

"You don't have to look after me," I said.

"Apparently, I do, even more than I first thought. I'm warning you, Laura. Don't defy me. I'll go to your father tonight and reveal what you have already done. Just think what such a revelation will do to your parents."

I shook my head, unable to speak.

"Now, quietly end the relationship, do well in your schoolwork, and continue to be a helpful, loving daughter. In time you will see my wisdom. After your next year, I'll see that you are admitted to the best of the Ivy League schools and you'll be admitted to the most prestigious sorority there. You'll meet a young man who is deserving of your name and your life will be wonderful."

"As wonderful as yours has been, Grandma?" I threw back at her. She stiffened. "With a sister locked away in a rest home and deserted by her family, and with a son who's been disowned. No, thank you," I said.

"Laura! Stop being impudent! You will do as I say or I will carry out my threat," she snapped back at me.

I felt myself wilt. Mommy and Daddy would be devastated to hear about my evening with Robert. All their trust in me would be gone.

"Now go home. Raymond's waiting for you outside. Study for your tests and put an end to this stupidity immediately. I will not have another member of my family be defiant and go astray. I didn't take action early enough with my sister and my younger son, but I am determined to do so with you," she vowed.

It was as if she spoke from the heavens. Her words rained down on me and landed like a heavy weight upon my shoulders.

There was no more to say to her. I turned and walked away, moving like someone in a trance. I didn't even remember the ride home. When I got into the house, I ran up the stairs and into my room before anyone could see me or ask any questions. I threw myself on my bed and started to cry. I cried until my chest ached and then I turned and sat up and wiped my tear-streaked face.

I got up and opened the desk drawer where I kept Robert's wonderful letters. I stared at them and started to think about him when something caught my attention. I lifted the pack and studied it for a moment. The letters were out of place and they had been bound again, but sloppily. My heart sank.

Cary, I thought, must have found them and read them and told Grandma Olivia what was inside them.

8

A Heart Betrayed

I had been the lead in several of our school plays, but I didn't think I was a good enough actor to keep Mommy and Daddy from seeing how sad I was that night. I was pale and tired-looking, no matter how I tried to smile or how I tried to make my voice sound happy.

Cary didn't ask me any questions about my visit to Grandma Olivia's house, and he hadn't even told Mommy that Raymond was waiting for me at the end of the school day. Mommy just assumed I had something to do after school and had walked home myself. Neither she nor Daddy heard or saw Raymond drive me up to the house in the Rolls-Royce.

May was the one who signed the questions, wondering where I had gone after school, what I had done, and why I looked so sad. I signed back quickly, just telling her I was busy with schoolwork. Daddy didn't notice and Mommy was too preoccupied with serving dinner, proud of the new recipe for meat loaf she had found in an old Provincetown newspaper. Cary kept his head bowed, his eyes on his plate throughout most of the meal. It was Daddy's turn to read the Bible and while he did, I kept my gaze locked on Cary.

He couldn't look at me and whenever he accidentally did, he shifted his eyes guiltily away. He was the first to leave the table, claiming he had better get upstairs and do some studying. Daddy was happy to hear that and didn't question his quick retreat. While I helped Mommy with the dishes, she talked enough for both of us, planning things for the summer, including a trip to Boston. Finally, she noticed me standing quietly beside her and reminded me that I should go up and study, too.

I was grateful for the escape, but once again it was hard, if not impossible, for me to focus on my schoolwork. My eyes drifted constantly from the pages of my books and papers and my attention settled on the drawer where I'd hidden Robert's letters as my thoughts wrapped themselves around images of his face and the sound of his voice.

Just before her bedtime, May came in to spend some time with me. I took a break and did some needlepoint with her while she talked about her friends at school and asked me questions about high school life. Finally, she got tired and went to sleep. I did, too.

Moments after I had turned off my lights and crawled under my blanket, I heard a gentle knock on my door. It was so light, I first thought it was just some pipes rattling in the walls. I listened again, heard it, and rose. When I opened the door, I found Cary standing there in his robe and slippers.

"What?" I said quickly.

"I tried, but I couldn't fall asleep without talking to you," he said.

"I'm not surprised," I replied curtly. I stepped away from the door and returned to my bed. I sat on it, my legs folded under me.

Cary entered and quietly closed the door. He stood there gazing down at the floor for a long moment. I turned on the lamp on my nightstand. The brightness made him squint.

"What is it, Cary?" I finally asked.

"I was just wondering what happened up at Grandma Olivia's," he said.

"Somehow, Cary, I think you already know," I said and looked quickly from him to my toes. I always thought I had ugly toes. They were too big, but Robert said they were perfect. He claimed everything about me was perfect. *How blind love can make someone,* I vaguely thought. *I'm far from perfect.*

"What do you mean, I already know?" Cary replied. He gazed at me and I stared back, undaunted.

"Someone told her I had been at the Sea Marina at night, alone with Robert."

"So? Anybody could have told her that, Laura. Anyone could have seen you go there. Maybe you told one of your friends at school. Maybe you bragged about it to Theresa Patterson," he added quickly. "Maybe—"

"Maybe you told her, Cary," I said firmly.

"I would never—"

"Cary, for as long as we have been alive, you couldn't lie to me easily. You're not doing a good job of it now either," I said. "I don't know whether to just cry or scream my loudest at you."

He stared.

"I might have said something to her," he admitted. "She's . . . well, you don't know what it's like to be interrogated by her. She called me to her house a few days ago and—"

"Why didn't you tell me, Cary?" He was silent. "Were you ashamed? Was that it? Ashamed that you betrayed me?"

"Yes," he admitted.

"Why? What happened?" I asked. "Cary, you might as well tell me everything and stop playing these silly games with me. You *might* have said something? You would know if you said something, Cary."

"Okay, I'll tell you what happened. She started with her questions about my taking you up to see Aunt Belinda. She was very angry about that and she bawled me out for not knowing better. She wanted to know what was so important about us seeing Belinda. I told her I didn't see her; it was just you and she got . . . I don't know . . . very mean-looking. She was really scary, Laura. I've never seen her like that. She told me to sit down and she stood up. She's only up to here," he said, holding his hand to about his chest, "but suddenly, she looked gigantic to me. She hovered over me and demanded to know why you went to see Belinda. What did you discuss? What did Belinda tell you? As fast as I told her I didn't know, she asked another question, firing them at me so fast, my head began to spin. I thought I was in one of those police stations you see in the movies. You know, interrogation rooms with the bright light in the person's face?"

"So then you told her about my letters, didn't you, Cary?" I asked directly.

His eyes shifted to my desk drawer and then back to me.

"I don't know what you—"

"Cary, you can't lie to me," I reminded coldly. "I know those letters were read. I had them folded and tied together a certain way. May wouldn't read them and Mommy and Daddy wouldn't read them. Who does that leave?"

"Well, I was worried about you. I knew you kept his letters in that drawer. I came in here to talk to you one day just as you were putting them away. When you started acting weird, I knew it had something to do with Robert Royce. So I came in here and just read a few."

"You read my personal letters," I said, shaking my head. It was one thing to suspect it and another to hear the confession from his lips.

"I care about you. I don't care about any personal letters," he claimed. Then he paused and softened his face. "Were they true, Laura? I mean, what he says happened between you and him in his place?"

I shook my head and looked away.

"I should have known you would read them," I muttered.

"The stuff in those letters, that was the girl stuff you went to talk to Belinda about, wasn't it?" he asked.

"No," I said. "It was far more than that."

"We never talked about those kinds of things, Laura. We

never really talked about sex, but I always thought that you would be different from the other girls in our school, that you would never—"

"I'm not like the other girls. I am different, Cary," I insisted, my voice cracking with emotion.

"That's what I think, too," he said, quickly nodding. "I think it's all his fault," he said firmly, twisting my words.

"It's not all his fault!" I cried, pounding my thighs with my small fists. The sight made Cary wince. I lowered my voice. "It's nobody's fault. I never did anything I didn't want to do. I happen to . . . I happen to love Robert, Cary, and he loves me, too. Now you've gone and made things very hard for us. You had no right to do that."

"I just did what I thought was right for you, Laura. I only wanted to protect you. I—"

"You had no right," I insisted, furiously shaking my head at him. "What did you tell her exactly? I want to know all of it, every ugly detail."

"I didn't tell her anything exactly. I told her how funny you had been acting and how suddenly you wanted to go see Aunt Belinda, that you said she knew about girl stuff.

"As soon as I said that, Grandma Olivia pounced. 'Girl stuff?' she demanded. 'Laura is still seeing that boy, then? How serious has it gotten?' she demanded. I tried to make it seem like nothing. Honest, I did, but she kept at me, asking if I knew if you had ever been alone with him. She's the one who suggested the inn, now that I think about it. Yes. That's what she said. 'Has she gone to that inn?' From the way she was asking me, I thought she knew and was just checking to see if I would be truthful. I told her you had been with Robert at his place for dinner. She asked if I knew if his parents were there. I said I didn't know, but I guess you're right: I'm not a good liar, because she asked me again in a sharper voice. I said I thought maybe his parents were gone and then she was the one who told me what you had done. It was as if she had read the letters herself, Laura. I swear," he added with his hand up as if he were about to take the witness stand in a courtroom.

"And you didn't deny any of it? You let her believe it," I concluded.

"She took one look at my face and said I didn't have to say another word. My eyes said it all. She's spooky. You know how she is. She's—"

"She's a very unhappy old woman, Cary. That's what she is, and now she's succeeded in making me unhappy, too," I said. "And you helped her. Are you satisfied?"

"No, of course not. But Laura, he shouldn't have . . ." Cary looked away. "If he loved you like you said, he would respect you more and that never would have happened."

"I don't want to talk about it anymore, Cary. I'm afraid that anything I say to you might get back to Grandma Olivia anyway," I added.

It was as if I had slapped him hard across the face. His head actually jerked to the side and his eyes filled with such pain, I couldn't look at him.

"I'm sorry, Laura, but I just did what I did because . . . because I love you," he blurted and turned quickly to rush out of the room.

I remained sitting there for a long, long moment, staring at the closed door and hearing Cary's words echo in my ears. How could I ever explain all this to Robert? Who could ever understand the madness of my family?

I tried to sleep, but fretted in and out of nightmares, waking with small cries, burying my face in the pillow and then falling asleep again, only to wake before the morning and then finally fall into a fitful sleep once again. I was in such a deep sleep when morning did come, I didn't hear anyone moving about the house. It was May who finally woke me, shaking my arm.

My eyelids fluttered and I looked at her without understanding why she was there. Then I gazed at the clock and flew out of bed. She followed me around my room, signing her questions. Was I sick? Was Cary sick? He wouldn't say a word to anyone, she claimed. I was fine, I told her. I just overslept.

Mommy was at me the moment I appeared.

"Aren't you feeling well, Laura? You didn't look so well last night, now that I think about it."

"I'm fine, Mommy. Just a little tired," I said. "I'm sorry I overslept."

"Your brother's acting strangely, too," she complained. "Just like when the two of you were May's age and younger. If one of you had a stomachache, the other did, too. Remember when you both got the chicken pox, not more than a day apart?"

"Yes, Mommy."

"Maybe it was something in that new recipe," she mused.

"No, Mommy. If there was something wrong with the food, you and Daddy and May would be sick."

"Yes, that's true."

"We're just a little tired," I said. It wasn't a lie. I was sure Cary hadn't slept much better than I had.

I drank some juice, had some toast and jam, and scooped up my things to join May and Cary, who were waiting at the door. Daddy had already left for work. Cary's eyes were full of remorse and sorrow, but I chose not to look at him. I didn't say a word as we started out for school. May was full of curiosity and signed questions all the way. After we dropped her off, Cary turned to me.

"I'm sorry, Laura," he said. "I didn't mean to get you in any trouble."

"Let's not talk about it, Cary. I'm still trying to come up with a way to explain things to Robert."

He nodded and walked a little ahead of me all the way to school. When we arrived, he quickly went to his locker and left me to talk to Robert alone. Robert took one look at me and the sweet, happy grin disappeared from his face.

"What's wrong? You look like you lost your best friend," he half-kidded.

"I think I did," I said.

The first warning bell rang before I could say anything, and I knew I didn't have enough time to explain it all.

"I'll tell you at lunch," I promised. "There isn't time now."

Robert nodded, his face darkly serious and full of worry. Between every class he tried to catch up with me so he could find out what was wrong.

"Are you all right?" he asked. "You look really tired, Laura."

"I *am* really tired," I admitted.

"Your brother's doing a good job of avoiding me today. I caught him looking at me and when I looked back, he turned away. He's back to muttering or grunting whenever I try to speak to him. What's going on?"

"We'll talk at lunch," I said, and I, too, hurried away.

However, when lunch hour finally arrived and I approached the cafeteria and heard the happy chatter of the students, all full of excitement about the approaching end of the school year and summer vacation, I stopped a few feet from the door. My feet felt frozen to the floor.

"What's the matter with you?" Theresa Patterson asked as she came up beside me. "You look like you've seen a ghost."

I turned to her. A tear escaped from my eye and I shook my head instead of speaking.

"Laura?"

I ran back down the corridor and out a side door, bursting into the afternoon sunshine and letting the tears come more freely now that I was alone. I walked to an old oak tree and plopped down in the shade, hugging my knees, gently rocking back and forth. My shoulders shook as I sobbed.

"Laura," I heard minutes later. Robert was rushing over the lawn toward me. "What happened? Why didn't you come into the cafeteria? I waited and waited until Theresa told me she saw you run outside."

He knelt beside me. I wiped my tears away and tried to smile.

"I'm all right," I said. "I just wasn't in the mood for all those eyes and all those inquisitive faces today."

"Why? Tell me everything," he demanded as he sat on the grass beside me.

"Oh Robert . . ." I started and then sucked in my breath. "Cary read the letters you wrote to me. He went into my room when I wasn't there and he read them," I wailed.

"Uh-oh," Robert moaned. "No wonder he's been treating me like someone with a contagious disease today. I'm sorry, Laura. I shouldn't have put any of that in writing. Has he been nasty to you or—"

"No, it's not just Cary," I said. I paused and looked around at the slow-moving traffic, the soft cotton clouds lazily crossing the horizon, and the songbirds flitting from tree to tree. The world looked so calm and beautiful that it made the knots in my stomach and the chill in my heart seem worse.

I told Robert about my great aunt Belinda and how my grandmother Olivia had questioned Cary at length about my visiting Belinda at the rest home.

Then I described how Grandma Olivia's interrogation had turned to my personal life and specifically my relationship with him. Before I could go on, Robert sputtered out, "You mean, Cary told her what I wrote in my letters?"

"Not exactly," I said, "but it had the same result."

Robert shook his head, amazed.

"What happened after that?"

"That was why she had the driver here for me yesterday, Robert," I said.

"Oh. You mean, she called you to her home to question you about you and me?"

"Yes."

He blew a low whistle through his closed lips.

"I'm sorry, Laura. I guess I really messed things up but I couldn't help myself. I had to tell you how I felt and you wouldn't talk to me. . . ."

"Don't blame yourself, Robert. Cary knows he was wrong," I said, grinding the tears out of my eyes and catching my breath. "It's just that Grandma Olivia is the head of our family and she could make things hard for everyone."

"What does she want? Should I go to see her? Maybe—"

"Oh no, Robert. Never. Don't even talk about it," I said and he saw the terror in my eyes. He nodded.

"Well, what should I do?"

"There's nothing to do at the moment," I said. "Except . . ."

"Except what, Laura?"

"Except stay away from each other for a while. At least until things calm down," I added quickly. He stared at me a moment and then shook his head.

"What's a while?"

"A while," I said, shrugging. "We've got our finals to think about anyway."

"You think I care about my finals now?"

"You have to, Robert. You want to go to college. If you did poorly because of me, I would feel ten times worse."

He plucked a blade of grass and put it between his teeth.

"I'm keeping you from eating lunch," I said, trying to joke. "You must be hungry. You're eating grass."

He stopped chewing and smiled. Then he shook his head slowly.

"I don't think you understand how much I love you, Laura. It's easy to say we should keep away from each other for a while, but it's nearly impossible for me to do. I'm going to camp out near your house and hope for a glimpse of you every night."

"Robert—"

"Seeing you in school will be like torture. What am I supposed to do, stay away from you here, too?"

My lips started to tremble, my chin quivering.

"I'm sorry," he said. "I'm doing it again. I'm thinking only of myself and putting you in a difficult position." He stood. "All right, I'll try to cool it, as they say. For a while," he added. "But Laura Logan, you mark my words. You will be my wife someday. You will be the woman I live with forever and ever, and no powerful grandmother, no over-protective brother, no one can stop it from happening."

I nodded, pressing my lips together and swallowing the lump in my throat. Robert smiled one last time before he turned and walked back into the school, his shoulders slumped, his heart as dark and as broken as my own.

Each succeeding day without Robert, without his smiles, without hearing his voice, receiving his phone calls, was a day of gloom. The sun might as well have kept its face behind a wall of storm clouds, as far as I was concerned. I did my chores, I studied and helped May with her work, but I know when I moved about, I resembled a zombie, a robot without a heart or soul. When I had time to be alone, I walked off and sat on the beach and watched the waves comb the sand, gently rolling over each other, beckoning. Sometimes I went down to the edge of the tide and walked barefoot through the foam. The terns followed me, circling, calling, gazing with curiosity at my sad, forlorn figure alone on a vast sea of sand.

Often I caught Cary watching me from afar, afraid to speak or to approach, distant, a sad figure himself, looking just as lost. He was struggling within himself to find a way to make me happy, to apologize, to win my forgiveness. I kept telling myself that I had to forgive him, that Grandma Olivia had forced him to talk, but that small voice inside me wondered if Cary hadn't told Grandma Olivia so that he could have me all to himself.

Mommy continued to ask questions about my health and even Daddy began to scrutinize me more closely. I blamed it on my studying.

The following weekend we all went to Grandpa Samuel's birthday celebration. It was an elegant party, a clam bake with two bars set up, one at each end of the grounds. There was a large blue and white tent under which tables were set up with linen tablecloths. Grandma Olivia despised the use of plastic plates and forks, so everything was served on real china and with real silverware. A small army of waiters and waitresses, servers and kitchen helpers was hired to help that evening. There were over a hundred and fifty guests, all wealthy businessmen, politicians, their families, and, of course, the best families from the Cape. People attended from as far away as Boston and Hartford, Connecticut.

A string quartet was set up in the gazebo and played all afternoon, culminating with everyone singing "Happy Birthday" to Grandpa Samuel. It was really one of Grandma Olivia's best parties, but I was still in no mood to be happy about anything. Late in the day, she pulled me aside.

"Apparently," she said, "you are following my advice. That's good, Laura. That's good for everyone," she added.

Before I could utter a reply, she called to one of her guests and went off arm in arm, leaving me feeling a little more empty inside. When I turned, I saw Cary was staring at me. I walked away and started toward the dock.

"What did she say?" I heard Cary ask and turned to see he had followed me.

"She said she was happy to see I had followed her advice and that it was good for everyone," I told him.

He shook his head.

"I'm sorry, Laura," he said for the hundredth time.

I folded my arms and looked at the sea.

"She has no right to run our lives," he continued. "I can see you're going to get sick from unhappiness," he added in an angry tone.

"I won't get sick," I said defiantly.

"You're as pale as driftwood," he remarked. "Look," he said, stepping closer, "there's nothing wrong with my being friends with Robert, is there?"

"What do you mean?" I asked.

"Nothing, except I was teaching him how to sail, wasn't I? So, I'll just invite him over to go sailing tomorrow and you and he can—"

"Can what, Cary?" I asked, my heart starting to beat with the possibilities.

"Go sailing yourselves."

"You would do this for me?"

"Yeah, I would," he said, looking away.

"You'll get into trouble with Grandma Olivia, Cary."

"I'm not afraid of that," he said boldly.

Just then the wind picked up and whipped the strands of my hair around my face. Someone shouted and we looked back to see a flower display topple.

"Uh-oh, some poor slob is about to be bawled out for not setting that up properly," Cary said and laughed. "Grandma Olivia might take away his breathing rights."

I couldn't help but laugh, too.

"That's more like it, Laura. Remember when I told you that your smile lights up the day?" he said shyly, breaking off in embarrassment. "Don't worry, I'll call him later. And this time, she won't get anything out of me either," he promised.

And suddenly, the sun did peek out from behind a cloud and the warm rays washed over me, making me feel reborn.

That night I dared a phone call to Robert. Cary had already called and invited him.

"I was going to call you," he said. "Cary's invitation was such a surprise, I didn't know what to make of it. What's going on? Why the change of heart? One day he comes at me like he's my biggest enemy and the next . . ."

"He's so sorry for what he's done, he's trying to make it up to me, to both of us," I said.

"Actually, I don't care what his reasons are. I'm going to spend the day with you. That's all that matters, Laura. You don't know how sick at heart I've been these past days," he moaned.

"I do know, because I've been the same way," I said.

"My mother's been asking questions constantly about you. She thinks I did something to drive you away and she wants me to know that if I did, I'm really stupid. She'll let up on me now that she knows I'm going to see you tomorrow," he said with a laugh.

It was as if the blood had returned to my body, my heart began beating once again. I caught myself smiling crazily, and I knew I was walking around with a glow around my face.

I was the first up in the morning, and started to make breakfast for everyone. Mommy was so happy at my display of energy, she talked a blue streak as she helped me set the table. Even Daddy looked more relaxed, amused. The only dark thing he said was we should keep an eye on the weather. He said the sky had the look it usually took on right before we get hit with a nor'easter.

To me the sky looked beautiful. Even the clouds gathering on the horizon were welcome to my eyes. The wind was up, but Cary thought it was perfect for sailing. He spent part of the morning with Daddy at the cranberry bog while I prepared our lunches for the picnic on the beach.

"I'm glad you're taking some time off, Laura," Mommy remarked. "You've been working too hard. There's no sense in getting sick before you take your finals and end the school year now, is there?"

"No, Mommy."

"We're very, very proud of you, Laura. Everyone in the family is proud of you. Why, just the other day at the party, your grandmother came over to me especially to remark about how delighted she was to hear about your accomplishments at school. She wanted me to be sure to tell you that, and that she had a special surprise for you."

"And what's that, I wonder?" I asked, keeping my eyes on the sandwiches I was wrapping.

"Well, we're not supposed to tell you yet, but Daddy said she told him she's established a fund in the bank to take care of your entire college needs. That's a lot of money, Laura. It's nice to know your grandparents care that much about you," Mommy added.

"Money's not the only way to show you care for someone, Mommy," I said.

"Oh, no, but it sure helps," she said with a light laugh. "Just think how that takes the worry out of your father's brow," she continued. "You know how he's been about the ups and downs in the business. He's not one to harp on bad times, but we've had our share," Mommy assured me. "Your daddy's very happy that Grandma Olivia thinks so much of you, too."

I swallowed away the tightness in my throat.

"I'm glad, Mommy," I said and hurried to pack the food in the basket.

I had wanted this to be an extra-special day. I had put my hair up, then down, then up again and tried on nearly everything in my closet trying to find the perfect outfit. I finally chose a pair of heather-gray shorts and a white tank top, a pair of sneakers with no socks, and just for a happy touch, I wrapped my navy silk scarf around my ponytail. I felt as light as air and floated up and down the stairs all morning until it was time to go.

Robert arrived just after Cary had returned from the bog. We all met outside. May had the smaller basket cradled in her arms.

"Well, thanks a lot for inviting me," Robert told Cary. "It looks like a perfect day for this, huh?"

Cary studied the weather a moment and nodded cautiously.

"As long as we come in before late afternoon. The wind's picking up a bit and it will be a good ride," he said. "But you're an expert now," he added with a note of challenge.

"Well, I haven't forgotten what I learned, if that's what you mean."

"Laura knows enough to be a judge of that," Cary said.

"Well, let's get going then," I said, impatient and worried that too many words would stir up old wounds.

"I'll carry that," Robert said, taking the bigger basket from me.

We walked down the beach, Robert and I glancing longingly at each other as Cary led the way.

"You want to test me?" Robert asked Cary when we reached the sailboat. "Go ahead, ask me anything," he challenged.

"The only real test is the test the ocean gives," Cary replied coolly.

Robert laughed nervously, his eyes flitting from me to the boat and then to Cary.

"Laura, why don't you take May to Logan's Cove while Captain Robert and I bring the sailboat over," Cary suggested.

"Okay. Be careful," I said to Robert and took May's hand. We had the blanket out and were sitting and organizing our picnic lunch when the sailboat appeared around the bend. Robert was doing all the work. The boat bounced hard on the waves and then straightened and turned toward us, the sea spray shooting up around it as it headed toward the shore.

"It's wonderful!" Robert cried. "Invigorating. Much more exciting than it was the last time, Laura."

"I can see that. How did he do, Cary?"

Cary busied himself with beaching the sailboat and then turned.

"Fine," he said. He gazed at the sky. The small dots of clouds had grown fatter and toward the south we could see longer strands of white. "But I think you two should go out right after lunch and if it gets too rough, head right back," he said.

"Boy, just that little bit worked up my appetite," Robert followed.

I was too excited to be hungry. Cary didn't eat very much either. He sat pensive, staring out at the ocean. Robert talked about the Sea Marina, how successful their first few weekends had been, and how they were close to being fully booked for July. Cary made little comment. I never saw him so deep in thought. He looked nervous, too, stealing glances at me and then quickly gazing back at the sea or down the beach. Finally, he stood.

"I think May and I will go looking for seashells while you two do some sailing," he said. "Keep your eyes on the sky, Laura," he added and signed to May, who rose quickly to take his hand. The two of them started down the beach.

"Well," Robert said with a sigh, "we're finally alone for the first time in a century. At least that's the way it feels to me," he said. "Ready for your maiden voyage with Captain Blood?" he asked, shooting to his feet and reaching for my hand. "M'lady?"

I laughed and let him pull me up. Then I took off my sneakers and threw them into the sailboat. I gazed down the beach at Cary and May, who were already some distance away. Cary looked like he was watching us and then turned back to help May hunt for interesting shells. Robert helped me into the sailboat and pushed off, jumping in quickly and taking hold of the rope.

"Let's sail all the way to China," he yelled into the wind.

The sea spray felt good on my arms and my face. More gracefully than I had anticipated, Robert took us out and filled the sail with wind.

"Not bad, huh? I guess the sea is in my blood after all, thanks to you," he said.

I sat with my back against him and screamed at the bouncing we endured until we got farther and farther out and the water calmed.

"The last time I went out with Cary, I saw another cove," Robert said. "It looked very private, too," he added. "Why don't we find it and call it Laura's Cove," he whispered.

He kissed my hair and my forehead and I turned and reached up to meet his lips with mine. The sailboat twisted and we both screamed.

"I better keep my mind on the business at hand," Robert said.

"Just let out a little line, Robert, and she won't spill us into the sea."

"Aye, aye, Captain."

We sailed on, the wind whipping the sail, the bow cutting into the waves. We were going at a good clip and as we made the turn around another bend of shore the wind died a bit and the ride became slower, smoother. Robert grew more confident.

"This isn't as hard as everyone makes it out to be," he declared.

"Don't get too arrogant, Robert," I warned. "It takes a

while to become as good a sailor as Cary. Cary says the sea
doesn't easily forgive mistakes, either."

"I know, but I do have a flair for it, don't I, Laura?" he
asked, fishing for a compliment. "Well? Don't I?"

"Yes, yes." I laughed. We kissed again and sailed on.
Finally, I felt relaxed and happy.

Perhaps all of our lives will be like this now, I thought.
We'll round another bend and find sunshine and happiness.
With the wind in my hair and Robert's arms around me as
our sailboat sliced through the water, it was easy to believe
in fairy tales. Cary and I had grown up with faith in the
magic of the ocean. Who could blame me for wanting
Robert to share it as well?

Who would ever blame me as much as I would soon
blame myself?

9
❧
Swept Away

*F*or a long time, I had no memory of that fateful afternoon. My mind locked it in a dark closet and threw away the key. As hard as it is to believe, I even forgot Robert's name.

I was lying comfortably in his arms as he turned the sailboat toward the shore. The cove was small, with just a patch of beach, really, but he had discovered it and claimed it as our special place. When we drew closer, I sat up. The wind had grown a bit stronger and the clouds flowing in from the south now looked a bit darker and thicker. I should have said, "Let's go back, Robert," right then and there, but I didn't. I, too, was hungry for love and I, too, was titillated by the prospect of our own private little world.

Robert leaped out of the sailboat and guided it onto the shore. Then he reached for my hand and I stepped out. He found a piece of driftwood nearby and planted it in the sand. Then he tied his handkerchief around it so it flapped in the wind like a flag.

"I claim this beach for Laura Logan and hereby name it Laura's Cove," he said, standing proud and strong like some historic explorer.

I laughed and clapped my hands. He took a sweeping bow

and I laughed again. Everything made me laugh that afternoon. All of it, the air, the freedom, the renewal of love and promises had made me giddy. I was drunk on dreams.

"We have to christen our piece of paradise," he declared and stepped up to me.

He embraced me and kissed me full on the lips. The wind whipped my hair and the sea spray felt cool and refreshing on my arms and neck.

"I missed you," he said. "Oh, how I missed you. I kissed you a thousand times in my mind, Laura. I held you every chance I could get."

He kissed me softly on the tip of my nose and then my chin before we joined our lips again. After that, he reached into the sailboat and pulled out the blanket. He spread it out and we embraced and lowered ourselves onto the sand. I lay back against his chest.

"We can't stay long, Robert," I remember saying. "Cary and May—"

"I know," Robert replied and stroked my hair, running his palm over my cheek as if he were blind and committing every feature of my face to his memory forever and ever. I wanted him. Oh, how much I wanted him.

He sensed my desire and began to kiss me on my neck. His hands moved to my waist and he gently pushed up my tank top. In moments we were both nearly undressed, embracing, clinging to each other as if the whole world had become water and we were floating on the surface.

"I will not let anyone take you from me," he whispered, "even for a short time."

His words filled my heart and drove away all the doubts about our love, about myself, about what and who we were. *Yes*, I heard myself begin somewhere deep down inside my very soul, *yes, yes, yes*.

Our kisses were long and hard and hungry, the kisses of two loving people who had been locked away from that love for too long. I don't even remember how we became totally naked, but we were, and without hesitation, almost without skipping a beat, we were making love, throwing all caution to the wind that whirled around us.

It began with a maddening rush and then slowed to an undulating rhythm that took me up and down, to heights and ecstasy and moments of quiet when I could catch my breath; but soon the hunger for another taste of ecstasy overpowered me and I tightened my embrace around him, holding him, refusing to permit it to end.

I remember hearing his small laugh of delight and seeing his face, his eyes full of so much love and pleasure. I told myself what we were doing couldn't be anything but good and beautiful. He smothered me in kisses; he chanted my name; he quieted my small cries and held me as tightly as I held him. We rode on each other's passion until we were exhausted.

He slid off me and lay beside me, his face against the blanket, but his eyes on me. I turned and looked into his eyes, into his beautiful smile of contentment.

"I love you, Laura," he said.

"I love you, too, Robert."

He put his arm over my shoulder, lay his palm against my naked back and closed the distance between us. We lay there, quietly, our eyelids fluttering, suddenly feeling heavy. We both decided to just rest for a little while, and then, like some magic spell, sleep washed over us and we both drifted.

I was the first to wake up. The wind had picked up considerably, spitting sand and water over us. I turned quickly and when I looked up, I saw only low, dark clouds whirling toward us. Seconds later, I felt the raindrops, but the worst and most terrifying sight was the sailboat drifting away. In our haste, we hadn't beached it securely. It was a good ten to fifteen feet from the shore already.

"Robert!" I screamed.

He opened his eyes and sat up quickly.

"Oh, no. The boat."

"We have to get it before it gets washed out too far!" I cried. He leaped to his feet and dove into the water, swimming as hard as he could to the boat. The waves were already at least two feet high. He struggled and reached the side of the sailboat, heaving himself up and over. The sail was flapping hard, the small mast swinging from right to left. Robert struggled to get a good hold on the line, but when he tightened the sail against the wind, the small boat began to turn over and he didn't let go fast enough. It looked like it jumped out of the water, spilling him into the ocean as it capsized.

"ROBERT!"

I was a good swimmer, but not strong enough to battle those waves for very long. It took a monster effort, nearly exhausting me, but I managed to reach the boat quickly. I grabbed hold of the boat and called to Robert again. He surfaced on the other side of the boat, looking dazed. It wasn't until he swam toward me that I saw why. When he had tumbled into the sea with the boat following after him, some part of it had struck him on the head. A thin, but steady stream of blood trickled from under his hair, down his temple, and over his cheek.

"Robert, you're hurt!" I cried. He nodded, but he still looked confused.

We bobbed with the boat as the waves grew higher, stronger. The wind was intensifying, too, and the rain had become stingingly sharp and cold. I looked back at the shore. All our clothing, the blanket, everything was being washed by the tide and slowly sucked into the sea. The shock of it all happening so quickly panicked me. I struggled with the boat in a vain and fruitless attempt to right it. Robert was just bobbing, holding on to the side, either unsure of how to right the boat or so confused he hadn't even thought to try.

"Climb over the hull, Robert, and start to pull the boat upright. Climb!" I cried. "Robert, do it now. We're being swept out farther and farther with every roll of the waves."

Finally, he seemed to understand. He pulled himself up and reached for the side of the boat, using his weight to turn it upright. He didn't weigh enough and wasn't strong enough, so I joined him as quickly as I could and both of us pulled desperately as the wind whipped against our backs like a cold, wet rope and the rain became a torrential downpour, blinding us.

More desperate, frantic, realizing the danger fully, we gave it all our might and the boat began to turn over. Robert was too excited by our small success and jerked wildly at the hull.

"Just let it turn, Robert," I screamed, but he continued leaping up and down, pulling and grunting, defeating his own efforts.

Finally, the mast came up, the wet sail came out of the water. We were doing fine. We would get it upright, I thought. We'll be all right. Then, another heavy, fierce gust of wind lashed at us and I lost my grip, sliding back into the sea. The boat began to turn over again and Robert lunged with all his strength to prevent it from happening. I saw him fly over with the boat and disappear on the other side. We were at least another twenty feet from shore by now. The rain was falling so hard, I could barely make out the tiny patch of beach.

"Robert!" I called when I didn't see him. "Robert, where are you? Robert!"

He didn't respond and he didn't swim back to me. I kept my grip on the hull and fought my way around the boat. At first I didn't see him, and then I saw his head, just under the surface, his hand floating toward the mast. I moved as quickly as I could, taking hold of the mast and then his hand, pulling with all my might until his head appeared. His eyes were glassy, dazed. There was a wider, faster stream of blood now on his temple and cheek. I thought he mouthed my name and smiled, but it was hard to see clearly with the salt water burning my eyes and the rain pounding my face.

I held on to him. He seemed incapable of moving on his own. His right arm never came out of the water and his head slowly lowered to his shoulder as his eyes closed.

"ROBERT!"

I tried pulling him closer, but I was losing my grip on the

mast. The water had made it slippery and difficult to hold. If I didn't let go of Robert's hand soon, I might lose my grip completely and get washed out to sea with him, I thought. My shoulders ached, my neck muscles screamed, and my hand felt as if it were being torn off my wrist.

"Oh, Robert, wake up. Help us. Robert!"

He bobbed with the waves that took us up and down. When I turned and looked back, I saw we were out of sight of the shore. The ocean was sweeping us away.

I remember thinking about Cary, expecting him to appear any moment in another boat, flying over the waves, coming to our rescue. He would be angry, but very, very worried. He would scoop us both out of the sea and wrap us in warm blankets and get us home.

"Please hurry, Cary," I moaned. "Please."

I held on to the mast and on to Robert's hand, but the weight of his body was pulling on my wrist and arm. His fingers lost their grip on mine and he started to slip away.

"Robert. Oh, Robert, wake up!" I pleaded. I thought about shaking his arm, but I was afraid the motion might cause me to lose the tenuous grip I still held on the mast.

The ocean water hit my face while I was calling to him and I swallowed too much. I gagged, coughed, choked, and felt myself losing my grip on Robert and I struggled to hold on to him. I couldn't let him go.

New England weather, I thought, famous for its quick changes. I should have known. I should have known better. It's my fault, my fault.

The ocean was relentless. It would not be denied its sacrifice. I made a desperate last effort to hold on to Robert and the mast and then I felt his fingers slide down over my palm. His body lifted in the waves as if he were rising up to say his last good-bye, and then he went under.

I yelled his name as hard and as long as I could. I started to let go of the mast to search for him, but my own desperation to survive wouldn't permit my fingers to loosen their grip. I know I screamed and shouted his name until my voice gave out, my throat ached, and then I closed my eyes and turned to put my other hand around the mast. I pulled myself closer to it and laid my cheek against the cold metal. The boat continued to bob, to rise and fall in the wind and the rain.

A deep and thick darkness fell over me. Even when I opened my eyes, I saw nothing. The last thing I thought was silly in light of what was happening and what had happened. I moaned and cried, "I lost that beautiful silk scarf Mommy gave me. I'm sorry, Mommy," I cried.

My body shook as much with my own sobs as it did from the cold water and the freezing rain. I lay there with my head resting against the mast and felt the hull on my left side. It was reassuring. I remember thinking, I'll just sleep a moment and then, the storm will stop.

The magic will return.

The sun will warm us.

We'll laugh again and make promises to each other again. Won't we?

We? I couldn't remember his name. I could see his face, see his smile, even hear his voice, but who was he?

And then, the worst terror of all struck me.

Who am I?

I have put together what happened next, working over time on the events, the vague memories, the words I had heard as if it were all part of some grand thousand-piece puzzle. Some of it was told to me later on, but I always had to measure what I remembered against what I was told.

The storm continued to build that afternoon, preventing any real search for us. The wind and the waves carried the overturned sailboat farther out to sea. A fisherman by the name of Karl Hansen was fighting his way back to shore. He had worked for Grandpa Samuel and Grandma Olivia for years, but was pretty much retired now, only venturing out now and again with his own net. He saw the overturned sailboat and drew close enough to spot me clinging desperately to the mast. He began to shout. I remember first thinking the wind had found a voice. I thought it was part of the magic and just listened with a small smile on my face,

my eyes closed as he called and called. Then I felt something
hit my shoulder and I opened my eyes to see a man tossing a
net my way as his boat bobbed in the rough seas.

"Take hold. Wrap it around you," he ordered, yelling
through his cupped hands. "Take hold!"

He threw the net again and again. Each time, I looked at it
but didn't move. I couldn't let go of the mast. My hands had
locked around it, and no matter how hard I tried, I couldn't
will my hands to reach out for the net he threw.

Finally, Mr. Hansen brought his boat closer until he was
able to leap into the sea. He had a thick rope tied to his
waist and when he reached me, he quickly untied himself
and wound the rope around me.

"You've got to let go," he said. "Don't worry. I'll get you
on my boat."

He was a short, stout man with a full gray beard and gray
hair. I should have recognized him, but I didn't. He
recognized me.

"Laura Logan?" he cried. "Mrs. Logan's granddaughter.
Sweet Mary and Joseph. Let go of the mast when I tell you,
girl."

I remember I screamed and screamed and tried to resist
his effort to pull me away from the mast, then finally he got
me free and swam back to his boat, towing me along behind
him.

The wind was furious; the rain unrelenting. The struggle
was getting to be too much for him. His own boat was in
danger. I'm sure he questioned whether he could continue
the effort, but continue he did. Finally, we reached the boat
and Mr. Hansen was able to lift me up quickly and swing
me on board.

I was naked and freezing, my teeth chattering so hard, I
thought they would shatter against each other. The waves
were tossing Mr. Hansen's boat mercilessly. He had to get
back to controlling the roll. He found a blanket and threw it
over me first and then he attended to the boat. We went
farther out until he found enough calm water to give him a

chance to tend to me. He returned and helped me into the cabin, where he set me on a small cushioned bench.

"What happened to you, girl? How did you get caught out here? Was your brother with you?"

Brother? I thought. I have a brother?

I didn't respond. I lay there, going in and out of consciousness. I don't remember how long it took for us to reach shore, but he made a tactical navigation decision and brought us to Grandpa Samuel and Grandma Olivia's dock. The wind had let up some and the rain had slowed.

The next thing I knew, Mr. Hansen was running for help. He returned to get me up and out of the boat, and then literally carried me into the house. A small, angry woman greeted us and directed him to bring me to a guest room downstairs, where he set me gently on the bed. The elderly lady stood behind him, waiting. I didn't know who she was then. All I saw was her face of rage as she glared down at me. It all seemed to be happening to someone else. It was as if I were watching a movie.

"Where did you find her?" I heard her ask.

"She was clinging to an overturned sailboat about a mile and a half off Dead Man's Cove," he replied. "Those things are too small for weather only half as bad as this."

"You found her by herself, then?"

"Yes, ma'am. I hope her brother wasn't out there with her," he said. "No one could survive that," he added.

"It wasn't her brother," she said. "She was naked when you found her?"

"Yes, ma'am."

"Disgusting," she muttered.

I was still so cold I couldn't move my arms or legs. I lay curled up in a ball, breathing heavily, my body shuddering. She drew closer.

"What were you doing out there, girl?" she demanded, glaring at me with cold eyes of steel.

I couldn't talk; I couldn't even shake my head.

"Something sinful, just as I predicted," she concluded, nodding.

"I'll get a search party up after this dies down," Karl Hansen said.

The old woman spun around.

"You'll do nothing of the kind, Karl," she snapped at him. "You won't mention a word of this."

"But . . . surely, there was someone else on that boat, Mrs. Logan."

"I know there was someone else. I'm sure he was naked, too," she added disdainfully. "It's not something I want anyone else to know," she said, nodding at me. "The both of them were caught in some sinful act."

"What sinful act?" I wanted to say, but I couldn't.

She turned back to him. I saw the look of surprise and confusion on his face, but I didn't understand why. I didn't know where I was and I had forgotten how I had gotten there. All I knew was I was very cold and no one seemed to be paying much attention to that.

"You never found her, Karl," she told him. "I need your word on that."

"Pardon, Mrs. Logan?"

"You never found her," she said firmly. "Leave it all to me now."

"But Mrs. Logan—"

"You will be handsomely rewarded for your loyalty to me, Karl. I know your wife is sick and you have been having a hard time making ends meet. You won't have to worry at all about her doctor bills anymore or anything else for that matter. As long as I can rely on your word," she added.

He gazed at me and then at the small, angry woman he called Mrs. Logan.

"Well. I suppose there's nothing more to do about this, really. You'll see to her and whoever else was out there. Well, God rest his poor soul," Karl Hansen said. "I'm sure he didn't survive. There's nothing we could do anyway except locate the body and there's no rush to do that."

"Exactly. Now remember, Karl, you never found her. You

just made your own way toward shore and got washed up here. It was hard enough for you."

"Yes, it was, ma'am. That it was. There's no lying about that."

"Precisely," she said. "Raymond will see that you get home and I will have something for you in the morning. I'll also see that Ruth gets the personal nursing care she requires."

"Well, thank you, Mrs. Logan. That's very kind."

"As long as we understand each other, Karl," she added, her small eyes very cold and threatening. He nodded quickly.

"Oh, absolutely, Mrs. Logan. Absolutely."

"Good," she said and turned back to me. "Good."

She escorted him out and then returned a few minutes later. She simply stood there, gazing down at me.

"How could you do this?" she demanded. "How could you deliberately lie and deceive me and do this?"

My teeth chattered and I moaned.

"Don't you have even the slightest concern for this family? Do you know what kind of a disgrace this could bring? Why, they might even put this in the newspapers. People from outside of Provincetown, friends, acquaintances from everywhere could learn of it. Well? Don't you have anything to say?"

"I'm cold," I finally said.

"Cold? That's the least of your problems. Fortunately, Mr. Hansen won't tell anyone a thing, but . . . don't you hear a word of what I'm saying to you?" she snapped. "You're staring at me as if I were speaking Greek. And wipe that silly smile off your face," she ordered. "I won't have it."

"I'm sorry," I said. "I'm not smiling. I'm just cold. My hair is soaked," I said. I started to rub the blanket up and down my arms and legs.

"I'm sure you are sorry now. Although it does us no good to have you say it," she said and wagged her head. "How did this happen?"

"What?" I asked.

"What? Are you an idiot? This!" she exclaimed, thrusting her hands toward me. "You've lived here long enough to know when to come in from a storm and when to be cautious. What were you doing out there? Were you so wrapped up in your lust that you ignored the weather? Well?"

"Out where?"

"In the ocean, you fool. What is wrong with you?"

Then I remember giggling. I couldn't help it. She was a funny little old lady to me. Her hair was held tightly back with pearl combs and she wore a flower print dress with a rope of pearls around her neck. When she got excited, the blood under her skin rose up her neck like mercury in a thermometer, and she seemed to bounce on her feet after every sentence.

"You think this is funny?" she asked, astounded.

I shook my head.

"What happened to him?" she asked.

"To who?" I responded.

She stopped being angry for a moment and stared intently at me.

"Don't you remember anything?"

I shook my head.

"You know where you are, don't you?"

Again, I shook my head.

She stared and then tilted her head a little as she thought.

"What's my name?" she suddenly asked.

"That man called you Mrs. Logan," I said. "Isn't that your name?"

"My God." She covered her mouth and stared at me. Then she lowered her hand slowly. "What's your name?"

I thought, but no name came to mind.

"I don't know."

She stepped back as if I had some contagious disease and stared at me again.

"Madness on top of disgrace. It's happening again. First, to my sister, and now to you, and I'm supposed to bear the

164

burden, face the community, hold on to my prestige and position, and keep this family name as respected as it once was, as it should be?"

She paused and then raised her small fist toward the ceiling as if she were threatening God.

"This will not happen," she declared. Then she turned back to me. "Don't you move from that bed," she ordered.

I didn't think I could move. I had just barely managed to straighten my legs.

Minutes later, she returned with an armful of big, fluffy towels and then went into the bathroom. I heard her run water in the tub. She was moving quickly, and she looked like a goblin to me and I couldn't help smiling again. It made her angry when she emerged from the bathroom and saw the smile on my face.

"Get up," she ordered. "I'll handle this myself. Go on, get up!"

I swung my legs out slowly, the muscles in my thighs screaming, and when I pushed to sit up, I felt my shoulder stinging. The blanket fell away. I looked at my arm. Blood vessels had burst all along it, so that there were black and blue marks from the inside of my wrist, up over my elbow, right to my shoulder. Even she gasped.

"Everything hurts," I complained.

"And rightly so," she said, regaining her regal, stern demeanor. "Stand up and walk into the bathroom. Go on. I don't have the strength to lift you," she added, her hands on her hips. I realized she had put on a light blue housecoat over her dress. I tried to stand, but my legs wobbled.

"I can't," I moaned.

"You can and you will. Stand!" she ordered. She reached forward and seized the top of my hair, tugging me hard.

I screamed. The breath nearly left me, but I rose. I reached out to brace myself on her shoulder. She stepped back and at least gave me her hand.

"I can't carry you. Walk," she commanded.

Each step was excruciating. My back, my legs, even my feet ached. I made my way toward the sound of the running water, reaching out to steady myself against the doorjamb, and then I entered the bathroom. She moved ahead and shut off the water.

"Get into the tub and soak yourself. Go on. Do what I say and do it now," she ordered again.

I don't know how I did it, but I reached the tub and lifted my leg to step into the water. It was so hot, however, I howled and pulled my foot out quickly, losing my balance. I fell back and sat hard on the floor.

"You're disgusting," she cried.

"It's too hot," I moaned.

"It has to be hot, you fool. Now get up and get into the water. Go on. Do it." She hovered over me. "If you don't, you'll surely get pneumonia."

I got to my knees and crawled to the tub. Then I took a deep breath and rose to put my foot in again. It took the breath out of me and I grew so dizzy, I thought I would faint. She put her hands on my hips and held me steady, permitting me to rest against her for a moment.

"All right, now lower yourself into the water. Just do it quickly," she commanded.

I took a deep breath and did so, crying out as I settled into the steamy liquid. My body began to itch and then tingle. I kept taking deep breaths. Finally, I grew more comfortable and then it did suddenly make me feel better. I closed my eyes.

Suddenly I felt something being poured over my head.

"You have to wash out the salt," she said. She scooped water onto my hair, scrubbed it, and then forced me to lower myself until I was under the water so I could rinse my hair. She kept me down so long, I thought she wanted to drown me in the tub. I came up gasping.

"Just lie there and soak," she said and left the bathroom.

I'm sure I fell asleep for a few minutes. Then I sensed her nearby again. She had returned and stood above me, looking down at me with an expression of utter disgust.

"Well?" she demanded. "Do you know who you are now?"

I thought and thought. Then I shook my head.

"I don't know," I wailed. "Who am I?"

"You're a fool and I don't suffer fools in this family anymore," she declared. She sighed deeply. "Who am I?"

I tried to remember. I had even forgotten what that man had called her before.

"I don't remember what that man called you," I moaned.

"What, has your brain turned to cranberry jelly?" she asked.

"Cranberries? I remember cranberries."

"Well, I'm glad about that. What else do you remember? Do you have any family, friends?"

I thought and just found a blank, dark place in my mind with no faces, no words, no voices. I shook my head.

"I don't know," I said.

She stared.

"Maybe you don't. Maybe . . . this is a blessing in disguise. Yes," she said, her face lighting up and her eyes widening, "it is."

She left again and for what seemed like quite a long time. When she returned this time, she had a white terry cloth robe in her hands.

"Get out. Dry yourself off and put this on," she said. "Someone will be here for you soon."

"Someone?"

Good, I thought. There was someone. Surely, I would remember everything soon. I crawled up and out of the tub with great effort. My body was beyond exhaustion, the muscles working on their own memory and not my commands. It seemed to take me forever to dry myself. She grew impatient.

"For God's sake," she said and seized one of the towels. She began to rub me vigorously. I felt as if she would peel away my skin. My every movement was still filled with pain and I ached everywhere.

"There," she said. "Now put on the robe and return to that bed," she instructed.

I did what she said. The moment my head hit the pillow

and I closed my eyes, I fell asleep. I woke when I heard voices near and above me. My eyelids refused to stay open at first and then, with stubborn effort, I did get them to do so.

Coming into focus was a tall woman in a starched white uniform. She stood next to the small elderly lady. The woman in white scrutinized me a moment and then made a small, tight smile.

"Hello. My name is Clara. What's your name?" she asked and took my wrist into her fingers to feel for my pulse.

"My name's . . . My name's . . . I can't remember!" I cried.

The woman looked at the elderly woman and then back at me.

"Do you know whose home you are in?"

I shook my head.

"How old are you?"

"I don't know."

"How did you get here?" she followed quickly.

"I don't remember. Where am I?"

"Are you home?"

"Am I?"

"See?" the elderly lady said.

"Yes. It's classic, I think," the woman in white said. "Her pulse is strong."

"It's not her pulse I'm worried about," the small elderly lady said.

Clara nodded.

"You understand what I want and how I want it done," the elderly lady said.

"Precisely. You have made the appropriate phone calls, I imagine?"

"Of course," the elderly lady said. "It's all arranged. I'm relying on your discretion. You will be rewarded," she added.

Clara smiled. "You won't be disappointed."

"Good."

Clara turned back to me.

"I'm going to help you now," she said, "but I need you to help yourself, too. Okay?"

"Yes," I said.

"Good. I want you to get up and walk with me. We're going to get into a car outside. I'm going to take you to a nice place, okay?"

"Okay," I said. I raised myself up on my elbows and Clara reached under my left arm and helped me get out of bed. When I stood up, I felt terribly stiff and said so.

"That's all right," Clara said. "You won't be stiff too much longer. I'll help you," she said. She smiled. She had a nice, friendly smile, a much nicer smile than the elderly lady could ever have, I thought. I was glad to be leaving.

The elderly lady followed behind us as we continued out of the room, down a long corridor to the front doors of the house. I remember thinking it was a big house and there were things about it that looked familiar, but I didn't remember coming here. The elderly lady walked ahead of us and opened the door.

It was still lightly drizzling out, and the cold air hit me like a slap in the face. I shuddered and Clara wrapped her arm around my shoulders.

"There, there, now," she said. "We'll be warm soon."

She guided me out and to the dark car that was waiting. I didn't see the driver. Clara opened the door for me and I was guided carefully into the rear of the car. Then Clara stepped back.

"You want to say anything to her?" Clara asked the elderly lady.

"No. Tell them I'll be there tomorrow to make the arrangements and give them a check," she said.

"Very good, Mrs. Logan."

I snapped my head around. Mrs. Logan? I remembered that name, but who was she? She glared at me, her eyes beady, icy, her mouth pinched tight. I was glad when the door was closed and she was out of sight.

Clara got in from the other side and sat beside me.

"All right now?" she asked. I nodded. "You'll be fine," she said. "Soon, you'll be fine."

I smiled back at her. She nodded at the driver and the car began to move away from the big house and into the rain, into the darkness that lay ahead.

I stared for a moment and then spun around and looked back, but the lights of the house were already gone and the darkness had closed in behind me. It was as if I had walked through a door and the door had been shut tight. I wanted to go back; I wanted to open the door again, but I couldn't find my way.

"Where are we going?" I asked Clara.

"Someplace else," she replied. "Is that okay?"

I thought for a moment.

"Yes," I said. "It's okay."

I wasn't sure why, but vaguely I realized that yes, yes, it was better to be someplace else.

10

My Name Is . . .

I fell asleep again in the car and didn't wake until the car hit a bump and jarred me from my trancelike slumber. It was very dark outside because an overcast sky kept the moon and the stars hidden. When I gazed out the window, I saw only my own reflected face in the glass, the face of someone so lost and confused, her eyes were filled with question marks and her lips frozen in a vain struggle to find some word, some thought to voice.

I turned and looked at the woman in the nurse's uniform dozing beside me. Her eyelids fluttered as the automobile jerked and turned, but they didn't open. I gazed at the back of the driver's head and I wondered who these people were and where I was going. Should I know? Had I been told?

I struggled with the questions, but it was as if I had fallen into an echo chamber because all I could hear were the questions coming back at me. The answers were like schools of fish swimming in the opposite direction, far, far out of reach and uninterested in turning back. I could only watch them disappear, their scales glimmering for a moment and then gone, perhaps forever.

My body was sore, yet I couldn't remember why that was either. It hurt to straighten out my arms and legs and the back of my neck felt as if someone with powerful fingers had grabbed it and squeezed for hours. My eyes ached even when I kept them closed. I groaned and twisted to make myself more comfortable and the woman beside me woke with a quick jerk of her shoulders. She looked about, seemingly confused herself for a moment, and then turned to me and smiled.

"How are you, dear?" she asked. The driver turned a little but didn't look back at us.

"I'm sore," I said. "Why am I so sore?"

"Don't you remember anything about what happened to you, why you are in pain?"

I thought and thought, but it was like opening a book and finding it had only blank pages. I turned one after another and saw nothing written on any of them.

I shook my head, my lips trembling, my tears feeling more like smoldering ashes under my eyelids.

"Don't worry," she said. "It will all come back to you someday."

"It would be better for her if it don't," the driver muttered.

"We'll be needing none of your comments," she snapped at the back of his head. "You're here to drive and nothing else," she added sternly. He cringed as if her words were actually slaps and then he grunted and drove on silently.

Suddenly, there were lights ahead cloaked in what looked like banks of fog. As we drew closer, I strained to make out the shape of what appeared to be an entryway to an estate. It was a very tall iron gate with a wide, red brick column on each side. The light came from a large ball lamp atop each column. The driver slowed to a stop at the gate.

"One moment, dear," the nurse said, patting me softly on the knee. She got out of the car.

The fog twirled about us like smoke. I leaned forward to watch her poke numbers on a pad built into the side of the column on the right. The iron bars groaned loudly as the nurse returned to the car.

"Where are we?" I asked.

"Just relax, dear," she said in reply.

When the gate was completely opened, we drove through and began a climb up a winding hill, climbing up out of the sea of fog.

After the second turn, a five-story, gray brick and wood structure loomed above us, rising out of the darkness like the bow of a great ship. As we drew closer, it looked like a medieval castle because there was a large cupola at the center of the roof. On both ends there were dormers with windows that caught the reflection of the light below cast by tall pole lamps illuminating the parking lot. Most of the windows in the building were dark, but there were some dimly lit rooms on the first floor.

When we turned into a parking space, I saw there was a cement stairway up to the front entrance. It was really too dark to see much of the grounds, but I could make out some large weeping willow trees to the right. They looked like giants with their heads bowed.

"What is this place?" I asked. The sight of it had stirred no memory, recent or otherwise.

"It's sort of a hospital," the nurse replied with a small, but quick smile. The driver snorted. She glared at him a moment and then turned back to me. "You'll be well looked after here," she said.

"Is this where I live?" I asked.

"For now," she said.

She got out and came around the car to open my door and help me out. The driver remained behind, slouching down and lowering his chin to his chest. The nurse knocked on the window and he lowered it.

"I'm not going to be that long," she told him, but he didn't act as if he heard her or cared. She turned back to me. "Come along, dear."

She led me toward the stairs. There was an iron railing on the right. I held on to it as we climbed the steps because I felt a little dizzy. When we reached the front entrance, she pressed the buzzer and then looked at me and flashed another snapshot of a smile.

The doors looked heavy and thick. They were tall and wide and had no windows. I leaned back and looked up at the roof. I thought I saw a bat fly from one end to the other. It was so quiet and the air was very moist and enveloping. I could practically see the droplets of moisture dancing like small fairies around us. Off to the right, a streak of lightning sliced through the blackness, and then instantly disappeared. My stomach felt as if it were filled with broken glass. I felt so lost, so detached, floating in space, longing for the pull of gravity to bring me back to earth, back home, back to my name.

We waited and waited. Finally, the door opened and a tall, lean man with hair that looked like it couldn't decide whether to be red or blond stood before us. He, too, wore a white uniform. He looked very sleepy, his eyelids drooping. He seemed to be in his twenties and had freckles all over his cheeks and forehead, even on his lips.

"Weren't you expecting us, Billy?" the nurse asked him gruffly.

"What? Yeah. Sorry, Clara," he said. "I fell asleep waiting," he added dryly.

"Well now that we're here, we'd like to come in," she said sharply. He stepped back quickly and we entered.

Nothing looked familiar inside either. It was a large room with gray-and-blue cotton–covered sofas and chairs. There were about a half dozen light maple wood tables. Only three of the small lamps in the large room were turned on, but I could see that there wasn't much on the walls, just some paintings of ocean scenes with sailboats and fishing boats and a few paintings just of colors in rectangular shapes. The floor was a dark wood with oval area rugs here and there. At the far end, there was a large fireplace made of fieldstone.

The freckle-faced man she called Billy looked at me for the first time, his gaze sweeping up from my feet to my face as if he were measuring me for something to wear. His eyes widened with a little more interest and alertness when I gave him a friendly smile.

"This is her?" he asked, his voice filled with surprise.

"Of course it is. Who did you think it was, the new Miss America?" Clara quipped. He smirked.

"She looks pretty good. I just thought . . . Mrs. Miller said we should just show her to her room and get her to bed," he concluded once he saw the expression of impatience on Clara's face.

"So let's do it," she said. "I don't have all night to dilly-dally with you."

He turned and started toward the stairway, pausing at the bottom step.

"She's going to be on the second floor. She can take care of her own basic needs, right? She looks like she can," he added, gazing back at me.

"Why don't you leave the diagnosis and treatment to the doctors and just take us to her quarters. It's late and I'm tired, too, Billy," Clara replied with more fatigue in her voice than anger this time.

"I'm just asking," he whined and started up the stairs. The nurse guided me up. We turned at the landing and went down a long hallway. The lights above were very bright, creating a glare off the gray tile floor. Occasionally, the clean white walls were smudged. Here and there I saw what looked like squiggly lines made with dark crayons. Suddenly, I heard someone wailing. Moments later I saw a woman and a man in white hurry through the corridor.

"That's Sara Richards having another whopper of a nightmare, I bet," the young man said. "The last time that happened, she scratched her face so badly they had to cut her nails back to her knuckles. She's headed for upstairs, for sure," he predicted.

"Thanks for the cheerful news," Clara said.

What was upstairs? I wondered.

Billy paused at a doorway and reached for a set of keys hanging on his belt. He rifled through them, chose one, and opened the door. He switched on the light and we entered.

The first thing I noticed were the bars on the windows. How odd, I thought, for a hospital. Other than that, the room looked very pleasant. There were pretty blue and white curtains around the windows and a pretty blue flowered wallpaper on the walls. The bed was twin size and looked comfortable. It had a light blue comforter and two plush pillows with a thick, dark mahogany headboard. Beside it were two matching nightstands, on the right one of which was a lamp shaped like a ship lantern in brass. Across from the bed was a small dresser and to the right of that was a desk and a chair. There was a cushioned, blue-and-white patterned chair between the two windows. On the wall across from the bed was a painting of a garden with lawn furniture. The word Impressionist came to mind, shooting out of some dark closet, followed by the face of someone I should be able to remember. Was it a teacher? A friend? Family? It was gone too quickly for me to come to any conclusion.

"Isn't this nice?" Clara said.

"Yeah, you know the facilities here are quite good when you consider," Billy said before I could respond.

"Consider what?" Clara asked. He shrugged.

"That most of them don't know where the hell they are anyway," he said.

"You've got a great attitude, Billy. Mr. Sensitivity himself."

He laughed.

"I just call it like it is," he said.

"Spare me," Clara told him and he laughed again.

Clara crossed the room and opened the closet. There was what looked like a hospital worker's powder blue uniform dangling on a hanger and a pair of white terry cloth slippers beneath it. Other than that, the closet was empty.

"All right," she said to Billy, "I'll settle her in."

"What about the paperwork?" he asked.

"I'll be down in a little while to take care of it. Just have it ready for me."

"Aye, aye, Captain," he said with a mock salute. He gazed

at me and then nodded at her. "Good," he said as if I had done something difficult by merely walking in and up the stairs. He turned to me again before leaving. "What's her name?"

She hesitated a moment as if she had forgotten and then said, "Lauren."

Lauren? I thought. That didn't sound right.

"No, that's not my name," I said.

Her eyes widened and her eyebrows curled up.

"Oh? You remember your name?"

I thought and then shook my head.

"So how do you know it's not Lauren?" she asked.

I stared at her and then at him. He was wearing a wide, silly grin.

"I . . . just . . . know," I faltered.

"Until you remember your name, that's your name," she replied dryly. "Now, Lauren," she said, pronouncing it emphatically so I would not contradict her again, "come over here and get into this." She took the shirt and pants off their hangers and handed them to me. "You should get settled in and get some sleep. Tomorrow is a big day for you."

"Yeah, the first day is always the hardest," Billy commented.

Clara turned to Billy, shooting him an angry look. He flashed another smile at me and then left quickly.

I got into the shirt and pants while she turned down my bed. The sheets smelled freshly starched and the blanket felt brand new.

"Comfortable?" she asked me as she tucked me in and arranged my pillow under my head.

"Yes, but I still ache all over. Why can't I remember what happened to me? Was I in some sort of accident? A car accident? Did I fall?"

"Tomorrow, the doctor will see you and then we'll see what can be done to help make you more comfortable," she said instead of answering my question. "In the morning, another nurse, the head nurse, Mrs. Kleckner, will show you around and take you to breakfast. You're going to be fine," she added.

"How long will I be here?" I asked.

She stared at me a moment.

"I don't think you'll be here as long as your grandmother thinks," she said.

"My grandmother?" I thought about the small elderly lady back at the house. "That woman was my grandmother? Why was she so angry and mean to me?"

"Never mind now," she said quickly, as if she had already told me too much. "There's plenty of time to work on your return."

"Return? From where?"

She thought a moment.

"From . . . oblivion, I guess," she said. She paused and looked at me, a small smile on her lips. "Can't you remember anything about yourself? How old you are? Any member of your family? Anything?"

I closed my eyes, tried to remember and then shook my head.

"Everything is so muddled. I hear voices and see quick flashing pictures, but it's like my mind is full of bubbles that keep bursting when I try to seize one," I replied.

She laughed.

"You'll be fine," she said and patted me on the hand. "Get some sleep."

"Will I see you again?" I asked quickly as she turned and started for the door.

"No. I don't work here. I work for a doctor who has patients here," she replied from the doorway.

"My doctor?" I asked.

"No, not exactly," she said. "Don't worry about all those details. Just do what they tell you to do and you'll get better sooner than you think," she said. "For now, what you need the most is some rest."

"I know I want to go home," I said, "but I just can't remember where that is."

She smiled warmly.

"You will. Someday," she said. Then she looked sad. "Good-bye, Lauren." She switched off the lights, and as she closed the door behind her, I heard the distinctive click of a lock.

Trying to forget that I had just been locked into my room, I lay there in the darkness, listening. Through the walls I could hear someone crying softly. Above me there were footsteps moving rapidly and then a deep, long silence that was soon filled with the sounds of creaking walls and floors, the slam of a door and more footsteps.

Why was I here? Why did Clara call that old lady my grandmother? She didn't act like a grandmother, I thought. Why wouldn't Clara tell me more? Who told her to call me Lauren? Maybe that was my name.

I closed my eyes. All these questions and thoughts were giving me a headache. A myriad of faces flashed against the insides of my eyelids, some smiling, some laughing, a young man looking serious and then someone began to whisper. I struggled to hear what he was saying, but his voice drifted back until there was only silence and blackness.

I was so tired. Clara was right. I needed rest. Maybe in the morning, I would remember who I was. All my questions would be answered and this would all be over.

For now, that was my only prayer.

I woke when the door to my room was thrust open with such force and abruptness, it sent waves through the air. A much older nurse than Clara stepped in carrying a package under her arm. Her hair was the dirty gray color of old silver coins and the strands cut just below her earlobes looked thin and harsh as wire. Her forehead had rows of deep wrinkles that exploded at her temples to produce spidery webs extending to her cheeks. Her cheeks were a bit puffy, making her small, wide nose look like it was sinking into her face and would soon be swallowed up by those cheeks. She had a thin, uneven mouth, the right corner of her lower lip dipping just enough to reveal some teeth. The roundness in her face fit her chunky, short body, yet she had long arms with wide hands and thick fingers.

She paused, breathing in and lifting her hefty bosom as she contemplated me for a moment. I thought she looked like a pigeon with her chest out as she strutted to the bed. She placed the package at my feet.

Her appearance had startled me so that my heart thumped. As soon as I regained my senses, I sat up and gazed about in confusion, trying to remember how and when I had been brought here. The soreness in my body had gone deeply into my muscles. My arms felt heavier and just the thought of standing was exhausting.

"Good, you're awake," this new nurse said.

She went to the windows and when she turned her back to me, I saw she had a rather prominent birthmark at the base of her skull. Small hairs grew along its perimeter so that it looked like a large black bug had landed there. She opened the curtains wider to let in more sunlight. I could see clear blue sky.

She spun on me, her hands on her hips.

"I'm Mrs. Kleckner," she said. "I'm the head nurse here. Your bathroom has all that you need in it. You'll find a toothbrush, toothpaste, a new hairbrush, soap, and shampoo in the cabinet. Can you get up and give yourself a shower this morning or do I have to take you to the special bathroom for the disabled?"

"I think I can do it myself," I said.

She approached the bed.

"Hold out your hands," she ordered. "Go on."

I did what she asked and she watched them tremble and then turned them over and watched them again.

"Touch the tip of your nose," she commanded. "Do it," she said when I didn't move quickly enough.

After I had done that, she took my pulse, looked at my eyes and then stepped back.

"Do you remember why you were brought here? Do you remember how you were brought here?" she asked before I could answer the first question.

"I came in a car. There was another nurse named Clara. She said I had been with my grandmother." I looked up. "The nurse kept calling me Lauren, but I don't think my name is Lauren," I said.

"Really? Then what's your name?"

I thought a moment, but I couldn't think of anything that sounded right.

"I know it's not Lauren," I said.

"That's nice. You know it's not Lauren. You know it's not Susan, too. And you know it's not Joyce and you know it's not Matilda, I bet," she rattled with a smirk. "You probably know you're not fifty or sixty or seventy names, but do you know how old you are?"

"How old? I can't remember," I said. "Why can't I remember my own age and my own name?"

My lips started to tremble.

She nodded as if confirming what she thought to be true.

"A shower is the way we begin the day. There are clothes for you in this package," she said, indicating what she had brought in with her. "Underthings, socks, a pair of shoes, a skirt, and a blouse. Other things are being brought for you today. First, I'll show you the cafeteria and you'll have breakfast. After that, you'll meet Doctor Southerby and have your first session. I understand you have some trauma on your arms and legs," she said and drew closer again.

She lifted the blanket away from me.

"Lower those pants," she ordered.

I started to do so and once again, I didn't move quickly enough to satisfy her. She finished lowering them herself and inspected the bruises on my thighs and my calves as well as my hips and ribs.

"You did take a beating," she remarked.

She lifted the shirt over my head so roughly, I cried out.

"My arms, my shoulders!"

She held my arm up and inspected the black and blue marks. When she released it, I studied my hands and my forearms, too. My fingers looked scabby where the skin had been peeled away. What could I have done to myself?

181

"What happened to me?" I moaned, near tears.

"You'll live," she said dryly, lifting the right corner of her mouth so that it put a bulge into her cheek. "This will all go away in time."

"But I don't understand. How did this happen to me?" I asked her.

She didn't smirk exactly. She pressed her lips together, puffed her cheeks out a bit more, and made her eyes small.

"It's your responsibility to tell us," she said. "When you do, you'll be on your way to recovery."

"What's wrong with me?" I asked in a shrill voice. "Why can't I remember anything about myself? No one wants to tell me anything. Please!"

"The doctor will tell you all about that. My job is to get you ready and see after your basic needs first," she said calmly, clearly unmoved by my emotional outburst. Then she fixed her eyes on me. "I'll warn you now," she continued, stepping back and folding her thick arms under her heavy bosom. Her elbows looked dry, the skin scaly like a fish. "This is not a five-star hotel. I don't want to hear complaints about the food or the service or the size of your room. I don't want to hear how we don't have enough to do to entertain you. I'm a nurse, not some camp counselor for wealthy, spoiled children."

"Am I a wealthy, spoiled child?" I fired back. I thought she almost smiled.

"That's something you'll have to learn for yourself. The plan is for you to make your own discoveries about yourself, with our help, of course. That's how you get better. My telling you everything I know about you doesn't help you."

"I don't understand. Where am I?" I asked.

"Where are you? You're in a mental clinic, my dear," she said.

"A mental clinic?"

"One of the best in the state, if not *the* best, and very exclusive, too. Now, take your shower. I'll be back in twenty minutes and I expect to see you dressed and ready for breakfast. There's no reason why you can't do it all for yourself. I have a few patients on this floor who really do need my assistance and I must get to them now."

My lips started to tremble. I thought my whole body would soon start to shudder uncontrollably. She saw something was about to happen and stepped closer.

"Get hold of yourself," she ordered. She put her hands on my upper arms and shook me. "I don't permit any of my patients to sit in their rooms and feel sorry for themselves. The quicker you get better, the quicker you get out of here," she said, "and make room for someone else who really needs us. Shower," she concluded, pivoted on her soft shoes, and marched out of the room, closing the door behind her.

I took a deep breath.

Remember, I chanted. *Try, try to remember. Please. If you remember, you can go home.*

I squeezed my eyes closed and searched my brain, but it was as if my shouts for help were locked in a small part of my mind, shut up and smothered. I looked down at my hands and my feet, seeking some mark, something that would stir a memory. Nothing happened.

I sighed with frustration, rose, took off the shirt and pants, and went into the bathroom. There was a mirror over the small sink. I stared at my face, bringing my fingers to my lips, my nose, even touching my eyes. I was like a blind person trying to identify someone through my fingers, but what I felt, what I found rang no bells. I leaned in to look very closely at my reflection. I was looking at the face of a complete stranger. It was as if I had been dropped into someone else's body.

"Who are you?" I asked the image in the mirror and waited.

Suddenly, I heard a roaring in my ears. A memory flashed, the memory of holding a seashell to my ear and listening.

The ocean is in there, someone was saying. I sensed I was just a little girl.

Look inside. Do you see it?

I closed my eyes. There were smiling faces and there was laughter and there was the ocean in the seashell. Everyone who looked at me smiled.

"Who am I?" I screamed at them, but they just continued to smile. "WHO AM I?"

I directed my screaming at the image in the mirror and the image just screamed back. I don't know how long that went on before Mrs. Kleckner returned. She spun me around with those strong hands of hers and then she slapped me sharply across the face and I stopped.

"What are you doing? You frightened some of my other patients."

"I don't remember my name," I wailed. "I don't know who that is in the mirror. I'm afraid. I feel like I'm dangling in space. It's terrifying!" I cried.

"Don't be ridiculous. You're safe here. You're not dangling. Now, didn't I tell you to take a shower and get dressed? You'll see the doctor this morning and your therapy will begin. Now, get into the shower," she said and reached over to turn it on. "Go on, get in and stop this nonsense now. No one is going to pamper you. You have to cure yourself and help yourself."

She glared at me.

"It will go better for you if you cooperate," she said, not cloaking her threats.

I ground the tears away and stepped into the shower, adjusting the water so it wasn't as scalding hot as she had it. She waited a moment and then left me alone.

Despite the shower, I felt deeply exhausted after drying off. It took great effort to dress, get on my socks and shoes. Where did this clothing come from? I wondered. Was it mine? Everything did fit well.

The door opened again and Mrs. Kleckner stood there inspecting me.

"Good," she said. "Come along. I'll show you the eating facilities now and tomorrow morning, you'll get yourself up and to breakfast on your own, understand? Do you understand?" she repeated when I didn't answer quickly enough.

184

"Yes," I said.

"This way." She turned and I joined her. We walked down the corridor toward the stairway. A tall, dark-haired girl was there ahead of us. She didn't glance our way, but instead bounced happily down the steps, waving her hands as if she were sweeping cobwebs away from her head.

Mrs. Kleckner sighed deeply and shook her head, but she said nothing. We started down the stairs. The dark-haired girl was already down and away. I was moving too slowly to satisfy Mrs. Kleckner, so when we reached the bottom of the stairs, she seized my hand and jerked me along.

"It's time to wake up," she declared and forced me to stride step for step alongside her until we reached a large doorway, from which I could hear dishes and silverware clinking and voices in a low but continuous murmur, punctuated by some laughter. When we turned into the doorway and entered the cafeteria, everyone stopped talking and looked at us.

There were a little more than a dozen people, all looking relatively my age, whatever that exact age was. The dark-haired girl who had been sweeping the air around her as she descended the steps broke into a long, shrill laugh. She was at the counter getting her food from a sweet-looking elderly lady in a white uniform.

"Quiet," Mrs. Kleckner cried. The dark-haired girl stopped with such abruptness, I couldn't help but be impressed with Mrs. Kleckner's authority. All eyes were on us now. There was a boy close by who didn't look much more than ten or eleven, gazing at me with a small smile on his lips. Sitting at his table was a tall, very thin girl with hair the color of ripe apricots. She had big dark eyes and a mouth with soft, perfect lips. Her cheekbones were clearly visible under her tissue-like skin, which was pale and thin enough to pass for transparent. I saw how thin her arms were, too. Despite her fragile appearance, she sat straight and firm and looked at me with a soft, friendly air.

Across from her, his eyes down, was a handsome young man with hair as dark and shiny as black pearl. He wore it brushed neatly on the sides and long down the back of his neck. For a moment I thought of someone else. A name almost appeared, but when this boy flashed a quick, timid look at me, I forgot the face in my memory and smiled back at him.

"We have a new resident," Mrs. Kleckner said.

"Hooray for her," a chubby boy with blond hair cried. The two boys at his table laughed, but then stopped as if they could turn it on and off like a television set, their faces moving from comedy to tragedy in a split second.

"That's enough of that, Carlton," Mrs. Kleckner chastised. He laughed silently, his cheeks jiggling, and then he suddenly looked as if he were going to cry. I glanced at Mrs. Kleckner, who didn't seem to notice or care.

"Her name," she continued, "is Laura."

I turned and looked at her, seeing a small smile on her face. All along she knew I had been right. The other nurse had mistakenly called me Lauren and not Laura, but I had been unable to remember. However, even though I sensed Laura was my real name, I couldn't connect it with anything else, especially a surname.

"I want you all to make her feel at home here," Mrs. Kleckner added.

"Home sweet home," someone in the back muttered.

The dark-haired girl by the counter suddenly spun around and then spun around again as if she were dancing a ballet. One of the attendants nearby moved quickly to her side and seized her hand. He spoke to her quietly and she gazed at the floor.

When I looked to the right, I noticed a female attendant hand-feeding a boy who looked at least twelve or thirteen. She encouraged him to feed himself, but he merely stared ahead, opening his mouth and chewing mechanically as she scooped the food into it and then wiped his lips.

"Go to the counter and get what you want," Mrs. Kleckner said. "There's juice, cereals, and eggs, if you like. Mrs. Anderson is our cook. She can make some special things for you if your requests are reasonable and she has enough notice. You can sit anywhere you like," she added.

I crossed the cafeteria, feeling all eyes upon me. The dark-haired girl had been moved along and sat with the attendant at her side. She sipped on a glass of orange juice and stared ahead.

"Hello, Laura," Mrs. Anderson said. She had a wonderfully happy smile, her eyes bright and cheery. "Would you like some scrambled eggs this morning?"

"Yes," I said. "Thank you."

I suddenly realized that I was very hungry. I chose grapefruit juice and plucked a roll from the basket. Mrs. Anderson scooped the eggs onto a plate and put a piece of melon beside them.

"Enjoy your first breakfast with us," she said.

"Thank you."

I took the plate, put it on my tray, and turned. Many of the other residents were still staring at me, but a number had gone back to their own breakfasts and conversations. Some looked absolutely terrified that I would stop at their tables as I made my way through the room.

"Sit here. You'll be safe," a pretty red-haired girl said. There was another, shorter and younger-looking girl with her. The younger girl wore a jeans skirt and a frilly white blouse. Her blond hair was tied in two long, thick pigtails.

"Thank you," I said and took the empty seat at their table.

"My name's Megan Paxton," the red-haired girl said. She had a button nose and a small mouth. Her eyes darted about as if she expected trouble.

"I'm Laura," I said, confident of that little bit of information.

"Laura what?" the younger girl asked. She looked like a doll because of her tiny features.

"I can't remember my full name," I said. "I can't remember anything," I admitted, as if that were a crime and this was a jail instead of a clinic.

"Around here, that's an advantage," Megan said. "You're lucky," she said dryly. "I can't forget anything. When did you arrive?"

"Some time last night. I think," I said. "It all still seems fuzzy in my head." I drank my juice.

Megan darted her eyes about again. I began to look in the directions she was surveying to see if there was something I should notice, too.

"Is something wrong?" I asked.

"I'm just waiting to see if he's still here. They claim," she said, widening her eyes and hoisting her eyebrows, "that they fired him yesterday."

"Who?"

"Garson Taylor, one of the attendants. He tried to rape me," Megan said.

"Really?"

"Of course, really," she snapped. "What do you think, I'm making it up? Well, *do* you?" she drove at me, her face full of fire, her eyes wide.

"No, I'm . . . I'm sorry. I was just surprised by what you said."

"Well don't be surprised. Be alert. All the men here have one thing on their minds and you don't have to take two guesses to figure out what it is either," she said. "When they look at you, they're looking through your clothes."

"That's terrible."

"Tell me about it." She considered me a moment. "Maybe you were raped," she said. "And it was so traumatic, it caused you to forget everything. That's very common." She nodded, firmly convinced in her diagnosis.

I stopped eating and gazed at her. I started to shake my head.

"Why are you shaking your head? You said you don't remember anything. I bet that's it. Right, Lulu?" she asked the young girl. The small girl nodded.

"Yes, Megan," she said obediently. Megan looked satisfied.

"Her name isn't really Lulu. I named her that," Megan explained with a smile. "That's because she's a real lulu. Right, Lulu?"

The small girl laughed.

"My daddy's coming to see me today," she said.

"Oh, will you stop? She's been saying that for two years. Her father doesn't even write her letters," Megan said. "You would think she'd understand, face reality by now."

"Yes, he does."

"Okay, Lulu. Believe what you want. Fathers are the biggest liars of all anyway," Megan said. "Can you remember your father?" she asked me.

"No," I said.

"He's the one who raped you then," Megan threw back at me.

I nearly choked on my eggs.

"I never said I was raped."

"Of course you didn't, but it's a very logical reason why you can't remember." She leaned over to whisper. "Be very careful after you've gone to bed. They all have keys to our doors," she said, leaning back, "that is how Garson Taylor got into my room. Fortunately, I was able to shout loudly enough to bring others. He claimed he wasn't even in my room. Can you imagine?"

She looked about nervously again and then turned back to me, her haunted eyes wide and full of alarm.

"If he's still here we're all in danger, especially a new girl like you. Watch the doctors, too," she added.

"The doctors? Why?"

"They like to touch you here all the time," she said, touching her small breasts, "and pretend it's necessary."

She stared at me and then bit down on her lower lip so hard, I thought she would draw blood.

"You'll be all right," she said. "We'll all be all right. Someday. Right, Lulu?"

"What? Yes. My daddy's coming today," she told me. "He's going to take me home."

V. C. ANDREWS

"I'm happy for you," I said.

"Oh, spunks," Megan said. "Let's go to the rec room. We can listen to some music and talk."

"We can just leave and go there?" I asked.

"We can do anything we want," she declared. "We're paying the rent. At least you know this much about yourself, Laura: You're rich."

"I am?"

"Of course you are, stupid. It costs about forty thousand dollars a year to stay here."

I sat back, amazed.

"I didn't realize," I said. "I—"

"Just don't let any of them take advantage of you. You don't have to put up with any of it." She gazed at the door. "If he's still working here, I'm going to raise holy hell," she said. Then she gazed at my plate. "Finish your breakfast. We've got things to talk about," she ordered. "I've got to make you aware of all the dangers!"

190

11

Return to the Land of the Living

I didn't get the chance to spend time with Megan after breakfast because as soon as I was finished and rose from the table, Mrs. Kleckner approached me to tell me Doctor Southerby was waiting for me.

Megan seized my wrist as I turned to follow Mrs. Kleckner out of the cafeteria.

"He's the worst," she whispered, "because he's young and unmarried. Watch yourself."

I nodded as if to thank her for her warning and she relaxed her grip on me so I could walk after Mrs. Kleckner. We went to the right and down the corridor to an office on the left. A pleasant-looking dark-haired woman of no more than forty looked up from her desk and smiled as we entered. She wore a dark green dress and had pretty pearl earrings that matched a pearl necklace on a gold chain. She looked as perfectly put together as a mannequin in a showcase window. Not a strand of her hair was out of place, but she had a warmth to her smile that made me feel welcome.

"Mrs. Broadhaven, this is our new patient," Mrs. Kleckner declared.

"Yes. Doctor Southerby is waiting to see you, Laura," she said to me and rose from her desk.

Despite Megan's warning, I was eager to meet the doctor, eager to find out what was wrong with me and finally be cured.

"When you're finished here, maybe Mrs. Broadhaven will show you around the clinic," Mrs. Kleckner said, nodding at Doctor Southerby's secretary. Mrs. Kleckner's tone made it clear it wasn't a request as much as it was an order.

"I'll be very happy to," Mrs. Broadhaven said, apparently not bothered by the sharpness in Mrs. Kleckner's voice. She went to the door to the inner office, smiling at me as she turned and waited.

I took a deep breath and followed her. Hopefully, the answers to all my questions and the light to wash away the darkness lay behind that office door.

"This is our new patient, Doctor Southerby," she announced as soon as she stepped in.

Even though Megan had warned me, I was rather surprised at how young the doctor looked. He rose immediately from behind his dark cherry wood desk, a desk so large it looked like it was wrapped around him. Everything on it was neatly organized with folders in a neat pile and an open pad before him. On the wall behind him hung his framed diplomas and awards. There were two large windows behind his desk that looked out at the grounds. I saw the weeping willow trees I had seen silhouetted in the dark the night before. Everything looked green and plush today.

"Good morning," Doctor Southerby said. "Please. Come right in." His voice was deeper than I would have expected and he had a Southern accent. His light brown hair was trimmed short at the sides, but with a small pompadour at the front.

"Please," he said quickly, nodding at the chair in front of his desk, "make yourself comfortable. Thank you, Mrs. Broadhaven," he told his secretary.

She gave me a smile of reassurance and left, closing the

door softly behind her. Doctor Southerby turned back to me.

He had turquoise eyes that radiated a warmth and friendliness that immediately put me at ease. His smile brightened them even more.

Not a very tall man, perhaps only five feet ten, he nevertheless projected a strong, firm demeanor with his shoulders back, his handshake assertive, definite. He had a firm, straight mouth and a taut jawline. In his dark gray suit, light blue shirt and matching tie with a jeweled tie clip, he appeared very distinguished and confident despite his youthful look.

He returned to his chair behind the desk.

"Did you get some rest last night?" he asked. "I always find it hard to sleep well in a new place, myself."

"I was so exhausted I didn't have time to think about it," I said and he laughed.

"Most likely, most likely," he said. "Well, let me introduce myself properly." He leaned back in his chair and pressed the tips of his fingers together. "I am Doctor Henry Southerby and I will be in charge of your case."

He spoke calmly, relaxed, while I felt like butterflies with their wings on fire were circling madly in my stomach. I could barely sit still.

"What is my case? Why am I here? What happened to me? Why can't I remember the simplest things about myself?" I blurted out all at once. "I couldn't even remember my real name! I still can't remember my surname."

The high notes of hysteria in my voice didn't seem to faze him. He simply nodded, gently.

"I can understand your anxiety," he said, "and I want to put you at ease as quickly as I can. That way, you'll recover faster. It would be best," he continued, "if you remember things on your own. My simply filling up the empty spaces won't be enough. For one, you might reject the information again and then we could be worse off than we are now."

"Reject the information? I don't understand," I said, shaking my head. The calmer he was, the more anxious I felt. "Why did I reject such important information about myself, my name, my family, where I live? It's terrifying. Am I crazy? Is that why I'm here? What's wrong with me?" I pursued, my voice so shrill it hurt my own ears.

"I assure you that what's wrong with you at the moment won't last. And once you are cured, there's very little chance this will happen again," he replied in a mellow voice. It didn't satisfy me, however.

"What will not happen? What do I have, a disease? What?" I asked. He couldn't talk fast enough for me.

"From what I understand about your situation, I feel safe in a preliminary diagnosis of psychogenic amnesia," he said, although he looked uncomfortable about committing himself so quickly.

"I know what amnesia is," I said, shaking my head, "but that other word—"

"Psychogenic simply means your amnesia probably isn't due to any organic mental disorder. There's no physical reason for you to be unable to remember things. You didn't suffer any injury to your brain; physical injury, that is. There are no drugs or alcohol involved. You're not an epileptic, and," he said with a smile, "you're not pretending to be forgetful."

"What happened then? What's caused this?"

"What's happened is you have experienced a very traumatic event, an event of such emotional and psychological magnitude that your brain has shut down its memory chambers to prevent you from suffering," he said softly, leaning over the desk toward me. "It's really a self-defense mechanism the mind employs and is not uncommon in situations such as yours.

"This trauma arose from an event that overwhelmed your coping mechanism. Another term for this today is dissociative amnesia, the inability to recall important personal information."

"What was it?" I asked, my heart pounding. "What was the traumatic event?"

"It's important you remember that on your own, Laura," he said.

"Laura, but Laura what? What's my full name?" I demanded. "Tell me."

He nodded.

"Your full name is Laura Logan," he said. Then he stared at me for a moment. "What does that do for you, hearing your full name? Do you remember any more about yourself? Close your eyes and repeat your name. Go on," he urged.

I did so and then I shook my head.

"I don't remember anything," I wailed. "I can't," I cried more desperately.

"You will," he promised me. "I'll take you back gradually until it all rushes into your consciousness again. If you're just patient and—"

I shook my head.

"I can't stand it!" I cried. "I look in the mirror and feel like I'm looking at someone else. It's horrible. I'm walking around on pins and needles. My head keeps echoing with questions, over and over and—"

"Easy, Laura. Don't upset yourself," he said, but the tears were already flowing down my cheeks, burning as they traversed my face and dripped off my chin. I shook my head violently, shook it so hard, it revived the ache in my neck.

"No, no, no. I want to be cured *now!* I want to remember *now!* Tell me everything. Tell me why I'm like this!" I screamed at him.

He stood up.

"Easy, Laura. Please. You're just upsetting yourself and making it all that much more difficult for us to help you here."

"I don't want to be here. I want to be . . . where do I want to be? I don't even know that!" I shouted. I gazed down at my arms, the black and blue marks still vivid. "Look at me. What happened? Tell me everything! Please, tell me," I begged and then I rose and looked about the office, looked

195

for an avenue of escape. I felt like running and running until I couldn't run anymore.

He was around his desk instantly and at my side.

"Laura, relax now. Sit calmly. Come on," he said, putting his hand on my arm gently but firmly.

Megan's terrified face flashed before me.

"He's the worst," she whispered.

Who were these people who knew more about me than I knew about myself but kept it secret? What was going on?

"NO!" I screamed again. I pushed him away and then I heard a terrible ringing in my head. I pressed my palms to my ears. Someone was shouting *Laura*. There was water everywhere, water rushing over me until I couldn't hear my name anymore.

"NOOOOO!" I cried and then, all went black.

I woke on a gurney in a treatment room someplace in the building. The walls and the ceiling were stark white. Mrs. Kleckner was at my side and Doctor Southerby was on a telephone, talking softly to someone when I opened my eyes.

"She's regaining consciousness, Doctor," Mrs. Kleckner declared. I started to sit up, but she put her hand on my shoulder. "Just relax for a while," she commanded. "Doctor?"

He cradled the receiver and approached.

"How are you feeling now, Laura?"

"My head hurts," I said with a grimace. The pain felt like a metal band being tightened from one temple to the other.

"We'll give you something for that," he said.

"What happened?"

"You got too excited." He smiled. "You know how a circuit breaker works?"

I thought. Yes, I did know, but I had no idea why.

"Yes."

"Well, the mind works the same way. When it gets overloaded, it shuts down. Now you see why I've got to get you to relax first before I can help you?" he asked. "I want you to learn to trust me, Laura. Only then can I help you, and I want to help you," he said firmly. He held my hand and gazed down at me, his eyes washing over my face and then fixing on mine. "Do you believe me?"

I nodded, but not with enough confidence to please him. He smiled nevertheless.

"In time you will and then you'll cure yourself, Laura. This unfortunate situation won't be long. I promise," he said. "Really." He patted my hand.

I wanted to believe him. He was saying the things I wanted to hear.

"Sit up now and take this pill," he said, indicating the pill Mrs. Kleckner was waiting to give me. She placed it in my mouth and gave me some water. I drank and swallowed.

"For now," Doctor Southerby continued, "I'd like you to return to your room, get some more rest, and then we'll talk again."

"I want to talk now," I insisted.

"I know you do, but I don't want to chance any recurrences of what just happened. You're very fragile right now, Laura, more fragile than you can imagine. You need to rest up a bit so you can go about your recovery with full strength. Trust me about this. I promise," he said, "you won't be here a minute more than you have to be." He nodded at Mrs. Kleckner.

"Try to stand up now, Laura," she said.

I sat up and my head began to spin so rapidly, I actually lost my breath for a moment and thought I was going to black out again.

"Easy, easy," Doctor Southerby said. "You better wheel her over," he told Mrs. Kleckner. Moments later they both eased me into a wheelchair. I lay my head back and felt myself being moved out of the treatment room. I kept my eyes closed all the way back to my room.

Once there, Mrs. Kleckner helped me into bed.

"Just rest," she said. "I'll be back to check on you in a little while."

"I want to go back to Doctor Southerby's office and get my treatment," I moaned. "I want this to be over."

"You will go back," she said sternly, "but you heard the doctor. He wants you to be rested, stronger, otherwise he's just wasting his time and his time is very important. He doesn't only work here with the privileged. He works at another clinic, too."

"The privileged?"

What was privileged about being here, about being disturbed and sick? I wanted to ask. I tried to open my eyes, but whatever they gave me made my eyelids feel so heavy. In moments, I was asleep.

I woke when I felt my whole body shaking. Megan Paxton was at my bedside, tugging on my hand. She looked at the door and then back at me.

"What happened?" I muttered. My eyes felt like cobwebs had been built over them. My eyelids remained glued shut.

"They gave you something," she whispered. "You've got to be careful. One of them can come in here and rape you while you're asleep," she said. "They did that to me. Stay awake," she warned. "Or sleep with one eye open."

"I'm so tired," I muttered. She shook me again.

"Stay awake," she ordered.

"What are you doing in here?" I heard and forced my lids open enough to see Mrs. Kleckner in the doorway. "Come out of there immediately, Megan," she commanded, her hands on her hips.

"I'm just seeing how she is. What's the big deal?"

"You know you're not supposed to go into anyone else's room without permission from me. Now come out and let her rest, Megan. Now!" she insisted.

"Stay awake," she whispered to me as she left.

My eyes shut closed again and when I woke the next time, Megan's presence in my room seemed more like a dream. I felt groggy, but I wanted to get up and move about, so I lifted myself from the bed and went into the bathroom. I washed my face in water as cold as I could get it and that

helped some. When I came out of the bathroom, I found
Mrs. Kleckner waiting.

"I see you got yourself up. That's good. How do you
feel?" she asked.

"Weak, but I don't want to sleep anymore," I added
quickly, afraid she had another pill waiting.

"Very well. As long as you feel up to it, I'll show you
about the facility myself then," she said.

"When do I see Doctor Southerby again?"

"Tomorrow," she said. "He had to leave the clinic for
other appointments. If you're strong enough, you can go to
the recreation room and meet some of the other patients.
It's good for you to interact with other people. Doctor
Southerby left strict orders about that. He doesn't want you
hibernating in this room."

"I don't want to hibernate. I'd like to get some fresh air,
too," I said.

"I'll see that one of the attendants takes you out before
dinner," she told me.

"Dinner? What about lunch?" I asked. She laughed, a
short laugh that sounded more like a cough.

"You slept through lunch. There's tea and crackers or
cookies in the recreation room, if you like, and soft drinks
in the refrigerator. Come along," she said and I started after
her, my steps not as steady as I would have liked. She
noticed and held my arm in the corridor.

"Once you move around, get your circulation going,
you'll get stronger," she said.

"What did you give me? What was in that pill?"

"It was just a light sedative. Doctor Southerby has
prescribed it for you to take at night so you get a good rest."

"I don't like taking pills," I said. She paused and looked
at me.

"You remember not liking them or you just decided?" she
asked.

"I . . . just don't like them," I said.

"Well, we all have to do things we don't like to do once in

a while. You're no different just because you can't remember who you are," she commented and led me to the recreation room.

There were only seven patients there, two boys who looked about twelve or thirteen playing a game of chess and the rest of the patients sitting and reading or just staring out the windows at the walkways and gardens behind the building. Megan, Lulu, the very thin girl, and the good-looking young man I had seen in the cafeteria were sitting on two sofas facing each other with a table between them. There were magazines and books on the table. Lulu was writing feverishly in a long, yellow pad and didn't look up as the others did when I entered.

On the right I saw a small stove, a refrigerator, a sink, and some cabinets.

"There's hot water for tea there," Mrs. Kleckner indicated, "and some cookies, if you like. Tea bags are in the cabinet and milk and soft drinks are in the refrigerator."

"Thank you," I said.

She brought me farther into the room.

"This is Mark and Arthur," she said, referring to the two boys playing chess. "You two remember Laura, don't you?" she asked. They looked up at me and then back at their chessboard with hardly a smile of greeting. It was as if nothing more than a breeze had blown by them.

"You already know Megan Paxton and Edith Sanders," she said, referring to Lulu. "This is Mary Beth Lewis and Lawrence Taylor," she added.

Mary Beth gave me a warm smile of welcome. Lawrence glanced at me quickly and then looked down.

"I'll leave Laura with you so you can all get to know each other better," she told them with a mechanical smile. "If you need anything, ask Miss Cranshaw," she told me and nodded at the attendant sitting in the corner and reading a magazine.

Miss Cranshaw gazed our way for a moment and then folded the magazine and sat back to watch us. I thought it was because of the look Mrs. Kleckner had given her. She didn't look much younger than Mrs. Kleckner. In fact, she could easily be older, I thought.

Mrs. Kleckner left us.

"Sit here," Mary Beth said, moving over on the sofa to make a place for me. Lawrence looked up, but quickly shifted his eyes from mine.

"Have you remembered your full name yet?" Mary Beth asked.

"It's Laura Logan," I said.

"How come you didn't know your own name?" Lulu asked, perking up.

"She's got amnesia, stupid," Megan said. "Why do you think she's here? For the food? Or for the stimulating company?"

"Oh," Lulu said, turning to me meekly. "I'm sorry. Does it hurt?"

"Not the way you think. It is painful not to be able to remember anything though," I said. Lawrence gazed at me and smiled softly before looking out the window.

"Do you know why you have amnesia?" Mary Beth asked.

"If she knew why, she wouldn't be here," Megan answered for me.

"She's right. I don't know," I said. "All I know is it's because of something terrible that happened to me."

"If that was the case, most everyone in this place would have amnesia," Megan quipped.

"What can you remember about yourself?" Lawrence asked and then pressed his lips together as if the words had escaped before he could stop them. He had thick eyebrows and dark eyes that flashed with interest before shifting away.

"Not very much, really. Actually," I said, looking at all of them, "nothing."

"Nothing?" Mary Beth cried. She started to smile.

"I didn't really remember my full name. Doctor Southerby told me," I said.

Mary Beth stopped smiling. She formed a big O with her lips. It looked like she had blown a bubble.

"He wouldn't tell me what had happened to me either. He wants me to remember on my own."

"It's classic," Megan said as if she were a doctor herself. "Once I heard her story, I knew she had suffered some terrible experience, and as a result, her mind's gone completely bonkers. Remember that girl they moved to the Tower," she continued, "the one who tried to cut her wrists with the broken plate? Every day she couldn't remember what she had done or said the day before. It was as if her mind erased itself every morning and started over. Remember? What was her name?" she asked Lawrence. "You tried to talk to her all the time."

He turned beet red.

"I didn't try to talk to her all the time," he said, flashing a look at me.

"Fine. You didn't. It was all in my imagination. What was her name?" Megan demanded.

"Lydia," he said quickly. "Lydia Becker."

"Right. Lydia Becker. Every day we each had to introduce ourselves to her again. It was as if she had just arrived. Remember, Mary Beth?"

"Yes."

Megan laughed.

"I started giving her a different name for myself each time just to see if it mattered. It didn't."

"What did you mean when you said they moved her to the Tower?" I asked.

"She's still here, but on the top floor. We call it the Tower because Megan thinks once you are taken up there, you are shut away for the rest of your life, like in a tower," Mary Beth explained and shrugged.

"You are! No one who's been brought up there ever comes back to this floor, do they?" Megan fired at her. She glared angrily for a moment and then turned to me. "You can just imagine what goes on. She could be raped and not even remember it the next day. If they ever want to take me up there, I want you all to promise to kill me."

Lulu laughed.

"I mean it," Megan said. "I'd rather be dead." She glared at Lawrence, who immediately looked down.

"Why are you here?" I asked Mary Beth.

Megan laughed loud and hard.

"Are you kidding? Why is she here? Look at her. She thinks she's fat."

"I am overweight for my size," Mary Beth said.

I started to smile, but saw the look on Lawrence's face that told me not to.

"She eats and then throws it all up," Megan said. "One of these days, they'll tie her to her bed and shove a tube down her throat."

"Oh, I'm sorry," I said, not knowing what else to say. I had the feeling words were like footsteps on thin ice here.

"Go on, ask Lawrence why he is here," Megan taunted. I looked at him. He held my gaze for a brief time and then blushed and looked down at his hands. They looked long and graceful. He had them folded and was twirling his thumbs. "Can you guess why he's here?" Megan continued.

"I have no idea," I said. "He looks very healthy."

His eyes lifted to mine and I thought he smiled, but then I realized he had the sort of face that could easily be deceiving. Was it a smile or a look of pain? As if to answer, he moved his lips slightly, lifted them almost imperceptibly in the corners, brightened his eyes and fixed them for a second on me, but almost as soon as he realized I felt his interest, he shifted away. Was he merely overly shy? That wouldn't be enough to keep someone here, would it? I wondered.

"Well, Lawrence, tell her what's wrong with you," Megan challenged. "Go on. Don't leave her hanging and guessing."

He shook his head.

"Oh, go on, tell her," Megan taunted. "It's a sign of improvement when you can talk about your own problem," Megan explained.

He glanced at me again and then looked away. I thought his eyes were starting to look a bit teary.

"Lawrence hasn't made much improvement yet. Young

Mr. Taylor," she continued, "has what the doctors describe as a panic disorder. Don't you, Lawrence?"

"Can't you leave him alone?" Mary Beth said.

"What am I doing to him? Lawrence, can't you speak up for yourself?"

"I—"

"Yes, Lawrence? Hold it, everyone," Megan said, raising her hands. She turned and looked toward the two boys playing chess. "Quiet down over there. Lawrence Taylor the third is about to say something. Go on, Lawrence," she said.

He looked at me and then rose quickly, his face flushed.

"Where are you going?" Megan cried.

"Will you leave him alone," Mary Beth said.

Lawrence glanced at me and then hurried out of the recreation room.

Megan laughed.

"Lawrence," she said, "is unable to perform today. Everyone gets his money back."

"That wasn't very nice," I told her.

She smirked.

"As Mrs. Kleckner says, if we baby each other, none of us will get better."

"And what's wrong with you then?" I demanded, still feeling sorry for Lawrence.

"Me? I'm . . . unable to have significant relationships. I don't trust anyone. Can I trust you?" she asked, her eyes growing watery. "Can I trust you?" she asked Mary Beth. "What about you, Lulu?"

"I'm writing to my father," Lulu said with a smile, "telling him about our new friend."

"Oh great. Another letter to the dead. I have to go to the bathroom," Megan said, rising. "Will everyone please excuse me?"

She folded her arms over her breasts and walked out.

"Megan is not a very happy person," Mary Beth said. "So she's not satisfied until everyone around her is unhappy, too."

"I can see that," I said. My stomach rumbled. "I think I'll have some tea. Would you like some?"

"No," Mary Beth said quickly. "I never eat between meals."

"Tea isn't really eating," I said.

"I've got to go to my room and get something," she said with a voice of panic. "I'll see you at dinner." She rose and left quickly as I got up to go to the stove and pour hot water into a cup with a tea bag. I took one of the cookies and looked at Lulu. She was so sweet, so dainty. How could her parents let her be here and not with them? I wondered. When I returned to the sofa, she looked up from her notepad.

"How do you spell acquaintance?" she asked me and I told her. "I'm describing you as a new acquaintance," she explained and wrote on. "Is that all right?"

"Of course," I said.

"I like making new friends and my daddy likes to hear about them. He told me to write him a letter every day. Sometimes, I write two a day. And I have piles and piles of letters from him," she said. Then she paused, put the notepad down and looked at me. "I think I'll have a cookie, too."

When she got up, I leaned over and looked at her pad. I went from surprise to shock and confusion.

There wasn't a word written on it, just lines scrawled in every direction.

At Mrs. Kleckner's directive, Miss Cranshaw took me out to the gardens and walkways to get some fresh air.

"We like you to stay on the pathways," she said. "You can sit on the benches, even on the grass or under a tree, as long as you remain in this area," she added, gesturing at the boundaries.

The grounds were beautiful, with beds of flowers, bird-baths, some stone and marble statuary, and tall, thick oak and maple trees. The hedges, the grass, and the gardens were all well maintained. A groundsperson was weeding in one of the gardens as we walked through. None of the other patients at the clinic were outside, as far as I could see.

"I'd like to just sit here for a while," I said, moving to a wooden bench halfway down the long, center path. The sight of the soft clouds, the scent of the grass and the flowers, and the touch of the breeze on my face was deliciously familiar. I liked being outdoors; I liked nature. What else did I like? It was strange, discovering such basic and simple things about yourself.

"You have about an hour before dinner," Miss Cranshaw said. "I have to look after a few patients and then I'll come get you when it's time to come in," she said.

I thanked her and sat back, watching two songbirds flit from the birdbath to a statue of a cherub. They paraded on the small angel's shoulder and then gazed at me before lifting off to fly toward the oak trees.

It's so quiet, so beautiful and fresh here, I thought. It was a perfect place for recuperation. The only problem was I didn't know from what I was recuperating and now a part of me was afraid to know, afraid to go back. If it was something so terrifying that it would cause me to forget the most basic things about myself, it must be horrendous, I thought, too horrendous for the doctors or nurses to want to tell me.

A movement near one of the sprawling oak trees caught my eye and I turned to see Lawrence Taylor emerge from the shadows and step onto a path. He walked slowly with his head down. When he drew closer, he looked up and saw me and he stopped quickly.

"Hi," I said. "It's so pretty out, I wonder why there aren't more people outside."

For a second he looked like he might run off. Then he took a deep breath and replied.

"No one comes out here this time of the day. It's too close to dinner," he said. "Everyone usually follows a strict routine here," he added. He looked to his right and then glanced at me as if he had to steal each and every look.

"How come you're outside then?"

"I like being alone now," he said. "Out here."

"Why do you like being alone?"

He shrugged.

"I always have," he said. "Well, not always. I used to be afraid to be alone," he confessed. "That's why they think I'm improving."

"Do you have any brothers or sisters?" I asked.

"No." He smiled and looked away.

"What's so funny?" I asked. He didn't reply. "Well?"

"I was going to ask you if you did and then I remembered you don't remember anything," he said.

"That's funny?"

He looked down. I was angry at first and then, I suddenly laughed. He looked up, a puzzled expression on his face.

"Maybe it is funny," I said. "I do feel ridiculous." He held his gaze on me for the longest time yet and then he drew closer.

"Doctor Thomas told me sometimes it's better to laugh than cry," he said. "If you have more of a sense of humor about yourself, you don't take things as seriously and you don't worry as much," he explained. "I try to follow his advice, but I still don't laugh all that much."

"Sounds like good advice though," I said. "How long have you been here?"

"Two years," he replied. "It seems like forever."

"Two years! You didn't go home and come back?" He shook his head. "Why can't you go home? You seem fine to me," I said. I wanted to add, "unless shyness is now considered an illness."

"I have these spells. I get chest pain, dizziness, and I start to shake uncontrollably."

"Why?"

"It's what Megan told you. I have a panic disorder," he admitted. "I have very low self-esteem, but as I told you, I'm getting better," he added quickly, as if he were afraid I would be frightened away. "At least now I can take walks by myself. It used to be, I never left the building. However," he continued, "every time I think about leaving the clinic, I break out in a cold sweat and feel faint."

"You want to leave though, don't you?"

"Yes. I'm trying. I really am now. I wasn't trying so much in the beginning. I didn't care as much."

"Did you always have this . . . panic disorder?"

"No," he said.

The whole time he spoke to me, he kept squeezing his right hand with his left and nibbling on his cheek.

"Why don't you sit here for a while," I suggested. "Relax. Tell me what it's like here. I've only been here one night," I explained.

He looked at the space beside me on the bench as if it were a high hurdle he could never reach.

"I don't bite," I said. "Or, at least I don't think I do. I don't remember biting people, but maybe I did," I added, tilting my head and pretending to think about it. "Since I can't remember, I can't swear I didn't. I might even be a killer." He smiled. "See, I have a sense of humor," I told him.

He widened his smile and then, with a sudden, abrupt, and definite move, like someone charging into a fire, he sat beside me.

"You really can't remember anything? Nothing?" he asked. When he spoke, he avoided looking directly at me for more than a fleeting second.

When he did look at me, I could see the sensitivity in his dark eyes. His pupils looked like two shiny black pearls. They made me think of another face, but I saw only the eyes in my memory, and then, when I saw the mouth, the eyes faded.

"I have these flashes, pictures, sounds, but as soon as I try to understand them, to trace them back to something, they disappear," I complained.

"What's an example? What do you see, hear?" he asked with interest.

"Water, the beach, boats, but little boats, toy boats."

"You mean like model boats?"

"Yes, yes, model boats, but it makes me shiver, even now, even in the sunlight, to think about boats," I said and hugged myself. My teeth actually chattered.

Very tentatively, inches at a time, he reached out to touch my hand.

"You are cold," he said, impressed.

I nodded and he wrapped his hand around mine.

"That feels good," I said, smiling. He smiled and held on to my hand. The longer he held on to it, the more confident he became.

"Well, what do we have going on here?" we heard, and Lawrence let go as if my hand had shocked him.

We turned to see Megan coming toward us. She marched stiffly with her hands clenched at her sides and her arms unbending.

"Hi, Megan," I said.

"I wondered where you were when I came back. Lulu said you had asked to go outside. Isn't this cozy?" she added, looking from Lawrence to me and back to Lawrence. "You don't know each other five minutes and you rendezvous in the garden and I find you holding hands."

Lawrence moved away from me quickly.

"We just bumped into each other out here," I said. "I didn't know Lawrence was outside."

"Really?" she said, her eyes narrow with suspicion. "How'd he get you to let him hold your hand?"

"He didn't get me to let him, Megan. I told him I was cold and he was just trying to warm me up," I said.

"Sure. That's how it starts," she said. "I'm surprised at you, Lawrence Taylor. You haven't touched another person here since I've known you. You must be someone special," she said to me.

Lawrence's face was crimson, but his lips were white with fear. He shook his head.

"I just—"

"The male in you has woken," Megan declared like a doctor diagnosing a terminal illness. "I'll warn the girls and the female attendants and the rest of the world. Everyone should know to be on guard. Lawrence Taylor's lusts have been miraculously resurrected. His hormones are raging. Beware!"

"No . . . I—"

"Oh, stop it," she snapped and then looked around. When she turned back to us, her expression was completely different. "I have a private, secret place I'll show you later," she told me, "if you're good. However, I hope you're not like Lydia and forget everything every day. I really don't like wasting my time on people."

"I don't think that's my problem, forgetting things I learn," I said.

"You don't know what your problem is. *That's* your problem," she replied. "Look at him," she continued, nodding at Lawrence. "Pathetic."

I turned and saw he was trembling and that sweat had broken out on his brow.

"Lawrence," I said, reaching out to touch him.

"I'm okay. I'm okay. I think it's time to go in for dinner." He stood up. "I didn't mean anything. I just . . ."

"It's all right, Lawrence. Really," I said. "Please stay with us."

He looked at Megan.

"Yeah, Lawrence. We're hungry for your wonderful company," she said.

"I'll see you inside." He glanced at me and turned away. "I've got to do something before dinner," he added and walked toward the building.

"I wonder what that could be, Lawrence," Megan called after him. "What could you do alone in your room? I hope it's not what I think it is. I hope it's not what other boys your age do with themselves."

Her words and laughter made him walk faster.

"Why do you pick on him like that?" I demanded. "He was doing so well."

She looked at me as if I spoke another language.

"I don't pick on him. I don't pick on anybody." She paused, making her eyes smaller. "Are you siding with them already? You just got here and you're siding with them?" she accused.

"With whom?"

"With whom?" she mimicked. "You'd better be careful," she warned. "You just better be careful. First they win your trust and then . . . then . . ." Her lips trembled and her chin quivered. She had her hands clenched into fists and her arms extended and against her sides again. She looked like a soldier frozen in place.

"Megan? Are you all right?"

Her eyelids fluttered. Then she looked at me and relaxed.

"Of course I'm all right. I have to be all right. I have to be sharp, aware. I'm . . . going back inside. I've got to get Lulu. She doesn't know enough to get herself to dinner. She keeps waiting for her daddy. Her daddy. Daddies," she spit, as if it were a profanity. "She should be happy he never comes around."

She turned and walked after Lawrence.

Why did she hate daddies?

12

Shadows of My Mind

Everyone seemed more subdued at dinner. Their voices were low and there was very little laughter. Those who were unable to feed themselves were seated together and served by the attendants. The rest of us moved through the cafeteria line. There were two choices for an entre: turkey or halibut. Everything smelled and looked good. Mrs. Anderson supervised with pride. If I closed my eyes and listened, I couldn't tell I was in a clinic.

"Does this cafeteria remind you of your school?" Lawrence whispered from behind me.

"It's familiar," I said, "but I can't recall anything specific."

"I went to a private school," he said. "I always did. The food was pretty good there, too, and it didn't have many more students than there are patients here," he added, but he sounded like it wasn't a happy experience.

"Some of us back here are hungry," Megan said to prompt us to stop talking, take our food, and move down the line.

I hurried along, noticing how Mary Beth skipped taking

bread or dessert and then pushed her food apart, as if to let anything touch would contaminate everything.

This time Megan, Mary Beth, Lulu, Lawrence, and I all sat at the same table. No one else seemed to want to join us.

"What are you waiting for?" Megan asked me. "Eat before it gets cold."

I hadn't realized I was sitting there, not touching any silverware, while everyone else, even Mary Beth, had begun.

"I don't know," I said, sensing a blank that wanted to be filled in desperately, "but you're right. I feel like I am waiting for something before we eat, something that should happen first . . ."

"My daddy used to tell us all about his day at work at dinner," Lulu said. "And then he would tell us stories about when he and my mother were young."

"He was probably never there for dinner. Didn't your parents get divorced when you were a baby?" Megan reminded her.

"I still remember," Lulu said and glanced at me to see if I believed her. I smiled at her and she smiled back.

"Maybe you said a prayer first," Lawrence suggested. "At my private school, the headmaster led us in saying Grace before every dinner."

"Yes," I said. "Maybe . . ." I nodded. "I think that's it," I added excitedly.

"Okay. I'll say it. Everyone wait. Hold your fork, Lulu." Megan stared ahead and raised her arms slowly toward the ceiling. "Grace," she declared, clapping her hands. Then she dug into her potatoes, laughing.

"Yes," I said, nodding. "Yes, that's it. You're right, Lawrence. I can remember that. I think I can remember . . . the Bible. We read from the Bible," I continued. Lawrence smiled, his eyes happy for me as he nodded softly.

"This is good," he said. "If everything comes back to you this fast, you can leave before you know it."

"Goody, goody for her," Megan said. She started to eat again and then paused to consider me. "Do you really remember something?"

"Just vaguely, someone reading . . . it's like I'm remembering myself reading." I shook my head. "It doesn't make any sense. I hear a different voice, but I see a face so similar to my own, it's like . . . I'm looking at myself."

"That doesn't sound like anything," Megan said after a moment of thought.

"Sure it does," Lawrence said, suddenly assertive. Megan widened her eyes and he turned back to me. "You better have something to eat," he suggested softly. "You'd be surprised at how much strength all this mental work takes."

"Yes," I said and started. Even that tiny bit of memory returning filled me with encouragement and stimulated my appetite. I really am going to get better, I thought.

Halfway through the meal, I glanced at Mary Beth and saw she was eating, but after every bite, she wiped her mouth with her napkin and put the napkin on her lap. I caught sight of it after she took another mouthful of fish and saw that the napkin was filled with the food she had spit back into it. Actually, she was barely eating anything.

The attendant named Billy, who had greeted Clara and me at the door when I first arrived, had been standing on the side with another attendant watching our table. Suddenly, he rushed over and pounced.

"Mary Beth, you're spitting out your food," he accused, his hands on his hips. He nodded at her plate.

"No, I'm not!"

"Let me see your napkin," he demanded. "Come on. We've got strict orders from Doctor Thomas about you."

"I'm eating!" she cried, on the verge of tears.

"Leave her alone," Megan said. He turned to her.

"Mind your own business, Megan. There's plenty to mind there," he said. He turned back to Mary Beth.

Mary Beth's panic had flushed her neck and face. She looked like she was trembling in her seat. I felt sorry for her. Her eyes were darting about, searching for some avenue of escape.

"You're scaring the hell out of her!" Megan cried. Billy ignored her and continued to hover over Mary Beth.

"The doctor said if we see you spitting out your food, we've got to tell him and then they'll put you upstairs and force-feed you," Billy reminded her.

"The Tower!" Megan declared. "Don't even think of trying it," she told Billy. She even poked him in the rear with her fork. He spun on her again.

"Look," he said, "if you interfere with our work with other patients, you'll end up there, too. And don't you ever poke me with anything. That's an exhibition of violence," he chastised with a smile that revealed his row of glitteringly white teeth. "And you know what *that* means," he threatened.

While he glared with fury at Megan, I reached under the table, took Mary Beth's full napkin off her lap and dropped mine in its place. She glanced at me gratefully. Billy turned back to her.

"Well? Hand up that napkin. Come on," he said, gesturing with both hands.

She reached into her lap and gave it to him slowly. He seized it. The disappointment registered on his face when he opened it and nothing fell out. Megan roared and then clapped.

"Billy Screwball screws up again!" she cried, clapping her hands over her head. Conversations throughout the cafeteria stopped and everyone looked our way.

"Cut that out," he told her.

Megan continued to clap, which caused one of the boys I had seen playing chess earlier to start clapping, too. His friend followed and then the whole table joined in. Soon, everyone in the cafeteria who could clap was clapping.

Billy's face took on a look of rage and he threw the napkin back at Mary Beth. Then he marched back to his position in the cafeteria, shouting at the patients to quiet down. Megan finally stopped clapping and soon everyone followed. One boy, however, kept breaking out into applause and laughter for no reason every once in a while during the remainder of the meal.

"Thanks," Mary Beth whispered to me.

"That was pretty smart," Megan told me. "You saved her butt with quick thinking."

Lawrence smiled at me, too, his gaze steadier now and full of pride and admiration.

"You better eat something, Mary Beth, or I'll feel responsible and guilty if you get sick," I told her.

She took a forkful of fish and put it in her mouth, chewing demonstrably and turning toward Billy as she did so. He looked away with disgust.

"Billy's such a dork," Megan said. She glared back at him until he turned his back to her and kept his eye on the other patients. "He doesn't scare me with his threats. He knows if he so much as put a finger on me . . ."

She turned back to me and stopped talking and eating.

"What's wrong with you?" she asked.

"That girl," I said, nodding to a girl who sat across the cafeteria from us, "what is she doing?"

Megan looked.

"Oh, that's Tamatha Stuart. She's mute. She won't talk, so she does that sign language to communicate. It's so stupid. She's not deaf. I don't know why they pamper her. She should have been given shock treatment. I—what?" she asked me when she saw the expression on my face get more emphatic.

"I know what she's saying with her hands. I understand it!" I said, even surprised myself.

"Really?"

"That's awesome," Lawrence said. "Someone you know must be deaf," he added.

I looked at him. It was as if a thick, heavy door had been opened just an inch or so, and there was light streaming through. I thought I saw a face peeking out at me through the darkness. But who was it?

My eyes began to blink rapidly, uncontrollably. I wanted to see who was behind that door. I felt as if I were struggling to tug that door open just a little bit more, pulling, pulling. . . . I couldn't stand the effort.

"Laura?" he said. "Are you all right?"

216

"You're upsetting her," Megan said.

"What am I doing? I'm not doing anything," he moaned. "Laura?" he said, turning back to me.

Suddenly, it just came over me. I heard a cry, the cry that had been haunting me ever since I arrived, someone was desperately crying out for my help.

I spun around in my seat and looked behind me and to the sides.

"What is it?" Lawrence asked. "Laura?"

"Someone . . . is crying . . ."

The noise in the cafeteria became the roar of the sea. There was water everywhere. The wind itself was calling my name: *Laura! Laura!*

My heart started to pound. I felt the whole room turn. It was as if I were in a boat and not a chair, and the boat was being tossed violently. I grasped the table.

"No!" I cried. I closed my eyes and felt myself swaying.

"What's the matter with her?" I heard Lulu say.

Lawrence reached over and touched my hand tentatively.

"Are you all right?" he asked. "Laura?" His voice merged with the voice in my mind, especially when he repeated, "Laura?"

I felt nauseated. I started to shake my head and then my whole body began to tremble. I was holding the table so firmly that the dishes began to clank. A glass fell over.

Megan shouted to Lawrence because I was tipping over backward. He seized my chair, but I started to slide off it. My body felt as if it had turned to liquid, all my bones melted. I was pouring toward the floor. Lawrence held me, but I slipped from his grip and fell down, down, down, waving my arms about me. Billy and a female attendant came rushing over to us.

"What's wrong with her? Does she have epilepsy or something?" someone asked. It sounded like Megan.

My tongue was swelling and I couldn't get any air. I felt myself drooling and then I started to scream, or at least I thought I did. Then, all went black.

When I woke this time, I was back in my room. A man in

a white lab coat was taking my pulse and one of the night nurses was beside him.

"She's stabilizing," he said. "Laura? How are you doing?"

I blinked rapidly.

His voice echoed.

"Laura, how are you?"

"Laura . . . Laura . . ."

"NO!" I screamed, or at least I thought I did. My whole body began to tremble terribly. It was as if the bed were coming apart beneath me. "I'm sinking!"

"Hold her!" the man said. "Easy . . ."

There was a pinprick in my arm and then, after a few moments, a wave of darkness washed over me. My body sank deeper and deeper into the bed. I felt like I was going underwater. I tried desperately to stay conscious, but wave after wave of blackness was rushing in, pushing me farther and farther down. The sound of my name drifted off, and then, I was asleep.

When I woke again, there was sunlight streaming through the curtains. I heard the sound of water being run in a sink and then a nurse emerged from the bathroom with a washcloth and a pan. She put the cloth on my face as I blinked and blinked, trying to focus in on something that made sense to me.

"So you're finally awake. Good," she said, twisting her mouth. "You gave everybody a bad time again, I heard."

She lifted the cloth from my forehead and gazed down at me. I opened my mouth, but my voice wouldn't work.

"So, let's hear about it. How are you now? Do you have any pain? Any nausea? Well?" she demanded when I was silent. I shook my head. "Are you hungry?"

I thought about it. I was a little hungry, but when I went to say yes, nothing happened.

"Well?" she asked. "Can't you talk this morning?"

Talk? I thought. Could I ever talk? I tried to speak and only a deep guttural sound emerged. The nurse looked surprised.

"What is it?" she asked.

I lifted my hands and as naturally as people speak, I began to sign.

"What the . . ." She stepped back and watched as I spoke through my hands.

"Yes, I am hungry," I told her, "but where am I?" I asked. She shook her head.

"This is a surprising turn of events," she said, looking quite impressed. "The doctor will be here in an hour. If you want to eat any breakfast, you should get up now," she said.

I signed okay and rose from the bed. I felt groggy, but strong enough to stand.

"Some more clothes were brought here for you last night," she told me. "They're all brand-new apparently. Everything still has a tag on it. Some of it is in the closet and some is in the dresser. Choose what you want to wear, get dressed, and come out to breakfast," she said. "Well?"

I signed okay.

"So you can't talk now, is that it? Fine. I could use a little more quiet around here," she said. "I'll see you in the cafeteria. Get dressed," she ordered and left the room before I could ask her where the cafeteria was.

Confusion resembled a great cloud of smoke circling me. I moved slowly, unsure of myself, making discoveries about the room and the bathroom as if I had never been here before. How long had I been here? And where was here?

I paused in the bathroom and looked at myself in the mirror. The face I saw seemed to change right before my eyes, and for a moment, I thought I was looking at a boy. It only lasted a second or two, but it made my heart pound and took my breath away.

After I dressed, I poked my head out of the room and looked up and down the corridor. The floors gleamed under the rays of sunshine that came through the windows. Suddenly, the door across from me opened and a girl about my age stepped out. She looked sickeningly thin.

"How are you?" she asked softly. "We were all worried sick about you last night."

"I don't know," I said with my hands. She started to smile and stopped.

"Why are you doing that?" she asked.

"Doing what?" I signed. She seemed to understand.

"Why are you doing that stuff with your hands, sign language?" she asked. "Has something happened to your voice? Can't you talk?"

I shook my head. She just stared at me, her face so thin her eyes looked like they were floating in their sockets. I could even see the bones in her jaw and cheeks through her thin skin. A thought brought a strange, soft smile to her thin lips.

"You look like you don't remember me," she said and then asked, "Do you?" I shook my head again. "I'm Mary Beth."

"Who am I?" I asked her, pointing to myself and then raising my hands and shaking my head to make her understand my question.

"You don't know who you are?" After I shook my head emphatically, she said, "You're Laura Logan. I don't know anything else about you because you didn't remember anything to tell us when you first came here," she said. "This is terrible," she added, gazing down the hall and looking for someone, as if I were hurt and bleeding.

I rubbed my stomach and indicated my mouth.

"You're hungry?"

I nodded and she relaxed.

"Just come with me," she said. "Come on," she urged, reaching out for my hand. I took her hand and we went down the hallway together to the cafeteria.

"How's she doing?" a dark-haired girl at the table Mary Beth had brought me to asked as soon as we appeared. The handsome boy beside her looked up with interest, as did the young girl on her other side.

"She can't talk. She's using sign language and she's forgotten everything, Megan. I don't mean about herself either. Now she doesn't know who we are, where she is, everything!" Mary Beth wailed.

220

"Oh no," Megan said, gazing back at the attendants who were standing and talking to each other. "They'll put her in the Tower right next to Lydia Becker, for sure. Look, Laura, I'm Megan, Megan Paxton. This is Lawrence and this is Lulu. You're at the clinic. You go up there and get what you want to eat and come back. Act as if you remember everything, okay?"

I looked at Lawrence, whose look of concern impressed me. Then I nodded.

"If you tell them you forgot everything about this place, they'll want to give you some other treatment, something like electric shock maybe. That could mean you'll be going to the Tower!"

I signed question after question, but no one understood. I wanted to know how long I had been here. Why was I here? Where had I come from? And what was this Tower?

"You sure you can't talk today?" Megan asked with a grimace. I shook my head. "Great. You're in deep water, I'm afraid," she said. "It's hard enough around here to protect yourself when you can talk."

"I'll take her to the cafeteria line," Mary Beth offered.

"That's like the blind leading the blind," Megan quipped. "If you help her pick out her food, she'll starve."

"Don't worry. I'll make sure she gets what she wants to eat," Mary Beth insisted.

"I can take her," Lawrence said, rising.

"Me too," Lulu said.

Why was everyone so concerned about me?

"Remember. If you make it look like she's helpless, they'll notice and that will be it," Megan warned. "Sit down, Lulu."

"Just follow me," Lawrence said softly. "I'll do all the talking and you just nod, okay?"

"All of a sudden he can help someone. Before this, he couldn't tie his own shoelaces if someone was watching," Megan remarked with a twisted smile.

Lawrence ignored her and directed me to follow.

"I can understand a little sign language," he said. "And I

221

can learn the rest fast. Don't worry. I'll protect you," he promised.

After I got my food and returned to the table, I did feel less tentative and insecure. I listened to their conversations and ate. Every once in a while, Lawrence turned to me and asked me how I would say or ask for something through signing. I showed him and he committed it quickly to memory.

Someone else, someone in my past, learned sign language that quickly, I remembered. I could see myself teaching him. Who was he? Everything I did raised another question about who I was and where I belonged, and every question felt like a needle in my side demanding attention.

"You shouldn't be encouraging her," Megan warned. "She won't snap out of it as fast."

"She'll be fine," Lawrence said, smiling at me.

"Listen to him, Doctor Lawrence Taylor. Hang a shingle over your room door," Megan said. She looked at the doorway and then leaned in toward me. "Here comes Mrs. Kleckner. You better not act too stupid," she advised.

"How are we doing now?" Mrs. Kleckner asked after she approached our table.

"Fine and dandy, Mrs. Kleckner. We're an absolutely happy little group of idiots and screwballs," Megan remarked with a fat smile.

"You're not really very funny, Megan. I'm hoping you'll realize that soon. For your own sake, as well as everyone else's," she added.

"Oh, I'll try, Mrs. Kleckner," Megan promised with a false smile on her lips.

Mrs. Kleckner turned to me.

"I understand you've lost your voice."

I looked at Megan and Lawrence and then at her before I nodded.

"Very well," Mrs. Kleckner continued, "you have your session with Doctor Southerby now. Come along, Laura," she said.

I looked at the others. Their eyes were wide with concern.

"Good luck with *your doctor,*" Megan said as I stood up. "I hope things go better for you *this* time," she added, telling me I had met him before. I smiled, signed my thanks, and left with Mrs. Kleckner.

Doctor Southerby wasn't in his office when I was brought there. Mrs. Kleckner had me take a seat in front of the big desk and then left. I sat quietly waiting, gazing at everything and wondering how it could be that I had been here before. None of it looked even vaguely familiar. A side door opened and Doctor Southerby entered. He smiled softly and went to his desk.

"So," he began as soon as he sat, "you've had a little setback, I understand. Lost your voice?"

I didn't know what else to do, so I nodded.

"You can use sign language," he said. "I know it well."

I felt like I was in a foreign country and had finally found another person who spoke my language. The questions flowed out of me so quickly, my hands could barely keep up. Doctor Southerby's eyes followed and his smile widened and widened.

"Whoa," he cried. "Let's take it one at a time. You're in a clinic for people who have mental and psychological problems. It's a clinic mainly for young people. It was established by a foundation funded by wealthy people and has become one of the more prestigious and successful institutions of its kind in the northeast, if I may say so," he added proudly. "I'm one of the chief therapists here and your case has been assigned to me.

"As we were discussing yesterday, you suffered a serious traumatic experience and it has affected your memory. You have a form of general amnesia, but it is the sort of amnesia that won't last long. I feel confident of that."

"Yes," he said after I signed my question, "when you first arrived here, you could speak, but you couldn't recall anything about yourself."

I signed, "Why can't I speak now?"

"I don't know yet," he said, looking very thoughtful. "I'm just learning about your background myself and the information I need is slow in coming, unfortunately," he said with a grimace. "However, since you know sign language so well, it is something that is obviously in your background. Someone close to you is deaf. Does that jog your memory a bit?"

I thought.

"Yes," I told him, "but I can't remember much about her right now."

"You will. Suddenly, you will see someone else doing it and you'll realize who it is," he promised. "Until then, since you are unable to speak . . ."—he reached into a drawer and came up with a notebook—"I would like you to write down everything you remember; everything you think and anything that occurs to you about yourself, or people here, anything," he said, handing me the notebook.

I took it gingerly.

"I know you have a lot of anxiety. Do you experience flashbacks, hear voices you don't recognize?"

I nodded.

"You're eating well, apparently. That's good. Do you have any numbing, any part of your body that feels detached?"

I shook my head.

"Good. Just so you'll know what to expect from me . . . I'm going to try to get you, slowly, of course, to relieve the trauma you have suffered. We have to undo any unnecessary shame and guilt. It's all right for you to get angry and eventually to grieve, Laura. When you're able to do so, you will return fully to yourself. I might employ hypnosis. We'll see, okay?" he said, his voice soft, comforting.

I nodded.

"That's good. Okay, Laura," he said, "let's do something now. Let's both relax and you tell me whatever comes to your mind . . . words, pictures, anything. Go on," he said, "close your eyes and just let your mind wander."

I did so. Pictures flashed, but each for only a split second. I saw sand and water, faces that I couldn't attach to names, small boats, and cranberries in a bog. I described each thing to him.

"That's good, Laura. That's progress. In a short time, all these apparently unconnected images will start linking up for you and you'll start to find meaning. You're on your way home. I promise," he said.

"The best thing for you to do here is relax. Enjoy our facilities, write in your notebook, and rest. You're going to cure yourself," he said. He sounded so confident and sincere, I felt better.

He talked about other patients with similar problems and how they overcame them to return to active, healthy lives. He assured me that whatever was wrong with me would end and I would never return to the clinic once I left.

"Try to say something to me before you leave today, Laura," he concluded. He got up and walked over to me, taking my hand into his and looking so intensely into my eyes, I couldn't look away. "Go on, say your name. Try," he urged.

I opened my mouth and moved my lips.

"That's it," he coaxed. "Go ahead."

My tongue lifted and fell. I felt the muscles in my neck and throat strain.

"Lawwwww." I started to gag, tears burned under my eyelids, and I felt my cheeks turn red and hot.

"Okay," he said, patting my hand. "Okay. It will come back."

He patted my hand and returned to his chair.

"I have to do some research on you, Laura. I have calls out to gather the information I need. You and I will meet again tomorrow," he said, "and in a week's time at the most, you'll see some dramatic changes. Okay?"

I nodded and smiled. I decided he was a very nice young doctor, someone I could probably trust, only at the moment I had nothing to trust him with except my immediate feelings. He took me out to his secretary.

"Mrs. Broadhaven didn't get to show you some of our facilities yesterday, Laura. She wants to do that now, okay?"

I nodded and the pretty woman rose and led me out.

"We have a very nice arts and crafts studio here," she explained. "It's just down the hall from the lounge."

I gazed through the door at some patients watching television, playing chess, and reading. In the rear, a young man was playing Ping-Pong with an attendant.

"Here's the studio," she said, pausing at another door farther down the corridor. I looked in and saw Megan wearing a frock and dabbing roughly at a soft clay figure she was forming. Lulu and Mary Beth were painting with watercolors at a table in the corner. A tall woman with beautiful red hair and a milky white complexion approached us.

"This is Laura," Mrs. Broadhaven said. "I'm showing her around, but she might come right back here," she added, seeing the interest on my face. "Laura, this is Miss Dungan, our art therapist."

"Hi, Laura," she said, offering her hand. "You can choose any format to work with: clay, oils, watercolors, wood. We can make ceramics, too."

I sensed something familiar. I know an artist, I thought, but I couldn't remember his name. Miss Dungan saw how hard I was staring at Megan's sculpture.

"Do you want to try that today?" she asked.

"It might help you remember things," Mrs. Broadhaven suggested.

I nodded.

"I'll bring her right back," Mrs. Broadhaven told Miss Dungan.

She then showed me the library, where I saw Lawrence sitting at the table, poring over a book. He had a small pile of other books beside it. As soon as he saw us, he blushed.

"We're very proud of our library facilities here, Laura," Mrs. Broadhaven said. "It's as good as many small college libraries. Isn't it, Lawrence?" she asked him.

"What? Oh . . . yes," he said. He looked frightened, I thought, and I wondered why. His eyes shifted quickly and I saw that his hand was shaking.

"Well, Laura. What would you like to do? Go back to the

studio?" Mrs. Broadhaven asked. Either she didn't see what I noticed about Lawrence or she chose to ignore it.

I nodded, looked back once more at Lawrence, who now had his hands over his eyes, and then we left to return to the art studio. Miss Dungan set me up with a smock and then placed me at a table with a mound of clay. After showing me how to use some of the tools, she went to attend to other patients. Megan, who had been working intently on her piece, paused and came over to sit beside me. She looked at my formless mound and then at me.

"They're hoping you'll do something revealing. You know, something they can analyze. They like to get into your head, dissect you like a frog." She laughed. "I know what Doctor Thomas expects me to say every time I do a piece. He sits back and nods and nods and then asks me what do I think I've made. Without hesitating, I say, 'A phallic symbol.' You know," she added when I didn't respond, "a penis." She laughed. "I don't. I try to make something else, but just because everything I make has some vaguely similar shape . . ."

She paused and shook her head at me.

"How long are you going to be dumb? I talk to myself enough as it is. Can't you talk to me and pretend to be dumb with the others? Forget it," she added quickly. "Do your own thing. Everyone else does."

She looked away and when she turned back, the crazy look in her eyes startled me.

"Today's visitors' day, you know. They'll be around to see their precious children working and playing in therapy. My mother probably won't come. You *know* my father won't. No, you don't know that, but I'm telling you he won't. Maybe my mother will come," she added. She looked at me. "I wonder if anyone will come for you," she said.

And suddenly, that became the most intriguing idea of all.

Visitors came throughout the remainder of the day. Some spent the time with their children in the lobby or rec room, but most went outside and walked in the gardens. I saw that Lawrence's mother and father came to visit him. They were an elegant-looking couple. His father was tall, easily six feet two or three, with graying hair. When he turned my way, I saw he had a strong, handsome face, his features chiseled much like Lawrence's. His mother was an attractive woman who wore her light brown hair in a stylish bob. She wore a pretty flowered dress and shiny black heels. From where I watched, it looked like Lawrence's parents were doing all the talking. Occasionally, Lawrence nodded and then he turned and saw me staring at him and his parents through the window of the art studio. He looked embarrassed, but smiled nevertheless and then moved his hands to wave hello. I waved back and smiled. Both his parents looked my way and Lawrence quickly turned and continued to walk. His mother's gaze lingered on me a moment before she joined him and his father.

After that, I caught a glimpse of Mary Beth walking with her mother. Mary Beth had her head down and her mother was talking so quickly it looked like she was giving a lecturing. Her mother was a very pretty woman, tall and thin with shoulder-length blond hair that curled slightly around her face. She looked like a model or an actress. They disappeared around the corner, Mary Beth never raising her head and her mother never stopping her lecture.

Megan, Lulu, and I remained in the studio working throughout the afternoon. No one came to see Lulu, and Megan let me know that her own mother had sent word she couldn't be here today.

"It's not hard to figure out why she hates seeing me," Megan muttered, sitting at my side again as I worked on my sculpture. "She blames me for what my father did to me. Can you imagine that? She gets a divorce and she blames me for her life now? I know it's true. You don't have to look at me like that. The doctor agrees with me. Oh, he won't come right out and say it, but he's met my mother and he agrees.

"So what? So let her blame me. Who needs her?" she said.

"What did your father do to you?" I signed.

"What?" she said, as if suddenly realizing she had been talking to me. "What are you saying? I can't understand all those stupid hand movements. I don't know why you suddenly can't talk. I thought finally, finally I would have someone with some brains to talk to and then you go and lose your voice and start doing this. What are you saying?"

"She's asking you about your father," Miss Dungan said as she passed us with an armful of colored paper.

"My father?" She turned to me. "Why are you so interested all of a sudden? You think I'm making things up? Is that it?"

I shook my head vigorously.

"Just mind your own business," she snapped and returned to her clay figure. Suddenly, she began pounding it madly.

Miss Dungan came rushing over.

"Megan, what are you doing! Please honey, stop that," she said calmly. Megan continued to batter the clay until it lost all shape. Then she sat down hard in her chair and started to laugh.

"Sorry," she said, "I guess there's nothing to analyze this week."

She laughed again and then began to cry; but strangely, although there were tears flowing from her eyes, her face remained still, her lips unmoving.

"You better take a little rest, honey," Miss Dungan said and put her arm around Megan's shoulders. "Come on," she urged. Megan stood and let herself be led out of the studio.

I returned to my own sculpture for a while and then gazed out the window and saw that Lawrence's parents had gone. He was alone, sitting on a bench, staring in at me.

When Miss Dungan returned, I asked her if I could go outside now.

"I suppose so, sure," she said. "We'll leave your piece just as it is and you can return to it tomorrow, okay?"

I nodded and left the studio. Lawrence looked up and smiled warmly as I came down the pathway.

"Hi," he said. "How's your artwork coming along?"

I shook my head.

"I wouldn't exactly call it a work of art," I signed. He seemed to understand and nodded. I liked the fact that he didn't try to convince me otherwise and fill my head with false ideas about being talented.

"You want to take a walk? If we go down the path there, we can get a view of the ocean."

I turned and gazed in the direction he indicated.

"It's still pretty nice out," he continued. "My parents had to leave early. They had a social function to attend. They usually do."

I turned back to him, hearing his note of displeasure.

"They're not crazy about coming here in the first place. It's an embarrassment. I'm the only member of my family to end up in a loony bin. Oh, I didn't mean it that way," he said quickly. "I mean, I don't think of you as loony. I'm loony, Megan's a real loon, but you're not."

"Something's wrong with me," I signed. I pointed to my head and shook it.

"Whatever's wrong with you will be easily cured. You won't be here anywhere near as long as I've been, I'm sure. Want to walk?"

I was reluctant, but I finally agreed and we started down the path.

"My father's a stockbroker," he said. "Very successful one, too. He's got some high-profile clients, big portfolios. I don't know exactly how rich we are, but I know we're really rich. My mother usually buys whatever she wants. You should see her closet. It's as big as some people's bedrooms. She even has a vanity table in there.

I smiled.

"I'm not exaggerating," he said. "When I was a little boy, I hid out in that closet. She always yelled at me for it. She's got clothes hanging in there with the tags still on them. I don't think she even remembers half the things she buys.

"And you should see her jewelry. She's got enough to stock a small store. What about your mother? Have you tried remembering her? Did you live in a big house?"

I thought and shook my head.

"No? That's strange. I bet your mother is probably the first person you're going to remember. Well, there it is," he said, stopping. I looked up.

Through the tall maple trees, I could see the ocean, its blue sheen glimmering in the late afternoon sunlight.

I stepped back.

"What?" he said.

I shook my head.

"You're afraid of the ocean?" He thought a moment. "It has something to do with what happened to you then. I was reading about your problem. I looked it up in our library. That's what I was doing when you came in with Mrs. Broadhaven. The only way you're going to get well is for you to confront what happened," he said. "That's Doctor Southerby's job, to get you to do that."

He looked at the sea and then at me.

"You want to try to get closer? Maybe it will revive your memory and—"

I shook my head emphatically.

"Okay," he said. "We'll go back, huh?"

I nodded, but chanced another glimpse of the water. Images began to parade through my mind: faces, lobster traps, boats, the beach, a cranberry bog, someone singing, and then someone calling my name, whispering at first, and then calling me louder, louder. It seemed like . . . I was calling myself.

I felt my throat tighten with the effort to pronounce someone else's name.

Lawrence's eyes widened as I brought my hands to my neck and shook my head.

"Is something wrong? Are you all right? Laura?"

Impulsively, I threw myself into his arms and buried my face against his shoulder as I sobbed, cried for reasons I couldn't explain. All I wanted to do was cry and keep crying until my well of tears went dry.

At first, Lawrence just stood there with his arms at his sides, not knowing what to do. Then he embraced me slowly and held me closely, kissed my hair, my temples, stroked my back and kept repeating my name.

"Laura . . . Laura . . ."

Finally, my sobbing ended and I pulled back slowly. He looked happy, but very concerned.

"Are you all right now?"

I nodded and he wiped the tears from my cheeks with his handkerchief.

"I better get you back before they come looking for us," he said.

He turned me around and reached for my hand. We started along the path again. This time, I didn't look back at the ocean, not even for a second. I was happy when it disappeared behind us, but I knew that soon, very soon, I would have to return, perhaps by myself, and stare at the water until the truth and my memory broke free of the chains I had thrown around it.

Only then would I get those chains off myself.

13
&

Close Call

I had three sessions with Doctor Southerby the following
week. He was happy to see I was following his advice and
filling my journal with thoughts and feelings. He spent the
first ten minutes reading them and then asking me questions about the things I had written, never insisting I try to
answer if I showed any reluctance. I performed my sign
language so spontaneously and gracefully, he joked about
my having once been deaf. Then he grew serious and
returned to the idea that I talked to someone who was deaf
on a daily basis.

"That seems logical, doesn't it, Laura?" he asked.

I nodded, even though I felt I'd rather not answer. He had
a way of holding his kind eyes on me firmly, but not with
intimidation. I felt so captured by that gaze, a gaze filled
with sincerity and compassion, that I could barely turn
away. His eyes were mesmerizing. In fact, during our third
session, he decided he would try hypnosis. I had no idea if
he learned anything. One moment, I was staring ahead and
the next, I was blinking and wondering how long I had been
in his office. Did he get me to speak under hypnosis? If he
did, he didn't mention it afterward.

"It's very good that you feel less and less anxious, Laura, especially about being here," he explained after I had agreed to be hypnotized. "Trust is essential if we are to make any progress with your problems."

I smiled and nodded. I did trust him more and more, and I even looked forward to our sessions. Some of the others, especially Megan, thought that was strange.

"It's like enjoying someone putting his fingers through your skull and feeling around in your brain," she said after she had asked me a little about our sessions and saw I was happy talking and listening to Doctor Southerby.

When she heard I had permitted him to hypnotize me, she went bonkers.

"Are you really crazy? When you're out of it like that, you have no idea what he's doing to you. Maybe he took your clothes off," she suggested. I started to laugh and her face crumbled not with anger, but with sadness.

I tried to sign an explanation, tried to tell her how good Doctor Southerby was and how he would never do something like that, but the tears were filling her eyes quickly.

"I thought you were different. I thought you believed me and understood. Everyone else laughs at me."

I shook my head.

"I'm not laughing at you," I signed.

However, the tears were already streaming down her cheeks. She had her hands clenched into tiny fists and for a moment, I was afraid she might hit me.

"You mark my words," she flared. "You'll be sorry you didn't listen to me someday. You will," she concluded, her voice strong and hateful, as if she were pronouncing my death. Then she marched away, her body straight, her arms extended and stiffly swinging like a toy soldier's. Lately, she was doing more and more of that, leaving us all and going off by herself, closing her door in her room or wandering about outside, avoiding people.

My own periods of depression, my feelings of nervousness, had diminished, but not the inner voices and the flashbacks. Doctor Southerby made me think as much as I could about those I had described in my journal. He probed my mind, his suggestions and questions resembling a scalpel in the hands of a skilled and graceful surgeon, knowing just when to push forward, when to pull back. If something became too sensitive, my lips would begin to tremble. In fact, my whole body would start to shake and my heart would pound so hard and fast, I had trouble breathing.

He would stop, touch my shoulder, ask me to close my eyes and take deeper breaths. Then, he would change the subject, and soon, I would relax again. During our fourth session, he had Miss Dungan bring in the needlework I had completed and we talked about the picture, why I was attracted to it and what I thought about when I looked at it.

Most of my free time was spent in the arts and crafts studio now. During my second visit there, I went from sculpture to needlework. That day, I saw another patient sewing quietly in the corner and I walked over and watched her for a while. My fingers felt as if I were doing the work along with her. Miss Dungan noticed my interest and suggested I try it. In minutes I was doing it comfortably.

"From the way you're at that," Miss Dungan said as she nodded gently, "I would safely say you've done it many times before. I guess your fingers don't have amnesia," she said, smiling.

She let me choose my own picture and I had selected one of a little girl playing on the beach. As I filled in her legs, her dress, and her face, the little girl became clearer and clearer in my mind, flashes of her smile, her eyes, and even the sound of her voice popping in and out of my memory. It was someone I knew and loved very much. But who? Her name was on the tip of my tongue and her voice tingled inside my head. All I had to do was think harder.

Yet, every time I started to open one of the secret doors holding the truths about my past, I found it locked up tight. Something in me knew that as soon as I remembered one thing clearly, it would all come tumbling out of the remaining dark places in my mind and with it, one terrible, terrible memory. Sometimes, the effort literally took my breath away and I had to stop, close my eyes, and wait for the trembling and the pain in my heart to pass.

"This is not unusual," Doctor Southerby told me when he saw how distressed I was after he read about this in my journal. "There's a tug-of-war going on inside you, Laura, and one day soon, the side of you that wants you to return to the world will win and it will be over. I promise," he said.

He really made me feel good; he gave me hope.

I discussed most of this with Lawrence, who was there waiting for me after every one of my sessions. He pretended he had just happened to be in the corridor on his way to the library or the rec room. I knew he was pretending, but I didn't mind. I enjoyed teaching him more sign language and then using what I taught him to explain and discuss things with him.

"Maybe the whole world should use sign language, Laura," he told me one afternoon. "When you have to draw a visual idea of your thoughts, you think about it more and don't say as many stupid or cruel things to the people you supposedly love and care for," he said.

I guessed from the way he lowered his eyes and then looked away so I couldn't see the hurt on his face that he was really talking about his parents. Only his mother had visited him this last time and when I asked about it, he said his father had to go off on a business trip.

"It's harder to lie to people through sign language," he continued. "It's a greater commitment because it involves more of yourself. Afterward, it's more difficult to tell people, 'I didn't say that,' or 'That's not what I meant.'"

He turned to me and sighed deeply, smiling through his fog of depression.

"Maybe you're lucky not having anyone visit you," he said. "That way no one close to you can lie to you."

I started to shake my head.

"We've always lied to each other in my family," he continued bitterly. "My mother always says it's better to tell little white lies and avoid unpleasantness. The thing of it is, everyone knows everyone else is not telling the truth, but we all make believe we don't. It's like . . . like we tiptoe over thin ice and it will just take a little nudge of the truth to crack the world under us and drop us into oblivion.

"All I had to do this last time is say, 'I know you're lying, Mom. Dad's not away on any trip. He just wouldn't come this time.' He can't stand coming here. Every time he comes, he wears this sour face, gazes around disgustedly. I know what he's thinking. He's thinking, What's he doing here? What's a son of his doing here?

"I don't want to be here either," Lawrence protested. "I don't. I . . . I don't like being thought of this way. I lost all my friends on the outside. How am I ever going to go back out there? What am I supposed to say when people ask me where I've been and what I've been doing all this time? Most of them know anyway and will just treat me like some sort of leper."

He dropped his head and didn't raise it until I reached out to touch his cheek. Then he smiled again.

"Now that you're here, I guess I don't mind it as much," he said. "At least you listen to me and I'm not afraid to talk to you."

"That's because I don't talk; I just sign, so you can get your words in faster," I signed and he laughed. Then he stopped abruptly.

"I don't laugh with anyone else," he told me. "Really, not even with my parents. Especially not with my parents," he added. "You're a special person, Laura. I know you are. That's why I made myself concentrate and learn as much as I could about sign language. If that's the way you're going to communicate for the rest of your life, I'll be here to understand and talk to you for the rest of mine," he pledged.

The softness in his eyes reminded me of someone else's eyes. Even the sound of his voice was more than vaguely familiar. If I closed my eyes and listened to him talk, I almost . . . almost fell back through the darkness toward the light.

I told Doctor Southerby about Lawrence, about our little

V. C. ANDREWS

talks, when he asked me if I had made any friends. I asked him about Megan and Mary Beth and Lulu. He didn't go into detail, but just said they all had serious problems, too. He assured me that everyone would get better in time, if they truly made the effort.

"You've got to want to help yourself. That's the key," he lectured. I knew he meant it as much for me as anyone else in the clinic.

I told Lawrence that and he nodded.

"I admit I don't want to help myself as much as I should yet," he said. "Not yet. But," he added quickly, "the day you walk out of here, I'll work hard at following you."

Is that a promise? I inquired.

He nodded, and I was so happy for him that I leaned forward on the bench and gave him a quick kiss on the cheek. His eyes nearly exploded. He raised his hands slowly and touched the place where my lips touched him, as if to confirm they had indeed been there.

From that day forward, Lawrence looked at me differently. His eyes would linger on my face longer. He wasn't afraid to be caught staring at me, and if I did catch him, he simply smiled. Most important, he stopped shaking whenever he was with me. I saw he was growing stronger in small ways, eating better, participating more in the recreational activities, talking more to the others.

One visitors' day, he appeared abruptly in the art studio. Megan, Lulu, and I were the only ones there. Once again, Megan's mother hadn't appeared and Lulu's mother had written to say she had an important legal obligation. Megan told her it probably had to do with her finding another lover.

"She'd rather be with him than with you here in the nuthouse," Megan said.

I wished she hadn't said such a thing. Whenever Lulu had trouble with her family, she acted even younger, behaving like a baby, crying and sulking until she had to be taken to her room.

The moment I saw Lawrence in the doorway, I knew

238

something dramatic and serious had happened. His face was flushed, but he stood firm, his eyes full of excitement. He hurried across the studio to me. I looked up from my needlepoint, a small, quizzical smile on my face.

"I did it," he bragged and strutted to the window. He looked out at the gardens, at the other patients and their families and then turned back to me. "I burst the bubble today. I risked falling through the ice."

He turned. I held my smile.

"She came without him again. This time it was supposedly because of some major company problem. It's Sunday!" he cried, raising his voice and his arms. "How can there be a major company problem? I told her she was lying for him and she couldn't deny it!"

The commotion caught Megan's attention. She left her mound of clay and approached, her tools still in hand.

"What's going on?" she demanded.

Lawrence turned and looked at her and then at me.

"Nothing," he said quickly.

She stared at him and then at me and then looked at him again.

"Ooooooh, I see," she said, "secrets. You two have secrets now," she said, smirking. Then her face filled with fury, her eyes blazing madly, her lips thinning. "So, keep your stupid secrets. See if I care. See if anyone cares."

"That's right," Lawrence said suddenly, surprising me by not backing down as usual. "We do have secrets. So mind your own business, okay?"

Megan's mouth dropped and she turned to look at me. I tried smiling at her, but she narrowed her eyes and shook her head. There was no retreat in her. A strange smile twisted her lips.

"You two have done it, haven't you?" she asked, stepping toward him.

"What?" He shifted his eyes to me and then to her, stepping back as she stepped forward.

"You've done it, haven't you, Lawrence?" she asked

disdainfully, her smile sharper. "You and Miss Laura Perfect have joined at the waist."

"What? No," Lawrence said, shaking his head more vigorously.

"Sure you have," she pounced. "Where did you do it? In your room? In hers? In the grass? Where?" Megan screamed.

"What's going on over there?" Miss Dungan said, looking up from across the room. She had been helping another patient with his fingerpainting so intensely, she hadn't noticed what was happening in my corner of the room. She hadn't even seen Lawrence enter the studio.

He looked her way anxiously, his eyes full of panic.

"Well, go ahead, Lawrence. Tell Miss Dungan what's going on. Tell her where you two did it," Megan challenged.

Lawrence grew more terrified. He seemed unable to move. It was as if his feet had been nailed to the floor.

I started to sign to him, but he was beginning to tremble harder, faster. Megan laughed. Miss Dungan rose and started toward us. Lawrence looked at me helplessly.

"I'll tell her myself then," Megan said. "I'll tell her what you two have been doing. I'll tell everyone," she taunted and started to turn toward Miss Dungan.

Lawrence rushed at Megan. I raised my arms and managed a guttural noise, but it was too late. He grabbed Megan around the neck. Miss Dungan screamed as he pulled Megan back. Her face turned crimson and she stuck her carving tool into Lawrence's wrist, but he didn't relinquish his grip until Miss Dungan grabbed his arm and I rose to push him away from Megan. Then he charged out of the art studio.

"He's bleeding," I signed at Miss Dungan.

"I know. Megan, are you all right?"

She was leaning against the table, gasping for breath, coughing and rubbing her neck.

"Yes, I'm all right," she managed. Then she blinked hard, as if she were trying to get something out of her eyes before turning back to Miss Dungan. "You saw it," she said. "He tried to rape me."

"What?"

I shook my head when Miss Dungan looked to me.

"He tried to rape me. All of a sudden, he was at me and if I didn't fight him off—" She looked at me. "He raped you, too, didn't he? Tell her! He came into your room one night," she continued, her eyes widening with the elaboration, "and put his hand over your mouth and—"

I shook my head more vigorously.

"No, no," I signed.

Megan stopped, the tears rolling down her cheeks. She took a deep, painful breath.

"Why don't you people believe me?" she asked tearfully.

"Maybe you should go to the infirmary, Megan," Miss Dungan said softly. She stepped up to her and put her arm around Megan's waist. "Come along. Let Mrs. Cohen check you over."

"I'm all right," Megan insisted, pulling away abruptly. "I fought him off. He didn't do anything. But he could have," she added quickly. She fixed her wild, angry eyes on me. "You weren't much help," she told me. Then she spun around and returned to her clay, as if nothing had happened.

Miss Dungan and I watched her for a moment. She was humming and working more vigorously on her clay.

"I have to see about Lawrence," Miss Dungan said. "Are you all right?"

"Fine," I signed, "but I'm worried about Lawrence."

"I'll see about him," she said and went to her intercom.

Lawrence frightened himself more than anyone else. The attendants found him down by the ocean, sitting on a rock. He had walked through the water, soaking his shoes, socks, and pants, and was hugging his knees, his head down, when they located him. He was shaking so badly from his panic and the chill of the ocean water, he had to be taken to the infirmary. Later, I found out his hands were clenched into fists so tightly, he nearly stopped the blood circulation to his fingers and he dug his fingernails into his skin until his palms bled. He had to be put on tranquilizers. They called his parents, but neither his mother nor his father visited. I was worried so much about him, I didn't think much about myself for days and my session with Doctor Southerby didn't go as well as usual.

A week later, Lawrence was released from the infirmary. In the meantime, Megan had behaved as if nothing at all had happened. She hadn't told a soul about the incident and had never brought it up with me. She often abruptly went from being as mute as me to talking incessantly about everything and everyone, mainly at the dinner table. Lulu and Mary Beth inquired after Lawrence and were simply told he wasn't feeling well. In this place, everyone accepted that as enough and didn't follow up with more persistent inquiries.

As if she felt she had to direct her slings and arrows at someone new, Megan zeroed in on different patients in the cafeteria and complained about the way they ate, talked, or moped about. She seemed to know everyone else's problems and always laid the blame on his or her father. She was so cruel to Lulu at times when it came to Lulu's father, I had to intervene, pulling Lulu's attention away and teaching her sign language.

"Why don't you just stop this already," Megan fired at me. "You were talking when you came here. It's just an act, an act to get them all to feel sorry for you. Oh," she said suddenly, her eyes shifting away from me, "look who's better."

Everyone turned to see Lawrence enter the cafeteria. He looked like his old self; unfortunately, that meant that once again he was unsure, timid, eyes downcast. He avoided looking our way and walked directly to the food line, stepping back when another patient went to reach for a second dessert. He didn't come to our table after he had gotten his food either. Instead, he sat at the first table available, one at which two younger boys ate, neither showing any interest in him, nor anyone else for that matter.

"Why doesn't Lawrence sit with us?" Mary Beth asked.

"He's probably too ashamed of himself," Megan said. "He peed in his pants," she whispered to Lulu. "Just like you do sometimes. Did you know that Lulu here has to wear diapers every once in a while?"

"Stop it!" I shouted emphatically with my hands as I stood up.

"What's the matter with you, Laura Perfect?" Megan teased. "You never wore diapers?"

I marched away from the table and joined Lawrence. He looked up with surprise as I sat beside him. I smiled and asked him how he was.

"I'm okay," he said softly, dropping his eyes. "I'm sorry if I embarrassed you."

I forced him to look at me and told him I wasn't embarrassed. Megan was the one who should have been embarrassed. Now she was pretending it never happened.

He shot a quick look her way. She was glaring at us.

"You don't have to worry about her," I continued. "She doesn't want anyone to talk about it. It's almost as if *she* suddenly came down with a case of amnesia."

He looked a little relieved, but I noticed how peaked and tired he was. Later, I learned that was probably an effect of the medication he had been given. It took the better part of another full day before he regained some of his newfound courage and outgoingness. He joined us in the rec room after lunch the next day and watched me play a game of checkers with Mary Beth.

Megan was in one of her mute moods again that day. She had barely uttered a word, and when Lawrence sat down beside me, she looked away and then started singing under her breath. After a while, we all turned to her. She was staring out the window and we heard, "Twinkle, twinkle, little star, how I wonder what you are. Up above the world so high, like a diamond in the sky . . ."

She turned when she realized we were all staring at her.

"My daddy . . . used to come into my room and sing that to me and tell me to look up at the ceiling and the stars would appear. So, I looked while he . . ."

Tears rolled out of her eyes.

"I hate secrets," she said, staring at Lawrence. "I hate having to keep secrets!"

She got up and walked out quickly.

"What's with her?" Mary Beth said.

I shook my head and looked at Lawrence, who gazed after her and then back at me, his face full of sadness and pity. I smiled at him. He didn't hate her for what she had done to him. He truly felt sorry for her.

Megan didn't appear for the rest of that afternoon. At dinner, we all got our food and sat, but she didn't come into the cafeteria. Billy, the attendant, approached our table suspiciously.

"Where's Queen Megan?" he demanded. "She knows what it means if you don't show up for dinner," he said pointedly, directing himself at Mary Beth, who quickly looked down at her lap.

"She said she would be right along," Lawrence told him firmly. Billy raised his eyebrows.

"What are you, her lawyer?"

Lawrence turned crimson. Billy laughed and returned to his position, but he kept looking at our table and at the door.

"I'm going to go get her," I signed to Lawrence and rose as inconspicuously as I could. I left the cafeteria and hurried up the corridor to the residential wing.

Megan's door was closed. I knocked and waited and then knocked again. We weren't able to lock our doors from the inside, so I knew I could enter her room, but she wasn't exactly the type of person who would forgive you for barging in. But I wanted to warn her about Billy and what he would do if she didn't show up soon, so I opened the door slightly and peeked in.

At first I thought she was gone. She wasn't sitting in a

chair or lying on the bed, but I heard what sounded like water running in the sink so I entered the room and knocked again on the door to get her attention. She didn't appear. I walked slowly to the bathroom and gazed in.

There she was, sitting on the closed toilet cover, her arms over the edge of the sink. I stepped forward and looked. Her wrists were under a sinkful of ruby red water, so dark it looked like she had cut off her hands. She gazed up at me, her eyes wet with tears, her cheeks streaked, and she smiled.

"Hi, Daddy," she said. And then she began to sing, "Twinkle, twinkle, little star . . ."

I felt my throat close and then open, as the shock of what I saw hit me. I ran to the door, gasping for breath as I tried to summon up my long-lost voice.

"He . . . hel . . . help!" I screamed, finding my voice. "HELP, HELP! HELP!"

Two male attendants and Mrs. Kleckner came running down the hall.

"What is it? Why are you shouting?"

"Megan!" I cried and pointed. "She's trying to kill herself!"

They sped past me and I fell back against the wall, sliding down slowly until I was crouched along the baseboard. The commotion drew some of the staff from the cafeteria and Lawrence and Mary Beth came out, too. Lawrence saw me sitting on the corridor floor and came hurrying over.

"What happened?" he asked.

"Megan tried to commit suicide," I said gravely. He looked down the hall at the staff gathering around her room and then looked back down at me.

"You've got your voice back," he said.

I nodded. Sometimes miracles happened at the strangest times.

Thankfully, I had found Megan in time. She needed only a day in the infirmary. However, they took her upstairs afterward, instead of permitting her to return to her room and to us. We all felt just terrible for her.

"She's probably heavily sedated," Lawrence said at dinner that night.

"When she comes out of it and realizes she's in the Tower, she'll get even more depressed," Mary Beth said. "You know how she is about the Tower," she reminded Lawrence and Lulu. They nodded.

"Maybe she won't be up there long," Lulu said hopefully. Despite the way Megan had often treated her, Lulu really liked and needed Megan.

"You know, when someone goes up there, they usually don't come down," Mary Beth reminded her. Lulu started to cry and rock in her chair.

I reached over and took her hand in mine.

"Maybe it will be different for Megan," I said, stroking her hand. "She's pretty tough and knows how to take care of herself around here, right?"

Lulu smiled and nodded.

"Why give her false hope?" Mary Beth insisted.

"What do you mean?" I asked. "They can't keep her up there forever."

"If they can't make any progress with you upstairs, sometimes they move you someplace else," Lawrence said. "Someplace where they handle only serious cases, not a rich person's country club clinic like this."

"Oh."

"I'm glad you found your voice," he said, smiling. "It's really nice to hear you talk again."

"Yes," Mary Beth said and I noticed she looked a lot healthier—like she had gained a couple of pounds since I had first arrived. Lawrence told me she had made significant progress in that she finally admitted she wasn't overweight. The end of her ordeal was in sight.

I felt bad for Megan. Despite her bouts of nastiness, I missed her. I told Lawrence how I felt when we went for a walk together after my work in art therapy. Lulu trailed along with us. She seemed to be the most lost without Megan, who in her strange fashion had defended and looked after Lulu as much as she ridiculed her.

"Poor Lulu. Maybe we shouldn't call her that anymore, Lawrence."

He laughed.

"I think it's gotten so she wouldn't answer if someone called her Edith," he said.

"I'm going to start doing that. She's never going to get better if we don't help her face reality, too."

"You're right," Lawrence said. "Here you are worrying about everyone else's problems but your own."

"You once told me helping others helps you, too."

"Yes," he said, smiling, "I did, but that was more of an excuse to get you to let me be involved with you more."

"You didn't need an excuse for that, Lawrence," I said and his smile widened.

We sat on our favorite stone bench, the one that had become a symbol of the boundary for me, because beyond it was the hill that led to the view of the ocean, a view that put ice into my veins.

Lulu walked around us, occupying herself with wild-flowers.

"I'm looking for a four-leaf clover," she said. "My daddy told me it brings good luck. If I find one, I'll give it to him when he comes to visit."

"Why doesn't her father ever visit her?" I asked.

Lawrence turned to me, a strange look on his face.

"I thought you knew," he said. I shook my head.

"I know her parents got a divorce. At least that's what Megan said."

"Yes, but not long after that, her father was killed in a car accident. Lulu won't believe it. She never went to the funeral."

"Megan never said—"

"Megan can be cruel, but not *that* cruel; at least to Lulu," Lawrence said. "Maybe . . . maybe she didn't want it to be true. She seems to hate all men, especially all fathers, but I think she really wants to love one, to have a real father. We all know what her father did to her. He put her here. Just like my father put me here," he added angrily.

"Who put me here?" I wondered aloud. "You know so much about everyone else, Lawrence. What do you know about me?"

"Nothing more than what you've told me, which isn't much," he said, smiling. "Everyone's asked about you, but it's like you're the top secret patient. A nurse brought you here one night and that's it."

"Yes," I said, "that's it."

I stood up.

"Going back?"

"No," I said firmly. "Going ahead." I started toward the crest of the hill and then paused.

Lawrence came up beside me and took my hand.

"I'm going to confront my demons, Lawrence." Determined, I took another step forward. "I'm going to do it."

"I'll go with you, Laura. Let me help you."

I took a deep breath and nodded. Then I took another step and another, until we were going down the hill. Lulu remained at the crest, watching us. We walked slowly until we rounded the turn in the path and the ocean came into view. It was as if someone had knocked the wind out of me and I closed my eyes as I struggled to take slow, deep breaths. Lawrence squeezed my hand.

"I'm right here," he whispered.

I opened my eyes and we walked ahead. The waves became more vivid, the spray splashing off the rocks, the breeze harder, faster. Seagulls screamed through the sky and swooped down to feed. The scents of seaweed and salt air made my head swim. The ocean's roar grew louder, stronger.

I paused and closed my eyes again. The darkness lifted like a curtain and I saw a young man, tan and strong, standing shirtless on the deck of a boat. He had eyes like mine and his nose and mouth were also similarly shaped. He was waving, beckoning. . . . I looked down. There was a small hand clasped in my own, a girl no taller than Lulu, smiling.

"Laura . . ."

Was that Lawrence or the boy on the boat calling me? I released my grip on the little girl's hand and she started to sign.

"She's deaf!" I cried.

"Who?" Lawrence asked.

I opened my eyes. We were close enough to the rocks and the sea so that the spray reached our faces. I turned to him, my heart thumping.

"I have a little sister who's deaf," I said, "and I have a brother who is . . ."

"What?"

"My twin," I declared and turned away to run back up the hill. I dug into the ground with my feet so hard my legs ached, but I charged up, terrified by the rush of memory. Lawrence called to me, but I didn't turn back. Instead, I kept running, passing Lulu, who looked surprised and confused, and then down the walkway and back toward the clinic.

I burst through the door and charged madly down the corridor, nearly knocking over the janitor who had just finished scrubbing the tile floor.

"Sorry," I cried as I ran toward Doctor Southerby's office. Mrs. Kleckner was just coming out of the staff quarters. She shouted and stepped in my path, holding her arms out so that she could stop me.

"What's wrong? Why are you running through the building, knocking into people? You know that's not allowed," she chastised.

"I've got to see Doctor Southerby right away," I said, gasping for breath.

"You just don't burst in on Doctor Southerby, young lady. There are other patients here. You wait for your appointment," she said.

"No, I have to see him. You don't understand. I have a little sister who's deaf. That's why . . . I know how to sign, and I have a brother—"

"That's wonderful," she said. "Congratulations. Now just turn around and get yourself cleaned up for dinner. You look like a wild woman. You'll frighten the other patients half to death."

"But, I have to see him now!"

"If you don't listen to me, I'll have to have you confined to your room or worse," she threatened. "I don't condone wild behavior here, no matter what's supposedly wrong with the patient. Those who can't follow the rules are placed elsewhere. This is not a high-security clinic for the mentally disturbed," she added.

I stepped away from her.

"No, this isn't, although I know you would like it to be," I said defiantly. "Well, we shouldn't be treated like criminals just because we have mental problems. We're people who have had difficulties in their lives, serious difficulties."

"I know," she said dryly, "overindulgences. Having too much can become a problem. Where do you put everything? How do you handle all the special privileges? Very serious difficulties," she said with a sardonic smile.

"Why are you working here?" I asked, shaking my head. "You don't care about the patients. You have no respect for us. You should be working in a prison hospital. That's really where you belong," I fumed.

"Really? How come all you blue bloods know what's good for everyone else but yourselves? Spare me the career guidance and behave yourself."

I straightened up as if a rod had been inserted in my spine and fixed my eyes on hers.

"I want to make an appointment with Doctor Southerby," I insisted. "I can do that at least, can't I?"

"I'll make the arrangements for you," she said. "Go on, get ready for dinner. You look a mess."

I hesitated a moment, debating. She looked like she was made of stone and if I tried to move her, I would only anger her and delay my visit with Doctor Southerby.

"I have to see him as soon as possible," I said and then turned and walked back toward my room. Lawrence and Lulu had come in and were looking for me.

"Are you all right?" Lawrence asked when he caught up with me outside my room.

"Yes, I just had a real memory and I wanted to share it with Doctor Southerby, but Mrs. Kleckner stopped me and told me to clean up for dinner. She said she would make my appointment for me."

"That's good," Lawrence said. "I'm happy for you, Laura. This might be the beginning of the end of your time here," he said.

"Maybe," I said and went into my room. I was too frustrated and furious to appreciate my progress at the moment.

However, when I looked at myself in the mirror, I saw that Mrs. Kleckner was right about one thing: I did look wild. My hair looked like I had run my fingers through it for hours, my face was flushed, and my eyes were bright with excitement. I decided to shower and change for dinner.

I was just putting on my shoes and going in to brush out my hair when Mrs. Kleckner appeared in my doorway.

"I've made you your appointment," she said. "Tomorrow at ten."

"Thank you," I said.

"Go to room one-oh-one in the morning," she added and started to leave.

"One-oh-one? But that's not Doctor Southerby's office," I cried. "Why do I have to go there?"

She turned back to me slowly.

"Your case has been transferred to Doctor Scanlon," she said, not without some pleasure.

"But I don't want to be transferred. I want to talk to Doctor Southerby," I said. My heart was racing. Why would I be transferred now?

She sighed and rolled her eyes toward the ceiling.

"I want, I want, I want. Don't you people have any other words in your vocabulary? It's not important what you want; what you *need* is decided by the people in charge here," she said. "Your transfer to Dr. Scanlon has been decided and that's that," she added, her words hammering into my brain.

"I won't talk to anyone else but Doctor Southerby," I insisted just as firmly. I faced her with all the defiance I could muster.

She stared at me a moment and then stepped toward me, a cold smile on her face.

"If you refuse your therapy, you'll have to be transferred upstairs, and if we can't help you upstairs, you'll be transferred to a different sort of institution, one that suits your needs better," she said. "Believe me, that's what will happen." She started to turn away.

"But Doctor Southerby is helping me," I moaned. How could I fight such raw power over me?

"Doctor Scanlon is just as good. In fact, he's Doctor Southerby's superior. You should be grateful you've been given the opportunity, that he has made time for you, but being grateful for things is not in the character of most of the patients here. Why should you be any different?" she added. "Don't be late for dinner," she warned.

She left me staring after her, wondering what I had done to deserve to be transferred to Dr. Scanlon. After all, getting my memory back wasn't something to be punished for. Was it?

14

Out of the Shadows

My mind wandered all through dinner that night. I kept drifting back to the memory of walking with my little sister on the beach toward the boat where my twin brother was waving, beckoning. The images burst like flashbulbs in the backdrop of my empty and dark mind: a tiny smile, a lobster trap being pulled up from the bottom of the sea, castles in the sand, starry nights on the beach, and the deep voice of a man I knew must be my father reading, reciting. It sounded like a chant, and then the woman I knew must be my mother singing a lullaby. My early memories mingled with later ones in a hodgepodge of faces, voices, and sights. I felt like I had fallen into a giant crossword puzzle. I was just another letter searching for the others that joined me to an entire word: family. The letters spun around and around in my head until they spelled out a name.

"May," I suddenly said.

"What's that?" Lawrence asked. Everyone stopped talking and looked at me.

I turned to him.

"Her name is May."

"Whose name?" Lulu asked.

"My little sister. Her name is May," I said more enthusiastically. "I just can't think of my brother's—"

"Easy," Lawrence said, reaching to touch my hand. "Don't try to remember too much at once."

I looked at his concerned face and nodded.

"It must be exciting for you, though," Mary Beth said, "regaining your past, your identity. Pretty soon, it will all come back to you."

"Yes." I nodded. "Yes, it will. Doctor Southerby was right."

I finished my dinner quickly because I had let most of it get cold while I sat there thinking. After dinner we usually went to the rec room to watch television, read, or play board games. This evening I didn't feel like doing any of those things. I was too excited by the closeness of my memories. I just wanted to sit in a corner by myself and struggle with images and words until I put together more of the puzzle.

Mary Beth, feeling sorry for Lulu, spent more time with her, playing the games with her that Megan used to play.

Lawrence sat across from me reading *A Tale of Two Cities*. He read a lot, and when he talked about some of the books he read, I remembered having read them, too.

"You must have been a good student," he remarked, "to have remembered all the characters."

Now I wondered. Was I a good student? Where did I go to school? Who were my friends? What did I want to become? Not having the answers to the simplest of questions had become more than an irritation. I sat there feeling as if an explosion might happen any time in my mind and send me rushing back to my past. I guess I looked like a hen about to lay an egg, because Lawrence suddenly looked up from his book and laughed.

"I wish you could see the expression on your face, Laura. You look so poised, so tense sitting forward like that. You look like you might jump up and yell 'Eureka!'"

"It's the way I feel. The images keep floating by, circling, circling, drawing closer. I can hear my mother's voice, my father's, too, and I'm beginning to see their faces. It's like a continually growing light is bringing them out of the darkness. Does that make any sense?"

"Yes," he said. "Actually, it makes a lot of sense, Laura. You're one of the really lucky ones here. You're going to get better," he said, "and very soon," he added, not without a little sadness in his voice.

"So will you."

"Yes, I will," he said. "I'd like to meet you again on the outside and do something . . . normal, like take you to a movie or go dancing. Something."

"Me, too," I said, smiling, "but who knows where I live? Maybe it's hundreds, thousands of miles from where you live."

"Distance wouldn't matter to me." He looked at me intently, his eyes burning bright.

Noticing the way he gazed at me made me wonder if I had had a boyfriend before my accident. I knew Lawrence would be disappointed, but that wasn't what kept me from remembering. I realized it had to be something else. But what? Why did my heart start to pound just at the idea?

Suddenly Mary Beth got up and came over to us. One of the younger girls had been talking to her and what she said made her look unhappy.

"Denise says she overheard Billy and another attendant talking about Megan. She says they said Megan's mother is having her transferred to a real nuthouse. From the way they described it, it doesn't sound nice. They called her a straitjacket case." She looked back. "Lulu's very upset. She heard most of it. Now she's just sitting there sucking her thumb. I don't know what to do. I don't want her to end up in the Tower, too."

"Poor kid," Lawrence said. "And poor Megan."

"When does she stop being a victim?" I asked aloud.

Lawrence fixed his eyes on me thoughtfully for a moment.

"When she wants to," he said.

"You think she wants to be like she is?" Mary Beth asked him angrily.

"I've been doing a lot of reading lately about some of this. Megan feels responsible for what happened to her. She blames herself and she looks for sympathy. It's all she knows how to do at the moment," he said. "The doctors have got to make her see what happened to her was not her fault."

"Maybe you're talking about yourself," Mary Beth snapped, her eyes furious.

He gazed up at her.

"Maybe," he admitted and then looked at me. "Maybe I'm talking about all of us."

I shuddered and looked around at all the other patients. Someone from the outside sticking their head in the doorway to gaze at us might not easily understand how troubled most of us were. For the moment, everyone looked as normal as anyone on the outside—playing cards, games, watching television and laughing, talking, and reading.

It struck me how difficult it was to know about someone simply by looking at them. Maybe it took years and years before anyone really knew anyone. Lawrence was growing more and more attached to me, but what if all that I remembered would devastate him? What if I were exactly like the people he despised? Would my true self, my identity, come rushing back over me and wipe away any identity I had established with him? He and I were truly strangers, a pair of lost souls who happened to meet for a while and soon had to return to our bodies, and those bodies might not be so attracted to each other afterward, I thought.

"I feel like going outside," I said and stood up.

Mary Beth and Lawrence looked at each other and then smiled.

"What? Why are you two looking at me like that?"

"You can't go outside now," Mary Beth said. "The doors are locked, and if you tried to open them, the alarms would go off."

"We *are* prisoners here," I moaned. "All I want to do is walk in the garden, look up at the stars, feel the night air.

What's so terrible about that? Why won't they let us out at night?"

"It's dark," Mary Beth said. "They can't keep watch over you as easily."

I flopped back into my chair, sullen, my arms wrapped around me.

"I could get you outside," Lawrence whispered.

Mary Beth widened her eyes.

"No, Lawrence. You'll get into big trouble."

"How?" I asked.

"The cafeteria staff is gone by now. They go in and out through a side entrance off the kitchen. It's not locked and there's no alarm on it."

"How do you know that?" I asked.

He hesitated and then leaned toward me.

"I did it once. I thought I was going to run away, but the moment I stepped out the door, I froze," he confessed.

We were silent a moment.

"I'm going back to Lulu," Mary Beth said. The conversation was obviously frightening her. Lawrence watched her return to the table before he continued.

"I know how she feels. When darkness falls and the doors are locked, the outside of the building feels and looks like the outside world. It's as if the boundaries of this place shrink. She's not ready to return, so she's even afraid of the thought of going out at night," he explained.

"You know a lot about everyone, Lawrence. You could study and become a doctor yourself," I said. I really meant it. He blushed at the compliment.

"It's just that I spend a lot of time in the library. Most of the people here don't know what's available." He leaned toward me again. "There's even a book by the head doctor, Doctor Scanlon," he said. *"Causes of Family Dysfunction.* After I read it, I thought he was using my family as his resource material for the book."

I knew he was waiting for me to comment, but I couldn't stop this feeling of restlessness. It felt like a hive of bees was buzzing inside me. I had to see the stars, feel the night air.

"Will you take me to the kitchen?" I asked finally.

"Really?"

"I want to go outside and look up at the stars. I think it might help me. There's something about the stars. . . . Something that's teasing my memory," I explained. "It would mean a lot to me."

He grew serious.

"All right," he said after a moment's thought, "we'll do it." He gazed at the attendants. "You go out first so we don't look suspicious. Go to the bathroom, wait a minute, and then come out. I'll be down the hall and if it's all clear to the cafeteria, I'll wave you on. Are you sure you want to do this? They could send you or me or both of us upstairs and you know what that could mean," he added.

"I don't want to get you into trouble, Lawrence. Maybe you should just tell me where it is instead of showing me."

"No," he insisted. "I want to do this for you. Go ahead. Go to the bathroom and give me a minute."

I still hesitated. He nodded toward the door, urging me on. I looked at the attendants and then rose as quietly as I could. Nevertheless, one of the attendants gazed at me as I approached the door. I smiled at her and mouthed the word "bathroom." She smiled back at me and I left the room. I waited just as Lawrence had told me and then I stepped out of the bathroom. The hallway was empty, but up toward the cafeteria, Lawrence appeared, stepping out of a doorway. He gestured for me to hurry.

I practically ran to him and we went through the doorway and then into the cafeteria. All the lights were out now, but there was enough of a glow from the lights outside to silhouette all the tables and chairs so we didn't bump into anything and make any noise. Lawrence moved quickly to the kitchen doors, then held up his hand for me to stop and be still as he listened. He slowly opened the doors.

There was a small light on over the stove. From what we could see, there was no one around.

"This way," he whispered. We walked through the kitchen to the pantry and then to a small hallway. "That's it," he said, nodding at a metal door at the end of the hallway.

"Thank you," I said. I approached the door slowly and then looked back at him.

"They're going to start looking for you soon, Laura. When they don't find you in the bathroom, there's going to be trouble."

"If they ask, tell them I went to my room for something," I said. "I won't be long."

"I'd like to come with you," he said, but he seemed incapable of taking another step forward. "It's just that . . ."

"It's all right. You've done enough, Lawrence. Go back before you're missed, too. I'll be fine," I said.

I reached for the door. When I opened it, I hesitated, afraid there might be an alarm he didn't know about, but nothing happened except the cool night air came rushing in at me.

"If you don't come right back—"

"I will. I promise," I said.

I could see that he was shaking. He wanted to pierce that invisible border so much. I stepped out and closed the door behind me quickly to end his suffering as much as to give myself the courage. For a moment, I simply stood there, listening to the sounds of the night. Then I walked away from the building so I could get away from all the lights.

It was a night filled with stars, clear and sharp so that the constellations were easy to locate. My eyes traced the length of the Big Dipper. The mere sight of the luminous dots sparkling above me took my breath away. I had to sit. I didn't even notice the coolness anymore. Words, pictures, and thoughts were rushing at me like shooting stars themselves, approaching and then veering away just when I was about to understand something or see something clearly.

I closed my eyes and sat back, my arms stretched out, my hands open, palms up, waiting to be touched, to accept my identity and everything that would follow. I thought I felt another hand in mine and I could hear a voice, a young man's voice, whispering, his lips so close I could almost feel them brushing against my ear.

I moaned. His face began to rise out of the black pit of forgetfulness, first his eyes and then his lips and then—

"What the hell do you think you're doing?" I heard and opened my eyes to see Billy standing there, smoking a cigarette. He had a wry smile on his face. "Huh?"

"Nothing," I said.

"How did you get out here?" he asked sharply.

"I just wanted to see the stars," I said. I started to stand and he stepped toward me, flicked his cigarette, and continued to move until he was between me and the building.

"Tell me how you got out," he demanded.

"I just found a door that wasn't locked and walked out," I said. He was close enough so that I could see his eyes narrow suspiciously.

"Just found a door, huh? Are you sure you didn't come out here to meet someone? Huh? Someone named Arnie by any chance?"

"What? Who?" I said, shaking my head.

"Arnie's had his eye on you."

"I'm not meeting anyone. I don't even know who Arnie is," I insisted and tried to go around him, but he stepped quickly into my path.

"I know how you young girls can get, locked up like this, away from your boyfriends," he continued, drawing closer. I retreated a few steps. "Arnie's a joke. I know how to treat my girls." The right corner of his mouth rose into an impish, lusty smile.

He reached out and put his hands on my waist.

"Let me show you," he said, pulling me toward him and bringing his lips toward my mouth. I turned away just in time and started to struggle as his hands moved over my ribs toward my breasts.

"Let me go!"

"Come on. There's nothing really wrong with you," he said, trying to get me to turn my mouth to his. "You're the prettiest girl here. I've been watching you ever since you arrived here, and I know you've been looking at me, too. Come on," he urged, cupping my breast with one hand while the other lifted my skirt.

I squirmed and struggled.

"If you don't cooperate, I'll turn you in," he threatened. "I'll get you and whoever helped you into big trouble. You'll end up in a straitjacket like Megan. Stop fighting," he insisted. "Stop it!"

I was afraid so I stopped squirming and his hand moved up my leg, over my panties, his fingers tracing the trim along the edge and then he lifted them away. I sobbed as he ran his fingers over me.

"You're sweet," he said, putting the tip of his tongue in my ear.

"Please," I pleaded.

"I'm not going to hurt you. You'll like this," he said, moving me back to the bench. I could sense he was undoing his trousers with his left hand as his right continued to move over my breast and then moved to undo the buttons of my blouse, slipping in to struggle with my bra.

"You're beautiful, so beautiful," he muttered.

I started to cry and to pull away again.

"Laura, don't make me angry," he said, stopping my resistance.

Suddenly, both of his hands were under my skirt. He pulled my panties down as he nudged me onto the bench. I was afraid to scream. I thought I would faint and then . . . someone whispered my name. Although the voice wasn't loud, it was close.

"Laura!" Billy froze, still holding his hands on my thighs. "Laura, you better come back inside."

"Who the hell's that? Lawrence?"

"Let me go," I said, pulling free and stepping away from him. I pulled up my panties quickly.

"LAURA!"

"Get out of my way," I told Billy. He thought a moment, looked toward the building, and then let me pass.

"You tell anyone about me and I'll tell about you," Billy cried as I ran toward the kitchen doorway. Lawrence was standing there with the door open. I ran toward him.

"What's wrong?" He looked at me aghast, jumping back as I pushed him out of the way and slammed the door.

"Let's get back to the rec room," I said. I didn't want him knowing about Billy and doing anything rash. It would only get him in trouble, I thought. It struck me that even in her madness, Megan might not have been so wrong about some of the men in this place.

Lawrence caught up with me outside the cafeteria and seized my hand, turning me back to him.

"What happened out there?" he demanded. "You look like you've seen a ghost. You're so pale and—"

"I almost . . . remembered someone," I said. "Someone special."

"Special?"

"Someone very special," I added.

He understood. His eyes flinched with pain and he released my hand.

"Oh. Well that's good," he said. Then he smiled. "That's good, only . . . I wish that someone were me."

I woke the next morning feeling as if my bed had been a boat adrift on the sea as I tried to sleep. That was how much I had tossed and turned. I was exhausted, drained. It was as if all the memories that had drifted away had come back during the night and added weight to my head. They lay in waiting now, bunched in a knot, anticipating my unraveling them and returning them to their rightful places.

I strained to sit up, my head spinning for a moment. I grew so dizzy, I lost my breath. When something like this had happened earlier, Doctor Southerby described it as an anxiety attack. He advised me to try to relax, take deep breaths, and concentrate on something pleasant.

Even after I had done what he had advised, my head still felt like it might just snap off my neck. I wobbled when I walked and a number of times, stopped to press my hand to the wall to steady myself. My stomach was hollow, empty, but I had no appetite. When I gazed at myself in the mirror, I saw how drained I looked, how pale my face was and how my eyes were empty, without thoughts behind them, orbs of glass that merely reflected whatever was in front of me.

My hands shook when I went to wash my face. Had I caught Lawrence's panic attacks? I had a ten o'clock appointment with Dr. Scanlon today. I realized I was afraid, afraid of having to meet and confide in a new doctor, especially after it took me so long to trust Doctor Southerby.

Somehow, I managed to get myself to breakfast, although I couldn't remember walking there. I must have looked like someone floating in a dream, sleepwalking her way through the clinic. Everyone was there already and starting to wonder about me.

"You don't look so good," Lawrence said.

I blinked and realized I was standing in the middle of the cafeteria. He was just heading back to the table with his tray.

"I don't feel so good this morning."

"Why don't you sit at the table and I'll go get you what you want," he offered.

"Thanks, but I'm not that hungry. I'll be all right," I said and went to the line.

I barely picked at my breakfast. Lawrence grew more and more concerned about me.

"Maybe you should go see the nurse," he said.

"No, I'll be all right. It will pass," I assured him, even though I wasn't so sure myself.

He wanted to stay with me and be sure I was okay, but he had his therapy session right after breakfast and had to leave. He did escort me to the rec room lounge before he went off to talk to his therapist.

As the hour of my first meeting with my new doctor drew closer, my heart began to thump and my dizziness became so intense, I had to sit with my eyes closed and wait for the spells to pass. Finally, I felt someone nudge my arm and looked up at Mrs. Kleckner. She was squinting, her forehead creased in thick folds. Her complexion was as gray as her hair, the tiny veins at the crests of her bony cheeks more vivid and more like crimson spiderwebs than ever.

"It's nearly ten o'clock. You're going to miss your appointment," she said.

"I don't feel so good," I groaned.

She stared down at me.

"Do you have any pain?" she asked.

"Not pain exactly. I have these dizzy spells and feel nauseated every once in a while." I put my hand on my stomach.

She lifted my wrist and took my pulse. Then she felt my forehead. The palm of her hand was clammy, cold, and rough.

"You're fine," she said.

"But I'm sick. I feel very sick," I insisted.

"It's all part of your condition. That's why you have to see the doctor," she concluded abruptly. "Get up. I'll escort you to his office. Come on. He's a busy man. You should count yourself one of the luckier ones to have Doctor Scanlon look into your case. Frankly, I think there are a number of far more serious patients for him to consider, but I'm not the one who gets to make that decision. Unfortunately."

She held out her hand. Reluctantly, I took it. I was afraid I might topple over if I didn't. After I stood, she put her hand behind my back and gave me a firm push, keeping the pressure against my back until I started walking out of the room. I felt a little stronger as we continued down the hall. My eyes went longingly to Doctor Southerby's closed office door as we passed it.

"Keep going," she said. "Come along. The clock is ticking. Even the wealthy can't bribe Father Time," she muttered.

We stopped at room 101 and she opened the door for me.

"Laura Logan," she announced as I entered.

A small woman in her late fifties looked up from her desk.

Her light brown hair was streaked with gray and she had gelatinous dull brown eyes hidden behind a pair of thick-rimmed glasses with rather large lenses. Her thin nose had a bump at the bridge that seemed to have been made specifically for her glasses. She stretched her uneven lips a bit in a weak effort to smile and turned to find a folder on the desk.

"One moment, please," she said, rose, and walked to the inner office door. She wasn't much more than five feet tall, wide in the hips with thick calves barely visible beneath the hem of her lavender knit dress. She knocked, entered, and closed the door behind her. A moment later she reappeared.

"The doctor will see you now," she told me.

"Behave yourself," Mrs. Kleckner advised and released her grip on my elbow.

I glanced at her disgruntled face and then walked into the office, past the receptionist, who stood like a statue, her back straight, her shoulders against the door. It was as though she were afraid I might touch and contaminate her. She stepped out and closed the door as soon as I had entered. I looked back and then turned to Doctor Scanlon.

Now that I was in his office confronting him, I recalled seeing him in the building a number of times, but I had never thought of him as a doctor, much less the head doctor. I thought he was always in a great hurry and imagined him to be some sort of salesman. He never looked at anyone in particular or smiled, nor had I ever seen him in a conversation with a patient, as I had other therapists, especially Doctor Southerby.

Doctor Scanlon wasn't much taller than his receptionist. He had hair the color of weak tea. The strands were so thin his scalp was visible and I could see that his head was covered with spots that looked like enlarged freckles.

At the moment, Dr. Scanlon had his back to me and was gazing out his window. His office faced the rear of the building and the pathway that led down toward the ocean. It was where I had sat on the bench the night before, when Billy had accosted me.

He turned and looked at me, his hazel eyes wide with

interest, but an interest that gave me the feeling I was under a microscope.

"Take a seat please," he ordered, nodding to the chair in front of his desk. "I like my patients to face me during their initial consultation. Later, you can lie on the couch if you like. Patients," he continued, pronouncing the word as if it designated an alien species, "can sometimes free associate easier when they're lying down. Did you sit or lie on the couch with Doctor Southerby?" he asked quickly after I sat.

"I sat," I replied.

He nodded and then gazed down at the folder his receptionist had brought in before I had entered. Still standing, he turned the pages, reading as if I weren't even there. Then he nodded and closed the folder. He dropped himself into his oversized chair, folded his hands on his desk, and leaned toward me.

"I'm Doctor Scanlon and I'm going to try to help you," he began.

"Why can't I stay with Doctor Southerby?" I demanded in response.

He didn't answer immediately. First, he closed his eyes, and held them that way for a moment, as if my question had given him great pain, and then opened them.

"Doctor Southerby works at another clinic as well as here. Actually, he has more responsibility at the other clinic. His patients at the other clinic now need more of his time and he had to cut back on his responsibilities at this clinic," Doctor Scanlon explained with obvious reluctance.

"We are a bit short of professional help these days," he continued. "Normally, I don't take as direct a role in the treatment of our patients. I'm here to consult and assist and confirm a diagnosis and treatment, but he left a gap and a gap must be filled," he added, giving me what I thought must have been his best efforts at a smile. I didn't think I liked being referred to as a gap.

"So," he went on, leaning back in his chair now, "after you were brought here, you were diagnosed with psychogenic amnesia and Doctor Southerby was helping you return to your past, helping you find your identity. I see from his notes that he was happy with your progress."

"I remembered more yesterday," I said quickly. I wanted to get this session over with as soon as I could. I felt very uncomfortable. It was clear to me that Doctor Scanlon didn't have Doctor Southerby's sincerity. He saw me less as a person and more as a patient, another statistic. In my way of thinking, the patients were lucky he usually didn't take a direct role in their treatment.

"Oh? And you had some sort of a reaction to that, I see. I have a report here," he continued, opening the folder again, "that you exhibited some acting out yesterday."

"Pardon me? Acting out?"

"You were running wild in the corridors, nearly knocked over a custodian, screamed hysterically, made demands, and nearly had to be restrained."

"I was excited. I wanted to see Doctor Southerby," I said. "I didn't mean to be loud, and I don't think I needed to be restrained."

"Umm-hmm," he groaned, without looking at me. He continued to stare at the papers before him. How quickly Mrs. Kleckner had written me up, I thought.

"I wasn't hysterical. I was excited about my memories," I added firmly.

He did smile, but it wasn't warm.

"You're here because you're having trouble evaluating and controlling your own behavior, Laura. It's best we give consideration to the way the professional staff evaluates your behavior, don't you think? Now, what was it that got you so excited?" he asked, but looked down at the folder again.

"I remembered my little sister's name and I remembered I had a twin brother," I blurted, impatient with the pace of things. If he kept reading something after everything I said, I would be here all day, I thought. And besides, why hadn't he prepared for me better?

"Really?" He fixed his eyes on me. "What else did you recall?"

"Visions of faces, memories of voices I know belong to my parents. I think we have something to do with lobster fishing and we have a boat and we live near the ocean and my little sister is deaf," I said, trying to contain my exuberance so it wouldn't be misinterpreted. However, as I told him these things, they began to reappear in my mind. My heart began to pound again and I closed my eyes.

"Why do you think you had forgotten them and yourself?" he asked.

"I don't know."

He sat back, again lifting the corners of his lips into that arrogant smirk.

"Well, I can see from Doctor Southerby's notes that you have at least come to the understanding it might have something to do with an event that disturbed you greatly. What we call psychological trauma. Is that still true?"

"Yes," I admitted, my lips trembling again.

He leaned forward, once again fixing me under his microscopic gaze.

"You look very tired. You didn't sleep well last night?"

"No," I said. "I kept waking, hearing voices, hearing someone call, someone who sounded like me. And then I felt very cold. It was as if I . . ."

"What?"

"I was soaking wet," I said, realizing just at the moment exactly what it was I had felt. "Yes, that's what it was: something to do with water . . . the ocean."

His eyes widened.

"I see. I don't like this," he suddenly added. "Take a deep breath and try to stop yourself from thinking about these things for the moment."

"What? What do you mean? Stop? Why should I stop?" I fired my questions like bullets that seemed to just bounce off his coldly analytical face.

"I don't like what's happening to you physically. It's classic. You're rushing back too quickly, I'm afraid. You're in danger of crashing into your trauma and that could cause irrevocable damage, psychological damage. There are a number of similar cases in my ward for severely disabled patients. Some have become comatose and live off intravenous feeding, and some have to be led around like lobotomized people, mere shadows of themselves, never smiling, never laughing, blind and deaf, the walking dead. You don't want that to happen to you, do you?"

"No," I said, terrified. "Could something like that really happen to me?"

"Of course it could. I wouldn't tell you otherwise. I read here that you've already lost your ability to speak once. I'm telling you not to frighten you as much as get you to be more cooperative. I like a patient who wants to cooperate with his or her own treatment. It makes it easier for all of us, especially the patient."

He widened that short, tight smile.

"The brain is the most complex part of our bodies. There are layers and layers of conscious and unconscious thoughts. Your memories are like buried treasure right now," he continued, "and the pathways to them have been shut down. If we reach too quickly or too clumsily for them, they could fall deeper and deeper into the abyss. We must be very, very careful how we go forward."

He paused and flipped through the folder again, shaking his head with disapproval.

"I see that Doctor Southerby failed to prescribe any medication for you. From the way you've described your nights, I think it would be wiser at this stage if we did. I want to be very careful with you, Laura. You're very tender, very sensitive, raw at this moment, and we have medication that can cushion you, protect you."

"I don't like taking medications."

"No one likes taking them, except those who become addicted to them, of course," he added. He wrote something on a pad.

"Won't I ever see Doctor Southerby again?" I asked mournfully.

"Hopefully, you will be cured and gone by that time," he said. "I'm sure you'd like that better, wouldn't you? You do want to go home, home to that little sister who needs you, and your twin brother and your parents, who I am sure miss you."

"Well, where are they then?" I asked. "Why don't they come to see me?"

My question startled him.

"In your case, it is not advisable just yet. Too much too soon, as I said, could cause you to have a breakdown and do what I just described: drive your past even farther away."

"Why?"

He hesitated.

"I'm not sure it's wise to tell you that just yet."

"I have to know. Why?" I insisted.

"Very well. It's because what happened to you is something you blame yourself for. You are the way you are because of guilt," he explained.

"So then, whatever happened was my fault? What did I do that was so terrible?"

"Maybe nothing," he said, "or maybe something that contributed to a tragedy," he continued. "You have to proceed in steps. First, gradually return to yourself and then deal with the guilt. Okay?"

"No. It's not okay. Why doesn't my family come to see me?" I exclaimed.

"There are frequent reports," he said.

"Reports? I would never be satisfied with only reports. Did I do something that hurt them? Is that why I suffer this guilt?"

"You know it's better if you make your own discoveries," he said rather dryly.

I thought for a moment. Could it be that my parents weren't any better than Lawrence's or Megan's?

"No, I don't want to wait anymore. I want to know everything, and now," I said.

"Miss Logan—"

"And I want to see Doctor Southerby. I have to see him. I have to tell him what's happened. He can help me. I know

270

he can help me. Please." I started to cry, my sobs growing stronger, longer with every passing second.

"Miss Logan, get hold of yourself."

"WHY . . . DON'T MY PARENTS . . . COME TO SEE ME?" I screamed.

He pushed a button on his desk and then he rose. The office door opened and Mrs. Kleckner and a male attendant came rushing in. The look in the attendant's eyes frightened me.

"We're acting out again," Doctor Scanlon announced, as though he and I were conspirators. "I think it would be better for now if she went upstairs."

"Upstairs?" I said, looking at them. "NO!"

I leaped up and stepped away from them, shaking my head.

"Easy," the attendant said, moving slowly toward me. "My name is Arnie. Don't worry, I'll take good care of you."

"I'm not going to the Tower!"

"Whoever gave that floor that ridiculous name?" Doctor Scanlon asked Mrs. Kleckner.

"One of our patients, I'm sure, Doctor." She turned to me. "Now, don't make this any harder on yourself than it has to be. You have to do what the doctor says. Come along," she said.

I shook my head.

"Please, I'll be good. I swear I'll be good. I'll go back to my room. I won't complain. I won't ask for Doctor Southerby anymore. Leave me alone. Please," I pleaded.

"Now, now, don't be afraid," Doctor Scanlon said. "We're here to help you, Laura. We won't let anything bad happen to you. You know, you have a grandmother, too, and she would be even more upset than your parents if we did anything to harm you," he added with a cold smile.

"My grandmother?"

Flashes of an older woman standing outside a car, looking in at me, shaking her head with disgust, returned. She had sent me here and I couldn't recall any expression of love in her angry face. What had I done to displease my whole family?

"NO!" I cried. "Stay away from me. Leave me alone." I held my hands out.

Arnie came around behind me and swiftly brought my arms down to my sides. I had little strength to fight him and soon he held me tightly in his grasp. Doctor Scanlon rushed around the desk and Mrs. Kleckner pulled up the sleeve on my blouse. I struggled and squirmed, but Arnie was too strong. Doctor Scanlon poked me with a syringe.

"You're going to be fine. Everything will be all right," he murmured. "Take it easy. Relax. That's it."

"My head," I moaned, "feels so heavy. It's felt so heavy all morning."

"That's right. Close your eyes. Get a wheelchair," he ordered.

Moments later, I felt myself being lowered into a wheelchair and then a strap was pulled tightly around my waist. Arnie's strong hand kept my shoulders back when I tried to sit forward.

"Just take it easy," Mrs. Kleckner said.

"Put her in three-oh-seven," Doctor Scanlon said.

As they began to wheel me away, I had barely enough strength to utter one last request.

"I want . . . Doctor Southerby. He can help me. I want to see him."

"I want, I want, I want," Mrs. Kleckner chanted behind me. "That's all you patients ever say."

Arnie laughed. I heard an elevator door open and opened my eyes as they wheeled me in. The door closed. Mrs. Kleckner smiled down at me.

"I knew this one belonged upstairs," she said.

And then, all went black.

15

∞

I Remember You

When I opened my eyes again, I thought I was still asleep, still dreaming. I felt like I was floating, hovering just above my bed, looking down at the empty shell of my body. My surroundings were white and sterile, more like an examination room. The walls were bare and the small windows had their dark gray curtains drawn closed so tightly they looked sewn together. The door of the room was slightly ajar and through the crack between it and the jamb came the only light, a dull, yellowish glow.

My bed smelled strongly of starch. The sheet was stiff and tucked tightly around me. Because my pillow was so soft, my head was barely raised. When I turned to look around the room, I saw there was a table with a long top drawer and a counter of some imitation wood beside the bed. On it was an ivory-white bedpan and a metal bowl with a washcloth draped over the edge.

When I tried to sit up, I was shocked to discover I was strapped down, thick belts of leather across the top of my body, just under my breasts, my arms tucked against my sides, and another belt across my legs. I could barely move.

It put a hot ball of panic in my stomach that rolled from side to side.

"Help me!" I cried. "Someone, please."

I waited, but heard nothing, no footsteps, no voices, nothing. I cried out again, waited, and cried out once more. The silence was maddening. Wasn't there anyone else here? My struggle against the straps was futile, even painful. I sighed deeply and gave up, closing my eyes and whimpering softly.

I must have fallen asleep again, because when I opened my eyes, I heard water running in the sink. There was someone in my bathroom.

"Who's there?" I called.

Moments later a tall, thin woman with rust-color hair stepped out. I could see her shoulder bones outlined against her white uniform. She had long arms with jutting wrist bones and very long hands, hands that looked strong and capable. When she circled the bed and came around on my right, I could see her face more clearly.

She looked half asleep herself, her eyelids drooping so that there were barely two slits revealing small hazel pupils. She had a long thin nose and a very wide mouth above a cleft chin. She reminded me of Mary Beth and I wondered if she were suffering from anorexia, too. If so, why wasn't she a patient instead of an employee?

She didn't seem impressed with the fact that I was awake. She moved about the room as if she had been taking care of me for weeks and weeks. It made me wonder just how long I had been here. Without greeting me, in fact barely looking at me, she placed the basin of water on the table and pulled back the sheet to undo the straps.

"You have to sit up. I'm going to wash you down a bit," she mumbled. Her voice was so deep it sounded almost manly. This close to me, I could see tiny black hairs curled at the side of her chin. "And then I'll give you something to eat," she said.

As she spoke, she avoided looking directly at me.

"What happened to me?" I asked. "Why was I strapped into bed?"

She paused and finally glanced at me.

"I don't know," she said and continued undoing the straps. "Can you sit up by yourself?" she asked.

"Where am I? Who are you?"

"My name is Clare. You're in room three-oh-seven," she said. "Can you sit up please."

I thought hard and vaguely recalled the events that led to my being brought upstairs.

"I need to see Doctor Southerby," I said. "Can you tell him Laura Logan needs to see him as soon as possible? It's very important."

"I'm just a nurse's aide," she said. "I don't tell anyone anything."

She began to wash my right hand and my arm with as much interest as she would have in washing a dirty dish.

"I can do that myself," I said, anger rushing in to replace fear. "Why was I strapped down in bed? Why can't I get up and walk around? Can't I just take a shower or a bath?"

She kept washing and rinsing as if I hadn't said a word. My anger began to simmer my blood into a rolling boil.

"Can't you tell me anything?" I demanded as forcefully as I could.

She paused.

"I have some meat loaf, mashed potatoes, peas and carrots, some bread, apple juice, and strawberry Jell-O."

"What?"

"That's your supper," she said. "That's all I can tell you. That's all I know."

She started on my other hand and arm. I pulled it back abruptly.

"I said I can wash myself."

She held the cloth a moment and then shrugged.

"Here. Do it. I'll get your food," she said and dropped the cloth in my hand before turning and walking out of the room. I put the cloth on my face and took a deep breath.

I have to get out of here, I thought. I have to find Doctor Southerby and get out of here. I put my legs over the bed and stood. My whole body swayed like the pendulum in a grandfather's clock. Nevertheless, I turned to the closet, hoping to find my clothes. At the moment, I was wearing a loose hospital gown and was barefoot. The tile floor felt like ice beneath my feet. Taking a deep breath, I stepped away from the bed and walked to the closet. However, when I opened the door, I looked in at empty hangers. There were no clothes, no shoes, nothing but a layer of fine dust.

"What are you doing out of bed? Get back in, quick, or I'll get fired," the tall woman cried. She had my tray of food in her hands and moved across the room to the table quickly. As I turned, she took hold of my arm to help me back. The room spun around me.

"Why am I so dizzy? What did they give me? My legs feel like rubber."

"I don't know anything about medicines. Just get into the bed."

"Why don't you know anything if you work here? Where's the doctor? I need to talk to someone who knows something," I moaned.

She practically lifted me onto the bed, tucking the blanket around me. My head fell back against the pillow.

"I'll crank the bed up for you," she said and pushed a button that raised my head and upper torso until I was nearly in a seated position. Then she moved the tray table so the food was in front of me. "Can you feed yourself, or do you want me to feed you?"

"I can eat by myself," I said. "I can do everything for myself if you people will just let me."

"Good. I got two other patients on this floor and neither can do much for themselves. They can't even wipe their own noses most of the time and they're not much older than you."

She started away from the bed and then stopped and returned to fasten the straps over my legs.

"Please, can't you leave them undone?" I asked.

"You might fall out and then I'll get fired," she said.

"Why do you work here if they'll fire you for anything that happens?" I asked.

She finally smiled.

"It's a good job. They pay me more than I can make most anywhere else, and there's just me and my mother now. She's too old to do anything for herself and she doesn't get much social security."

"How long have I been here? You can tell me that at least," I said.

She shrugged.

"Not more than a day, because I would have seen you before," she said.

We heard the sound of footsteps in the hall.

"Uh-oh," she said, her face whitening with fear. "That's Doctor Scanlon making his rounds along with Mrs. Roundchild. She cracks the whip here."

A woman of about forty with hair the color of pencil lead turned into the doorway, a step ahead of Doctor Scanlon. She had gray eyes and a narrow face with a strong, full mouth and a nose so straight it could be used as a ruler. She wore a dark blue cardigan sweater with pearl buttons over her uniform. I thought she had a nicely shaped figure and a rich complexion. However, all that was feminine and soft about her body was negated by the firmness in her lips and the piercing chill in her eyes.

"What are you doing?" she asked Clare.

"I was just on my way to three-oh-four. I got her settled with her dinner and—"

"Well then, get on with it. See to the others. They can't complain for themselves, you know." Her words were sharply pronounced with an English accent.

"Yes, Mrs. Roundchild."

"Wait. Why is that closet door open?" she demanded, nodding at it.

"Closet door? Oh." Clare looked at me, her eyes frantic. She reminded me of some small creature looking for a way to escape.

"I was trying to find my clothes," I said. "I want to go back downstairs, Doctor Scanlon," I explained, turning my attention to him.

"You will," he said. "Soon."

Mrs. Roundchild spun on Clare.

"You let her get off the bed and open the closet?"

"When I went to get her food, she did it herself," Clare said.

"You undid the straps and left the room?" Mrs. Roundchild practically lunged at Clare.

"She wanted to wash herself, so I thought to save time, I would go get her food and—"

"That's a demerit, Miss Carson. It will go on your record. You know all about our liabilities here and you've been told what to do and what not to do. It clearly states on the door that this patient does not have off-bed privileges at the moment."

"I know, but—"

"There are no buts when it comes to regulations. You've been here long enough to know that."

"It's not her fault," I said. "I insisted I wash myself."

Mrs. Roundchild considered me.

"It's admirable that you want to take the blame, but it's not honest now, is it?"

"Yes it is," I said.

"Are you a liar?"

"What? No, I just . . . it *was* my fault. I told her I would wash myself."

"She knows she's supposed to be in charge, not you. Why are you still standing here, Clare?" She swung around to look at the meek woman paused in the doorway.

"I'm sorry," Clare whined and hurried out.

Doctor Scanlon approached the bed with Mrs. Roundchild right beside him.

"That's good, you're eating," he said, nodding at my food. I hadn't touched a morsel.

"I'm not hungry," I said. "Doctor Scanlon, why can't I go back downstairs? Why am I being kept here?"

"You have to remain under strict observation for a while, Laura. Here, you can get more personal treatment," he added and glanced at Mrs. Roundchild.

"I don't need more personal treatment. I was doing fine until you wanted to start giving me some drug," I complained.

"First, it's not just some drug, Laura. I'm giving you something that's designed to keep you from being too anxious and having a bad reaction to your returning memories," he explained calmly. "Second, I really don't think you're in a position to know what's best for you."

He glanced at Mrs. Roundchild, who looked like she disapproved of his taking the time to defend his decision.

"I want my clothes," I moaned. "And I don't want to be strapped into bed like this."

"The medications I'm giving you can have some side effects, Laura. They can disorient you sometimes. This is just to protect you."

"I feel like a prisoner," I cried, the tears gathering under my lids and making my eyes watery and my vision hazy.

"You're not a prisoner. You're a patient, and we're here to help you get better. Mrs. Roundchild is one of the two specially trained head nurses who run this floor. I have the greatest confidence in her. She will see to all your needs."

"What's happening to me?"

"I feel you are on the verge of a complete recouping of the past with a minimum of selective amnesia. My sense of this is you could at any time remember the trauma and when that happens," he continued, "it will be like being hit by a freight train. Believe me. I've seen situations similar to yours many, many times."

His words frightened me. I settled back, my tension and resistance melting away. I saw that pleased him. He looked at Mrs. Roundchild and she stepped forward, reaching down to bring up a button attached to a plastic wire.

"If you need any assistance, you press this and someone will come in due time, but don't think they will fall out of the ceiling. We're understaffed here and people are always

busy. Have patience," she warned, "and we'll do our best to
see to it that you are comfortable and safe."

"Can't I at least have my arms free? I'd like to get a drink
of water for myself or scratch myself when I itch," I said.

"I think that will be okay as long as you promise not to
undo the strap around your legs. That will guarantee you
won't fall out of the bed," Doctor Scanlon said. "What do
you think, Mrs. Roundchild?"

"I'd like to keep the top strap around her waist as well. At
least until she's stronger," she added.

"Fine. All right, Laura?"

I nodded. What else could I do?

"If you undo them," Mrs. Roundchild threatened, "we'll
have to restrain your arms again."

Doctor Scanlon took my pulse and then checked a chart
dangling from the end of the bed. While he did so, Mrs.
Roundchild tightened the straps securely.

"Let's remain with this current pharmaceutical proto-
col," he told Mrs. Roundchild.

"Very good, Doctor," she said. She looked as though she
were going to salute as well.

He turned back to me.

"I'm going to let you rest now, but Mrs. Roundchild will
keep a close eye on your condition. If there are any dramatic
changes, she'll inform me immediately and I'll be here as
soon as I can," he promised.

"Does Doctor Southerby at least know what's happened
to me?" I asked softly. He didn't like the question and
hardened his mouth, turning his eyes to granite as well.

"Doctor Southerby knows you are now under my direct
care. He has no concerns," he replied sharply. "Just so
you'll know," he added after a moment, "Doctor Southerby
interned under me. He thinks of me as his mentor. Do you
know what that means, mentor?"

"Yes," I said. "You were his teacher."

"More than that. Doctor Scanlon was his idol," Mrs.
Roundchild corrected. "And rightly so," she finished. Doctor Scanlon smiled at her and the two of them left my room.

I gazed down at my food, my appetite still gone. Nevertheless, I nibbled on some of the cold meat loaf, drank some juice, and lay back. A little over an hour later, Clare returned for the tray.

"I'm sorry I got you into trouble," I said.

"I got myself into trouble," she replied, took the tray and left without a word.

Fifteen minutes later, I had to use the bedpan. I pushed the buzzer for it to be taken away, but no one appeared for more than a half hour. Finally, Mrs. Roundchild came with Clare right behind her.

"Empty that," she told her, nodding at the bedpan. Then she handed me a cup with two pills in it, and gave me a glass of water. "Your medication," she said firmly.

"Will it make me tired? I'm still so weak and tired from before," I complained.

"Your medication," she repeated, holding it out. "Doctor Scanlon wouldn't prescribe it if it wasn't necessary, Laura. I'm sorry to have to be so firm with you, but it's an awesome responsibility to care for people who can't care for themselves."

I plucked the pills out of the cup and put them in my mouth while she hovered over me, watching me swallow the water and the pills. She nodded.

"Good," she said. Clare returned the bedpan to the table and they left me.

Never did I feel more alone. Strapped down, in a barren room with no one to talk to, nothing to look at, not even anything to read, I did truly feel more like a criminal than a patient. It was as if I were being punished, not helped. I listened hard, but the sounds that I heard from the corridor were few and meaningless. There were no voices and little movement. If they were so understaffed, why wasn't there more going on?

I had to close my eyes. The pills are working, I thought. They're making my eyelids heavy again. In moments I was asleep, and soon after, I was dreaming. Wonderful, familiar faces began to reappear, rising out of the darkness. My mother was smiling at me and my father was looking at me with love in his eyes. A little hand reached for me. It was May and she was afraid. My brother stepped up beside her. His name seemed to be closer, my tongue struggling to form it.

"Come home, Laura," he said. "Please, come home."

"Laura," my mother called. "Laura, come home."

"We need you back here, Laura," my father said.

May was signing and crying.

I struggled, twisted, and pulled against the straps in my sleep so violently, that I woke myself in the middle of the night. My skin burned where I had chaffed my waist and my legs. I groaned and cried out. The door to my room was nearly closed completely, so that most of the dim light from the corridor was gone. I was alone in the dark.

I closed my eyes again, drifting off. This time I immediately felt a wave of cold ocean water wash over me. I gasped. There was a hand reaching up and the top of a head emerging from the water. I struggled to get a grip on that hand and then . . . I really felt something in my hand and my eyes snapped open.

"Shh," I heard, and turned to see Lawrence kneeling by the bed.

"Lawrence? What are you doing here?"

"Don't talk too loud," he said. "I snuck up to see you. We heard what happened to you and I tried to get information all day, but no one knew or would say a thing. Mary Beth and Lulu send their love."

"How did you get up here?"

I sat up until the strap cut into my waist.

"There's another stairway that's used to bring up supplies mainly. It's right near here. I didn't know what room you were in, of course. I checked two others before finding you. The chart on your door says that they don't want you to be disturbed. Has something terrible happened to you, Laura? Have you remembered something horrible? Is that why they brought you up here?"

I told him what had happened with Doctor Scanlon and what he wanted done with me and why.

"I don't see why that meant you had to be brought up here," Lawrence commented.

"Neither do I. I want to go back downstairs, be with people, move about on my own."

"Did you tell him that?"

"Yes, but he keeps saying they're doing this to protect me, to ensure that I don't hurt myself."

"I don't know why they can't protect you downstairs just as well," Lawrence said. I nodded.

"Anyway, at least I know where you are now. I'll come up to see you as much as I can, but it will have to be at night. If I get caught, they'll lock me up someplace, too, or ship me away like Megan."

"I can't believe you got up here. You know everything about this clinic," I said. He was barely visible in the dim light from the hallway, but I saw him smile.

"I've been here long enough to know every corner of the place," he said. "Are you going to be all right?"

"I'm scared, Lawrence," I said, holding on to his hand. "I don't want to be here, but I'm frightened of putting up too much of a fight. What if Doctor Scanlon's right? He's the head doctor, isn't he? They said even Doctor Southerby learned from him."

"I don't know, but I don't want you to be frightened, Laura," Lawrence said softly. He rose and brought himself closer to me. I knew what courage it took for him to come up to see me, how much of his own problem he had to have overcome.

"Thank you for coming up here, Lawrence. I want you to know that it means a lot to me that you snuck up to see me."

"I couldn't sleep, thinking about you and worrying about you," he said.

We heard footsteps in the hallway.

"Someone's coming," I whispered and watched frantically as he crawled underneath my bed.

Moments later, the door opened and Mrs. Roundchild

stood silhouetted in the hallway light. She stared in at me. I closed my eyes and waited, praying she wouldn't come in. She stood there for the longest time and then she left, closing the door behind her. Neither Lawrence nor I spoke or moved until we heard her footsteps die away. Finally he got to his feet.

"That was close," I said. "You'd better go."

"All right."

I started to sob. I didn't want him to go. I felt more secure, more at ease with him holding my hand. He leaned toward me again and I touched his face. His lips drew closer and closer until they met mine. It wasn't so much of a kiss as it was a brush of lips and a sigh.

"I wish I could stay here with you all night," he whispered. "I wish I could put my arms around you and hold you and protect you from your own fearful thoughts. When I'm with you like this, I don't think about myself and I don't get panicked, Laura. I need to be with you as much for myself as for you," he admitted. "We're good for each other, Laura."

"I don't think I'm good for much right now, Lawrence. I'm no better than an invalid. I can't even get off the bed to go to the bathroom."

"You'll get better and I'll get better. You'll see," he promised.

"You've been so nice to me, Lawrence. I'm glad we got to know each other," I said.

"I hope we can get to love each other," he followed quickly. I think the darkness made him brave. It brought a smile to my face.

He held his face close to mine for another moment and then he kissed me again, only this time, he held his lips to mine longer and made it into a real kiss.

I moaned softly, desperate for a loving touch, for affection.

He kissed me again, moving his lips over my cheeks and back to my lips. Then he kissed my forehead and held me.

"Robert," I said softly, my cheek against his chest.

"What did you say?" He pulled back. I opened my eyes.

"What's wrong?" I asked quietly.

"I thought you called me by another name just now. I thought you said Robert."

Neither of us moved a muscle.

I searched my thoughts and waited, but it was as if a dark cloud had suddenly appeared, shutting away the light and enveloping me in darkness once again.

"I don't know," I said, frustrated. "I don't understand." I started to cry. "You see, Doctor Scanlon is right. I am disturbed, too confused to be on my own."

"Don't, Laura. Please." He kissed away a tear.

We heard the sound of a cart being wheeled in the hallway and we waited until it passed my room.

"You'd better go," I whispered.

"I'll be back tomorrow night," he promised. He kissed me again. "Good night, Laura."

"Good night," I said. He held my hand until he started away and had to let go. I watched him walk to the door and peer out. Then he was gone.

Moments afterward, alone in the dark and quiet room with only my thoughts for companionship, I had to wonder. Had I dreamed Lawrence's visit or had he really been here?

In the morning, I realized I must have cried most of the night in my sleep because my pillow was soaked with my tears. I knew my dreams were full of sadness, but I couldn't remember the details of a single one. It was as if everything had been written in the sand and as soon as I woke, the ocean came up and washed out each and every word, carrying them back to the depths of the sea. There was nothing to do but start all over.

A different nurse's aide brought me my breakfast. She was just as closemouthed as Clare and seemed even more afraid of doing anything wrong. All I learned about her was her first name, Della. She was a heavy black girl with very pretty ebony eyes. She wore her hair very short, which made her look even chubbier than she was, I thought. She emptied the bedpan, gave me fresh water, and helped me wash.

"When can I take a bath or a shower? These sponge baths aren't enough."

"I don't know," she said. "You have to ask the nurse."

Just like Clare, Della avoided looking at me most of the time she was in my room. It made me feel as though I were ugly, a hideous creature that no one could bare to look at.

Doctor Scanlon finally appeared late in the afternoon. He gazed at my chart and then pulled a chair up beside the bed.

"I see that you had a restful twenty-four hours. That's good," he commented.

"Restful? I woke with a soaked pillow and my arms and legs are chaffed from all the tossing and turning I did against these straps. Please take them off. Please," I begged.

He considered.

"All right. I'll trust you to watch yourself." He scribbled something on his pad. "Now, tell me about your memories. How are we doing on that score?"

I described my visions, the ones I could remember. He seemed to tiptoe gently about the descriptions I gave him of the ocean, the waves, the hand coming up.

"Your memory is returning, Laura. We're handling this right. I'm more convinced than ever. Continue to cooperate, take your medication, and let your mind feel at ease enough to permit the past to seep back into your consciousness slowly. It won't be long before you walk out of here," he promised.

"However, with the trauma threatening to make itself heard dramatically and completely, I'd like to increase your medication a bit. Just to play it safe," he added and made another note. "Okay?"

"Okay," I said and he gave me the phoniest smile he had given me yet.

"To reward you for your cooperation, I'm leaving instructions for you to be taken on a short walk through the halls so you get some exercise. How's that?"

"I'd like that," I said. At this point, I thought, I'd like anything that resembled or suggested a normal life.

"We'll do it before it's time for your next dosage of medicine so you can be a little more alert."

He rose.

"We're in control of your problems rather than permitting them to be in control of you, and as long as we keep it that way, we're on the right track," he concluded.

Clare returned at the start of the late afternoon shift and announced that she had been instructed to take me for a short walk. For that purpose, I was given a light blue cotton robe and a pair of cotton slippers. She undid my restraints and helped me put on the robe and slippers.

"Maybe this will help your appetite, too," she commented, noticing how much food I had left over from lunch. Then she bit her lip as if she had said something blasphemous.

"I hope so," I said. "It's not because the food is terrible. I'm just not hungry," I added quickly, imagining the same people prepared the food for the Tower floor.

She helped me to my feet. I was shaky at first, but as I took one step and then another, my blood began to circulate and I felt stronger. We left the room and paused in the corridor.

It was very different up on this floor. The hallway was just as immaculate, but there were no paintings, no chairs, and the windows were covered with heavy drapes that blocked out all signs of the sun. I noticed also that there were very few rooms at the far end of the hall. Instead, there was a glass double door through which I saw Mrs. Roundchild talking with another nurse. To my right was a sharp turn in the corridor.

"What's around that way?" I asked.

"At the very end of this corridor is the Zombie Ward," Clare said.

"Zombie Ward?"

"The patients in there don't talk except to scream or cry. Many of them just sit or stand for hours staring at nothing, shaking their arms or their heads madly. They've got to be fed and washed all the time. There are young people in there who took too many drugs and burned out their brains," she added.

"How horrible."

"You're lucky compared to them," she said.

We walked in that direction. After a while, Clare lessened her hold on me and I took stronger steps. When we made the turn, I looked down the hallway and saw there were glass doors there, too. I could make out some patients sitting in chairs and a couple of young women standing.

"I'm not supposed to take you that far," Clare said, nodding toward the glass doors. I kept walking in that direction anyway. "You got to turn back now, Laura," she said.

Suddenly, from a room on our right, we heard a loud crash, the sound of a bedpan slamming to the floor and then a shrill scream.

"Oh no, it's that Sara Richards again. Just wait here," she ordered, and went into the room. I continued to walk toward the doors.

As I drew closer, I thought I saw a familiar face. It intrigued me and I sped up until I was only a few feet from the doorway and could look through the windows. There, standing with her wrists all wrapped in bandages and staring at the doorway, was Megan. Her mouth was open, drool seeping out and down the sides. Her eyes were wide but vacant.

"Megan?" I whispered.

Clare came up beside me quickly and grabbed my elbow. "You can't be down here. Come on, let's go back, Laura."

"But that's a friend of mine from downstairs, Megan Paxton. I thought she was being moved to some other hospital. What happened to her? She looks terrible."

"I don't know, but if she's in there, it wasn't good. Please, let's get back before Mrs. Roundchild catches us and gives me double demerits. When you reach ten, they fire you. Come on, Laura," she urged and turned me.

I looked back as we walked.

Megan seemed to recognize me. She lifted her arms and held them up and then, I thought she screamed. I couldn't hear anything. Maybe she wasn't making any sounds, but she was trying to scream. A nurse moved to her quickly and directed her into a room and she was gone.

"Megan," I murmured.

"You have to get back into your bed now," Clare said as we rounded the turn and headed toward my room.

Mrs. Roundchild was gazing our way suspiciously.

"Poor Megan," I said.

And then I wondered, could that happen to me? Would I end up on the Zombie Ward, too? Maybe no one gets better here. Maybe they all just end up locked away in the Zombie Ward. Or worse.

"Time for your medicine," Mrs. Roundchild said, bursting into the room moments after Clare had helped me into bed. She thrust the cup of pills at me.

"I don't need them. I want to try to sleep tonight without them," I said.

"You have to take your medication. Besides, you told Doctor Scanlon you would. Why are you being obstinate now?"

"I'm afraid," I said. "Too many drugs might burn out my mind."

"That's ridiculous. Who told you such a thing?" She turned to Clare, who was hurrying to clean up the bathroom and leave.

"No one told me," I said. "I'm just afraid."

"I'll stand here all night if necessary until you take your medication. And if you don't, we'll have an I.V. hooked to your arm and we'll feed them to you intravenously," she warned.

"But they make me so groggy. I'm already exhausted just from that little walk," I moaned.

She held out the pills, her expression unchanging and unsympathetic.

"Are you going to take these pills voluntarily?" she finally asked.

Reluctantly, I took them from her. She watched me wash them down, her hands on her hips, her eyes beady.

"Strap her in," she said.

"But Doctor Scanlon said I don't need to be strapped in. He promised," I cried.

"As head nurse I have to make decisions on the spur of the moment if necessary. You just said the walking made you tired. I don't think you'll be safe tonight without being strapped in," she said.

"Look at my legs, how red they are," I said.

"That's nothing compared to what could happen if you fall on your face. Strap her in," she commanded.

Clare moved quickly to obey her.

"I want to see Doctor Scanlon," I demanded.

"He'll be here tomorrow at his usual hour."

"I want to see him now!"

"Don't raise your voice to me, young lady. Your grandmother might be paying for your treatments and making big donations, but you're still a guest of this clinic. We don't take just anyone—no matter who they are," she said and marched out of my room.

Clare gave me a look of sympathy and then quickly followed after her.

"I want to see the doctor!" I shouted at the nearly closed door.

No one returned or responded.

Soon, the pills began to take effect again. My eyes drooped and I felt weaker. It was futile to struggle against them. Sleep and remember, I thought. Sleep and remember who you are and then you will be free.

Vaguely, I thought about something Mrs. Roundchild had said . . . something about my grandmother. What did all that mean? That was my last conscious thought.

I knew the dosage Mrs. Roundchild had given me was considerably greater, as Doctor Scanlon had promised, because I didn't wake during the night. Lawrence had been in my room, too. I knew because when I woke, I found a tissue in my hand with the words *"I love you. Guess who—"* scribbled on it. It made me smile, but also put fear in my heart because I was afraid someone would find it. I quickly crumbled the tissue into a ball and put it in my bedpan. No one would want to look at it now, I thought.

Doctor Scanlon didn't come to see me the entire day. I kept asking about him, but as usual, neither nurse's aide knew anything and Mrs. Roundchild simply said, "He'll be here when he'll be here."

The only thing I could count on regularly was my medication. They had me taking it twice now, once in the morning, once at night. The night dosage affected me just the way it had the night before. Soon after I took it, I was asleep, but this time, my dream woke me, or at least I thought I woke.

Once again, I saw a hand come out of the ocean and then a head began to rise to the surface. When I saw his eyes, I started to scream. He was sinking again and I was struggling to reach him. I heard his voice. I heard him say, "Help me, Laura. Help me. I want to be with you always. Help me. Come to me."

I felt his lips on my face and reached out to embrace him and cradled his head against my breast where he could fall asleep safely. Just before morning, I woke with a start. I wasn't imagining it now. I did feel something against my breast and turned to see Lawrence, his head resting on me, his body curled up beside me.

"Lawrence," I cried. His eyes fluttered. "When did you come? I don't remember."

"I was here, Laura. I've been here for hours and hours."

"They're giving me more medicine, Lawrence. It makes me so tired. I'm afraid not to take it, I'm afraid of what might happen to me. Lawrence," I said, seizing his hand, "Megan, Megan wasn't transferred to another hospital. She's here. She's in what they call the Zombie Ward. I saw her. She looks terrible."

"Zombie Ward? I know about that place. She's really that bad?"

"I almost didn't recognize her. She looked so wild she frightened me. Oh, Lawrence," I moaned, "what if that happens to me? What if the medicine and my dreams drive me mad? Don't let them put me in that place."

He shook his head sharply.

"Never. I'll never let them lock you away in there."

"If only I remembered everything they would let me go," I said with a small sob.

"I think it's happening, Laura. I heard you cry out in your sleep for someone, someone you were losing. That must be your traumatic experience, the event that caused your illness," he said.

"You did? Who was it? Did I say a name?"

He hesitated.

"I'm afraid to tell you. After what you just told me, I'm afraid of doing something wrong," he said.

"You've got to tell me. I can't stand this emptiness, this darkness. Please. Whom did I cry for?"

"It was the same name I heard you say before."

I thought a moment.

"I can't remember what I said before, Lawrence. The medicine that they're giving me has already turned my mind into a glob of mush. Whose name did I call out?" I repeated more firmly. "You must tell me, Lawrence. I don't want to end up like Megan. Please."

"Someone named Robert," he replied.

The sound of his name took my breath away. I stared at Lawrence.

"I think it was someone you cared for very much," he said sadly.

"Yes. Yes," I said, seeing the darkness begin to retreat and the light begin to slip in from behind the cloud of my memory. "He was. He is."

And I knew that today, today I would remember everything. I was filled with mixed emotions, anxious, terrified, and yet hopeful it would mean the end of my ordeal. Finally I would be free.

16

❧

Reunited

"*I* hate to leave you," Lawrence said.

Through the slight opening in my window curtain, we could see the dawn beginning. The light that cleared away the darkness gave me hope that something similar would happen to the darkness in me as well.

"You have to go, Lawrence. I'll be all right now," I said, smiling. "I will. Somehow," I said, my eyes shifting as I gazed ahead, "I know I will."

"I wish they wouldn't give you so much medicine. It doesn't seem right," he worried aloud. He leaned over and kissed me softly on my forehead and then smiled. "I'll see you later," he promised, squeezing my hand and walking toward the door. He paused to check the hallway and in moments, he was gone.

"Robert," I whispered in the silence that followed. It was as if my lips were trying on the word to see if it fit. "Robert."

I closed my eyes and a series of pictures rolled maddeningly by. I concentrated, slowing them down until I saw my family clearly, heard their voices clearly, the sounds of their laughter, their chatter at dinner, Daddy reading from the

Bible, and then—Cary. His name emerged in a bubble rising out of the confusion, and with his name came a litany of his words: his compliments and his complaints, his warnings and his hopes.

A small sailboat bobbed on the surface of a pond. I understood it to be one of Cary's models. I had memories of him working hard on them, hunched over his table with his soldering gun and his glues, his fingers turning and fitting the miniature parts into their tiny places. I realized I was remembering his workroom. With each memory, each vivid picture, my home was returning. I saw my own room, my stuffed animals, my beautiful, beautiful bed. I saw Mommy in the kitchen making a delicious clam chowder. I saw Daddy sitting in his favorite chair reading the newspaper and mumbling over some event. May was at his feet putting a puzzle together, waiting for me to help her with her homework. They were all waiting for me to come home, to come back.

I saw myself running up to the front door and tugging on the door knob when it didn't turn. The door wouldn't open. Why was it locked? I pounded and called.

"MOMMY! DADDY! CARY!"

No one came to the door. I turned and looked around desperately, but instead of seeing my front yard, I saw the sailboat, only now it began to grow larger. The pond became the ocean. Someone was in the boat, steering it toward shore. He was calling to me, beckoning. The boat drew closer and closer until I saw him vividly, my Robert.

"Laura," he was calling. "Come back. Laura . . ."

Now I was running down the beach toward the boat, but the more I ran, the farther away it became. I ran harder and began to call to him. I seemed to run over the same sand repeatedly, never making any progress as he continued to call and to beckon.

"What's wrong with you?" I heard someone ask and instantly all my memories evaporated. Mrs. Roundchild stood by the side of my bed with my medication in hand, gazing down at me. "Why are you crying?"

"I . . . can remember lots of things now. I remember my family and my home," I said. "And I remember Robert and a boat and—"

"That's good. Here," she said, "take your medicine. Clare's bringing your breakfast."

"Maybe I shouldn't take any more medicine now," I said. "Now that I'm really remembering things, maybe it's better I have a clear mind."

"Why is it everyone wants to be a doctor here?" she asked, almost with a smile. "I'm sorry, but you have to spend a little time in medical school first."

"I'm not trying to be a doctor, but it just feels right that I shouldn't take anything."

"Really? Well, up until now, has Doctor Scanlon been wrong? Haven't you begun to remember things and do it in a fashion where you don't hurt yourself or get mentally incapacitated? Isn't that true?"

"Yes," I said. "I suppose."

"You suppose? Well, I know. I've been a head nurse on this floor for nearly five years now and I've seen many, many different kinds of illness, a number of cases similar to your own. I've seen Doctor Scanlon treat them successfully, too. So, I don't have to suppose," she said.

Tears filled my eyes once more.

"I just want to go home," I said.

"You will if you do what you're told." She paused for a moment, her expression softening. "I don't mean to be cruel to you, Laura, but I must be firm. I have an awesome job here. I am responsible for a number of people who are not able to be responsible for themselves. Many of these people have and will continue to hurt themselves if I don't follow doctor's orders in regards to them. There is a lot to do and little time to do it. Everyone needs specialized, personal treatment. It makes it hard to waste time, do you understand?"

"Yes," I said in a small voice.

"Good. Then take your medicine. Doctor Scanlon will be here to evaluate you and your progress and we'll see what he wants to do after that."

With trembling fingers, I plucked the pills out of the cup and put them in my mouth. She handed me the glass of water and I swallowed them down.

"Very good," she said. "Your breakfast is on its way."

She left the room and moments later, Clare arrived with my tray. She raised my bed and moved the table over me.

"I'm getting better," I told her. "I'm remembering things quickly now. I'll be able to go home."

"That's nice. I'd like to have less to do," she said. She paused. "But whenever someone leaves the floor or gets moved to the Zombie Ward, there's always someone else to take their place. I heard they have a waiting list as long as my arm," she added.

"Can you find out about a patient for me? Can you find out about Megan Paxton?"

"They don't like me asking about patients. If anyone working here is caught talking about the patients, they could be fired instantly," she said. "I gotta get breakfast to the others," she added before I could plead with her any more. She quickly left the room.

I sighed with disappointment and frustration and began to pick at my breakfast. I ate what I could, then closed my eyes, and dozed off. When I woke, my bed had been lowered and my tray taken away. I stared at the white ceiling.

Robert's face began to form on the white background. It looked like he was emerging from a cloud. I saw his soft eyes and gentle smile. Strands of his light brown hair fell over his forehead. He was laughing and then suddenly, the white background began to whirl around him. His head started to spin along with it and the white ceiling turned into water. His arm emerged, his hand reaching out for me.

"Laura . . ."

I screamed.

Maybe I fainted. Maybe I fell back to sleep. I don't know,

but when I woke this time, Doctor Scanlon was seated beside the bed. He had just taken my pulse and was making some notes on his pad. He looked very calm, so calm that I couldn't imagine he heard me scream.

Suddenly, I noticed there were two younger men in doctor's hospital coats standing at the foot of the bed looking at me. Both carried clipboards. One had dark brown hair and wore glasses; the other had longer, light brown hair and light blue eyes. He was taller and wider.

"Hello, Laura," Doctor Scanlon said. "This is Doctor Fernhoff and Doctor Bloom. They're both interns, studying with me. From time to time, they'll each look in on you, too. So," he continued, "Mrs. Roundchild tells me you've remembered a lot more about your family and your home. Is that so?"

I nodded.

"Good. Now, let's talk a bit about those memories. Were they all pleasant?"

I shook my head.

"I see. What was unpleasant?" he asked.

I gazed at the two interns. Doctor Fernhoff, the man with the glasses, was staring at me so intently, I felt self-conscious.

"I . . . remember . . . there was someone," I said, "someone I cared for and something happened to him."

"Yes," Doctor Scanlon said. He glanced at the two interns. Neither cracked an encouraging smile nor changed expression. "Go on. What happened to him?"

"I think . . . it has to do with the ocean. He was in a sailboat."

"Yes, go on, go on," he urged, as if he were playing a tug-of-war with my mind.

"I don't know. I . . . think he might have fallen out of the boat."

I gazed at Doctor Bloom. Something in his softer face told me I wasn't far off.

"What else do you think, Laura? You must tell me what you remember and what you believe happened."

"He and I were in the boat," I said, "and I think we were caught in a storm. Is he all right?"

"Who?" Doctor Scanlon pursued. "Who is this person in the boat with you?"

"Robert," I said and it all tumbled out. "Robert Royce, a boy from my school."

Doctor Scanlon sat back, a look of satisfaction on his face.

"That's good, Laura," he said, nodding. "You've come a long way."

"But is he all right?"

"Is he?" Doctor Scanlon fired back at me.

"I don't know. I can't remember," I cried frantically. "He's not all right. He can't be all right. Please, say I'm wrong. Tell me!" I begged.

"You must not think of it as your fault," he said.

"Why would it be my fault? Was it my fault? What did I do?" I demanded.

"That's enough for now," he declared with finality. He gathered up his charts and stood.

"No, it's not enough. How can it be enough? You've hardly been here five minutes."

"The length of time I'm here isn't what's important. It's what happens *during* the time I'm here," he said, as if I were one of his interns, too.

"I can't remember everything, but I remember a lot. Can't you help me remember it all, finally?"

"I think it's best we take it one step at a time, Laura. Tomorrow is another day," he declared with a regal air. His two interns made quick notes on their clipboards as he turned to them.

"I want to go home," I moaned. "I remember my mother, my father, my little sister, and my brother. Why don't they come to see me now?"

"Perhaps they will very soon," he said. "Classic case," he said, nodding at me. The two interns widened their eyes and pressed their lips simultaneously. "As you know," he lectured to them, "dissociative amnesia most commonly presents a retrospectively reported gap or series of gaps in recall for aspects of the individual's life history. As illustrated here, these gaps are usually related to traumatic or extremely stressful events."

"It's a common battle-fatigue syndrome," Doctor Fernhoff said.

"Precisely. However, today, we're seeing it more and more with early childhood abuse. I'd like you both to keep a close observation on this case. She's on the verge of crashing through her trauma and the immediate aftermath is most instructive."

They nodded and stared at me. I felt like an amoeba under a microscope. The way their eyes fixed on my face made me cringe.

"I want to go home," I moaned.

"We have to deal with the patient's perception of the event," Doctor Scanlon continued. "It's critical we deal with her sense of guilt as soon as she recalls nearly one hundred percent, for it is precisely that sense of guilt that put her into dissociative amnesia. Again, classic symptoms for classic cases, i.e., mothers who survive accidents when their children don't, husbands or wives who survive, et cetera.

"I'm giving her a series of EEGs. As you know," he continued in his teacher's voice, "regions of the brain that are involved in memory function also affect the stress response. Traumatic stress results in changes in these brain regions; alterations in these brain regions in turn may mediate symptoms of posttraumatic stress disorder.

"Unfortunately," he continued, looking at me, "Doctor Southerby neglected to give her an EEG on admittance, so we lost a potential comparison there, but . . ." He smiled at them. "We'll make the best of it."

He gestured at the door and they turned.

"Please let me go home," I cried. Why wouldn't they answer me?

"Our next patient is a more classic case of child abuse,"

he rattled on as they walked away. "We have a twelve-year-old Caucasian male . . ."

I watched them leave the room and then I dropped my head to the pillow because it suddenly felt like it had turned to stone.

As Doctor Scanlon had explained, later that day I was taken for tests. Electrodes were placed on my head and machines read my brain waves. Doctor Scanlon's interns supervised and studied the results, although no one told me what they were. I was simply brought back to my room and put to bed. When I complained, Mrs. Roundchild permitted me to sit in a chair for a while, as long as I didn't walk around or try to leave the room.

I sat there all day, thinking about my memories, feeling the details fill in, the colors and shapes growing richer and richer with each passing minute. It was as if my recollections, which began as simple line drawings, were now being painted by a wonderful artist. Not only did pictures and words return, but aromas, scents, and tastes did as well. More than ever, I wanted my mother. I cried for her all day, but no one listened. Every time Mrs. Roundchild or one of the interns appeared, they offered me promises, punctuating every hope with "Soon."

Soon was not soon enough, I thought. Only right now was soon enough. Because I became more vocal in my demands, Mrs. Roundchild had me returned to bed and strapped in again. She called Doctor Scanlon and then came back to my room to inform me that he wanted me to take my medication earlier than usual tonight. She said he claimed I was about to make a dramatic breakthrough. Once again, they held up the promise that this would all be over . . . soon.

I took the pills after dinner and immediately fell asleep. In moments I was drifting on the sea. I was in the sailboat and Robert was smiling with pride at his ability to guide us over the waves. We were heading for a cove. It was coming back to me with the promise of love and all that lay just around the bend.

* * *

MUSIC IN THE NIGHT

In my dreams I saw Robert and this girl who appeared to
be me pull the sailboat onto the shore quickly and, laughing
and teasing each other, go up the beach. I saw her fall to the
sand and then I saw him fall first to his knees, and then to all
fours above her. He gazed down at her, his eyes full of love,
and he reached out to touch her hair, her cheek, to let her
hold his fingers to her lips so she could kiss the tips of them.
The girl moaned and the boy leaned over to kiss her softly
on the lips, moving his mouth up her face, over her cheeks
to her closed eyes.

For a while, he touched her only with his lips. He held
himself above her, moving to her forehead, her hair, and
then back to her lips before moving to her neck and then,
ever so gently, lifting up her shirt.

In the distance the clouds began to gather. Neither the
boy nor the girl noticed the change in the wind, the hectic
and nervous cries of the birds, or the lift of the water as the
tide rushed in faster, higher. They were completely en-
tranced with each other, mesmerized, lost in the whisper of
their own voices pledging endless love, promising.

I saw them undress, peel their clothes away quickly, but
not roughly. Naked beneath the sky, they held each other
first gently, and then desperately, wanting their lovemaking
to be bigger, greater, more intense than it had ever been
before. And it was.

Exhausted, they collapsed against each other, held each
other tight. With this exquisite exhaustion came contentment. They closed their eyes and remained entwined, soon
falling asleep. I tried to cry out a warning, but they couldn't
hear me.

The sky darkened. The wind grew stronger. The water
rose and fell with a slam against the rocks, and the small
sailboat was washed away from shore. By the time they
finally woke, the boat was out to sea.

Suddenly, I was no longer a third party, an observer. I was
on the beach, shouting. Robert was swimming desperately
for the boat. I saw it all and rushed forward to help him.
That was when the darkness fell again, slamming my

memory closed, ripping the sounds away, leaving me in a terrifying silence.

"Robert," I called. I started to swing my arms about madly until I felt someone holding me and opened my eyes to see Lawrence at my side.

"Laura, Laura," he cried.

I reached up for him and he embraced me.

"Were you having another bad dream?" he asked. "Maybe the medicine is causing your nightmares."

"I don't know," I sobbed. "I've got to get out of here, Lawrence. They don't really want to help me. They just keep giving me drugs that make me sleep and keep me weak. I want to go home, Lawrence. I know who my parents are and I know where I live. I remember almost everything! I've got to go home right away."

"You want to leave the clinic now? Tonight?" he asked.

"Yes, desperately. They're turning me into some sort of guinea pig, using me for a study. They want to prolong my treatment for as long as they can. I know they do. I want to go home. Help me, please," I begged.

He thought a moment. I pressed my fingers around his hand firmly.

"Okay, Laura," he said. "I'll help you, if that's what you really want to do."

"Thank you, Lawrence. Thank you."

I undid the strap around my waist and ripped the blanket away. Lawrence undid the strap around my legs and I started to get out of bed.

"Wait," he said. "Let me think first."

"There's no time to think. Get me out of here, Lawrence. Please."

"You need clothes, Laura. You can't go outside like that," he said. "I know. When we get downstairs, we'll go to your old room and get something for you to wear and then we'll go to the door off the kitchen, the one I showed you," he said.

"Yes, yes. But we've got to hurry."

"We've got to be careful," he corrected. "If we're caught,

they're sure to take more drastic measures with both of us."
He went to the door and peered out. "It looks clear," he
said.

I swung my feet over the side of the bed and stood. For a
moment I swayed and nearly fell, but I steadied myself
quickly. He came to me to take my arm, and we both went
to the door. He looked again.

"When we go out, we go around the corner and take the
first door on the left, Laura. We'll go down the stairway and
stop at the bottom floor so I can check the corridor again.
I've done this enough times already to be an expert. Don't
worry," he added.

I nodded, eager.

Lawrence took my hand and led me from the room to the
doorway. We slipped away quickly and started down the
steps. My head was spinning, but I didn't let on how dizzy I
was until I slipped on the landing and he had to catch and
hold me.

"You're so weak, Laura. How can you leave the clinic?"

"I can do it, Lawrence. Once I'm away and out in fresh
air, I'll be fine."

He held me for another indecisive moment, and then he
guided me down the next flight of steps, until we were at the
bottom floor and he was checking the hallway. After a few
moments, he nodded and we scurried out and down the
hallway to the residential area. Minutes later, we were in my
old bedroom. We didn't put on the lights for fear of
attracting attention. I went to the closet and found a pair of
jeans and a sweatshirt, but there were no shoes or sneakers.
I had to wear my slippers.

Lawrence remained at the doorway with his back to me as
I dressed.

I paused by the small table and looked at the journal I had
been keeping for Doctor Southerby. No one had bothered
giving it to Doctor Scanlon. I was tempted to take it with
me, but hesitated. I didn't want any reminders of this place,
if I could help it, I thought. I wanted to leave this place
behind me for good.

"I'm ready," I announced.

Lawrence looked at me and shook his head. He didn't move.

"What?" I asked.

"I can't let you do this by yourself, Laura. I'm going to go with you."

"You're going to leave the clinic, too?"

"Yes," he said. I could almost feel him trembling in the dark. Lawrence had told me that he hadn't been off the grounds for years.

"You don't have to do that, Lawrence."

"I want to," he said.

He watched the corridor and indicated I should be still. Seconds later, we heard talking and through the crack in the doorway saw Billy and Arnie walk down the corridor. They paused near my door. Billy whispered something to Arnie and they broke out into laughter as they continued down the hallway, disappearing around the corner.

"Now," Lawrence said, and we shot out and hurried down the hallway to the cafeteria. Just before we reached the kitchen, the doors opened and a janitor stepped out pushing a pail on rollers. He didn't look right or left or he would have seen us with our backs against the wall, watching him go through the cafeteria and out into the hall. We waited.

I looked at Lawrence. He seemed suddenly frozen against the wall.

"Shouldn't we go now?" I asked him. He nodded, but he didn't move.

"Maybe you should go back, Laura. I don't know if this is the right thing to do. No," he concluded. "It isn't. I shouldn't have done this. Please, let's go back," he said. He was trembling badly, and even in the subdued light, I saw how white his complexion had turned.

"No, I can't go back. I have to leave," I said. I started away and entered the kitchen myself. Moments later, Lawrence was behind me.

"How will you get home?" he asked when we confronted the metal door.

"I don't know."

"You don't even know which way to go. Laura, this is wrong," he said, seizing my arm to hold me back. "Laura . . ."

His voice seemed to die away after he pronounced my name, the word falling lower and lower as if everything he was saying were being said from the top of a deep well and I was on the very bottom. I felt like I was shrinking.

"Laura . . . don't go. Laura . . . come back."

"Yes, Robert," I said. "I'm coming back."

"What? Laura, it's me. Lawrence."

I went to the door.

"Laura! Wait!"

I pushed the door open and stepped out into the night, and then, I heard him calling again.

"Laura, come back! Come back!"

"Yes," I said. "I'm coming, Robert. I'll be there soon."

I turned and started around the building. Above me, the sky was thick with clouds. There were no stars, no promises for tomorrow.

I stumbled, but ignored the pain. I could hear his voice in the wind. Sometimes it was loud and sometimes it sounded far, far away.

"Laura, wait. Where are you going? You can't get to the highway that way. Laura."

Lawrence grabbed me at the elbow and spun me around.

"Laura, what are you doing? You lost your slipper back there," he said and gave it to me. I stared at it a moment and then at him.

"I'm not going back," I said. "Tell my grandmother I'm not going to give him up."

"What? You're not making any sense, Laura. Aren't you cold?" he asked, embracing himself. He looked around us. The weeping willow trees shook in the wind. "That wind is wild tonight. There's a storm brewing."

"Of course there's a storm brewing," I said, "but that won't stop us. You can tell her I said that."

I slipped my foot into the slipper and continued down the path, past the benches and the gardens.

"Tell whom? Laura, you're not making any sense. Laura!" he shouted.

Someone inside the building heard him. A light went on and then another. I heard doors opening and voices calling out into the night. It drove me on faster. I was running down the hill now, slipping and sliding, losing the slippers again, but not slowing down. Something inside me told me not to slow down for an instant or it would be too late.

And besides, he was calling louder and more desperately each time.

"I'm coming, Robert. I'm coming, my darling Robert," I cried into the darkness.

Ahead of me, the ocean thundered as the waves slammed against the rocks and the sea spray flew into the night. My eyes had grown accustomed to the darkness, but shapes were still only silhouettes. Some of the rocks had been stroked so long by the water, they gleamed like jewels in the night.

I fell and scraped my arm on a rock. It stung, but I didn't pay any attention to the pain. Instead, I got back to my feet as quickly as I could and listened. His voice was gone. The ocean was drowning him out.

"Robert!" I screamed.

"Laura! Where are you?" The voice seemed to come from behind me, but then I heard it again, this time from directly in front of me. "Laura. I'm here. Laura!"

"Yes, yes, Robert. I'm here."

I moved more carefully over the smaller rocks, until I reached the water and the tide slapped at my legs. Concentrating hard, I could see the boat rising and falling. The small mast was broken and lay over the side, the sail soaked. I started into the water.

"Robert!" I called. "Robert!"

The boat lifted again, only this time it came down on its

side and then turned completely over, and after it had, I saw him, bobbing in the water, his arm up.

"Laura . . ."

"Robert, I'm coming. Wait."

He disappeared for a moment. I charged ahead, the water now up to my waist.

"Laura!" I heard someone scream behind me, but I didn't turn back. That was Grandmother Olivia's trick to get me to give him up. Don't look back, I thought, or you'll be like Lot's wife and turn into a pillar of salt.

I started to swim toward the boat. His head reappeared and then that arm slowly emerged from the dark water, just as it had many times before in my dreams. I tried to shout to him as I swam, but it was difficult because the water slammed into my face and I swallowed some, gagging for a moment. The waves lifted and threw me back, but I continued, swimming as furiously as I could now. I wasn't far from the boat.

His head lifted slowly and his eyes—even in the darkness without a moon and stars—his eyes were luminous and full of love.

"Robert, my darling," I called to him and swam and swam and swam. When I looked up, the boat wasn't any closer. Was it just the strong tide keeping me back?

My arms ached. My clothing weighed me down. I treaded water and stripped off my jeans and then my shirt. The tide carried off its bounty quickly and I turned back to my swimming, putting all my strength into every stroke. I felt myself lift and fall with the water and when I looked out again, there was the boat, but not any closer.

"Robert, I can't lose you. I won't lose you. Don't let them take you from me. Please."

Miraculously, he appeared only inches away, his head emerging from the sea, his arms out toward me. I stretched until our hands joined.

"Robert—"

"Laura," he said. "My Laura."

I felt him draw me closer to him until his arms were

around me. The water didn't matter anymore. I didn't feel how cold it was or how rough it was. In his arms I felt safe and warm. We kissed.

"I waited for you," he said. "I knew you would come back to me, so I waited for you."

"I'm so glad, Robert. I'm so happy."

I turned toward the shore. Someone was waving madly. He was up to his waist and waving.

"Let's go back," I said, "together."

"No, Laura. We can't go back," Robert said. "Come . . ."

He gestured with his head toward the overturned sailboat.

"Oh," I said. I smiled, understanding.

We swam together for a few moments and then I reached forward to touch the boat. Robert did, too. We turned to each other and we brought out lips together and kissed as the darkness swept in over us.

But I was happy, as happy as I had once been.

I was with my love.

Forever.

Epilogue
&

The black Rolls-Royce climbed the hill to the clinic slowly, rising over the crest of the knoll. The automobile came to a stop in front of the main entrance as the sun was covered by a long, dark cloud. The driver got out and quickly opened the door for Olivia Logan. He reached in to take her at the elbow, but she shook him off.

"I'm all right, Raymond," she snapped. She paused after emerging and looked at the building as if it were alive and the windows now glittering like mirrors were the dozens of eyes greeting her.

"Just wait right here," she ordered and made her way to the steps.

Raymond watched her obediently for a few moments before getting back into the Rolls. He reached for his newspaper and lowered the back of the seat.

Before Olivia Logan reached the entrance, the door opened and Doctor Scanlon, with Mrs. Kleckner on one side and Mrs. Roundchild on the other, stepped forward to greet her. She paused and looked at them, her eyes full of contempt and accusation. The three seemed to wilt; Herbert Scanlon, the most. It was as if his clothes were growing on his body. His shirt collar widened and he pressed the knot of his tie between his right thumb and forefinger before reaching out to take Olivia's hand.

"Where is she?" Olivia asked.

"We have her in the infirmary. I'm sorry," Doctor Scanlon began. "I—"

Olivia put up her black-gloved hand, palm forward.

"Save your explanations for later," she said. "Take me to her."

The three separated, Mrs. Roundchild stepping back so Olivia could enter the building.

There wasn't anyone in the lobby. The patients were all at lunch. Olivia paused, struck by the silence, and then continued as Herbert Scanlon directed her to another doorway and the corridor beyond. The two nurses trailed behind, neither looking at the other, neither saying a word.

"The patients are all in the dining room," Doctor Scanlon said.

"Except one," Olivia remarked.

He glanced back at his nurses and continued walking. When they reached the end of the corridor, they turned right at a door labeled INFIRMARY. Dr. Scanlon opened it and stepped back for Olivia to enter. The nurse, wearing a nametag, Suzanne Cohen, rose so quickly from her desk chair it looked like she had been sitting on springs. She looked at Doctor Scanlon, her face gray with concern.

"This is Mrs. Logan," he said. "She's here to see Laura."

"Oh yes," the infirmary nurse said. "I'm so sorry," she added.

Olivia closed her eyes and shook her head.

"I'm not interested in hearing apologies," she replied. Sue Cohen glanced at Doctor Scanlon and saw from the expression on his face that she should move quickly.

"This way," she said, and led them through the small lobby to a rear door and down a short hall, on either side of which were examination rooms, radiology, a laboratory, and at the very end, a room that fortunately was used rarely. It had no label on the door, but everyone who worked there knew it to be their morgue.

She opened the door and stepped back.

Olivia approached slowly and gazed in at the steel gurney covered with a sheet, on which lay the body of her granddaughter. The room had no particular odor. It seemed aseptic, devoid of any character, or light.

Olivia approached the gurney. Doctor Scanlon moved quickly to get beside her.

"Let me see her," Olivia demanded.

He lowered the sheet to her neck and Olivia gazed for a long moment.

Now, now that she was here and they were around her, she would make demands.

"How did this happen?"

Doctor Scanlon was prepared.

"Another patient with whom she had developed something of a relationship snuck up to our special floor and helped her escape down a stairway used by the employees. He knew of the one door we don't keep alarmed and showed her the way out of the building. He claimed she wanted to go home."

Olivia turned with interest.

"Home? Then how did she end up in the ocean?"

"You have to understand," Doctor Scanlon said, "that this other patient is a seriously disturbed young man himself. It's taken an enormous effort to get him to be lucid enough to give us any sensible details. This entire event has put him into a regression that—"

"I'm not here to discuss him," Olivia said sharply.

Doctor Scanlon nodded.

"Apparently, from what I've been able to garner, she heard voices."

"Voices? What voices?"

"Mainly the voice of her young man, the one who drowned. Lawrence—that's this other patient's name—said she kept calling for Robert. He said as soon as he showed her the way out, she turned toward the sea and ran. He tried to stop her, but she was determined."

"She went down to the ocean and deliberately drowned herself?" Olivia asked incredulously.

"That's not uncommon, suicidal tendencies in cases such as hers, Mrs. Logan."

"Then why wasn't she guarded, day and night?" Olivia snapped at him.

"I . . . well, she was on our most secure floor."

"Secure floor? And yet this other patient was able to get to her and take her away?"

"No one expected . . ." He looked to Mrs. Roundchild, who stepped forward.

"She was strapped in, medicated. We had just looked in on her. He must have been hiding in the doorway, watching," she explained.

"Send them away," Olivia commanded with a wave of her hand.

Doctor Scanlon nodded at the nurses and they all backed out of the room. As soon as they had, Olivia turned on him.

"You know I could sue this clinic and you for every penny you are worth. Word of this sort of negligence would destroy you," she said, her eyes small, but full of fire.

Doctor Scanlon could barely swallow. He nodded.

Olivia held her hateful glare on him like a spotlight, hot and intense. Finally, she turned back to Laura.

"It's your good fortune, however, that I don't want word of this to leave these premises."

"What? But in any death, there's an inquest, reports . . ."

"It's your problem," she said. "I don't want this in any newspaper. We're going to give her a proper burial and that will be all. This could devastate my family," she added and turned, "and I won't permit it."

"I understand. I'll do the best I can."

"No, you'll do what I ask; not the best you can." She looked at Laura again. "We see the results of the best you can do. I want more than that."

He nodded, sweat trickling down his brow.

"Do you want any of her things, anything you sent?"

"Not at the moment, no," Olivia said. "I hesitate to ask, because I have some doubts about your competence now, but was she making any progress?"

"Oh, yes. I think in time I could have effected a complete recovery," he bragged.

"What did she recall before . . . before this?" Olivia asked.

"Her family, her parents, her brother and sister, and most of the tragic event," he replied.

"She said nothing about me?"

"Not a word during my sessions and from what I see of Southerby's results, not a word with him either," Doctor Scanlon said.

"What about him?"

"That's taken care of," he said quickly.

"Good. I want it all taken care of, Herbert." She turned again and fixed her piercing eyes on him, turning his spine to ice. "I mean it."

"I understand. Is there anything special you want at the gravesite?"

"No," she said. "Leave me for a moment," she ordered.

"Yes, of course. I'm sorry, Mrs. Logan. Truly."

She said nothing and he left.

For a long while, she stared at Laura's face. Then she took a short, deep breath and looked up at the ceiling.

"I'm sorry about you," she said. "I know you won't ever understand now, but what I did, I did for my family. Family is all that really matters, family name, family loyalty. It's who we are when we come into this world and who we are when we leave it, and we must cling tenaciously to it all the time in between, Laura."

She gazed at her granddaughter and thought how beautiful she looked, even in death.

"Somehow I knew that after you lost your precious Robert, you would never have a really happy moment, Laura. Maybe . . . maybe you weren't so mad, as sick as the doctors think. Maybe you heard him calling.

"In a strange way," she whispered, "I envy you, my dear."

She reached out and touched Laura's cold face. Then she turned and left the room.

Doctor Scanlon escorted her to the front entrance.

"My lawyer will be in contact with you to be sure all is done as I instruct," she said.

"Yes, I understand," Doctor Scanlon said with a small nod.

"I want you to do something else for me."

"Of course," Doctor Scanlon said without hesitation, without hearing it first.

"I want you to tell that young man, that other patient something."

"Yes?"

"I want you to tell him I don't blame him for anything. Tell him I thank him for being her friend. Will you do that?"

"I will. It will help him, Mrs. Logan. It's very kind of you."

"I'm not doing it for him. I'm doing it for Laura and," she said, looking at the Rolls-Royce, "for myself."

She started down the steps. Raymond got out quickly and opened the door. Doctor Scanlon wiped his face with his handkerchief as he watched her get into her automobile. When the door closed, he backed up and closed the clinic's front door.

Raymond got in and started the car. It moved slowly toward the driveway.

MUSIC IN THE NIGHT

The sun escaped from under another cloud and shot its rays downward over the car, over the grounds, over the ocean, where the waves were now gentle, the whitecaps glimmering. Two terns lifted into the warm air and flew side by side, sweeping down together toward the sea, and then rose toward the sun as if it were a promise kept between them.

In moments, they were gone.

I was alone in Mrs. McGuire's office, waiting to meet the couple who had asked for me. When I sat properly on the straight-back chair beside Mrs. McGuire's desk, my feet barely reached the floor, but Mrs. McGuire, the chief administrator of our orphanage, pounced on any of us if we slouched.

"Posture, posture," she would cry out when she passed us in the cafeteria, and everyone would snap his or her back into an ironing board. Those who didn't usually had to parade about the building with a book on their head for hours, and if the book fell off someone, that person would have to do it again the next day.

"You're orphans," she lectured to us, "looking for some nice people to come snatch you up and make you members of their families. You must be better than children with parents and homes. You must be healthier, smarter, more polite and respectful. In short," she said in a voice that often turned shrill at the end of her small speeches, "you must become desirable. Why," she asked, sweeping her eyes over each and every one of us critically, her thin lips tucked in, "would anyone want you to be their daughter or son?"

My heart, which everyone told me must be as tiny as a pocket watch because I was so small, ticked faster when she fixed those steel-gray eyes on me. She was right. *Who would ever want me?* I thought. I was born prematurely. Some of the boys and even some of the girls here said I was stunted. One boy, Donald Lawson, called me the Dwarf.

"Even when you're in high school, you'll wear children's clothes," he said.

I suppose it made him feel better to make someone else feel bad. He strutted away with his head high. My tears were like trophies for him, and the sight of them didn't make him feel sorry. Instead, they encouraged him.

"Even your tears are tiny," he said. "Maybe we should call you Tiny Tears instead of the Dwarf."

Potential Mommies and Daddies had considered me before today. Margaret Lester—who was the tallest girl in the orphanage, fourteen years old, with legs that seemed to reach up to her shoulders—overheard some comments they had made about me and couldn't wait to regurgitate them.

"The man said he thought you were adorable, but when they found out how old you were, they wondered why you were so small. She thought you might be sickly and then they decided to look at someone else," Margaret said.

No potential parents ever looked at her, so she was happy when one of us was rejected.

"I'm not sickly," I whispered in my own defense. "I haven't even had a cold all year."

I always spoke in a soft, low voice. Mrs. McGuire said I had to appear more self-assured.

"It's fine to be a little shy, Janet," she told me. "Goodness knows, most children today are too loud and obnoxious, "but if you're too modest, people will pass over you. They'll think you're withdrawn, like a turtle more comfortable in his shell. You don't want that, do you?"

I shook my head, but she continued her lecture.

"Then stand straight when you speak to people and look at them and not at the floor. And don't twist your fingers around each other like that. Get your shoulders back. You need all the height you can achieve."

When I was called to her office today, she had me sit in the chair and then paced in front of me, her thin high heels clicking like little hammers on the tile floor, as she advised and directed me on how to behave once the Delorices arrived. That was their names, Sanford and Celine Delorice. Of course, I hadn't set eyes on them before. Mrs. McGuire told me, however, that they had seen me a number of times. That came as a surprise. A number of times? I wondered when, and if that was true, why had I never seen them?

"They know a great deal about you, Janet, and still they are interested. This is your biggest opportunity. Do you understand?" she asked, pausing to look at me. "Straighten up," she snapped.

I did so quickly.

"Yes, Mrs. McGuire," I said.

"What?" She put her hand behind her ear and leaned toward me. "Did you say something, Janet?"

"Yes, Mrs. McGuire."

"Yes what?" she demanded, standing back, her hands on her hips.

"Yes, I understand this is my big opportunity, Mrs. McGuire."

"Good, good. Speak loudly, and speak only when you're spoken to, and smile as much as you can. Don't spread your legs too far apart. That's it. Let me see your hands," she demanded, reaching out to seize them in her own long, bony fingers before I could offer.

She turned my hands over so roughly my wrists stung.

"Good," she said. "You do take good care of yourself, Janet. I think that's a big plus for you. Some of our children, as you know, think dirt belongs on their bodies."

She glanced at the clock.

"They should be arriving. I'm going out front to greet them. Wait here and when we come through the door, stand up. Do you understand?"

"Yes, Mrs. McGuire." Her hand went behind her ear again. "Yes, Mrs. McGuire," I said, louder this time.

She shook her head and looked very sad, her eyes full of doubt.

"This is your big chance, your best chance, Janet. Maybe, your last chance," she muttered, and left the office.

I wished I could remember my real mother, but my earliest memories began with my life in an orphanage. I had been in one other besides this one, transferred when I was nearly seven. Now I was almost thirteen, but even I would admit that I looked no more than nine, maybe ten. Because I had no memories of my real mother, Tommy Turner said I might be one of those children created in a laboratory.

"You might have been born in a test tube and that's why you're so small. Something went wrong with the experiment," he said. Those who heard him and understood about experiments in laboratories laughed.

"Janet's mother and father were test tubes," they chanted.

"No," Tommy said. "Her father was a syringe and her mother was a test tube."

"Who named her Janet then?" Margaret asked, her lips twisted into a smirk.

Tommy had to think.

"That was the name of her lab technician, Janet Taylor, so they gave her that name," he said, and some of the children actually came to believe it.

I wished with all my heart there was something, some fact, some item I possessed that would enable me to throw my real past back at them and shut them up, but I had nothing. I was like a butterfly who had metamorphosed and forgotten that she was once a caterpillar. In fact, now that she was a butterfly and flew above them squirming on the ground, she couldn't imagine how it was ever possible that she had been one of them. If a wise old butterfly would tell her that, she would laugh and say, "What a ridiculous old wives' tale. I'm too beautiful, too dainty. You're just saying that because you're old and will soon fall to earth like a dead leaf."

Then, the wise old butterfly took her to witness a metamorphosis and she saw what she had been. It broke her heart and she fell to earth much sooner than the wise old butterfly.

I told myself this story because I wanted to keep myself flying in the sunlight, above the chatter of the others, above their jokes and cruel remarks, and I knew, if I believed any of them, I would fall to earth, too.

"Janet!" I heard Mrs. McGuire stab at me, and my eyes snapped open. Her face was filled with fury, her mouth twisted, her gray orbs wide and lit like firecrackers. "Sit up," she whispered through her clenched teeth, and then she plastered a smile on her face and turned. "Right this way, Mr. and Mrs. Delorice," she said in a much softer tone of voice.

I took a deep breath and held it, my pocket watch–size heart suddenly sounding like a kettledrum in my chest. Mrs. McGuire stepped back and I nearly gasped aloud. A tall, thin, dark-haired man with sleepy eyes and a cleft chin pushed a wheelchair in which sat a pretty woman with hair the color of a red sunset. She had diminutive facial features like my own, but even more perfectly proportioned. Her hair floated around her shoulders in soft, undulating waves. There was nothing sickly or frail looking about her, despite her handicap. Her complexion was rich, like peach ice cream, and her lips the shade of fresh strawberries.

She wore a bright yellow dress, my color for hope, and a string of tiny pearls around her neck. Her fingers were dainty and I could see she wore a wedding ring; pearl earrings in gold settings were visible when she brushed her hair back. I had rarely ever seen them, but it looked like she was wearing ballet shoes, too. If she was in a wheelchair, why was she wearing ballet shoes? I wondered.

Her husband pushed her right up to me. I was too fascinated to move, much less speak.

"Mr. and Mrs. Delorice, this is Janet Taylor. Janet, Mr. and Mrs. Delorice."

"Hello," I said, obviously not loud enough to please Mrs. McGuire. She gestured for me to stand and I nearly jumped out of the chair.

"Please, dear, call us Sanford and Celine," the

pretty woman said. She held out her hand and I took it gingerly, surprised at how firmly she held her fingers around mine. For a moment we only looked into each other's eyes. Then I glanced up at Sanford Delorice.

He was smiling down at me, his eyes opening a bit wider to reveal their mixture of brown and green. He had his hair cut very short, which made his long, narrow face look even longer and narrower. He was wearing a dark gray sport jacket, no tie and a pair of dark blue slacks. The upper two buttons on his white shirt were open. I thought it was to give his very prominent Adam's apple breathing space.

"She's perfect, Sanford, just perfect, isn't she?" Celine said, gazing at me.

"Yes, she is, dear," Sanford replied. His long fingers were still wrapped tightly around the handles of the wheelchair, as if he was afraid to let go.

"Has she ever had any training in the arts?" Celine asked Mrs. McGuire. She didn't look at Mrs. McGuire when she asked. She didn't turn her head from me. Her eyes were fixed on my face and I was unable to look away.

"The arts?"

"Singing, dancing . . . ballet, perhaps?" she asked, this time turning toward Mrs. McGuire.

"Oh, no, Mrs. Delorice. The children here are not that fortunate," she replied.

Celine Delorice turned back to me. Her eyes grew smaller, even more intensely fixed on me.

"Well, Janet will be. She'll be that fortunate," she

predicted with certainty. She smiled softly. "How would you like to come live with Sanford and myself, Janet? You'll have your own room, a very large and comfortable one. You'll attend a private school. We'll buy you an entirely new wardrobe, including new shoes. You'll have a separate area in your room for your schoolwork and you'll have your own bathroom. I'm sure you'll like our house. We live just outside of Albany, with grounds as large as, if not larger than, what you have here."

"That sounds wonderful," Mrs. McGuire said as if she were the one being offered the new home, but Celine Delorice didn't seem interested in Mrs. McGuire's opinion. She stared at me and waited for my response.

"Janet?" Mrs. McGuire questioned when a long moment of silence had passed.

How could I ever refuse this, and yet when I looked up at Sanford and back at Celine, I couldn't help feeling little footsteps of trepidation tiptoeing across my heart. I pushed the shadowy faces out of my mind, glanced at Mrs. McGuire and then nodded.

"I'd like that," I said.

"Good," Celine declared. She spun her chair around to face Mrs. McGuire. "How soon can she leave?"

"Well, we have some paperwork to do. However, knowing as much as we do about you and your husband, your impressive references, the social worker's report, et cetera, I suppose—"

"Can we take her with us today?" Celine demanded impatiently.

My heart skipped a beat. Today? That fast?

Mrs. McGuire looked at Sanford Delorice and then at Celine.

"I imagine that could be done," she finally replied.

"Good," she said. "Sanford, why don't you stay with Mrs. McGuire and fill out whatever paperwork has to be filled out. Janet and I can go out and get more acquainted in the meantime," she said. It was supposed to be a suggestion, I guess, but it came out like an order.

"There are documents that require both signatures," Mrs. McGuire said dryly.

"Sanford has power of attorney when it comes to my signature," Celine countered. "Janet, can you push my chair? I don't weigh all that much," she added, smiling.

I looked at Mrs. McGuire. She nodded and I walked behind the chair. Sanford stepped back and I took hold of the handles.

"Where shall we go, Janet?" she asked me.

"I guess we can go out to the garden," I said. Mrs. McGuire nodded again.

"That sounds wonderful. Don't be any longer than you have to, Sanford," she called back as I started to push her to the door. I went ahead and opened it and then I pushed her through.

I made the turn and started down the corridor, overwhelmed and amazed with myself and what was happening. I finally found parents, but also a mother who wanted me to take care of her, perhaps as much as I wanted her to take care of me. What a strange and wonderful new beginning, I thought as I wheeled Celine Delorice toward the sunny day that awaited us.

The Phenomenal
V.C. ANDREWS®